PRAISE FOR NA

JANE CARVE

"First and foremost this is a rollicking adventure. Jane is tough, liberated and smart (and can wield a mean sword), and Long has fun subverting the stereotypes, sexual and racial, of the original novels. Tremendous pulp fun."

—*The Guardian*

"Not merely a parody, *Jane Carver of Waar* is a classic adventure novel and great fun. Think of it as a Burroughs homage by an accomplished modern fantasy writer."

—*City Book Review*

"*Jane Carver* just breathes excellence from page to page...once it takes a hold of you in the very first few pages, it refuses to let you go."

—*The Founding Fields*

"Long takes Edgar Rice Burrough's classic John Carter stories and gives them a modern bent with a strong, female protagonist. The novel reads like a pulp lover's fantasy with over the top action, humor, and a good amount of sex...a ton of fun to read and I highly recommend it."

—*Staffer's Musings*

"Planetary romance gets a fun update in this take-off on Edgar Rice Burroughs's *A Princess of Mars*... Add some sex scenes Burroughs would never have gotten away with, and the attitude's definitely different—but the flavor of adventure remains, from encounters with pirates and gladiator contests to swordfights atop airships."

—*Locus*

"*Jane Carver of Waar* is adventure fiction at its rowdiest. And it's Nathan Long at his freest, loosest, and most wildly inventive. Very much a voice-driven, character-rich narrative, Jane simultaneously pays tribute to and parodies Edgar Rice Burroughs' iconic John Carter of Mars stories."

—*Clarkesworld Magazine*

PRAISE FOR NATHAN LONG'S
JANE CARVER OF WAAR
(continued)

"In this affectionate and often raunchy parody of Edgar Rice Burroughs's *John Carter of Mars* books, Long mocks and critiques elements of space fantasy settings that a son of the Old South like John Carter would never have noticed. Long is sometimes amused, sometimes angered, and very familiar with his source material; his book will appeal to readers who share those characteristics."

—*Publishers Weekly*

"Nathan Long's devilishly entertaining homage to Edgar Rice Burroughs gets the updating right. *Jane Carver of Waar* features airships and romance and savage four-armed warriors, but in the John Carter role it has Jane Carver, a sword-swinging biker chick swashed in leather and buckled in a bronze bra."

—*The Plain Dealer, Cleveland.com*

"If Edgar Rice Burroughs were writing today, with 21st Century skills and sensibilities, *Jane Carver of Waar* is the book he'd have written."

—Mike Resnick, Hugo and Nebula Award-Winning author

"With Jane Carver, Nathan Long takes Burroughs' classic tales of interplanetary adventure and one-ups them on every level. It's funnier, brasher, and even more fun! Read it, and love it!"

—Matt Forbeck, author of *Amortals* and *Carpathia*

"...the future of pulp fiction! I turned the pages while Jane Carver quested in a world 'full of slaves and gladiators and naked sexists.' Give Jane a sword and a Marlboro, and send us back to Waar!"

—Nancy Holder, *New York Times* bestselling author of the Wicked series and *Unleashed*

"What a ride! Thrilling, hip, and all so clever. Nathan Long's keen wit and engaging characters kept me grinning the whole way."

—Brom, author of *The Child Thief*

JANE CARVER

SWORDS of WAAR

Other books by Nathan Long

Valnir's Bane
The Broken Lance
Tainted Blood
Orcslayer
Manslayer
Battle for Skull Pass
Elfslayer
Shamanslayer
Gotrek and Felix: The Third Omnibus
Bloodborn: Ulrika the Vampire Book One
Zombieslayer
Bloodforged
Jane Carver of Waar
Bloodsworn

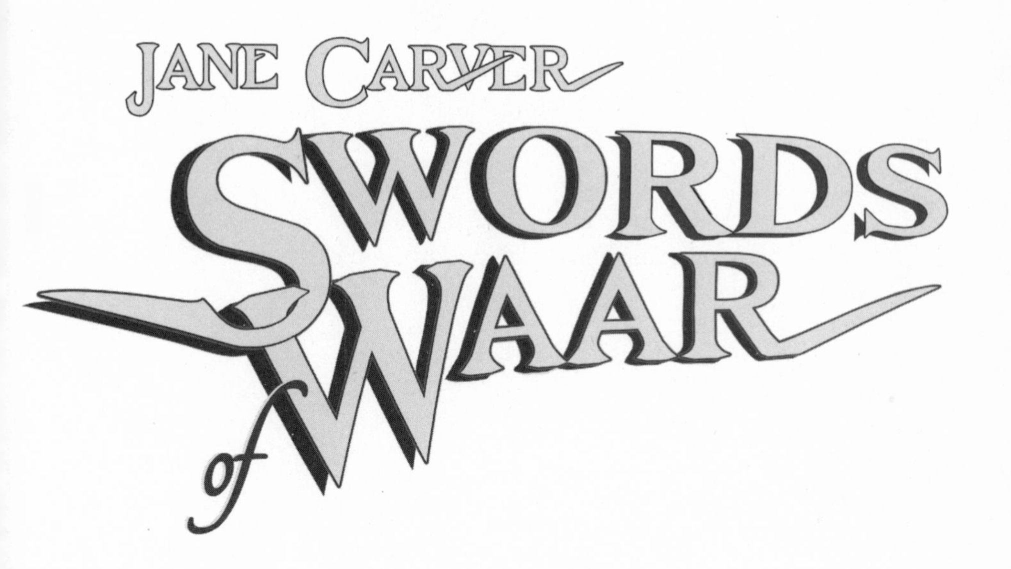

Nathan Long

NIGHT SHADE BOOKS
SAN FRANCISCO

Cover Illustration by Dave Dorman
Cover design by Martha Wade
Interior layout and design by Amy Popovich

Edited by Ross E. Lockhart

First Edition

ISBN: 978-1-59780-429-5

Night Shade Books
www.nightshadebooks.com

To Edgar Rice Burroughs, for inspiration,
and for having a sense of humor about it all.

CHAPTER ONE

EXILED!

Cut to a week later, and I was back standing outside that same fucking cave in the hills above Tarzana that had started it all. And standing was the right word, too. I was so petrified I couldn't go forward or back. Couldn't move a goddamn inch, which was stupid, considering I'd just hitch-hiked seven hundred miles to get there.

Did I mention I don't like tight spaces? Well that cave was tighter than a walrus's poop chute, and blacker too. I'd been up it once before, so I knew. It might be a quiet afternoon on that hillside right now, instead of a dark night with police dogs and whirly-birds chasing me like last time, and I might have brought a flashlight, but it didn't matter. I was still froze up like a statue.

And my claustrophobia wasn't the only thing keeping me out of that hole. It's a little long to get into here, but the last time I went in there, I found this weird clock-looking thing way at the back, and when I touched it, well, I went to another planet. Yeah, I know, but I did. Waar, it was called, and while I was there I got mixed up with this spoiled rich kid named Sai-Far, and helped him rescue his sweetheart, Wen-Jhai, from this grinning, grab-ass son-of-a-bitch named Kedac-Zir. More important than all that, though, was that I met Sai's best friend, Lhan-Lar, a sweet-talking sharpie with a face like a hot-rod devil and a heart of twenty-four carat gold, and I fell in love. At least it coulda been love, maybe, if it'd had half a chance. Our first night together sure went like gangbusters, but before we even had time to wake up and have our first morning sex, I got drugged by a bunch of sneaky little orange-robed priests and dragged away. No goodbyes. No nothing.

Next thing I know I'm wakin' up in a cave in Monument Valley with Lhan's smell still on my skin and good old Earth gravity crushin' me to the ground like an elephant sitting on my chest.

All I wanted to do as soon as I realized where I was was to get back to him, and fast—who knew what those fucking priests mighta done to him after they 86ed me—and the only way I knew how to do that was come back to this cave and touch the little doo-hickey again, which should have made me as eager as a bridegroom to push back into the dark, right?

Yeah, well....

Other things had happened on Waar, too, and some of 'em didn't sit well. I'd killed a guy. Lots of guys. And not by accident, either. I'd chopped 'em all up with a big-ass sword. It was that kind of place—guys with swords killing other guys with swords, giant centaur-tiger dudes tearing each other to pieces, creepy priests kidnapping people. I've been a biker chick since I got kicked outta the army. I've seen plenty of brawls, but Waar was just a whole 'nother level. Did I want to go back to that? And what about the *really* bad stuff? People owned slaves there. *Lhan* owned slaves. How could I love a guy who owned slaves?

So I stood there, thinking about all the things Earth had that Waar didn't. Rock and roll, Texas barbeque, Harley-Davidsons, equal rights—at least in some places—air conditioning, dive bars, Marlboros, guys bigger than me, blue jeans, leather jackets. But Earth also had cops, jails and a warrant for my arrest for killing that dumbass dude outside the Fly-By Nightclub—even though that had been an accident. And it didn't have the one thing that really mattered. Not anymore. Big Don was a rusty smear on the highway somewhere east of Sturgis now, and without him around, all the rest of it seemed kind of bland and washed out. Waar, on the other hand, had wide open spaces, wimpy gravity that let me run twenty feet a stride, no extradition to the US, and a chance to start again—at everything.

With a grunt, I shoved into the cave and worked my way to the back. It wasn't easy. My mouth got drier as the walls got narrower, and I'd completely sweated through my t-shirt by the time the flashlight finally found the opening to the back cave. It was a little hole halfway up a knife-cut wall, and so tight I didn't know how I got through it before.

I put the Maglight in my teeth and climbed up, then looked through. I knew it opened out again, but forcing myself to put my head and shoulders into that sphincter was as hard as reaching into a full toilet after a diamond ring. It made me shudder just to think about it.

I thought about Lhan instead, wondering if he was okay, wondering if he'd escaped the priests who'd grabbed me, if he was even still alive. That pushed me through, and I rolled onto a layer of sand, then pulled my legs in after me. I was in the little tent-shaped chamber where the dogs had found me and where I'd fallen back on the clock-thingy—and out of the world.

I flashed my light around. I didn't see it. Panic squeezed me like a python. Had the cops taken it? No, wait. There was a little mound of sand at the back. I crawled to it. It was surrounded by paw prints and boot marks, like it had been covered in a scuffle. I brushed it all away with the sleeve of my hoodie and saw metal underneath. I breathed a sigh of relief, then immediately tensed up again. The doo-hickey was there, but I didn't see the glow. When I had found it before, the headlight-sized gem in the center of it had been glowing—a kinda weak, lemonade light. Now there was nothing. I turned off the Maglight, just to be sure. Still nothing. I swallowed, afraid now that something was wrong, and turned the light back on. I still had to try.

I reached for it, then stopped an inch from the gem, all my misgivings coming back. Did I really want to go? I thought I did, but… Well, what the fuck. It wasn't going to work anyway. I slapped my palm across the gem.

Nothing happened. I was still in the cave.

And yeah, I know. I'd just said I knew it wasn't going to work. I wasn't exactly surprised.

I cried anyway.

***

I hadn't planned for after.

I walked back down the hill to Ventura Blvd. with just the clothes on my back—my hoodie, some dusty jeans, some dustier Vans and seven dollars—all I had left after the dead-run sprint I'd made from Monument Valley.

The race had started six days back when a couple of Arizona Park Rangers had caught me trying to hitch-hike buck-naked down US 163 and wanted to know what the fuck I thought I was doing. I'd been so cooked by sun stroke by then I think I told them the truth, which needless to say they did not believe.

Anyway, they took pity on me, gave me some clothes, a meal, and a lift to Flagstaff. I was desperate to get to LA as quick as I could, but I knew I wouldn't be going anywhere without a little traveling money, so I made some the old-fashioned way. No, not *that* old-fashioned way. That way doesn't work with girls as big and beefy as me. Instead I went and stood with the Mexican guys outside a Home Depot until a truck came by, and I made eighty bucks humping roofing tiles up ladders for two days.

Three days and six hundred miles of hitch-hiking later I got dropped off in the parking lot of a Ralph's supermarket on Victory Blvd; and spent my last intact twenty taking a taxi up to the top of Vanalden in Tarzana. I'd told the cabbie not to wait. I hadn't thought I'd be coming back.

Now that I had, I needed a plan, 'cause finding another way back to Waar might take a while—like the rest of my life maybe—and I was gonna have to make a living while I looked. I was also gonna have to avoid being arrested for murder. I squinted in the sun as I reached Ventura Blvd. and looked for a bus stop. Fortunately I knew a place where I could lay low while I figured shit out. At least I hoped I did. All I had to do now was figure out which buses to take to get there.

CHAPTER TWO

THUNDERSTRUCK!

"Well I'll be a son-of-a-bitch. I thought you were dead."

Eli hit the kill switch on the lathe and stared at me through his safety goggles as the thing whined to a stop. He pulled off his gloves.

"Nah. I just look that way." I ducked under the half-open roll door into Sun Valley Engineering, Eli's machine shop, and looked around. It was the same grimy little place I remembered, with a greasy film of three-in-one and metal shavings all over everything, and posters of girls with tattoos and betty bangs bending over low-riders on the walls. Eli specializes in reboring pistons, and there's always an assortment of bikes, hot-rods, lead sleds and trucks crowding his parking lot, but he also makes other, shadier, things on the side—lock picks, slim jims, gas tanks with hidden compartments. He could make a fortune if he was willing to pack and bore silencers, but he draws the line at accessory to murder, so he has to settle for being comfortably well off.

He tugged his goggles down to his neck, exposing his bifocals and a pair of bushy black eyebrows as he came around the lathe and spread his arms for a hug. Eli is in his fifties, with wild, greased-back gray hair, a face like a dry creek bed, and the dress sense of an Arkansas moonshiner—bib overalls, no shirt, tattoos from neck to wrists, and unlaced combat boots.

I crushed him to me and leaked tears on his tats as I sobbed like a school girl. After a while, when I'd petered out to sniffs and snorfs, he pushed me back to arms' length and gave me a once over, then squeezed my biceps.

"Well, where-ever y'went, it toned you up. You do a stretch?"

"Nah, I..." I wasn't ready to go into all that just yet. "Just went out of town."

Eli grinned. It was like brown paper folding up. "I'll bet. Last I recall, your face was all over the TV for killing some drunk hoopty outside a bar. You get that all cleared up, or are you still flyin' low?"

That was one of the reasons I came to Eli. He wasn't the type to call the cops on a gal for a little error in judgment—not without hearing her out anyway. He'd been one of Big Don's oldest friends—like since the navy—and had set me up with the construction job in Van Nuys after Don died. A true-blue guy, no matter what else he did on the side.

"Still on the lam, and guilty as charged." I swallowed as Polaroids of that night flashed through my head. I still felt bad about that guy.

"He put hands on you?"

I squirmed. "Not so much that he deserved—"

"Save it. It's good enough for me." He pulled a pack of Marlboros from the chest pocket of his overalls, lipped one, then shook another out toward me. I waved him off. Weird, I know, but I really didn't want one. Guess going cold turkey on Waar had worked. He shrugged and lit up. "So whaddaya need? Money? A bike? A fake ID? A lift over the border?"

"I—I don't know yet." I wiped my nose with the back of my hand, like I was the world's biggest five-year-old. "I guess if you could manage somewhere for me to sleep tonight? I got a lot of thinkin' to do."

He looked at the beer clock over the compressor. It said four o'clock. "Go lie down in the back for a bit. You look like you're gonna curl up and blow away. I got a job I gotta finish 'fore I close up, then we'll go out to the house and get some supper. Delia'd love to see ya."

***

I lay down on the old green couch in Eli's office, but I didn't sleep. For one thing, it smelled a bit too much like moldy towel. For another, my mind was stuck on the spin cycle. I couldn't stop it.

How was I gonna get back to Waar? I didn't even know where to start. Did

I spend the rest of my life snooping around in caves looking for little green glowy things? Both times I'd been teleported it had begun or ended in a hole in the ground, but that didn't guarantee any other caves had teleport gems. Hell, I didn't know if there were any more at all. I could have used up the only one on Earth!

That hurt too much to think about. There had to be more. There had to be! I couldn'ta lost Lhan forever. That just wouldn't be fucking fair! But where should I look? If they were just lying around, people would have found 'em long ago. They had to be hidden somewhere.

So where did I start?

By the time Eli came back to the office a little after five, I'd fallen asleep from all the walking in circles my mind was doing. It was a relief when he woke me up. I'd exhausted myself.

***

Eli's place was as rag-tag and rumpled as he was, a dusty redneck compound north of the 210 freeway with a dried out '50s ranch house up front, and various sheds, garages and stables out back. There was a horse carrier, an old tractor, a rusting Airstream trailer, a few dogs and chickens running around, a dozen vintage cars and bikes in various states of repair, and his daily driver, an old Ford pick-up with a "Keep honking, I'm reloading" bumper sticker on the back window.

Inside, the house was pretty much the same, a jumbled mess of mix and match furniture, old tin signs, a coffee table made out of an old door set on an engine block, more dogs, a kitchen with a half-built Moto Guzzi propped by the back door, and on every wall, floor-to-ceiling bookshelves, double stacked with battered old paperbacks—mostly sci-fi and fantasy, but with some spy and detective stuff mixed in.

Maybe that was another reason I went to Eli. Of the few people I knew in LA, he and Delia were the ones who just might believe me when I told 'em what had happened to me. *If* I told 'em. I mean, I was dying to tell somebody, but at the same time I was, uh, kinda shy about it too. Over the years I'd had people tell me plenty of times they'd seen a UFO, or been visited by angels, or lived a past life as Catherine the Great, and I knew how *I'd* acted. I'd given them the glassy smile and the noncommittal nod, the "Huh, whaddaya know," and the quick change of subject, and I wasn't sure I was ready to be on the receiving end of that kind of treatment—not without a six pack in me at least.

Eli passed me beer number one. "So, you decided what you wanna do yet?"

I was sitting at the kitchen table while him and Delia got some dinner together. Eli was pan-frying some steaks while Delia stirred up a salad made with mushrooms, tomatoes, and greens from her little garden out back. They looked like a pair of tattooed apple dolls pottering around the kitchen—both brown, greying and desert-hard. Delia was half Indian, half black and half Irish, and let her wavy iron-colored hair hang loose down her back.

I pulled on my beer. "I'm still not sure, but I guess it'd be good to skip town for a while."

Eli nodded. "I made a couple of calls while you were asleep. Some Mongols I know are goin' down to Tijuana on business this weekend. They could get you across no problem."

Mexico was a good idea. Easy to lay low down there. Easy to make a buck if you weren't too particular about the work, or the company you kept. But did I want to go? All I really wanted to do was hunt for a way back to Waar, but who was to say I wouldn't find it south of the border? Whoever sprinkled those teleporters around probably didn't give a damn about international boundaries.

Eli read my hesitation as reluctance. "Well, you got a couple days to think about it. And I'll see what else I can come up with. Let's eat."

He flipped the steaks on some plates with black beans and rice on the side and set 'em on the table as Delia dished out her salad. They sat down and Eli raised his beer.

"To safe returns."

Delia hoisted as well, but I hesitated. I knew he meant me coming back after six months, but all I was thinking about was getting back to Waar. Well, I'd drink to that.

I clinked their bottles. "To safe returns."

Delia had never been chatty, and I think Eli was giving me some space, so for a while there wasn't much to the conversation except, "Pass the salsa," and, "Another beer?" But finally, after second helpings and a lot more beers, Eli got out the tequila while Delia put some coffee on, and we all moved out to the back deck to watch the sun go down over the San Fernando hills.

"So," said Eli, and left it at that.

I knocked back my shot and held out my glass for another. He filled it and I settled back in my lawn chair, looking up at the stars that were just starting to come out overhead. One of those little lights might be where Lhan was. I didn't know which one to wish on, so I wished on 'em all. *Take me there now. I need to go back.*

Nothing happened. I downed the second shot and sighed. "You're not gonna believe me. It's *National Enquirer* kinda stuff."

"Try me."

I opened my mouth, but I still couldn't get started.

Delia put a hand on one of mine and squeezed. "I believe all kinds of things. Go on, sweetheart."

I nodded. "Well, I'll start from the beginning, then. The part you know about—punching that guy outside the Fly By Night."

So I told it. How the cops had chased me up into the Tarzana hills, how I'd hid in the cave, how I'd touched the stone. I could see them tense up a little bit at that, but I was drunk enough now that I just kept going, and when I told them I woke up on Waar, I could see the nervous smiles start to form on their lips, but they let me go, at least until I got to the part about the Aarurrh—the big tiger-centaur guys that captured Sai and me almost as soon as I got there.

I'd just finished describing One-Eye, the big alpha male Aarurrh who had been the leader of the hunting party, when Eli burst out laughing.

"Tiger-Taurs? Are you—?" He laughed again. "Shit, sweetheart, you really had me going there for a while."

I blinked at him, pulling myself out of my memories. "What do you mean?"

"I'm sayin' you picked the wrong guy to tell somebody else's story to." He motioned toward the bookcases in the living room. "I *have* read all of those, y'know."

I still didn't get it. "Somebody else's story?"

Delia was frowning too. "Be nice, Eli. Jane's been through a lot. Don't—"

"Yeah, but she ain't been through this!"

I balled my fists. I didn't expect them to believe me. But I didn't expect them to be so bare-faced about it either. "Are you calling me a liar?"

Eli held up his hands. "Now now, don't get your panties in a twist. I'm not saying you're lying. Maybe you got knocked on the head and you dreamed a book you read once." He laughed again and shook his head. "I'll give you credit for picking an obscure one, though. Most people haven't even heard of that one, let alone read it."

He hadn't calmed me down one bit. "I don't know what you're talking about.

I didn't hit my head, Eli. I didn't read about it in a book. It all happened. To *me*. Where do you think I've been for the past six months?"

Eli looked me in the eye for a long second, then sighed and put down his drink. He stood up. "Wait here."

Delia and I watched him go back into the house, then exchanged a glance.

"I'm sorry, Jane. It usually takes him to the second bottle before he's this ornery."

I shrugged. "It's fine. I didn't think you'd believe me. I just had to tell it is all."

"Well, when he comes back you can tell the rest of it. I want to find out what happens next."

There it was. I could hear the pity in her voice. She was being kinder about it than Eli was, but she didn't believe me any more than he did. She thought I was sick or something. I drank off another shot and turned away from her, looking up at the sky. There were a lot more stars out now. I had a lot more to wish on.

After about five minutes of silent sitting, Eli came back through the door.

"Here it is." He held out a book. "Knew I had it somewhere."

I took it and looked at it. It was battered old paperback. The title didn't mean too much to me—*Savages of the Red Planet* by Norman Prescott Kline—but the illustration made my heart do a back flip. Against a Ty-D-Bol blue sky, a big, square-jawed hero wearing nothing but a loincloth and an armored sleeve was fighting two half-man half-tiger centaurs, while a hot purple-skinned chick looked on all wide-eyed in the background. I turned it over. A sentence on the back jumped out at me. "Stranded on Mars, which its inhabitants call Wharr…"

CHAPTER THREE

HOPE!

I stared at the word for for a full minute, my mind spinning like a stripped clutch, then flipped the book over again and stared at the cover for another minute. The cen-tigers in the painting looked absolutely nothing like Aarurrh. They looked more like zebras with tiger-faced men where their necks should be, but combined with the armored sleeve, the purple chick in the corner, and *motherfucking* "*Wharr*" on the back cover, it was kinda hard to buy that it was all just some crazy coincidence.

I looked up at Eli, my jaw hanging by one hinge. "What is this? What the *fuck* is this?"

He sat back down in his chair. "That's the story you been tellin'. Except it was written in 1909 or so, by the guy whose name's on the cover, Norman Prescott Kline." He chuckled. "I still don't know how you got your hands on one of those. There ain't many copies around anymore."

"I've never seen this before. I told you."

"Well then maybe you heard someone talking about it some time." He nodded toward the book. "Lancer brought that out in the mid '60s, hoping to ride the Conan wave, but it tanked. Everybody thought it was just another Burroughs rip-off. Thing is, a lot of the hard-core fans think Burroughs ripped off Kline."

"Uh, who's Burroughs?"

Eli rolled his eyes. "You never heard of Edgar Rice Burroughs? The guy who invented Tarzan, and John Carter of Mars, and Carson of Venus? One of the fathers of science fiction?"

I shrugged. I'd heard of Tarzan, of course, but the rest of it meant nothing to me. I was more of a true crime gal. "I guess I have."

"Kline wrote *Savages* in 1909 and it was serialized in some crap pulp magazine, and Kline fans claim Burroughs must have read it before he wrote his own Mars stories." He sipped his tequila. "Anyhow, Kline's version didn't see the light of day again 'til Lancer Books went searching for old pulps to repackage in the sixties. Like I said, it didn't do too well for 'em—though it's a collectable now."

I shook my head, wishing I hadn't had quite so many shots on top of so many beers. It felt like the world had just pulled a rabbit out of a hat, and I couldn't figure out the trick. Had I made it all up after all? Had I heard somebody talking about this cheap-ass book back in the day, and just dug it out of my subconscious? I could swear I'd been to Waar. Hell, I had the scars to prove it, didn't I? But were they proof? I could'a got those scars anywhere. Maybe I'd hit my head when those dogs swarmed in and I fell in the cave. Maybe I'd spent the last six months in some kind of schizophrenic dream and I'd just now came out of it. But, no. That would mean Lhan wasn't real, and I wasn't ready to believe that. Not yet.

I held up the book. "Can I read this?"

Eli raised his glass. "Enjoy. Just go easy on the spine. It's the only one I got."

I got up, then realized I was being rude. "Uh, sorry. I—I just—I really want to..."

Delia waved a hand. "Go ahead, Jane. Go on. There's a bed made up in the Airstream. We'll see you in the morning."

I gave her a grateful look, then saluted Eli with the book. "Thanks, Eli. I don't... Well, goodnight."

"Night, Jane."

"Get some rest, girl."

***

I didn't get any rest. I read that book cover to cover in about six hours, then turned off the light inside the Airstream around 4am, but that don't mean I slept. I didn't. I lay there staring at the curved metal ceiling of the trailer until the sun came up, seven little words running through my head on an endless tape loop—*Norman Prescott Kline had been to Waar.*

I saw why the book had been a flop. It was a terrible story. Boring and predictable and corny at the same time. After the civil war, Captain Jack Wainwright, southern gentleman and officer of the Confederacy, heads out west to escape a bunch of evil carpetbagging creditors, and finds a strange object while prospecting for silver in Nevada. The thing transports him to "Wharr," which for some reason he thinks is Mars, and he falls in love with a local girl—a princess named Alla-An, who immediately gets kidnapped by an evil prince, and for the rest of the book, Captain Jack chases the bad guy from place to place, fighting his minions and trying to rescue Alla-An. Then in the end he saves her and they get married, even though they've said, like, three words to each other in the whole book.

Anyway, the fact that it was a stupid story didn't really matter, because behind all the noble speeches and the other hero bullshit, every detail about Waar was just how I remembered it. It was all there, the Aarurrh, the airships, the names of things. The princes were called Dhanans, the birds everybody rode were called krae, the big-ass gila-monster pit-bull bastards were called vurlaks. Some things sounded a little different. For instance, Kline spelled Ora's capital city Armlau, where I'd heard it as Ormolu, but shit, close enough, right?

All that book did was make me sure that this guy had been to Ora, and if he had, he might know the way back. I had to find him. I'd beat it out of him if I had to.

Around 6:30, I heard the back door of the house open, and boots crunching across the gravel of the yard. I got up and looked out a port hole. Eli was tip-toeing toward his truck, beer cooler and jacket in hand. I pulled on my jeans and t-shirt and stepped out barefoot, holding the book.

"Hey, Eli."

"Shit. I was tryin' to let you sleep."

"Forget it. I was awake. I, uh, finished the book."

He threw his jacket and cooler in the truck. "Uh-huh. Like it?"

"Ha. It was shit, but… but it was right." I held up the book. "Where can I find this guy? I need to talk to him."

Eli snorted. "Better find yourself a seance, then. Kline died broke sometime in the fifties, raving 'til the end that Burroughs and all the rest had ripped him off. Never even got to see that book published."

I sagged. Of course the guy was dead. He wrote the fucking thing in 1909. It had just seemed so immediate that I'd forgot, like nothing had changed on Waar for a hundred years.

"Well, does he have any family, then? Anybody I could talk to?"

Eli laughed and swung up into the truck. "I haven't exactly made the man my life's work, girl. I only know what I read in the fan mags, back in the day." He pointed toward the house. "You wanna look him up, there's a computer in Delia's office. Go nuts."

The look on his face as he drove away said he thought I already had.

***

I helped Delia feed her three horses and all the various dogs before she went off to work—she was an inventory manager for a company that rented camera cranes and lighting rigs to movie people—then made myself a cup of coffee and a bowl of Cheerios and sat down at her computer.

I am not what you'd call computer savvy. I've never owned one. Always felt riding a Harley with a laptop in my saddle bag was a little… wrong. But I have used one before. Whenever I've had to do any job hunting I'd go to the public library and use theirs and check the want ads, and I borrowed a friend's computer after Don died to sell his parts bike on eBay. Anyway, it wasn't hard to get the hang of it, and pretty soon I had a list of Google results for Norman Prescott Kline.

It got harder from there, slogging through sites owned by people with similar names, store sites offering his books for sale, forums for science fiction fans with post after post by people who really needed to get out more tearing each other new assholes over the most minuscule bullshit. I wasted an hour paging through those before I realized I wasn't going to find anything useful there.

I found a Wikipedia page for him, but it didn't have much more than what Eli had told me and his bibliography. Finally I found a fan site dedicated to him. It had a picture of him—a scrawny little guy with spectacles and a big mustache—and a more detailed biography than the Wikipedia page had. It also mentioned that his granddaughter, someone named Leigh Gardner, maintained a museum of his memorabilia at his old house, which was in Altadena, California. There was even an address and phone number.

I stared at the phone number for a minute, my heart pounding, then picked up Delia's phone and dialed. Someone answered in Spanish. They'd never heard of Norman Prescott Kline. I cursed. The number had been changed. Had Leigh Gardner moved? Did somebody else live in Kline's house? Was it even still there? There was only one way to find out.

I googled the address, which was on a street called Holliston, and scribbled down the directions, then went out to the yard. There were a couple of bikes out there that actually worked. I picked one, and was hunting around for a helmet when I realized what I was doing. If I found a teleport gem, I wasn't coming back. I guess I coulda left a note telling Eli to pick up his bike at Leigh Gardner's house if I didn't come back, but that seemed a pretty lame thank you for all his hospitality.

Instead I took ten bucks from the top of Eli's dresser, grabbed my hoodie, and went back to the computer to look at bus routes. It didn't feel right to be charging back to Waar on the Metro, but it was more right than stealing Eli's bike. I left the copy of *Savages of the Red Planet* on the kitchen table along with a note:

> Delia and Eli,
>
> Think I found a way back 2 Waar. If I don't come back U know I did. Thanks for everything. Especially the book!
>
> Jane
> P.S. Took $10

***

The Kline house was the kind of quaint, two-story bungalow that yuppies paint dark green or deep red and fill with fake craftsman furniture. No yuppies had got to this one yet. It was white, with a white picket fence and a white wicker porch swing, all a bit dusty and old-ladyish.

So was the gal who answered my knock. She was shaped like like an eggplant, narrow at the top and wide at the bottom, and very pink and grandmotherly. She wore a gray twin set and pearls, with white meringue-pie hair and a cardigan around her shoulders though it was the middle of summer. From what I could see beyond her, the house looked as dusty and old-fashioned as she was—couches with afghans over the back, dainty side tables with candy dishes, beaded lamps, a fireplace, the works.

She gave me a nearsighted once-over—holding for a while on my hoodie and the Jack Daniel's t-shirt I'd borrowed from Eli—then smiled like she was afraid I was going to set her house on fire. "May—may I help you?"

I opened my mouth, then shut it. I'd been so busy praying that the old girl had one of the glowing clock-thingies lying around that I hadn't thought how I was going to ask her about it once I got here. "Say, did your grandfather leave a teleport device lying around somewhere?" probably wasn't going to cut it.

I finally managed a grin. "Uh, hi. Is this Norman Prescott Kline's old house?"

"Yes, it is. But—"

"Oh great. Well, I'm a big fan, and I heard you had a—a kind of museum here. Of all his stuff. I was hoping. . . ." I trailed off as I saw her face go all sad and apologetic.

"Oh, I'm terribly sorry." She sounded like Julia Child. "I thought everyone knew by now. I no longer maintain the museum. There just weren't enough people coming. I—I hope you haven't come far?"

"You wouldn't believe. But, listen. I don't suppose you'd make an exception since I'm here already. I won't take too much of your time. I just want to see if—"

She looked like she was going to cry, she was so sorry. "But I'm afraid there isn't anything to see. I auctioned off all of my grandfather's effects five years ago. It was in the news. If you want to see them, you'll have to go to—" She frowned. "Oh, I don't know where it went—Iowa or some place like that."

I stared at her, open-mouthed. "Iowa?"

"Iowa. Idaho. I don't remember now. I'm terribly sorry. I'm afraid there's nothing I can do for you."

She gave me another sad smile and started to close the door. I stopped it with a hand.

"Please. Just one more question. Did they take everything? Are you sure they didn't leave anything behind? Something that might have looked like a—a glowing clock, or a hood ornament, or a lamp?"

Her lips pursed like she was going to get mad, but then she pulled up short and looked at me again, kinda uneasy. "Are you talking about the transmigration ray?"

My heart leapt. That's what Norman Prescott Kline had called the teleport gems. "Yes! The transmigration ray! I need to find one! Do you have one?"

I realized as soon as I said it that I should have been more discreet. That uneasy look spread all over her face and became the same kind of smile Eli and Delia had given me when I was telling them about going to another planet—that tight little, "Get the net!" grimace. I was getting sick of it.

"You do know that my grandfather wrote works of fiction. There is no such thing as a transmigration ray. He made it up."

Maybe I could have played it off and said I knew it was fake, that what I meant was that I was looking for a "prop," as a memento, but I could tell, like a transvestite can tell when the red-necks in the corner have clocked her as a guy, that there was no putting the cat back in the bag. Nothing I could say now was going to convince Leigh Gardner I wasn't crazy, so I went for it.

"That's not true, and you of all people should know it! Norman Prescott Kline went to Waar, and he used the transmigration ray to do it!"

She backed up like I was going to hit her. I eased back, holding up my hands.

"Sorry, sorry. I didn't mean to shout, but come on. Even if you don't believe it, I bet there were rumors. Family stories. He must have told somebody. Was it you?"

Her face got very stiff. I'd hit a nerve. She started to close the door. "I will not discuss my grandfather in this way. He was a very sick man. Goodbye."

"Sick? Ha!" I shoved my foot in the door. "So there were stories! He *did* say he'd gone to Waar. Did he say how? Did he say he had a transmigration ray?"

Her pink face was turning red as she tried to crush my foot and close the door. "Please, if you don't leave, I will call the police!"

I was practically crying with frustration. I swear I put my hands together and pleaded like a schoolgirl begging for a pony. "Lady, Mrs. Gardner, please. I don't want to scare you, and I don't want to steal anything. I just want to look at the transmigration ray. If it doesn't do what I think it will, I'll leave. If it does… I'll leave even quicker. Please. It's the quickest way to get me out of your hair."

Leigh stopped pushing on the door and looked me in the eye. "Nothing like that was found among Grandfather's things. He claimed he had one, and said he intended use it to go to Waar and live forever before he got old and frail, but he never produced it. He died in his bed at eighty-one."

My heart sank. "And nobody's ever found one?"

"Never. Now would you please go?"

"Okay, okay. Sorry."

I pulled my foot out and the door slammed. I sighed and just stood there, head down, boiling with frustration. Was she lying? Did she know where the teleport gem was but didn't want to tell me? I kinda doubted it. She didn't seem like the lying type. Kline must have hid it before he died. Or maybe he lost it. Either way, I was at a dead end. Leigh Gardner didn't know where it was. Was I going to have to schlep all the way out to Iowa? That would take weeks! And there was no guarantee the thing would be there once I got there. And even if it was—and it worked—would Lhan still be alive after all that time when I got back to Waar?

I closed my eyes, fighting back tears. Shit, if I was honest with myself, I'd have to admit he was probably already dead. Those priests probably slit his throat at the same time they grabbed me. But I couldn't let myself believe that. I couldn't just turn my back on him and stay on Earth because of a "probably." I had to go back and see for myself. I…

A murmur in my ears made me lift my head. It sounded like the tinnitus I've got from all my years riding Harleys and going to see rock and roll bands. It's with me all the time, but I generally ignore it. This time, however, it caught my attention, pulling me out of my swirling brain.

I waggled a finger in my ear, but the sound stayed with me, right on the edge of my hearing. Maybe it wasn't my tinnitus. Now it sounded like traffic noise from down the block. Or somebody with a radio on static a few houses away. It wasn't letting me think.

I turned around, looking up and down the street, but the murmur still sounded like it was coming from behind me. I waved my hands around my head like I was swatting mosquitos. It didn't make a damn bit of difference. I still heard it. I stuck my fingers in my ears. I heard it louder—a whole planet full of people whispering gobbledy-gook inside my head.

And suddenly I knew what it was.

CHAPTER FOUR

CORNERED!

I'd heard that same whispering six months ago in the cave when I'd touched the glowing green gem and been dragged across the universe to Waar—a thousand voices all babbling to me in a language I didn't understand—*downloading it* into me. That's what the teleporter gem did. It took you to Waar and taught you the language. If I was hearing it....

I looked around, eyes wide. There *was* a gem around here! There had to be! That noise couldn't be anything else!

I took a step toward the house. The voices got a tiny bit louder. Was it inside the house or behind it? I stepped off the porch and started around to the drive. It got louder still, like bees buzzing inside my head. I frowned. Did Kline's granddaughter hear this all the time? How did she stand it? I woulda been climbing the walls. But maybe she didn't hear it. Maybe I only heard it because I'd touched a gem before. Maybe I was attuned to it now or something.

I stepped into the backyard and started toward the back fence. The whispering got softer. Okay. In the house, then. I turned around and saw the old lady through the kitchen window, on the phone, and staring right at me. Her voice came muffled through the closed windows.

"I'm calling the police!"

I waved my hands and started for the kitchen door. "Don't! Please! It's here! I can sense it! It's in your house!"

Yeah, I am aware how crazy that sounded. I *was* crazy. It was so close. I had to get to it. I had to find it.

Leigh shrank back as I ran up her back steps and rattled the kitchen door. She was crying into the phone. "Yes, Holliston Street! Hurry! She's trying to break into the house!"

"I'm not trying to break in, Mrs. Gardner. I'm not going to hurt you. I just want you to open the door. I know the transmigration ray is in your house."

Leigh hung up the phone and backed through a door, out of sight. "I—I have a gun!"

I didn't believe her. I banged on the door. "Mrs. Gardner! Open the door! Please! Just let me talk to you."

Nothing but whimpering. Goddamn it! There was no time for this. The cops were coming. I had to be gone before they came, and I would be if I could just find that gem!

"Mrs. Gardner! Are you there? Can you just—"

Right there in mid-sentence, my patience ran out. It was there one second, gone the next, like a drop of water on a hot skillet. I saw red. I snarled. I put my fist through the back door window, then cleared the shards with a couple more punches and reached down to the latch. A second later I was in, knuckles and arm bleeding.

I heard a scream from the living room.

"It's okay, Mrs. Gardner. I'm just going to look for the transmigration ray now."

I stepped into the dining room, dripping blood off my knuckles. The whispering got fainter. I backed out and crossed to the door to the living room.

BLAM!

I jerked back as a bullet splintered the door frame beside my head. The silly bitch *did* have a gun! A fucking Dirty Harry magnum revolver, of all things. Fortunately, firing it had knocked her on her ass, and she was heels-up across an occasional table with her head in a dish of butter mints, her forehead turning purple where the recoil had smacked her in the face.

I jumped across the room and snatched the howitzer out of her hand before she could recover.

She threw her arms over her face. "Don't kill me! Don't kill me!"

I flipped out the barrel and shook out the five remaining bullets onto the carpet. "I told you I wasn't going to kill you. Now, stay put!"

I stuffed the gun in the back of my jeans and stood stock still, trying to listen past the pain in my arm and hand and find the whispering again. My ears were still ringing from the gunshot. It took a while. Leigh looked up at me like I was crazy. Well, duh.

After another minute I could hear it again, and it felt like it was stronger above me. I ran for the stairs.

Leigh whimpered from the floor. "Where are you going?"

"Out of your life, I hope."

I heard sirens as I reached the second floor, and not too far away, either. Shit! The cops must have had a cruiser in the neighborhood. I didn't have much time.

There were bedrooms to the right and left, with a bathroom and a closed door in between. The whispering was definitely louder up here. I ducked into the left bedroom, Leigh's by the slippers under the bed and the curler set on the vanity. The whispering got quieter. I backed out and went into the other, a guest bedroom—neat as a pin. Quieter here too. Damn. The bathroom didn't give me any love either. What was behind door number two?

I threw it open, expecting a linen closet, but it was a set of stairs going up. The attic! Of course!

I bounded up the stairs, and nearly cracked my skull. The attic was an L-shaped space with a slanting bare-beamed ceiling coming to a point only a few inches over my head. I hunched down and looked around, then groaned. The place was packed with junk! Hat boxes, trucks, crates, piles of old magazines, clothes bags hanging from a rod, an ancient baby buggy. And the sirens were only blocks away. I was never going to find the gem in time!

It was almost impossible to stop myself from tearing into the boxes at random, but that wouldn't get me anywhere. I needed to clear my head and listen. I stopped, heart pounding, and closed my eyes. Right. It was to the right. I turned to the long leg of the L and squeezed down the narrow path between mounds of junk. The whispering got louder. I was on the right track.

I slipped around the rectangular brick pillar of a chimney and pushed to the far wall, which had a little window in it. The whispering was behind me now. I'd passed it. As I turned back, a flash of red and blue out the window caught my eye. The cops were outside. They were getting out of their car.

"Fucking cops. It's goddamn deja-vu all over again!"

I forced myself to go ahead slowly, feeling for the moment when the source of the whispering slipped behind me. Just past the chimney, it did. I turned and looked around. There were suitcases piled up all around it. I started tearing into them like a crazed badger, dumping out dusty clothes, old letters, silverware sets, diplomas, and throwing the luggage behind me. Nothing.

As I stomped open another case I heard a knock on the front door downstairs, and Leigh wailing, "She's upstairs! And she has a gun!"

She was answered by reassuring cop murmurs and the squawk of cop radios.

I flipped over the case, spilling it. Checkers, chess pieces and Monopoly money. I tore open another one. Postcards and souvenir spoons. I kicked it aside and spun around. I'd cleared all the suitcases around the chimney and it wasn't in any of them, and the whispering was going crazy now, like the last act of an opera. My whole head was ringing, and I was hearing creaks and squeaks as the cops tip-toed up to the second floor. Where the fuck was it! Under the fucking floorboards?

I leaned against the chimney and mopped my forehead with the sleeve of my hoodie, catching my breath and wondering how I was going to tear up heavy wooden planks. I froze. The singing was right here! It was drowning everything out. I stepped back and stared at the chimney.

"Norman Prescott Kline, you sneaky son-of-a-bitch."

I looked around for something heavy. There were a pair of greenish bronze statues of big-boned gals in long robes looking toward heaven and holding up laurel wreaths. I grabbed one under the tits and swung her at the chimney. She was sturdy and her base was marble. It did some damage.

I spit out brick dust and grinned. I'd be through in five.

"This is the police! Slide your weapon to the top of the stairs where we can see it and come forward with your hands on your head."

Goddamn it, not now! I was almost there! I had to stall 'em. Time to play as crazy as Leigh thought I was. The cops killed burglars, but they were always real nice to wackos who were a danger to themselves.

"Don't come up! I'll kill myself! I've got a gun!"

There was a pause. I could hear the cops whispering to each other. I swung the statue again, and cracked mortar. Bricks were hanging loose.

"Hey up there, take it easy! What are you doing?"

I laughed like a maniac and swung again. "I'm digging my own grave!"

A brick tumbled out of the chimney, and more cracked and shifted.

"Come on, now. Stop that. Put down the gun and let's talk this out. What do you want?"

Smash! I hit the chimney again. "I want out! I can't stand it anymore!"

"Well, we're here to get you out. We're here to help."

Another swing and the marble base went flying, spanging off a stack of cookie tins. But bricks went flying too, and through the gap I could see wood. I dropped the statue and started tearing out the loose bricks with my bare hands. There was an old wooden box back there, all scarred up, with writing burned into it—Army of the Confederacy.

"Hey, did you hear us? We're here to help."

I shouted over my shoulder as I worked my fingers behind the box and tried to lever it out of the hole. "I don't want your help! I wanna leave this world behind!"

I heard a step on the stair. "Listen, I'm just gonna come up there and we'll talk this—"

"Don't come up! I'll shoot myself! I swear I will!"

The cop retreated. "Don't do that. Come on. This is nothing to kill yourself over. You haven't hurt anybody. We can resolve this."

I braced a foot against the chimney and wrenched as hard as I could. The box ripped out, showering bricks everywhere, and caught me in the chest. It was like an engine block. I staggered back and went ass over tits over one of the suitcases I'd dumped, the box crushing my ribs then slipping off and slamming to the floor.

"She's down! She's down! Go go go!"

I sat up, gasping, and saw the shadows of the cops charging up the stairs, guns out. I looked at the box. The lid had split and something inside was glowing a pale lemonade green. Time to go.

I shoved the lid aside. There was another rocket-finned clock thing in there, just like the one in the cave. I stretched for the gem in its center.

The cops saw me reaching. "She's going for a gun!"

The last thing I heard as my fingertips touched the cold smooth surface of the gem was the double bang of two police-issue nine millimeters firing at my heart.

CHAPTER FIVE

TRAPPED!

At first I thought they'd hit me. It sure as hell felt like *something* hit me. There was an impact like a car wreck, but no noise except weird voices jabbering in my ears, and no sensation except a cold like skinny-dipping at the North Pole. Then I was falling.

Forever.

Okay, not forever. 'Cause, you know, eventually I woke up. It sucked.

Like when I'd done this before, I came to buck-naked with the bed-spins making me feel like I was doing loop-de-loops even though I was lying still. Unlike the time before, I hurt everywhere. All my various aches and pains, which I'd been a little too busy to pay attention to in my last minutes on Earth, all lined up front and center and shouted, "Ma'am, yes ma'am! All present and accounted for, Ma'am!"

My butt and legs throbbed where I'd landed on 'em after falling over the suitcase. The cuts on my knuckles and arm throbbed and stung like someone had poured rubbing alcohol on them, and they were still bleeding—like, a lot—but those were nothing compared the pain in my chest. My ribs ached like—well, like I'd dropped a safe on them—which I had. I felt like I couldn't catch my breath, and I got nasty zings all down my sides every time I tried.

Worse than that, I didn't know where I was. I didn't even know for sure if I was on Waar. I'd had the idea—stupid, I know—that I'd show up in the same place I had last time. No such luck. There were no wide, blue-flowered plains around me. No saw-toothed mountains on the horizon. No horizon at all. In fact, if I hadn't known better, I woulda sworn I'd ended up in some VIP lounge at the Hartsfield-Jackson International Airport in Atlanta.

I was in a high, round room that looked like it had been designed by Swedish people in the seventies—all egg shapes and white plastic walls and arched doors as tall and wide as the back end of an eighteen-wheeler—and no furniture, just the white marble disk I was lying on, and a console by the door that looked like an ATM. Recessed lighting glowed the same soft white as the walls, and an electronic chime filled the room with a mellow GOONG sound. I don't think I've ever been in a place so clean-looking in all my life, and it made the hackles rise on my neck, 'cause no part of Waar I'd been to had been this spotless, this white, or this high tech.

Where the fuck was I? Had the damn teleport thingy sent me to the wrong planet? It had to be. Waar had been nothing but stone and red dust, and they'd barely invented the wheel. I rolled over, groaning as my ribs stabbed me in seven different places, and looked for the gem in the center of the disk. I had to get out of here before whoever lived here found me and did science experiments on me.

The gem was glowing. It was working! I could get back! I reached out my bleeding hand to slap it, then stopped. What was I thinking? It was only seconds after I'd left Mrs. Gardner's attic. I'd be going back to the cops searching for me under the boxes, and if I suddenly popped back in front of them they were going to shoot first and ask questions later. Even if they didn't fill me full of holes, I'd be arrested for breaking and entering, assault, and of course the manslaughter rap I'd been running from the first time I touched one of these gems. Maybe I'd better see what was up on this end of the interstellar poop chute after all.

I got my arms under me and pushed up—and sent myself flying sideways to land on my face and shoulder. It hurt, but I couldn't stop laughing—which hurt more. What a fucking idiot. You woulda thought this time I woulda expected a different gravity, but, well, gravity is one of those things you take for granted—like a pocket you keep reaching for even when you're wearing the pants without the pocket. You're kinda surprised when it's not there.

I pushed up more gently this time, and got to my feet without falling over again. I was gonna have to go easy for a while, but it felt great to be so light again. I hadn't known what I was missing before I left Earth, but bouncing around like I was some kind of red-haired jackalope had been the coolest thing ever, and the thing I'd missed most when I'd been sent back—except Lhan, I mean. He was kinda fun to bounce around with too.

I bobbled over to the door like a Macy's Thanksgiving Parade balloon on its tip-toes but couldn't find a handle. It was just two plain white slabs that looked like they slid apart. I tried to get my fingers between 'em and pull, but they didn't budge, and the effort made my ribs creak and twinge like I was being stuck with needles. I stepped back to breathe and massage my ribs, then looked around at the ATM thingy. Maybe that was how you opened the door.

There was a red light blinking on it, and now that I was closer, I noticed the GOONG sound was coming from it too. Was it an alarm? Was it some kind of phone? Was there an incoming call? Was— My heart skipped as I realized that *I* was the incoming call. The thing was letting the natives know someone had come through the looking glass and was waiting on the doorstep.

Just as I figured this out, I heard voices through the door. They were too muffled to catch any words, but they were coming closer. I looked around. There was no place to hide in the room, so I backed to the far wall, praying that the guys who lived in this airport weren't as tall as their doors.

The door whooshed open, and a bunch of bald-headed purple guys in orange and white robes looked in, crossbows and spears raised and ready. I stared, my heart thudding with relief. I almost ran up and kissed 'em! Those little creamsicles were Priests of the Seven, and it had been Priests of the Seven who had drugged me and sent me back to Earth, which meant I must be back on Waar, right? Or, shit, maybe not. What if these guys planet-hopped as much as I did? I could still be anywhere. I mean, from the looks of things, I could be on a space ship.

It didn't matter. Wherever I was, the priests would know how to get me to Waar. They might even know where Lhan was. Maybe they had him locked up right here! I'd just have to beat it out of them. But maybe not just now. There were five of 'em standing in that door, three with spears and two with crossbows, and I was buck naked and bleeding like a stuck pig. I didn't wanna travel ten thousand light years from home just to end up dead on arrival.

I stepped forward, smiling and raising my hands like I'd been cornered by the cops. "Hey, guys. No hard feelings right? I mean, thanks for the ride home, but—"

They backed off, shouting. One of 'em fired his piece by accident, and the bolt pinged off the ceiling.

"A demon!"

"A demon has come through the portal!"

"Sound the alarm!"

I frowned, confused, then remembered. People on Waar thought demons were big pink chicks with red hair. Not real flattering, but what the hell. If it worked, I'd take it. I leapt toward them, laughing like the wicked witch of the west and shouting, "Swallow your soul! Swallow your soul!"

It wasn't much of a leap. I was still dizzy and not used to being a featherweight again, so I veered off like a bottle rocket and crashed into the left wall, spraying blood everywhere, then picked myself up, hissing in pain. That seemed to scare them even more and they turned and bolted down the white hall that stretched straight out from the teleport room door.

I ran after 'em, grinning. This was gonna be easy. All I had to do was run down one of these little goobers, beat the tar out of him, and get him to tell me where Lhan was.

They reached a T-bone intersection ahead of me and turned left. I bounced after them and caught the slowest one in a flying tackle, slamming him to the ground and sending his spear flying as we skidded across the floor to smack into a wall. I came up straddling him and got a hand around his throat, then raised the other in a fist. My ribs hurt like fuck, but I did my best not to show it.

"Alright, you purple pipsqueak, where's Lhan?"

"Wh-who?"

I bounced his head off the linoleum. "Lhan! Dhan Lhan-Lar of Herva! You know, the guy who was with me the night you and your fucking inquisition kidnapped me and sent me *back to Earth*!"

His pals had stopped by this time, and were looking back, weapons raised, but didn't look like they wanted to come any closer. One of 'em ran to another ATM on the wall.

Pipsqueak squirmed under me. "Please, demon! I—I know not this person! Let me—"

WHOOP WHOOP WHOOP WHOOP!

A deafening siren went off right over my head and I cringed down like I'd been slapped by the hand of god. Pipsqueak's pals fled down the hall and I looked up and around, taking in where I was for the first time.

The hallway we were in now was wider than the first one—much wider—and curved away to the left and right in a way that made me guess it would eventually make a circle at some point. In both directions, orange-robed priests stood staring at me with slaves cowering behind them, carrying their books and papers. Directly to my left was a pair of giant double doors with big looping silver symbols inlaid in them, but they only held my attention for a second, 'cause the wall they were set in stopped me cold.

Actually, it wasn't the wall that had me staring, even though it was pretty amazing—a seamless floor-to-ceiling glass window that went left and right down the hall as far as I could see. That just made the whole place feel even more future-seventies theme-park than it had before. And it wasn't the view behind the wall either. That was just a big circular open space, more than a football field across that looked like the atrium of one of those fancy hotels where all the floors look down to the lobby below, except so high and deep that it seemed to go up and down forever. No, what was making me gape like a hooked trout was that the floors on the far side of the atrium were all warped and distorted like I was looking at them through a bottle. The atrium was filled with water! I was looking at the biggest aquarium I'd ever seen, but there were no fishes. What the hell was it for?

The sound of running feet brought my head around. More guys in orange and white were jogging up the hall from the left, but these were wearing armor, and looked like they knew how to use their weapons.

"Fuck! Sorry, pal. Gotta go."

I hopped up off Pipsqueak, grabbed his spear, then jumped to the doors with the silver squiggles on them. They didn't open. I looked around for a button or switch and saw a glowing white circle to the right of the door at about shoulder height. I pressed it and the light pulsed a little brighter, but nothing else happened. The spear guys were jogging closer.

"Goddamn it."

I ran right, taking wobbly ten-foot strides and sending panicked priests and slaves scattering, but before I'd got more than a few steps I saw more guards coming in the other direction—a lot more. There musta been twenty of the fuckers.

I skidded to a stop and looked around for a way out. There. A door on the outer wall. It was smaller and plainer than the others, but at least this one whooshed open when I ran to it. I looked in. A little hallway, dark and empty.

I ducked in and the door whooshed closed behind me as I ran on. There were more doors along both walls and one at the end. All the curved white smoothness was missing here, replaced by unpainted concrete and exposed lighting fixtures, and a muffled roar came from somewhere below that sounded like an air conditioning system.

I tried the doors on the walls, which, though they were as big as the ones in the main hall, were just plain old doors, with plain old latches. They all opened into plain old store rooms. No way out.

Whoosh.

The door from the hall opened behind me and the spear guys stepped in, crouching low, with crossbow guys behind them, aiming over their heads. I ran for the far door, expecting to be a pin cushion at any second.

"Archers! Bring her—!"

"Wait! Don't kill her!"

I don't know who said it, but I was on their side. I felt exactly the same way.

"Wound her only! She is to be taken alive!"

Okay, so not exactly the same.

I slammed through the door as crossbow bolts zipped past my ankles and skipped off the floor. A blast of cold air hit me like a frozen fist, and the air-conditioning noise went from distant vacuum cleaner to in-your-face jet engine.

I squinted my eyes against the wind and ran out onto a metal catwalk that hung in the middle of a huge dark open space which went down so far I couldn't see the bottom, and up so far I couldn't see the top, and curved around to the left and right so far... Well, you get the idea. It was a big place, but also funny shaped. It was like a big hollow ring that encircled the water-filled atrium and the hallways around it like the space between the inside surface of a thermos and the outside, if you can picture that. And it was so loud I couldn't hear myself think.

The noise was coming from huge turbines which filled the ring like—okay, how am I gonna describe this? Have you ever seen the redwoods, up in Sequoia National Park? All those huge-ass trees, all standing a little bit apart from each other and going up forever before they have any branches? Well, imagine you're halfway up one of those big bastards, with miles of trunk above you and below you, and you'll get the general feeling, only here, the tree trunks are huge stacks of turbines, piled one on top of the other in endless columns and big around as houses, and all roaring like dragons inside heavy steel superstructures. Now imagine that, in between all the sequoias are other, thinner, trees, just as tall, but only as big around as your average grain silo, and looking like gigantic chrome Slinkies—big silver coils, dripping with condensation, that go up and down into the darkness just like the turbines. I don't normally have much fear of heights, but all that black space below me was making me a little weak in the knees, and I felt like clinging to the railing like it was a life preserver. Seriously, the place had a sense of scale like the Grand Canyon.

Unfortunately, the guys behind me weren't giving me any time to pull myself together. They spilled out of the service hall like an orange and white tide and started taking more potshots at my legs. I jumped to the end of the catwalk as bolts shot past me into the void, and found a spiderweb spiral staircase twisting down out of the darkness above and screwing down into it again below. It looked about as sturdy as a tinker-toy fire escape, but I didn't have much choice. I skimmed down the steps four at a time as I looked for a way out. It was freezing in that place and I wasn't wearing a stitch. My goosebumps were getting goosebumps. On top of that, the roar of the turbines felt like it was shaking me apart. My teeth were rattling in my head like castanets.

There was another catwalk a few twists down, but more guards were charging out of the service door at the end of it, so I kept going as they shouted after me.

"She's heading for the nineteenth floor!"

Was I? Okay.

The next catwalk was empty. I took it, hissing in pain as I ran across the cold grating with my ice-block feet. A bolt shot down from above and I flinched into a railing. It's amazing how cold makes every pain worse. I felt like I'd been rung like a bell. Everything throbbed. I picked myself up, groaning, and kept going.

The guards charged onto the catwalk behind me. I threw open the door at the end and stumbled into another service hall, moaning with relief as my frozen body hit the warmer air. This time I didn't bother checking the doors on either side. I just ran for the big door at the end. It whooshed, and I was back out in another glass-walled hallway exactly like the one I'd been in before. Where the fuck was the exit to this place? Was I gonna have to go all the way down to the bottom to get out?

I ran to the glass wall and looked down. There was no bottom to see. The distortion of the water blurred everything. But I could see something I hadn't noticed before. There were clear-walled tubes running down the aquarium walls at various points, and there were little capsules moving up and down inside them. Elevators! *That* was what was behind those big doors with the silver squiggles on them! Perfect!

I ran left toward the nearest one, and just like last time pushed on the glowing circle beside the door. Just like last time, nothing happened. I grunted, anxious, and looked back the way I'd come. The guards hadn't come out the door yet. I stepped to the glass wall and looked down into the aquarium again. Was it coming up? I didn't see it. I looked up. It was coming down! Finally! But then I saw through its glass walls. It was filled with guards!

Crap.

I looked right again. The guys from the turbine room were racing toward me out of the service door. I started left, past the elevator, but more were coming from that way too. The only direction open was a side corridor identical to the one that had led to the teleport chamber two flights up. Goddamn it! I didn't want to go back that way! I wanted to take the elevator!

But there was nowhere else to go. Pointy things were pointing at me from every other direction. I bolted down the side corridor, looking for doors to my left and right. There were none. Just the big door at the end. Two purple guys were guarding it, but they weren't guards. They were priests, and they were more hiding behind their spears than threatening me with them.

I leapt at 'em, raising my stolen spear like it was pool cue, and swatted theirs out of their hands as I came down. They yelped and tried to run, but I nabbed one and slammed him against the door.

"Open it! Now!"

He just whimpered. I looked over my shoulder. The guards were pouring into the hall and running straight at me, spears leveled.

"God dammit, if you don't open this door, I'm gonna feed you your own nuts!"

With a squeal of fright, he touched his hand to a circle next to the door—just like the one on the elevator—and the door whooshed open. Why did it work for him and not for me? Whatever. Now was not the time to figure it out. Inside was another teleport room with another marble disk and a glowing gem. Where the hell did this one go? Krypton? I dragged the priest into the room and shoved him at the ATM machine.

"Now, lock it! Hurry!"

He spread his hands, helpless. "The guards have the key, demon. I cannot keep them out."

I pointed to the ATM. "Come on. Can't you override the lock? Can't you break it?"

The priest frowned, confused. "Using the speaking box?"

Well, how was I supposed to know it was the intercom? It *looked* like a big deal.

The door whooshed open again and the guards stepped in, ranked up and spears ready.

"Shit!"

I jumped to the priest and got him in a hammer lock, then put the blade of my spear to his neck and started backing away from them. "Stand down or he gets it! I'll cut his throat!"

The spearmen stopped, but spread left and right. A priest with a neck like a turkey wattle stepped in behind them and raised his hands.

"Let him go, demoness. We mean you no harm, I promise you. Put down your weapon and let us talk."

"You put down your weapons first."

I took another step back and tripped over the lip of the raised disk. I flailed to keep my balance and lost my grip on the little priest. He squirmed like a cat trying to avoid a bath and ran behind me, straight for the gem. Fuck! He was gonna blip out and leave me without a hostage!

I spun around mid-fall and grabbed his ankle as he dove for the gem.

"No you don't, you little—"

The little priest's hand slapped the gem and I was back in the void, falling and frozen and wondering why I'd thought that room with the turbines had been cold.

CHAPTER SIX

CHASED!

We popped back out of the blackness into a stone room about the size of a walk-in freezer, only it wasn't cold in there, it was broiling, and it stank like an outhouse in July. There was nothing in the room except the teleporter disk and a heavy door in one wall with a pull chain beside it.

I came up hacking and choking and hauled on the little priest's ankle, pulling him away from the gem. "Where did you take us, you little fuck?"

He kicked at me with his other foot and cracked me on the jaw with the heel of his sandal. Sandal? Hey! He used a teleport gem and was still wearing clothes! What the fuck! He scrambled to the gem as I was staring and grabbing my mouth and, pop! He wasn't there.

"Goddamn it!"

I looked around, wondering where the hell he'd left me, and saw the door again, and the chain. I groaned to my feet and reached for it, then heard a soft "fump" behind me and looked back.

An orange and white guard was standing on the disc. Fump. Another one. Fump fump. Two more. Fump. Mr. Turkey-Wattle.

"Seize her!"

I yanked on the chain and the heavy door edged open. I shoved it open, then ran through into a dark tunnel with brick walls and the worst smell I'd ever smelled in all my life. It was enough to buckle my knees, but I had to keep going. The guards and the priest were charging out after me.

Little knife blades of light sliced down from the roof of the tunnel as I ran on, and showed me that there was a wide gutter down the middle of it, with a thick, lumpy river running through it, and steam rising up off it. I was in a sewer, and I don't think it had rained in a while. I gagged. There was a real danger that the Cheerios I'd eaten back on Earth were gonna come up again and mix in with the muck of wherever this was. Fuck. What if my breakfast combined with the local lunch to create some weird alien poop monster that destroyed the world?

"Catch her! Bring her back!" Turkey-Wattle's voice echoed down the tunnel from behind me. "Duru-Vau will have our heads if we let her escape too!"

"Fat chance, pal." I was skimming low so I wouldn't crack my head on the ceiling, but I was still taking ten feet a stride. There was no way they'd catch me.

Then his words sank in. Too? Who else had they let escape? Did he mean Lhan? Did that mean Lhan was free? Did they know where he was? All of a sudden I wasn't so interested in escaping. I had some questions to ask first, and I knew just who I wanted to ask.

There was an intersection up ahead, lit by a bigger shaft of light. I looked behind me. My eyes were tearing so bad from the smell I could hardly see a yard away, let alone fifty feet, but after blinking a couple of times I made out some shadows running through the blades of light.

If I could see them, then they could see me, so I made a big show of turning left at the intersection, and ran through the big shaft of light on purpose. As soon as I was around the corner, though, I stopped and looked around, searching for a way to separate Mr. Turkey-Wattle from his pals.

That's when I noticed that the beam of light next to me was shining down on a ladder that looked like iron staples half-sunk into the walls. I jumped to it and looked up. It went up into a little brick chimney, and the shaft of light was shining through a little slot at the top.

"A manhole. Perfect."

Quick as lightning, I zipped up the ladder until I was hidden in the chimney, then waited, staring down into the tunnel. I felt like a jungle cat, though I don't think any jungle ever smelled as bad. I put one hand over my mouth and nose and tried not to breathe. Didn't help even a little.

A couple seconds later I heard jogging footsteps and Mr. Turkey-Wattle's voice.

"Where is she? She's gotten too far ahead! Speed up!"

I readied myself as all the guards thudded by below me, then tensed as I waited for Turkey-Wattle to appear. Finally he staggered into view, winded and gasping. Like a naked ninja, I dropped down on him, knees first, and knocked him flat. His head hit the bricks, stunning him, and one of his arms went in the stew. I winced, but I couldn't be finicky now. I grabbed him by the collar and zipped back up the ladder like a rat up a drainpipe.

I was hoping to get away clean, but one of the guards musta looked back, 'cause suddenly I heard, "She's behind us! She has Brother Aln!"

I hauled the priest up the chimney to the manhole cover, which was more like an iron grate, but so caked with mud and crap that there was only one open hole. I shouldered it up and climbed out, dragging Turkey-Wattle behind me, and only then thought about what I might be dragging him into.

All around me was screaming and shrieking and people backing away. I blinked around in the blazing sunlight and saw I was in some kind of street market, with purple-skinned customers crowding around colorful little stalls and kids running around in rags. We'd come up in the middle of it all, and people were taking it big, gasping and pointing and calling for the cops.

"Demon!"

"It's got a priest!"

"Fetch the guard!"

The guards were already coming. I could see 'em climbing up the chimney beneath my feet.

"Sorry, fellas. We're closed."

With my free hand I grabbed the grate by one edge and dropped it down the hole. Back on Earth I couldn't have done that trick, because we're civilized enough to make manhole covers round so they won't fall down their own holes. These nimrods hadn't figured that out yet, and they paid for it. The grate wiped them off the ladder like the hand of god and I started looking around for a place where me and Brother Aln could have a quiet little chat.

Unfortunately, somebody *had* fetched the guard. I could see a troop of guys in green cloaks pushing through the crowd with a bunch of ragged children waving them on and shouting.

"This way!"

"A demon! A demon!"

"Look there!"

I locked eyes with the guard captain as he came around some kind of shish-kabob stand, then saw that a couple of the guys behind him had crossbows. Time to go. And time to go up.

The buildings around the square were all two and three stories, but their fronts were covered with awnings and fancy stone work, so it wasn't hard finding a way to climb one, but doing it with a stunned priest in one hand made it harder. I threw him up onto an awning, then vaulted up after him and slung him over my shoulder.

A crossbow bolt stuck in the plaster beside me as I climbed for a balcony, but then the guard captain shouted at his men not to fire in case they hit the priest, and they ran into the building instead.

I heaved Brother Aln onto the roof, climbed after him, and picked him up again, then stopped dead, staring out across the rooftops. Any doubts I'd had about what planet I was on were all washed away just like that, 'cause rising up out of the city like a giant white vibrator was the Temple of Ormolu, headquarters of the Church of the Seven, a windowless, spaceship skyscraper that looked as out of place on this medieval planet as a ray gun at a renaissance fair.

I blinked at it, a realization dawning. "That's where I just was. Duh. The inside matches the outside. That must mean there's local teleporters as well as long distance. Crazy."

I turned around to make sure, and saw the Aldhanan's palace, all red and orange sandstone up on its hill in the other direction. Yup, I was in Ormolu, the capital of the Oran Empire. I was back on Waar! Yay!

The sound of boots thudding on stairs inside the building snapped me out of my happy dance. The guards would be up there any second, and I didn't want to be waiting for 'em. I clamped Brother Aln to my shoulder, jumped for the next roof, and kept jumping until I was a whole block away, and had put a few cupolas and chimneys in the way besides, then stopped in the middle of a triangle of laundry lines and dumped him on his back.

"Alright, pal. Tell me where Lhan is."

He didn't answer, just lay there with his mouth half open. Shit. Had I killed him? I knelt down and listened to his chest. His heart was thumping along just fine. I slapped him, then slapped him again. He came to with a yelp and curled up, covering his head. I rolled him back over and pinned his shoulders flat with my legs, then clamped a hand around his neck.

"Where is Lhan-Lar?"

He stared up at me, whites showing all around his eyes. "I—I know not the name."

I slapped him again. "Liar! I heard you tell your guys you couldn't let me escape *too*. That means you let somebody *else* escape, and I'm guessing it's Lhan. Now where is he?"

He sneered up at me, my handprint turning his purple cheek maroon. "You may do your worst, demon. A priest does not give up the secrets of the—"

I reached behind me and clamped a hand on his junk. He squeaked like a dog toy.

"He has fled with the pirates!"

"What pirates?"

"The pirates with whom you defeated Kedac-Zir!"

My heart did a little dance in my chest. Lhan was alive? And he was with Kai-La and her gang of buckle swashers? This was the best news ever!

I gave his nuts another honk. "Where are they?"

"You will not save him. An airship went after them days ago. He will be dead with all the rest."

I rolled my eyes. "Tell me another one. Kai-La got the personal thanks of the Aldhanan. The navy's got no reason to go after them."

He smiled, smug. "The Temple has its own airships. And its own warriors. Besides, it was discovered they had betrayed the Aldhanan's trust."

My heart stopped dancing. "You framed 'em. You set 'em up."

"We did what was best for Ora, as we always have."

I let go of his sack and stabbed my finger at him. "I don't know what y'all are up to, but if Lhan is dead, I'm coming back here and burning your god-damned rocketship club-house to the ground. Now where is he? Where are the pirates?"

He shrugged like it didn't matter. "They are at Toaga, the pirate haven. Or they were. They are dead now, I assure you."

I slapped him. "And where is that?"

He spit blood and tried to hide his head against his shoulder. I grabbed his chin and forced him to look at me.

"Where?"

"To the south! Near the mountains!"

"Where *exactly*?"

"Do you think I have a map? It is to the south. I know no more."

I wanted to shake him, but he was right. Him telling me wasn't gonna do me any good. I needed to find a map, or somebody who could take me to this Toaga place personally. And how the fuck was I gonna manage that?

Through the flapping laundry I could hear the guards coming across the roofs. I stood up and grabbed a red blanket and a lime green sarong off the clothes line and started to cover myself.

"Thanks for the info. Remember my warning."

Brother Aln raised up on his elbows. "I did not lie before, demon. The church will give you mercy. Come willingly and you will not be harmed."

I sneered and backed for the edge of the roof. "Yeah, you'll just send me back to a place I don't wanna be no more. Thanks but no thanks, padre."

I turned and jumped for the street.

CHAPTER SEVEN

THE HUNT!

About eight hours later, looking like a color-blind babushka in my clashing blanket and wrap, I stared out from the branches of a purple tree at the ritzy country house of the guy Lhan and I had stayed with the night the priests had grabbed me and sent me back to Earth.

My first instinct had been to go to the Aldhanan's palace and ask Sai for help, or maybe even the Aldhanan himself. I mean, Lhan and I had saved his country for him, right? Couldn't he do us a solid and get the church off our backs? But then I remembered how many priests I'd seen in there, and how paranoid Lhan and Sai had been about them knowing what we were up to. They had ears everywhere, Sai had said, and even the Aldhanan watched his ass around them.

Then I remembered that Lhan and the guy who had put us up on our last night together had looked over a bunch of maps while we were trying to work out where we gonna go to escape the priests. If anybody knew where this Toaga place was, it was that guy. All I had to do was find him. I wish I'd had a map. It took me a while to work out where that was from the middle of Ormolu, but after a long day of sneaking and hiding and dragging my ass all over hell and back, and way too many wrong turns, rewinds and dead ends, I finally got to Lhan's friend's house about three hours past sunset. Now I was scouting the place like a spy in a movie. It looked like I remembered it, like a villa on some Greek island, with balconies and porches and wings, only all made out of hexagons the way all the buildings were on Waar, and I half expected to see it full of priests, all waiting to ambush me. Well, if they were, they were wearing some pretty good shrubbery disguises, so I made for the wall.

It isn't easy being a ninja when you're big and pink and dressed in red and green. You don't exactly blend in with the scenery. Fortunately, the big and little moons were down, and the lights were off in the house and probably nobody was watching anyway. I took a running start and jumped the wall long and shallow, then tucked and rolled on the blue lawn inside the compound and came up near the bushes outside the dining room.

Nobody called out. Nobody shot at me. Nobody opened a window. I let out a breath and climbed to a balcony on the second level, then rolled through an open door—and found myself in the bedroom Lhan and I had shared before the priests had grabbed me. I swallowed hard as little movies of that night flashed through my head. There was a lot of porn in those flicks, I admit, a lot of bouncing and grinding and licking and biting, but there was more too—kisses, hugs, stories back and forth, tears—all the stuff that makes a roll in the hay more than just a one-night stand, even if it only lasted one night.

"Don't be dead, Lhan. Please don't be dead."

I waited for my eyes to adjust to the darkness—and to stop leaking—then crossed the room to the door and out into the hallway. If I remembered the layout right, our host's room was two down to the left. The hall was darker than the rooms, so I made my way down by feel, and hoped my curses didn't wake anybody as I banged my shins and elbows into things.

Finally I found what I hoped was the right door, and opened it. It was the right door. Tubby, our host, was asleep on his bed, snoring softly at the ceiling. His name started coming to me as I looked at him. What was it? Ryan? No. Rian? That was it. Rian-Gi. I slipped in and closed the door behind me.

"Psst! Hey, Rian. Hey, buddy."

Have you ever seen a bulldog stuck with a cattle prod while napping? Neither have I, but now I don't have to. Tubby levitated about three feet off the bed and did some kind of spastic ballet move before coming down half-off the bed with one hand to his chest and his eyes as round as ping-pong balls.

"Who-who-who-who—?"

"Relax." I stepped out of the shadows. "It's just me."

He blinked at me for a second, then his eyes went wider than before. I was afraid they were gonna pop out onto his chest. "You! But you're the worst person it could possibly be! Go away!"

"I need your help to find Lhan."

He squealed. "By the Seven and the One! Go away! They may be watching the house!"

I looked toward the windows. He was making me paranoid. "Come on, dude. Nobody's watching. I promise. They all think I went south. Now, will you help me? I need a map to some place called Toaga."

He clapped his hands over his ears. "Do not tell me! They will ask again! They will put me to the question!"

"They questioned you? About Lhan? They…" A lump of ice slid down into my guts and grew into an iceberg. I clenched my fists. "Wait a minute. You told them. You're the reason they knew he went with the pirates."

Rian-Gi buried his face in his hands. "Oh, why did Lhan bring you here? The two of you have brought nothing but misery to this house. I wish they had caught you both before you ever darkened my door!"

That was too much. I grabbed him by the front of his robe and hoisted him off his feet so I could look him right in his fat little face.

"Listen, Madam Butterfly, I'm sorry we inconvenienced you. I'm sorry you've had storm troopers keeping you up past your bedtime, but if that's enough for you to wish your best friend killed by those orange house-coat wearing pricks then you're a fucking coward, and I oughta—"

He slapped me. It was like being hit with a silk glove full of tapioca, but it still brought me up short. He was red in the face. "Inconvenienced?"

He pushed away from me and tore out of his robe in a flinging frenzy, then stood there panting with his belly hanging out. There were red, half-healed whip cuts all over it.

"You see how inconvenient this has been for me?"

I stared, a hot flush rising in my face. I'd been too easy on Brother Aln. Way too easy. "The priests… The priests did that?"

He turned his head. "I—I was strong even then. Only when they threatened Wae-Fen did I—"

"Wae-Fen?"

He looked hurt. "You do not remember? He served us dinner. He ate with us."

I thought back to that evening. Everything before me and Lhan had hooked up had kinda ended up on the cutting room floor, but now that I thought about it, I remembered. Rian-Gi had given us dinner in his bedroom—this room—and we'd been waited on by this laughing little pretty boy with slim hips and lavender hair.

"Your, uh, servant?"

"It was I who was servant to… to…."

He started blubbing and slumped on the bed again. I looked down at him, feeling guilty about pressing him, but wanting to hear him say it. "So, to save your lover, you told them where Lhan was."

A hysterical laugh bubbled out of Rian-Gi's lips. "To save him from the whip. Yes. I did. They… they gave him the knife instead. As soon as I had betrayed my best friend, they cut Wae-Fen's throat from ear to ear. A corrupting influence, they said. A noble such as myself should not allow such perversion into my home. I must be a model for the morals of my inferiors."

His dimpled fists balled up and turned white at the knuckles. He hung his head. "I should have thrown myself at them, killed as many as I could before joining my beloved in death. I am a coward. That I live is proof of it."

I know it was shitty of me, but for a second, I was kinda inclined to agree with him. Then I felt ashamed of myself. Gay guys had it tough enough on Earth, and we were a supposedly civilized planet. Waar was still in the dark ages, and the church was the fucking Spanish Inquisition. Even a rich guy like Rian-Gi couldn't stand up for himself here. If you fought back, you got killed. End of story. No laws, no courts, no rights organizations, nobody had your back.

I squatted down beside him and put a hand on his shoulder. "I'm sorry. I didn't know. But… you don't really want Lhan to die too, do you?"

He raised his head, haughty and hurt, but then his face crumpled. "I fear I may have already killed him."

I was afraid of that too, but I didn't want to think about it. "There's still a chance. At least I hope so. But I need your help to find him, to save him."

"But he is with the pirates. They might be anywhere."

"They're in a place called Toaga. At least that's what a priest told me. I just need a map to get me there."

He pursed his lips, then nodded and stood. "This way. To my private chamber."

CHAPTER EIGHT

THE RACE!

From the way he said it, I was expecting his "private chamber" to be some kind of pervy pleasure room, and it was—at least part of it was. It was behind a secret door, just like it was supposed to be, and there were paintings of beautiful purple naked boys all over the place, and books of porny drawings open to the good parts on podiums. There was also a bed and a wardrobe filled with naughty costumes, but another part of the room was more like a professor's office. There were scrolls on the desk, and thick leather-bound books with titles like *The First Angao Dynasty* and *Heresies of the Khat Rebellion* in piles on the floor, maps on the walls, and ink quills and notebooks and scribbled-on scraps of paper everywhere, which Rian-Gi was digging through like a dog looking for a bone.

I laughed and held up a book called *History and the Nature of Divinity*. "You have to hide history books too?"

He looked up from his search and pointed to the porn. "They might shun me for owning that." His finger swung around to the history books. "They will kill me for owning that."

He was dead serious. I didn't get it. "What? Why?"

"You truly are from another world, aren't you? History is the most dangerous thing in Ora. The truth about the Seven and the One? The truth about the Wargod? The church has guarded those for centuries. Men have disappeared for only wondering aloud about their true origins. Professors, men of great learning, they all tread carefully around those subjects, choosing, for the sake of their own skin, to concentrate on the succession of kings and the wars between them. Those who do not? Gone. They fall out of windows, they die in tavern brawls, robberies, of strange sicknesses, of accidental poisonings."

I looked around at all the books again, shaking my head. He'd had all these in his house when the priests had come asking questions. "Damn. You're braver than I thought."

He shrugged. "Lhan and I and… others, are part of a loose circle of truth seekers, determined to learn the real story of our past, and we spent much of our youth hunting for forbidden books and digging in old dead cities." He smiled, and his eyes went all far away. "Those are some of the fondest memories of a sad and profligate life. Lhan and I, alone together, full of youth and curiosity and appetite."

Alone? Together? Appetite? I blinked. "Wait a minute. You and Lhan…?"

Rian-Gi smirked. "Surely, my dear, you knew he slept on both sides of the bed?"

"Well, yeah, but… but…." I couldn't help it, my eyes dropped to his gut.

He looked down, shrugging. "Well, I was more svelte then, and Lhan more beautiful, if you can imagine. Ah, here we are."

He pulled a map from the bottom of a pile and laid it across a desk. "It isn't shown as Toaga here, but it is marked nonetheless. This is a poor copy of an ancient map of the old kingdoms I made for one of our expeditions. You may have it. It shows the route from Ormolu…" He pointed to a big dot on the upper left side of the map, then trailed his finger down to a smaller dot near the bottom edge of the map. "To Udbec the Impregnable."

"The—the what?" I was still trying wrap my head around the idea of him and Lhan being together and was only hearing every other word.

"A great tower of rock rising from the forest—well, there is no forest now, but there was then. It was so high and so inaccessible that it was thought to be unconquerable, and the King of the Udar built his castle upon it. That, of course, was before the Seven granted us the gift of levitating air. After that it fell to the first Oran Emperor in a day. It has been abandoned since then, but for the pirates."

I squinted at the map. There wasn't much to it. I didn't see any lakes or oceans or roads, and it was hard to tell what the scale was. "How far is this? How long is it going to take to get there?"

Rian-Gi pursed his lips. "Hmmm. Riding a krae, four perhaps five days."

"And a ship?"

"Two days? Perhaps less."

I cursed to myself. Brother Aln had said the church had sent a ship after them days ago. That meant whatever they'd gone to do, they'd already done it, and I'd be getting there almost a week too late. Goddamn it! There was no way Lhan was still alive. But I couldn't give up. I had to go and see for myself. I *had* to.

I looked up at Rian-Gi as he started to roll up the map. "Thanks for this. I owe you, big time, but I gotta get going. I—I'd kill myself if I didn't...."

"My dear girl, there are tears in your eyes. You love him that much?"

I don't know why, but I snapped at him. Maybe I didn't like him seeing me cry. "What's it to you? You jealous?"

He looked miffed for a second, then shook his head. "No, not at all. I would not deny you your future with him. I hope you will not deny me our past."

I shrugged, uncomfortable. "Everybody's got a past. I got more past than most. No worries. And thanks again." I took the map from him and turned to the window, then stopped. I was still in my bag-lady outfit, and all of a sudden I was starving. Not the best way to hit the road. I turned back to him. "Uh, I don't suppose you can hook me up with some water and some chow? And... and if you had any old clothes, maybe a spare sword, I'd really appreciate getting out of this bed sheet."

He smiled. "I can give you better than spares. Wait here."

I studied the map while he left the room, trying to figure out if any of the places I'd already been were on it, and what cities and towns I was going to have to avoid on my way to Toaga or Udbec or whatever it was called. Before I'd made much sense of it, Rian was back, carrying something big and bulky and wrapped in a blanket that he had a hard time getting through the door.

He set it down with a clunk, then opened it. I almost cried. It was all the gear I'd had with me the night I was kidnapped—the heavy duty loincloth-bikini and the made-to-measure sleeve and chest armor I'd got when I was a gladiator in Doshaan, the riding boots and clothes Lhan's servants had made for me, and best of all, my custom-made six-foot-long Aarurrh-style sword, weighted and balanced just for me. And Lhan's clothes were there too.

"Fantastic! How do you still have these?"

He looked down, sad. "The priests left them behind on the night, so I kept them, hoping, though I had betrayed him, that Lhan would someday return, and need them. And you too, of course." He turned toward the door. "Dress yourself. I will ask my majordomo to prepare some food for your journey."

"Excellent. Thanks."

He paused at the secret door. "Mistress Jae-En. I hope that if—nay—*when* you find Lhan alive, you explain to him why I—why I did what I did, and ask him to forgive me."

I gave him a hard look. "I'll tell him what happened, but if you think I'm gonna plead your case for you, you got another think coming."

He turned a pinker shade of purple. "No no, of course not. It was cowardly of me to ask. I will ask him myself if—that is *when* you bring him back alive."

He bowed himself out, and I stared down at Lhan's clothes, looking very empty and forlorn without Lhan in them. "No, pal. I think you had it right the first time. *If. If* I bring him back alive."

***

Running on Waar was better than sex, maybe even better than riding a Harley. How could I hate bounding across the landscape with big twenty-foot strides like the kind you have in dreams, like the ones you see antelopes doing on nature shows? I coulda run like that forever and never got tired of it. I felt like Wonder Woman.

Of course I coulda had a nicer landscape to run through, not that it was all that bad at the beginning. The farmland around Ormolu was the same lush and neon-colored candy-land I remembered from before, with fields full of purple plants, pastures full of six-legged orange sheep-pig things, red shrubs with blue fruit, and little villages of hexagonal houses sprinkled all around, but the next day, as I got away from the center of the country, things started to get a lot drier and dustier. The fields were nothing but bare stalks and dead plants, and the pastures were filled with dead sheep-pigs and sick-looking maku, which were Waar's answer to buffalo—big shaggy six-legged bastards with heads like fists with eyes—only these all looked like they had the mange, and I could see their ribs through their hides. Dust devils whirled across the red dirt roads, and a whole lot of farms and villages were just plain empty. Half the time there wasn't anybody around to be scared of me as I ran through the town square.

And the further I went, the worse it got. By the third day, the fields were full of six-legged skeletons, baking white in the sun, and the villages looked like they'd been abandoned for years. I didn't understand it. I knew rain was rare in Ora. I knew they had to import a lot of wood from down south because there wasn't enough rainfall up north to grow forests. Lhan and Sai had told me all about it. But why wasn't there enough water for farming? Hadn't I seen a whole aquarium full of water back in the Temple of Ormolu? Why weren't they irrigating these fields? It made no sense.

On the fourth day the farms disappeared completely, and I was out on the plains—the same kind of area I'd showed up in the first time I came to Waar. That had changed too. The endless carpet of blue-stalked plants with little match-head flowers that I remembered from before had all wilted to a dry charcoal grey, and every now and then I'd see the dried corpse of a wild krae lying on the side of an empty creek bed.

I saw a few live animals too, and ran away from a few more. I surprised a pack of shikes, which are scary, screeching four-armed spider monkeys, tearing apart the corpse of a dead vurlak, which is like a fur-covered econo-van with teeth, and they chased me for a good half mile, and there was a run-in with a live vurlak later that day, but I jumped up on a jumble of rocks and hid from him and he gave up after a while.

At noon on the fourth day, I saw a tribe of Arrurrh, the four-armed centiger guys I'd been captured by once, off in the distance. They were hunting wild krae, and I was tempted to go see if it was Queenie's tribe. Fortunately, I'm not insane, so I didn't. If it wasn't her tribe, they'd have eaten me for lunch or taken me as a slave. If it *was* her tribe, the bulls woulda probably killed me as soon as they saw me. Her chief had tried to have me killed once before. He'd probably think I was back for revenge. Instead I looped wide around 'em and kept going.

Still made me wonder how Queenie's daughter Kitten and her sweetheart Handsome were doing. Probably had a litter of little four-armed, tiger-striped kids running around by now. I hoped they were alright. Them and Queenie had been better to me than just about anybody on Waar—except Lhan, of course. I wished 'em well.

Finally, later that day, just as the sun was touching the horizon, I saw through the heat shimmer what I first thought was another giant rocketship temple in the distance, and I wondered what the hell it was doing way out in the middle of East Bumfuck. As I got closer though, I saw that it wasn't a rocket ship, or a building, or anything man-made. It was a mesa, a wide, straight up shaft of rock, all red and majestic in the setting sun like something out of Monument Valley back home, only way taller, and all by itself. There weren't any others like it for as far as the eye could see. I also saw that there were ruins on top of it—a bunch of crumbling walls and towers so old they almost blended in with the natural rock.

And I saw one other thing too, an airship, endlessly circling the top of the mesa, and every now and then firing an artillery bolt into the ruins.

CHAPTER NINE

TOAGA!

As I got closer, I saw that the airship's balloon was painted the same orange as the robes of the priests of Ormolu and had their hexagon with a dot in the middle symbol painted on the side. I also saw something else—more than twenty other airships, all burned and broken and deflated on the rocks around the bottom of the mesa, and looking like the skeletons of dinosaurs right after the comet got 'em.

My guts clenched at the sight, imagining Lhan had been on one of those ships, and had fallen to his death with all the rest. I didn't get how it had happened, either. One temple ship against more than twenty pirate ships, and the priests didn't have a scratch? Even the Oran navy wasn't *that* good.

By that time I was close enough that the temple ship could have seen me if they'd known where to look, so I hid behind a rock and waited a half hour 'til the sun went down, then pulled on my hood and cloak to hide my light skin and started forward again.

It was creepy as hell tip-toeing through all those dead ships in the dark, with all their burnt ribs looming up on either side of me and their killer floating over my head like a circling hawk. In the dim light of the little moon I could see mangled bodies spilling out of the wrecks, and smell them too. The whole place stank of death and charred wood. Part of me wanted to stop and search through the corpses for Lhan, but I told it to go fuck itself. Looking for his body would mean I'd given up on him being alive, and I wasn't ready to do that. Not yet. I mean, the temple ship was still circling and shooting. That meant there still had to be somebody alive up there to shoot at, right?

I kept going until I reached the bottom of the mesa, then started to climb. It was obvious pretty quick why somebody woulda put a castle here back in the day. Even for me, with my Earth strength and my jumping ability, it was an almost impossible climb. The sides of the mesa were nearly as smooth and flat as a stone wall, and sometimes I had to search around for minutes for my next finger hold or foot rest. On top of that, I had to stop moving every time the navy ship came around my side of the mesa, just in case they were on the lookout for ninjas.

My fingers and toes were cramping before I was halfway up, and my muscles started to burn like I'd been running a marathon. Then, three quarters of the way up, the climb stopped being hard and became impossible instead. I reached a point where the rock face bulged out above me in a smooth curve, like I was looking at the underside of a balcony, except the bulge went as far as I could see in either direction. I was under a lip that seemed to go all the way around the mesa. The frustrating part was that I could see that the rock layer above the bulge was all rough and chunky and full of hand holds. If I could get there, the rest of the climb would be cake, but I couldn't get there.

Well, I might be able to, but if I went for it and didn't make it, I was dead—smashed to a pulp with all the other corpses down among the broken ships at the bottom of the mesa. See, I was in a good spot where I was. There was a two-inch-deep hole for my right foot, and good grips for both my hands. I had plenty of resistance to push off from if I wanted to jump, and I could see an easy hand hold on the lip of the bulge that I knew I had the power to reach, but power wasn't the problem.

Fear was the problem. Even just thinking about making that jump was making my sphincter tingle. I had to jump ten feet up and five feet out with my back to a twenty-story drop and no rope or safety net to catch me if I blew it. There would be no do-overs. There would be no take twos. There would be a Jane pancake on the rocks of an alien world and I would never know if Lhan had lived or died. On the other hand, what were my options? Was I supposed to climb down and give up? I didn't even know if I could. Some of those hand holds probably wouldn't work in reverse. And even if I could, I hadn't come all this way to say, "Never mind. I guess I'll go back to Ormolu and forget Lhan existed." It was up or nothing.

I crouched in close to the wall and tensed my muscles, ready to spring. Time to—

The warship came around the corner of the mesa only about twenty yards over my head. I nearly slipped outta my perch as I held myself back from jumping. Goddamn it! I'd been ready! Now I'd have to psych myself up all over again.

I waited for fucking *ever* until it floated past and slid around the other side of the mesa, then got ready again. Foot set? Check. Hands loose? Check. Target sighted? Check. Brain off? Check. Then go!

I kicked up as hard as I could, letting the weight of my sword and flapping cloak pull me out away from the wall as I shot up past the bulge—and kept going. Stupid idiot! I'd been so wound up that I'd kicked way too hard. I whooshed past my target hold like Superman headed for the sky, getting further away from the wall with every second.

I flailed at the jagged wall like I was trying to swat a mosquito, and snagged a knuckle of rock with my left pinky. The one-finger grip failed a second later, but I'd managed to pull myself closer to the wall and grabbed again. This time I caught a proper hold and clamped hard as the rest of me slammed into the wall all at once, knees, elbows, stomach, shoulders and face. I knocked my head so hard I didn't know where my arms and legs were, and for a sickening second I felt myself sliding down the rough wall without being able to tell my hands what to do.

Then everything snapped back and I grabbed on with all I had and just lay there, panting and bleeding and listening to my heart go BOOM BOOM BOOM BOOM!

Finally, after the warship had circled past one more time, I thought I could move again, and started up the lumpy wall with all my limbs as weak as lite beer. Five minutes later I was at the top, and pulling myself through a gap in a thick stone castle wall that looked like it had been knocked down a thousand years ago.

For a while I stayed where I was, which was the ruins of some kind of little hallway that had run through the base of the castle wall. There was another gap in the inner wall that seemed to lead to a big open space, but I wasn't going through it until I could catch my breath and stand up without my legs going all wobbly.

That took another five minutes, then I stood and looked through the other gap. The top of the mesa was bigger than I expected, roughly two football fields laid side by side, but otherwise what I saw didn't surprise me—a broken-down, high-walled compound, half town, half fort, with rubble and caved-in buildings everywhere, and a roofless castle in the middle, sticking sheered-off towers up into the night sky.

Set up among the ruins were multi-colored tents, and some of the more-or-less standing outbuildings looked like they'd been turned into bars and shops, with signs and tables outside, and there were others places that looked like they might be hostels, or maybe whore houses.

It was all deserted, though. All the campfires and torches were out, and there was nobody walking around the courtyard or in any of the tents that I could see. Were the pirates hiding? I didn't see any lights in any of the buildings, but they had to be here somewhere, or why was the warship here? I looked up and saw the big bastard floating by on the far side of the mesa. Yup, still there, and high enough up that it could look down into the compound and see anything that was going on. If I was gonna go looking for Lhan, I'd have to be sneaky, and the best way to do that was stay right where I was, inside the outer wall.

I started down the little hall to the left, peeking through the gaps as I passed them and hiding behind the standing sections when the warship had an angle on me. Halfway around I still hadn't seen any signs of life. I didn't even smell any cooking or a fresh latrine, but then, as I was sneaking past the castle, I heard a cough.

I hunched down behind a mound of rubble and looked up, thinking the sound mighta come from the warship, which was sailing so close to the mesa I could hear its sails flapping, but no, the ship was way on the other side just then, and that cough had been nearby.

I turned toward the castle. I still couldn't see any lights, but as I edged closer, I thought I heard a couple of people talking, low and quiet, then another cough. Yup. Definitely the castle, and definitely through that gap in the wall right in front of me. Hmmm. There was about forty feet of open space between me and it—so three or four long strides. I just had to time it so the warship was behind something as I made my run.

I looked up. It was circling past a long open stretch where the outer wall was completely down, but beyond that was a narrow three-story building that had three walls intact. When the ship went behind that, they'd be blind for at least five seconds. Perfect.

I waited until the prow of the ship just started slipping behind the building, then bolted, running as fast as I could across the courtyard. Not quite fast enough. I was still a stride away as the ship started coming out on the other side of the building, and I dove for the opening like I was diving for home plate.

Well, I didn't hear anything from the ship, and it didn't shoot at me, so I guess that was a win, but I scared the living piss out of the two pirates who were on guard inside the room I dove into, and they *did* shoot at me. Fortunately, they were so surprised that their shots went nowhere near me, and I came up waving my hands to show I wasn't armed.

"Wait! Wait! I'm on your side, don't—!"

I don't think they heard me. Their eyes were bugging out of their heads like they were on stalks, and their knees were shaking.

"A demon!"

"The priests have sent a demon after us!"

They'd been standing at the head of a stairway that went down through the floor behind them, and now they turned and ran down it, still shouting.

"Close the doors!"

"We're breached! Hurry!"

I ran after 'em. "Goddamn it! Wait! I'm not a demon! I—"

The double doors at the bottom of the stairs started to close. I jumped down the flight in one step and shouldered through just before they slammed shut, then went down on all fours as I tripped over one of the guys pushing them closed.

I came up in a little room with an open door in the far wall, and smack dab in the middle of a handful of pirates, all staring at me and raising swords and axes and crossbows.

"By the Seven, it's horrible!"

"The white skin! The red hair!"

A tall, bald guy with a braided beard edged toward me, holding a cutlass and dagger.

"Kill it, friends. Or we are all doomed."

"No you're not doomed! Now just shut up and listen to—"

They didn't listen. They just came in, screaming and slashing. It was too tight in there to draw my ridiculous sword, and I didn't want to anyway. I didn't want to hurt these guys, I just wanted them to not kill me.

Braid Face got to me first, and he was good, slashing with the cutlass to get me off balance, then stabbing at my blind side with the dagger, but all my months of gladiator training down in Doshaan hadn't been for nothing. I kept my feet under me and caught his dagger hand as it came in, clamping hard on his wrist, then whipped him around at the rest of 'em like he was a giant rag doll.

Guys staggered back with his knees to their jaws and his feet to their ears, but the guys with the crossbows were hanging back and aiming. I made to throw Braid Face at one of 'em and dive at the other, hoping my big-and-scary act would throw off their point blank aim, but before I could let go, a skinny pirate with a bandage around his middle limped into the room, waving his arms.

"Hold, friends! Do not fire! She is no demon! She is a friend! Hold!"

I looked around, still holding Braid Face by the wrist like he was a sack of laundry, and saw that the skinny pirate had a chin beard and a pencil-thin mustache, and the face of a hot-rod devil.

My heart started beating like a big bass drum. "Lhan?"

CHAPTER TEN

BESIEGED!

The skinny pirate looked up at me, a lopsided smile cracking his face. "Mis-mistress Jae-En! It *is* you. When I heard your voice, I could scarcely—"

"Lhan!"

I scooped him up in a big hug and held him tight—not too tight, 'cause of his bandages, but tight enough. He winced, but hugged back. I kissed him, hard and deep. It wasn't the freshest smooch ever. His mouth tasted like dirt and stale water, and mine probably wasn't much better, but I didn't care. He was alive and here and so was I, and I poured all the hoping and praying and crying I'd been doing since we'd been seperated into that kiss, trying to fill him up with it so he'd know how much I'd missed him, and how glad I was to be with him again. He gave as good as he got. He made my toes curl.

Finally we came up for air and looked at each other, grinning like idiots.

"Mistress, you live. I feared—"

"Not half as much as *I* feared! I thought I was gonna get back here and find out those fucking priests had—" I blinked. "Hey. You look terrible."

I'd been so staggered to see him again I hadn't noticed much more than the bandages, but Lhan looked like a zombie—gaunt, unshaven, dark under the eyes, and that bandage was disgusting, all black with dried blood and crusted yellow around the edges.

"Jesus, Lhan. What happened to you?"

Lhan swallowed, then looked around at the rest of the pirates, who were all standing around staring at us. They were as skinny and bashed up as he was. I stared back. I'd completely forgot they were there.

Braid Face got up from where I'd dropped him and pointed at Lhan, his eyes cold. "*He* happened to us. The fugitive. If not for him, the priests would not have come for us. Our ships would not have burned. Our men would not have died. We would not be trapped on this rock without water or food. And now he brings demons among us."

Lhan bristled. "Mistress Jae-En is no demon! I'll not deny the evils I have brought down upon you by my presence, but Jae-En is not one of them. She is flesh and blood just as you are, Lo-Zhar. A brave warrior from distant lands, and my… my great friend."

Lo-Zhar wasn't convinced. He took a step forward, his sword held low. "Well, perhaps it's time for you and your 'great friend' to go back to 'distant lands.' Maybe then the priests will leave us alone."

Lhan drew his sword and stepped in front of me. "I have already said I will give myself up, but you will not touch Mistress Jae-En. She has done nothing to you."

Lo-Zhar kept coming, his guys filling in behind him. "Nothing but knock my men flat and pull my arm from its socket. You will both go out, and—"

"Hold, Lo-Zhar! What is this fighting?"

I looked back as another handful of pirates piled into the room from the door behind me, blades out and all business. I put my back to Lhan's, ready for a last stand, but then I saw a big burly guy at the head of the new gang, holding a mace the size of a butter churn, and a little woman in a red bullfighter jacket beside him, glaring past me toward Braid Face.

"Kai-La!"

She blinked, then refocused on me. Burly did too.

"'Tis the barbarian girl!"

"The strong sister!" Kai-La lowered her sword and gave me a hug. She was skinny too. I'd remembered her being built like J-Lo with more bootie. Now she was more like Angelina Jolie on crack. "Where have you sprung from?"

"And what foolish notion inspired you to share our doom?" Burly clapped me on the shoulder. He'd been as big as a fullback when I first met him. Now his armor was hanging off him like a bad Halloween costume.

"I came to see...." I swallowed. "I was afraid you were already dead."

Lhan laughed bitterly and looked toward Lo-Zhar, who was giving Kai-La and her gang the stink eye. "We *are* already dead, mistress. And as Lo-Zhar has said, it was I who have killed us."

Kai-La slapped her hand on her flat chest. "And *I* have said that only makes you a pirate like the rest of us." She turned blazing eyes on Lo-Zhar. "We are *all* fugitives here! We *all* have a price on our heads! And so we must *all* band together against those who would destroy us, not fight amongst ourselves like shikes over a carcass. Do you hear me, Lo-Zhar?"

Lo-Zhar looked as sullen as a gangbanger in the back of a patrol car, but eventually he nodded. "Aye, Skelsha. But you best keep them away from me. Hunger makes my temper short."

"Then you should try eating your pride. That is a meal that would fill us all." Kai-La laughed, then turned and motioned for me and Lhan to follow. "This way, sister. Pay no mind to the growling of toothless vurlaks."

Lhan stepped back from Lo-Zhar, then sheathed his sword and offered me his arm like we were off to cotillion. "Aye. Come, Jae-en. Let us show you our palace in the sky."

A few yards down the low-ceilinged hallway, a door opened into a big room that looked like it had been a storage cellar at one point. Now it was a refugee camp, with rows of bedrolls laid out on every inch of floor, and little cook fires dotted around, though I had no idea what they were cooking. Nobody in that room looked like they'd eaten in a week. And half of 'em were as torn up as Lhan. I saw more slings and bandages and stitched wounds than I could shake a stick at.

There were a handful of openings in the walls of the room. Half of 'em looked original, with door posts and lintels, but the other half looked like they'd been dug out by hand.

Lhan noticed me looking, and nodded toward the holes. "The pirates have made extensive additions to these catacombs since they appropriated Toaga, all those centuries ago. There are tunnels and rooms all through the rock. None, alas, goes all the way to the ground. Not anymore. Those were sealed up long ago as a security measure. Ha!"

He laughed, bitter, and it turned into a hacking cough. He clutched his ribs. I held onto him until it passed.

"Goddamn it, Lhan. Y'all gotta get outta here. You gotta get fixed up."

He wiped his mouth with the back of his hand. "Impossible. Would the priests land and make a fight of it, we might win, but they are cowards. They have no stomach for meeting us steel to steel. They would rather float in safety beyond our reach and let us starve to death."

"There's no food at all? Not even upstairs?"

Burly shrugged. "Pirates are not known for planning for the future. There was some, but most was on the ships."

"And no water?"

"There is a great cistern, built by the old kings to catch the rain. But it has not rained for more than a moon, and it is nearly empty."

"And what water there is...." Kai-La made a face.

Lhan motioned me toward one of the carved-out doors. "But if you thirst, if you are hungry, I have a little left to share. I would not have you think us all as ungracious as—"

His knees buckled as he said it, and his eyes rolled up in his head. I caught him before he hit the floor, then laid him down.

"Lhan! Lhan, are you okay?"

Kai-La knelt beside us. "He took a bolt as we were rescuing those who fell in the priests' first attack, and I fear the wound festers. He will not let us see it, though, so I know not."

I looked down at him, tears filling my eyes. "Goddamn it, Lhan. Why you gotta be such a fucking hero?" I looked up at Kai-La. "Where's his bed roll? I'm gonna have a look at this wound, no matter what he says."

She shrugged. "There is little point. We are doomed here. You will only delay the inevitable."

"You're damn right I will. For as long as I fucking can."

She turned to Burly. "Find our medicine bag." Then she stood and motioned to me as he hurried off. "Come. Lhan-Lar has taken a cell for himself in the old dungeon. I will show you."

I picked Lhan up in my arms and followed.

CHAPTER ELEVEN

REUNITED!

Burly came into the cell as Kai-La and I laid Lhan on his bed roll. He handed me a leather pack. "There is needle and thread, and some salves and bandages, but I'm afraid there is no water here fit to clean a wound."

I pulled my canteen off my shoulder. It was still half full. "I have some, thanks."

Kai-La rose and joined Burly at the door, then looked back. "I know you will do as you will, but you would do better to let him drink that than to wash his wounds with it. Neither will save his life, but a drink will sooth him more."

"Go fuck yourself. He's not going to die."

"Then he will be the only one."

She walked off down the hall and I got to work. It took way too long. His bandages were so glued on with dried blood that I had to use his dagger to cut them away, and what I saw underneath made me wonder how he was still alive. He had scrapes and bruises all over, but the main wound was in his side, just under his ribs, and it smelled like a dead skunk. It had been neatly sewn up a while back, but it hadn't been cleaned in way too long, and was so inflamed now it was popping its stitches.

Lhan opened his eyes as I choked out a sob. "You cry, beloved?"

I wiped the tears from my eyes. I was so mad my hands were shaking. "Why shouldn't I cry? Look what being a hero got you!"

He looked down at the wound and pursed his lips. "Hero? I was the cause of the massacre. I deserve worse."

"Bullshit. You don't deserve any of this."

I gave him some of the water to drink, then got to work. Fortunately, I'd done this before. I'd had basic first-aid training in boot camp, and more advanced stuff in Ranger school, plus I'd spent years riding Harleys back and forth across the states, and had plenty experience patching up myself and my pals after some nasty wreck or bar fight. As long as there weren't any internal injuries I was good. I just hoped the arrow in his side hadn't punctured his guts. If it had, I was lost—and so was he. He gasped as I started to cut the stitches, then smiled like a skeleton.

"Ah, Jae-En. I feared I would never see you again. It seems impossible that you still live, that you escaped the priests. The Seven have answered my prayers."

I kept cutting. "I didn't escape."

"I—I don't understand."

"They sent me back. To my world. I—" I had to stop cutting and swallow. "I thought I was stuck there. I thought I'd never… never…"

Lhan frowned. "You… you came back? But I understood you wanted nothing more than to return to your own world."

"I—I did." I looked down at him. "But I changed my mind."

Lhan's confusion melted into a look of wonder. He tried to sit up. "Oh, mistress. Oh, Jae-En. Oh, ow—"

I eased him back down, shaking as much as he was. "Even when I came back I thought it was impossible. I thought you were… I thought you'd…."

Then I did lose it. I put a hand over my eyes and tried to hide the tears that were streaming down my face. Lhan gripped my other hand and squeezed with all his might, which right about then wasn't so much.

"I thought the same of you, Jae-En. But against all odds we have found each other again, and what e're occurs now, however brief our time, I am content, as you are at my side once more."

I snorfed and wiped my nose with my hand, then looked him in the eyes. Despite how sick and starved he was, they were still the same as they'd always been—warm, smart, sly and sweet all at the same time. "Yeah," I said. "Ditto."

I leaned down to kiss him, but as he raised up he winced and clutched his side and I remembered what we were doing. I pressed him back down.

"Time for that later. Now stay still."

He tried, but as I went back to cutting the stitches he flinched again and I nearly stabbed him. Maybe he'd be better if he was talking.

"Tell me how you got here, Lhan. From the beginning. When they grabbed me."

"I would rather not remember… my shame."

"Tell it anyway."

I cut the last stitch and the wound opened up like a diseased mouth. It was horrible, but at least it didn't go deeper than the muscle. I breathed a sigh of relief and started washing it out as best I could with the water from my canteen. He clenched up like a fist.

"Come on. Start talking. From the beginning."

"V-very well. I—I remember waking to see the priests reaching for you, and tried to rise, but there was a horrible lethargy."

"Yeah. They drugged us."

"Aye. But still you fought. It took all of them to hold your limbs. I think it is that which saved my life."

I looked at him. I fought? It was news to me. "What do you mean?"

"There was one, with a knife. I believe he meant to cut my throat, but he turned to help the others, and went with them to carry you to the balcony, leaving me alone."

I opened up a pot of goop from Kai-La's medicine bag and held it out to him to smell. "What's this?"

He sniffed, then wrinkled his nose. "An astringent, for clean healing. Be sparing. It stings."

I slathered it on like it was peanut butter. He twitched and yipped with pain.

"Mistress!"

"Keep talking."

Tears were running down his cheeks. "You are cruel, Mistress."

"Yeah, I know. Go on. You said they left you alone."

"Yes. I—I knew it was my only chance. I fought the drug, forced myself to stand, then found my sword and made it to the corridor, where it was easier to breathe."

I got a needle and thread out of the kit, sterilized the needle using Lhan's lamp, and started sewing the wound back together.

He gritted his teeth. "I meant to return and rescue you, but before I had recovered, he with the knife and another came looking for me. I fell upon them from the shadows, but the drug had me in its clutches. I did not fight well. They wounded me."

He touched a scar on his sword arm. It was long and fresh, but healed and clean—not like the rest. "I could not lift my sword, so I fell back and hid in..." He blushed. "In a secret room."

I smiled at that. I'd been in that room. I knew why he was blushing.

"Go on."

"Again, I meant to return to you immediately, but my head was muddled, and as I struggled to bandage myself I... I lost consciousness." He punched his leg, and almost tore my stitches. "An unforgivable weakness!"

I grabbed his arm. "Hey! Stay still! What happened next?"

He turned his head and went on. "What happened next is that I woke to Rian-Gi shaking me, and I discovered that it was morning." He hid his face. "Your pardon, mistress, the shame of it is still unbearable."

I rolled my eyes. "Lhan. You passed out. You can't control that."

"Can I not? The mind controls the flesh. The flesh does not control the mind."

"Yeah yeah, so then what?"

"Then Rian saw to my wounds and begged me to leave, for he feared the priests would return and find me there."

I bit my lip, not sure I should tattle, but then I caught myself. I didn't see any shame in what Rian did. It was the priests who were the murdering bastards, not him. "They did return. That's how they learned you were with the pirates. That's how they followed you here. Y'see. It's not your fault after all."

Lhan looked up at me, and his face went in about six directions at once—shock, horror, anger, sadness—okay, only four. "Rian-Gi talked?" And then. "Of course. Of course he did. Any man would. They know their business, those villains. Did... did they kill him?"

"Not him. His boyfriend. Rian talked to save him, but they killed the poor guy anyway."

Lhan closed his eyes and I stitched him up in silence for a full minute, then he shook his head. "You are wrong, Jae-En. It *is* my fault. It is I who killed Wae-Fen. And I who brought about Rian's torture. For it is I who foolishly told him my plans. Had I kept it from him—"

"They would have tortured him anyway. *And* killed Wae-Fen. Come on, Lhan. You can't blame yourself for the church's evil shit."

"I blame myself for knowing we were the subject of their scrutiny and not keeping away from my friends. My lack of proper caution allowed them to catch you, to torture Rian-Gi, to murder Wae-Fen and, by the One, I have hurt these poor pirates worse than all the rest. Thirteen ships burned, hundreds of men dead. Lo-Zhar is right to wish to cast me out and kill me. I am like a plague victim who kisses his children. I harm all I love. All I touch!"

He was close to popping his stitches again. "Lhan! You're gonna hurt yourself!"

He stayed clenched for a long minute, then sagged back and let out a breath. "How... how did you know? About Rian and Wae-Fen?"

"I went to see him. I came back to Waar inside the Temple of Ormolu, and found out that the priests were hunting you in some place called Toaga. So when I escaped, I went to ask him for a map, and—"

Lhan was staring at me like I'd just grown horns and turned green. "You... you escaped from the Temple of Ormolu?"

"Yeah. There was a teleport gem thingy, and—"

"No one escapes from the temple of Ormolu. But for the priests, no one who has entered it has ever come out again. There are no doors, no windows, and no one is ever seen to enter or leave."

I tied off the last stitch, then cut the thread and looked for more wounds. There was a nasty one that cut across his hip and halfway around to his butt. I started undoing his loincloth. "That's because they have teleporters like I was saying. They don't need—"

Lhan caught my hand as I started to strip him. "That is not necessary."

"Bro, I've seen you naked, remember. And that's infected."

"Very well, then I will do it. Give me the salve."

I started tugging again. "Come on, Lhan. Don't be a prude. Let me—"

"No! I insist. I—"

The fabric ripped as he tried to pull my hand away, and the loincloth fell apart. He had a thin strip of leather tied around his waist, and there was some kind of stone hanging from it. It hadn't been there the last time we got naked. He closed his hand around it.

I stared at his fist, shaking. The thing reminded me of the thing I'd seen around Kedac-Zir's waist when I'd stripped him naked in front of the entire Oran court—a balurrah it was called—only his had been silver. A balurrah was a secret token people on Waar wore next to their skin to remind them of their lover, and it didn't matter if you were married or engaged to somebody else, you were supposed to only wear the balurrah of the person you truly loved. It was meant only for their eyes. Nobody else's. And Lhan was hiding his from me.

"What's that?"

Lhan clenched tighter. "Nothing. Pay it no mind."

"Lhan, don't be a douche. Show me."

He didn't like it, but he opened his hand, then turned his head away. "Forgive me, mistress."

I took the thing in my hand and looked at it, heart pounding. It was a smooth pink pebble, about the size and shape of a pocket watch, and there was something scratched into one side of it. It looked like a drawing of a knife with a blade that curved at the tip.

"This is a balurrah, right?"

"Aye."

My heart sunk. "Whose is it?"

"It... it is yours, mistress."

"M-mine?"

"Aye. That crude etching is meant to represent your sword, while the pebble is the color of your skin."

Fucking hell. It *was* my sword. A breath went out of me that I hadn't know I'd been holding. "Oh, god, Lhan. I—"

He gripped my hand. "I beg you to forgive me, mistress. It was presumptuous of me to make such a thing without knowing your heart, but I believed I would die, and did not want to—"

"Lhan, you fucking idiot!" I lay down beside him and hugged him so hard I heard him grunt. "What the fuck do you need to be forgiven for? Didn't I tell you? I came back for you! All I wanted to do when the priests sent me to Earth was get back here. All I wanted was to find you again. I...." I held him away from me and looked into his eyes. "I decided I didn't want to go back home the second we kissed."

Lhan looked at me, still unsure. "Truly?"

"Truly." I held up three fingers. "Scout's honor."

It took a minute for Lhan's brow to unwrinkle, but at last he clasped my hands and smiled. It was like a bath in warm whiskey, that smile. It made me all hot and gooshy inside.

"And I decided I would ask you to stay at precisely the same moment. I believed I had not a hope to convince you, but I knew I must try, or lose half my world."

"Aw, Lhan."

I leaned in to kiss him, but he held me off and looked into my eyes, all serious. "Mistress. Jae-En. 'Tis sudden, I know, but I fear we have little time left to us, so I would speak now."

"Uh, speak about what?"

"This." He took my hand. "That if we are truly of like minds, then I would pledge myself to you as a dhan of Ora should—heart, soul and arm. From this day forth, however few they may be, you will be my dhanshai and I will be your dhan. Your safety and well-being will be my only concern. Your love will be my only goal."

He was so serious I wanted to laugh, but I kept it in. I couldn't keep the tears in, though. They were running down my cheeks.

He took my hand and kissed it. "Will you have me?"

There was a dirty answer to that, but I kept that in too. Now wasn't the time. "Yes, Lhan. I will," was all I said.

"The One be praised."

Lhan stretched up and kissed me, and that whiskey bath turned into a sauna. Wounds or no wounds, I was ready to push him down and "have him" as often as he could manage, but all of a sudden he went all floppy again and slumped back, his eyes fluttering.

"Lhan!"

He gripped my forearm. His hand was clammy and cold. "Forgive me... beloved. There has been no food for so long. I... I have little strength. At least we will be Dhan and Dhanshae when we die."

I stared down at him, feeling helpless, then shook my head, angry. "Sorry, Lhan. Fuck dying. I'm not giving you up after I just found you again. I'm gettin' us off this rock, and then we're gonna go have a happily-ever-after somewhere."

I stood and turned to the door. "Wait right here. I gotta go see some priests about a ship."

CHAPTER TWELVE

BREAKOUT!

"I don't get it. I've seen y'all take on a navy ship before, *and win*. And that was twice as big as that boat out there. How did that one little ship wipe out thirteen of yours?"

Okay, yeah, I know I made it sound like I was gonna go handle shit all by myself, but I ain't stupid. I knew going kamikaze wouldn't get me anywhere but dead, and as I'd said to Lhan, fuck dying. So, instead of going to see the priests about a ship, I went to see the pirates about the priests, and now I was sitting around a dusty stone table with Kai-La and Burly and Lo-Zhar—yeah, him too—in what looked like an old kitchen.

Kai-La curled her lip. "A single wand of blue fire."

I blinked. "Damn. Really?"

Lo-Zhar rolled his eyes.

Burly was a little more helpful. "The levitating air that fills our canopies is flammable, and the blue fire can burn through the envelope in the blink of an eye, and then... boom."

Kai-La sighed. "We saw the ship on the horizon and took our time preparing to fly, thinking we had at least an hour before it would be close enough to engage. But a wand of blue fire..." She shook her head. "I know not the limits of its range, but it destroyed us from more than an iln away, every ship that was anchored here."

Lo-Zhar bared his teeth. "I lost forty men."

It still made no sense. "But then how the hell do y'all operate at all? If one wand of blue fire can burn a whole damn fleet out of the sky, what's the percentage in being a pirate?"

Burly raised his head. "Because we never face them. Neither Ora's army or navy possesses one, nor have I ever heard of a temple ship carrying one either."

Lo-Zhar snorted. "Until now."

"That is why we were taken by surprise." Kai-La leaned back. "But for the two in the possession of the Aldhanan's guard, only servants of the Temple are allowed to carry wands, and they are so rare, and so valuable, that they are almost never used, for fear of losing them or allowing one to fall into the hands of the enemy."

"Huh. So why don't they just make more?"

All three of 'em laughed at me this time.

"The wands are gifts of the Seven, lass, made by the gods themselves, and beyond the ken of mortal man to understand." Burly chuckled. "The priests don't even know how to fix them, let alone build another. If one breaks, it is gone for good, and there are so few now that they are named—Tyrant Slayer, The White Death, The Guardian of Modgalu, and the like."

More Waarian Lord-of-the-Rings bullshit, giving a ray gun a fancy name. On the other hand, we did the same thing back on Earth all the time—The Peacemaker, Fat Man, Little Boy. Shit, I knew guys who named their dicks. Anyway, back to business.

"Okay. So there's only one of these wands on the ship?"

Burly grunted. "One is enough."

"I just wanna know what I'm gonna be up against once I get on board."

Lo-Zhar snorted again. "*Once* you get on board? Shouldn't your first worry be *how* you get on board? Do you mean to fly? That ship never comes closer than bows' reach."

Kai-La grinned. "You've not seen our girl in action, have you? She'll get on board."

I sat forward, trying not to look smug. "I hope I will, but what I want to know is, can you reel it in once I do? The last thing I want is to do something stupid and heroic and end up giving myself up to 'em."

Lo-Zhar smiled, nasty. "It wouldn't trouble me in the slightest."

Kai-La and Burly gave him a dirty look, then Kai-La patted me on the wrist.

"Worry not, sister. A pirate always has a grappling hook or two lying about. We'll hook your fish."

"I just hope you do it before it swallows the bait."

***

It took an hour for me and the thirty or so pirates who Kai-La and Lo-Zhar rounded up to get into position without being seen by the priests' warship. I felt like we were a bunch of mice, trying to sneak across the kitchen floor while a fat orange cat walked around on the counters above. We could only move when the ship's view was blocked by a wall or a tower, and we had to make sure wherever we stopped we couldn't be seen from any angle, because the ship was constantly circling. The whole scheme woulda been impossible during the day, but with the big moon down and the little moon low on the horizon, the shadows were as black as caves, and there were plenty of them.

The whole plan hinged on that three-story building which I'd used as cover before. The battlement at the top of it was the only thing tall enough and close enough to the edge to get me to the level of the ship. It also had a pretty much intact stairway inside it that would give me enough run up for my jump. Unfortunately, it also had one big problem. When I was in position in the stairwell, I couldn't see out, which meant I couldn't tell when the ship was coming, which meant I didn't know when to start my run. It'd be embarrassing as hell to do a perfect run up just to miss the boat and jump to my death.

In the end we worked out a system where Kai-La would stand watch outside the building and give me a whistle when the ship was coming in range. All I had to do was run when I heard her toot.

We finally got into position just as the ship passed the tower, and so we had to wait another endless fifteen minutes for it to circle all the way around again, but finally I started hearing the flap of its sails and the whispers from the pirates around the tower, and I went into a runner's crouch at the bottom of the stairs.

Ten seconds later, "Weet!"

I tensed, but didn't go. What if she'd whistled too soon? I better wait. One, two, three, four, five—okay go!

I launched like a sprinter coming off the blocks and pounded up the stairs as hard as I could, then kicked off the wall of the landing and ran up the second flight, skipping more and more steps with each stride. Another turn and there was night sky above me and I rocketed up onto the top of the tower, jumped onto the battlements, and kicked up into the air with the empty plains dropping away a thousand feet below me—and the priests' ship slipping out from under from me to my right.

CHAPTER THIRTEEN

ATTACK!

Fuck.

So, I guess Kai-La musta counted to five to make sure I didn't go too soon, and then *I* counted to five, and... and I was dead. The flank of the balloon was right in front of me, but too far out. My trajectory was angling me down toward the deck, twenty feet below, just like I'd planned it, except it was already passing me by. I was gonna miss the stern rail by about two yards. It was funny in Roadrunner cartoons. In real life? Not so much.

I had one chance—the trick I'd learned in gladiator school when we'd been trying to figure out some fancy moves I could do in the arena. I whipped my big-ass sword out of the sheath on my back and swung it as hard as I could to the right, then let the weight of it jerk me around after it.

It worked. Well, almost.

I needed six feet. I got five. The mid-air swerve swung me toward the ship just like I'd hoped, but I didn't quite make it to the deck. Instead, I bounced tits-first off the back rail and started to fall away again, head spinning and nose bleeding, but at the last second, I managed to throw out a desperate hand and caught the bottom of the railing.

Saved!

Sorta.

I really coulda used a minute to just hang there and catch my breath, but there were footsteps pounding across the deck above me. I had to move. With a grunt I braced my feet on the hull and vaulted onto the deck—and ended up face to face with a shitload of surprised priests and paladins, all staring like a shark had jumped in the boat.

"It's her!"

"The other one!"

"The demon!"

"But she was sent away!"

You know, back in the stairwell, waiting to charge out and do this, I hadn't been sure I'd be able to get it up to slaughter a whole bunch of people I didn't know, but that did it. These were the guys who'd sent me back to Earth. These were the guys who'd chased Lhan halfway across Waar and put an arrow in his side. These were the guys who'd tortured Rian-Gi and killed his lover. These were the guys who'd sent thirteen ships crashing to the ground and killed hundreds of men. This wasn't going to be a problem at all.

I jumped forward, hair flying, blood spraying, screaming like a banshee, and landed in the middle of 'em, chopping left and right. Four of 'em went down like pinatas, opened up and spilling their insides everywhere. The rest scattered, bellowing for help. I charged after 'em, howling, ready to lose myself to the red rage, but then I remembered I had a job to do, and changed direction.

The reason the pirates hadn't been able to pull this stunt before now was because every time they'd tried to hook the ship and reel it in, they'd been pin-cushioned with crossbow bolts or zapped with blue fire and had to fall back. That's what I was here for, to keep the firepower busy.

I leapt for the starboard rail, slashing wide and wild at the crossbowmen lined up along it. They scattered, screaming, but I caught 'em in a step, cutting the legs off one guy, and kicking two more over the side, then charged after the rest.

It was inevitable that some of 'em were going to start firing back, and I almost flinched myself overboard as a bolt glanced off my blade and nearly took my nose off. I hit the deck with more whiffing past me, and by the time I rolled back to my feet I was alone in the middle of the deck with the whole ship reloading and aiming at me.

I leapt straight up, screaming like a school girl, and a handful of bolts zipped under my feet, but a bunch more followed me, whizzing past my ears and sticking in the balloon over my head. I landed on the foredeck and charged another knot of shooters, my back tingling, expecting to be a pincushion with every step, but instead, all the crossbow guys started shrieking and falling and turning toward the rail.

Whew! Part two of the plan was a go. The pirates were finally firing from the mesa, shooting grappling-hook bolts over the rails and picking off the guys who were trying to pick me off. Now we had 'em in the crossfire. I attacked the crossbow guys from behind as they took cover behind the rail, and the pirates pegged 'em when I made 'em break cover. The poor fuckers were like chickens in a dog pen, they didn't know which way to run.

But just as the pirates started hauling on their hooks and I figured we had it in the bag, the door to the under-decks slammed open and a bald-headed, buzzard-beaked priest with an extra fancy robe strode out with six paladin spear carriers for an escort and a motherfucking wand of blue fire in his hands.

He aimed it at me and the world stopped like someone had hit the pause button. I stopped. He stopped. Everybody stopped. The only thing I could hear was the blood pounding in my neck. Then he spoke. He sounded like a juvie school principal giving a lecture.

"I have orders to spare you, demoness." He swung the barrel of his white plastic Casio-looking gun toward the mesa, where Kai-La and Burly and all the rest were still reeling in the ship. "But no such orders for your friends. Surrender or they die."

I'd seen one of those pop guns in action before, so I knew he wasn't bluffing. It might look like a vacuum cleaner tube with some Christmas lights on the side, but the fucking thing could carve a mountain in half if you wanted it to. It scared the living piss out of me. On the other hand, I could see it in his beady little eyes that I scared the living piss out of him too. Maybe I could bluff him.

I took a step towards him, sword low but ready. "And how many do you think you can kill before I cut you in half? You wanna try it? You wanna take your shot?"

He edged back, eyes twitching from me to the pirates and back, as his guards stepped in front of him, spears leveled. "You would not risk it. Your lover is among them. You—"

With a sound like a fastball hitting a catcher's mitt, a crossbow bolt appeared in his shoulder and he shrieked and fell and dropped the wand.

"Ha! Nice shot!"

Score one for my pirate pals, and more bolts started to thud into the deck all around him as the crew on the mesa reeled the ship into close range. A bolt took out one of Beaky's paladins. The others were ducking and backing away.

I sprang at 'em, hoping to finish 'em off and get a hold of that fucking zap gun, but they were a lot tougher than the guys I'd cut down earlier, even under fire, and kept me back with some fancy spear work, stabbing and backing and stabbing and backing as Beak-Nose staggered to his feet with the wand clutched to his chest and ran for the foredeck.

"Hold her! The wand must be saved!"

I had no idea what he was talking about, but I tried to go after him anyway, leaping high, dodging wide. No dice, those spears were everywhere. If I wanted to get past 'em, I'd have to go through the hard way. I turned all my attention to breaking the paladins' line, chopping through their spears, bashing 'em back, kicking their knees and shins, and all the while afraid Beak-Nose was gonna find a nice little perch and start sniping from on high.

But he didn't. As I fought through his dudes, I saw him up on the foredeck pulling a tarp off some big piece of equipment I hadn't noticed before. I thought it might be some kind of big-ass machine gun or sling shot, 'cause it was high in the middle and square on the sides, but when the tarp came off I saw it was a futuristic boat-bike looking thing.

Even knowing there were wands of blue fire lying around, this freaked me out. There was no way these sword-swinging, loincloth-wearing shit-kickers had built anything like that. It looked like a cross between a ski-doo and one of those crazy-ass souped-up racing boats that they always show crashing on ESPN. It was flat and square and wide at the bottom, like a big white plastic mattress, but with what looked like a snowmobile seat and handlebars sticking up out of the middle.

The weirdest part, though, was when Beak-Nose climbed on and fired it up. He was tiny on it. He looked like a kid sitting on his dad's Harley. In fact, it looked like there was some kind of booster seat on top of the bench just so he could reach the handlebars. I almost laughed until the thing whined like a rice rocket going eighty and rose up off the deck like a hovercraft. Then I stared—and almost got speared through the neck for it.

I snapped back to my fight with blood streaming down over my collar bone, and hacked off the tip of the spear that had almost shish-kabobed me, then bulled through the rest and leapt for the foredeck, trying to stop him.

The ski-doo had two rows of glowing white spheres—each about the size of a beer keg—sunk into its undercarriage, and they were vibrating so fast that the air around them was blurring, and this seemed to be the way it was flying. Yeah. No rotors, no jet engines, just an annoying high-pitched screech from the vibration. The goddamn things were levitating.

"Anti-motherfucking-gravity. Wow!"

I bounded toward the thing as Beak-Nose angled it around toward the back rail, but just as I was gonna land on it and cut his head off, it slipped out from under me like a watermelon seed and made a screaming bee-line for the horizon, its white globes glowing like tracer bullets in the dark.

I crashed down on the deck and stared after it with my jaw hanging open. "Look at that thing go. Goddamn."

There were footsteps on the stairs behind me, and a shitload of shouting, and I turned, ready to fight again, but it wasn't Beaky's paladins. It was Kai-La, a bloody cutlass in her hand, and a smile on her face.

"Well fought, sister! You have won the day!"

I looked around, amazed. The battle was already over, and I'd missed it. While I'd been fighting the paladins and chasing Beak-Nose, the pirates had pulled the ship tight against the mesa and swarmed it, and the priests and paladins were surrendering all over the place. Not that the pirates were paying any attention. I got a little queasy as I saw them grabbing priests who had thrown down their weapons and started tossing them over the side. I mean it was one thing to kill somebody when they were trying to kill you, but this was straight up murder.

I turned to Kai-La. "You're gonna kill 'em? All of 'em?"

Lo-Zhar turned from cutting a priest's throat and answered for her, snarling. "It will still be but one for every ten they killed of mine."

Kai-La nodded. "Aye. And priests of the Seven hold a special place in my heart. I would spare a vurlak's life before that of a priest."

I still didn't like it, but she clapped me on the back before I could say anything else, and waved back toward the mesa. "Now, come, your beloved lies in a cell, alone. Bring him aboard and you shall have a cabin to yourselves for the great work you have done today. You have saved us all!"

That snapped me out of my funk. I gave her a salute, then bounced down to the main deck and across to the mesa. A cabin to ourselves? Well, yippy-kai-yay! I'd hot-footed it across the entire universe to get Lhan alone again. It was about fucking time.

Heh.

Or about time for fucking?

CHAPTER FOURTEEN

WANTED!

Yeah, well, not so much.

The priests' warship had been circling the mesa for days, and didn't have much more food and water than the pirates did, so Kai-La gave orders to set sail for a burg three days to the south of us called Galok, a pirate-friendly border town which was the closest place they could resupply. That meant Lhan and I had three days with nothing to do but hang out in our cabin and get reacquainted. It shoulda been heaven. It was hell.

Lhan was just too hurt to get busy. Way too hurt. He needed food and drink and rest, but at the same time, being so close to each other and not being able to do anything was killing us. I'd lay down beside him to keep him company on his bunk, but just pressing up against him was enough to get my motor running, then my hands would start wandering, and pretty soon *his* motor would be running, and we'd start rolling around and pulling at each other—and then a second later he'd break away, hissing and holding his side, or bleeding, or wheezing like he was going to die, and I'd end up cursing and apologizing and have to go up to the top bunk and promise that *next* time I'd be good and keep my hands to myself.

You can guess how that worked out.

Anyway, we also did other stuff. Mostly talk about the future. That started the first morning, when I brought Lhan some breakfast in bed. I was handing him a cup of banana-smelling pink gruel when he gave me a little grin.

"So, beloved. Where shall we go?"

"Huh? Whaddaya mean?"

"I mean, my Dhanshae, that, with no obligations to chain us to place or purpose, we may go where we like. Therefore I ask you, where would you like to go?"

I laughed. "Not back to Ora, that's for damn sure. I'm sick of that place. And I bet we'd have the church cops on our ass in a hot second. Hmmm, maybe I should just take you back to Earth and—"

For a split second it seemed like a great idea. There wouldn't be any crazy priests hunting us on Earth. I knew my way around. I could show off *my* planet for a change, introduce Lhan to hamburgers and beer and fat-boy Harleys. With the hair and the goatee, he'd sure as hell make a damn fine biker dude—except...

Except he would be as weak on Earth as I was strong on Waar, and he was purple. We wouldn't have the church after us, we'd have the US government hunting our asses. They'd want to cut Lhan up and take samples. They'd want to know how to get to Waar. They'd lock us both up as a matter of national security. The *National Enquirer* would put us on the front page, BIKER CHICK AND SPACE ALIEN IN INTERSPECIES LOVE NEST. It would suck, and it would never stop sucking.

"Never mind. Stupid idea. Where do *you* wanna go?"

Lhan shrugged. "I? I would not be unhappy following the path we already tread. Kai-La and her crew are merry companions and lead an unfettered life. There would be worse fates than to sail under her banner."

My heart jumped in my chest as he said it, and I almost agreed then and there. Almost. But then my conscience, that fucker, caught me and I stopped. I'd been tempted to join Kai-La's gang before, and been put off by the same thing that put me off now. They were, as Lhan said, a blast to hang around with—my favorite people on Waar as a matter of fact—but they were pirates. They flew around, stealing other people's shit, and killing them if they didn't hand it over. On top of that, the pirates also sold people as slaves. Shit, they'd sold *me* as a slave once! I knew all that was different on Waar. Lhan's family owned slaves, for instance, and even the slaves dreamed of owning slaves, but I still didn't want any part of it.

I shook my head. "I can't do it. I was a biker, Lhan, not a Hell's Angel."

"I fear I do not understand the reference, mistress."

"I mean, there's a difference between a rebel and a robber, and I've never been a robber—well, not a lot. Also, I know Kai-La's gonna go after Oran ships, and after the Aldhanan gave me the keys to the kingdom and all that, I'd feel a little weird attacking his people."

Lhan smirked. "I fear you will find that the difference between the crimes of a pirate and an Aldhanan are but a matter of scale. Still, I understand your reticence. Indeed, I share it. If we were to make war only upon the state or the church I would not hesitate, but the thought of attacking some honest merchant and stealing his hard-won goods? No. It makes the dream ugly and common." He looked up at me, grinning. "Very well, with piracy dismissed, what other life calls to you? Where else would you like to go?"

All I wanted was the recurring dream I'd had ever since I'd drifted off to sleep at Lhan's side, that night when the priests had come for me, the dream where Lhan and I would wander Waar side by side, going wherever we wanted, seeing things nobody from Earth had ever seen before, living rough but easy forever and ever amen.

I leaned over and gave him a squeeze. "As long as it's with you, I don't care. Any place that's not Ora. Any place without priests."

Lhan squeezed me back, then smiled. "Beloved, there is a whole wide world of them."

***

Seeing Galok appear in the distance far below us on the third morning it looked like a joke—a seaside town without a sea. I could see where the water *should* have been. The stone docks were still there, sticking out over a steep sandy slope—and being used for airships instead of boats now—and the town still curved around what had once been a long winding shoreline, but there was no ocean anymore, only a deep dry valley which went on forever.

Leaning on the rail beside me, Lhan pointed to the west, which was lit up like fire by the sun coming up behind us. "You see yonder, that glint of gold upon the horizon?"

I squinted. There was a permanent haze of dust out there, but I thought I could see something winking behind it. "I think so."

"That is the Great Inland Sea—or was, hundreds of years ago, before the rains slowed. Now it is little more than a lake. It is called the Vanished Sea now."

I nodded toward the town. "So they don't do much fishing anymore."

"Indeed not." Lhan pointed down as we dropped toward the waterless docks, where about half a dozen airships were already tied up. "Now they mine salt."

On the slope of the exposed sea-bed beyond the docks I saw guys with picks and shovels digging up the dry earth and running it through hand-cranked sifting machines, while other guys loaded the sifted stuff into sacks and threw 'em on big vurlak-drawn carts, which then trundled up a zig-zag road to some kind of refining plant on the shoreline to the south of the town. It looked like Louisiana chain gang work, like hell on earth—or Waar. I wondered if the workers were prisoners or slaves.

"You take me to all the nicest places."

"But of course. Had I started with Waar's best, what would you have to look forward to?" He turned from the rail and started back toward the below-decks door. "Come. We must find you a disguise before we land. The edge of the vanished sea marks the end of Oran territory, but until we are safely upon another ship and sailing beyond it, you must not be seen as you are."

I groaned. I hated disguises. I'd had to disguise myself my last time on Waar, and I'd ended up slathered in purple paint and sweating to death inside a mask and heavy clothes that stank like the back end of a yak.

"Fantastic."

***

I groaned again as he opened a trunk in what had been the ship's surgery and pulled out what looked like a pair of red Ku Klux Klan robes. It was a hundred degrees in the shade out here in the sticks, and he wanted me to put on a cloak and hood?

"You gotta be kidding me."

"At least it is this time clean, beloved. And you will have the satisfaction that I must wear one too."

"That'll make it much better, thanks."

He handed me mine and I held it up to look at it. Yup. Pointy hood, robes, gloves, cloak—all blood-red and stitched at the collar and cuffs with zig-zagging black lines, and made of some kind of cloth that was thicker and heavier than denim, plus a black ninja-mask kinda thing that went with it to hide my face. The one good thing was that, unlike most robes and cloaks I'd tried on Waar, it actually reached down all the way to the ground, which meant I didn't have to find some way to paint my legs purple to hide the color of my skin. Of course I still had to wrap my boobs so I could pass as a man, but the bandages in the surgery were nice and clean, so it wasn't as bad as last time.

When I was all strapped down and dressed up, I looked at Lhan. His robes and hood matched mine, but instead of the ninja mask, he had a long-nosed gas mask kinda thing that completely hid his face, and a black leather satchel slung over one shoulder. He looked like a stork in priest drag.

"So what is all this? What are we dressed up as?"

Lhan smiled as he pulled on his gloves. "These are the traditional robes of a surgeon and a surgeon's assistant. They are red to hide the blood of surgery, and your robes are large because the surgeon's assistant is traditionally a large individual, necessary to hold down the patient when the cutting begins."

I winced at the image, then wiped my brow under the ninja mask. The robes were already hotter than fuck.

"Well, I hope we find a ship ASAP. I don't wanna wear this shit a second longer than I gotta."

"I do not expect any difficulty there. Galok is constantly visited by foreign traders. And if there is currently no suitable ship, we will take a room at the inn and stay out of sight until one arrives."

There was a bump on the hull that made us both side step, and a lot of shouts and thumping above us.

Lhan smiled. "Ah. We have docked. Come, let us see what Galok has to offer."

***

Not much, as it turned out.

Well, we did score passage on a ship, a tiny little merchantman bound for some place called Vedya, but other than that, Galok was about as exciting as a Tuesday night in Wichita.

There was one dusty street which ended at the docks on one end and the plains on the other, and had a dusty market square in the middle, with a few dusty hawkers sitting in the dusty sunshine selling dusty goods, and lots of dusty beggars with missing limbs reaching after us as we walked through them. Dusty tough guys hung out in doorways around the edges, watching everybody else and spitting dusty loogies in the dusty dirt, while dusty local cops strolled through with their spears on their dusty shoulders, eating what looked suspiciously like donuts.

I hardly saw any of it. I was too busy thinking about our room at the inn. Today was the first day that Lhan had seemed healed enough and chipper enough that something might actually happen if we had two hours alone together, and since the boat didn't take off until noon, we *did* have two hours alone together. I was getting hot and bothered just thinking about it. I might finally get the second helping I'd come back to Waar for in the first place!

"There it is." Lhan pointed across the square toward a two-story building with an open door and a bunch of shuttered windows. It looked like it would melt into mud if it ever rained around here. "And I have never seen a finer establishment."

"As long as the rooms have beds, it'll be the greatest hotel that ever lived."

I couldn't see Lhan's expression through his stork mask, so I didn't know if he was leering or not, but the way he squeezed my hand made me think he was.

"Precisely."

We crossed the square and were just about to step into the inn when a flyer nailed to a board on the outside wall caught my eye. It was a wanted poster, and the guy on the left looked familiar. I looked closer. It was Lhan. And to his right was a picture of—

"Jesus Christ on a fucking tricycle! That's not me! That's Dolph Lundgren in drag!"

Lhan turned at my squawking and gripped my arm. "Keep your voice down, *assistant*. I—" He saw the poster too. "I am sorry, mistress, that… that is appalling. But not unexpected. You said yourself there would be a bounty. And at least they won't be looking for anyone who looks like—" He stopped again as he read the fine print. "*What* is this?"

I'd been too busy staring at my "likeness" to read the thing, but now I did, squinting to unscramble the Waar alphabet and make it come out in English in my brain.

"Wanted dead or alive. A bounty of ten thousand tolnas is offered for the capture of Lhan-Lar of Herva, and his accomplice, the albino barbarian giantess Jae-En, for crimes against the Church of the Seven and for the kidnapping of—" I stopped and read it again. No *way* did it say what I thought it said. But it did. "For the kidnapping of Aldhanshai Wen-Jhai, daughter of our beloved Aldhanan, Kor-Har of Ormolu, and her consort, Dhanan Sai-Far of Sensa."

I stepped back, shaking. "What the fuck, Lhan? We didn't kidnap Sai and Wen-Jhai! What are they talking about?"

Then I knew, and my teeth clenched hard enough to crack. "Those fuckers. This ain't nothin' but bait on a hook. The priests kidnapped Sai and Wen-Jhai, 'cause they think we're going to drop everything to go rescue them, and walk right into their trap."

Lhan nodded. "Aye. 'Tis exactly what they think."

"And they're right." I tore the poster off the wall and started back toward the docks. "Vacation's canceled, Lhan. Let's go talk to Kai-La. We're goin' back to Ormolu."

CHAPTER FIFTEEN

DUTY!

Kai-La looked up from her map table and shook her head. "I sympathize, sister, but I'll not go anywhere near Ormolu. Not after Toaga. And certainly not in this ship."

"But..." I spread my hands and hit a bulkhead. The captain's cabin in the church ship was a lot smaller than Kai-La's quarters back on her old man-o-war. "But they're your friends too! Well, Sai is. Didn't you fuck the living daylights out of him all the way to Doshaan?"

Burly snorted from the built-in bench under the stern windows. "And sold him when we arrived."

Kai-La smirked. "If you went to rescue only his prick I might help you, but the fool attached to it? No. I'll not risk my crew for a pair of spoiled brats. I'm afraid you are on your own."

I sighed, but I couldn't really blame her. She'd just killed an entire shipload of priests. The church would never stop hunting her. Even if she wasn't on their shit list, I couldn't expect her or anyone else to wanna come along. Lhan and I were basically planning to go commit suicide. Nobody in their right mind would want a piece of that action.

Kai-La stepped around the table. "All I can do is wish you well and give you your share of the spoils. It might help open some doors."

Lhan and I exchanged a glance. Lhan raised an eyebrow.

"And what spoils are these?"

Kai-La nodded at Burly, who stood up from the bench, then opened it. He lifted out a heavy satchel and carried it to the table with both hands, then threw back the flap. It was filled to bursting with flat orange glass disks about the size of poker chips. There was a white hexagon symbol stamped on each one. I knew that symbol. It was painted on the side of the balloon we were sitting under.

Burly grinned. "As you did half the work, your share is half. We will divide the other half amongst ourselves."

Lhan whistled. His eyes had gone all glittery. "That… that is extremely generous of you."

I looked from him to Kai-La. "Church money?"

"Aye. Water Tokens. Anyone who possesses one can redeem it at a temple for a hundred weight of water. The priests carry them for bribes."

I still wasn't up to speed on my Waarian weights and measures. "How much is a hundred weight?"

"About as much as would fit in two large barrels."

I blinked. "As dry as it is around here, that's gotta be worth quite a lot."

Lhan patted the satchel, nodding. "Indeed. We gaze upon a fortune here. 'Twould be enough to buy my father's house."

I remembered his father's house. It was a castle—and not one of those dinky little castles, either.

Lhan crossed his wrists and bowed to Kai-La and Burly. "You are correct, friends. This will make our journey much smoother. Thank you."

Kai-La and Burly bowed back, then Kai-La reached up and gave me a hug. "Again you travel in the wrong direction, sister. Someday you will sail with me. I know it."

"Maybe I will, if I survive."

She stepped back and looked me in the eyes. "Then survive. We will be waiting."

***

Half an hour later we waved goodbye as the pirates lifted off and headed south. Even with the stupid orange church balloon, the warship looked so beautiful flying off into the sun it made my heart hurt.

"Totally having second thoughts now."

"Aye, mistress. As am I."

Lhan sighed and turned toward the other ships and I followed. My eyes were tearing up from looking at the sun anyway.

We got our fare back from the ship that was sailing to Vedya and bought a ticket on another one going to Ormolu. It didn't leave for three hours, so we went back to the inn to wait it out. Unfortunately, we were both too freaked out about Sai and Wen-Jhai being kidnapped and what we were heading into to get ourselves in the mood, so there were no hi-jinx, not even when I took off my robes and loosened my boob bindings because of the heat. Instead Lhan fidgeted and paced around while I just flopped on the bed, sweating like I was in a sauna and staring into space with a million thoughts spinning around in my head. Eventually, one of 'em popped out.

"Why are these little church fuckers so weird about me?"

Lhan turned from looking though the crack between the curtains. "As I said before, I believe you impinge on the divinity of the Wargod. You have his skin color, his strength, his leaping. Thus, by your mere existence, you make him less unique—less a god."

I sat up, pulling the sweaty sheets off my shoulders. "Yeah, yeah, I remember. But that doesn't explain 'em sending me back to Earth. Why didn't they just kill me in my sleep? Wouldn't that have been easier?" I looked at the crumpled wanted poster where I'd laid it on the bedside table. "And why are they gunning for you so hard? Whadda they got against *your* 'mere existence?'"

"As to the first, I know not, though I am glad beyond all measure they did not. For the second, I cannot be certain, but perhaps it is because I was witness to your capture." He smirked and leaned against the wall. "A bit awkward for the church to be caught kidnapping the savior of the Empire, eh? She who had been given honors and rewards by the Aldhanan himself?"

I shook my head. "Awkward, yeah, but to chase you halfway across the continent? To slaughter all those pirates? Would they really go to all that trouble?"

Lhan's smirk faded. "You do not know the church. Secrets mean more to them than life itself, and they fear anything that might reveal them or threaten their power. And you—" He stopped, staring at nothing, then refocused and sat down beside me, taking my hand. "It occurs to me that the priests fear you for more than just your possible diminution of the Wargod's divinity.

They fear you yourself, as they did the Wargod when first he arrived."

"I thought they worshipped him."

"Not at first. At first he fought against them, calling them corrupt and raising the Dhanans against them, but later, when he might have destroyed them, he joined them instead, claiming that he would change the church from within." He smirked again. "Heretics such as I believe it was the church that changed him, that it was they who turned him into the haunted, secret-hoarding hypocrite who ruled Ora for nigh on a hundred years. Or rather, we believe that the corruption had always been in his heart, and only revealed itself when he was given absolute control over the church and the state."

"But what has all that got to do with me? I don't want absolute control over anything—well, 'cept myself, I guess. I just want 'em to leave my friends alone and stay out of my life!"

"And that, I believe, is precisely what they are afraid of—that you are not corruptible. That if you were to rise against them—for their treatment of your friends, for example—you would not give up your ideals if offered the reins of power. That you would instead spurn their offers and tumble their ancient towers to the ground."

I snorted. "Are they kidding? I ain't got enough energy to do all that. All I wanna do is bum around with you and—"

There were running footsteps in the hall, then somebody was pounding on the door. "Surgeon! Surgeon, come quick! There's been a fight!"

CHAPTER SIXTEEN

DISCOVERED!

Lhan stood up and flapped a hand at me. "Don your robes, quickly!" Then shouted at the door. "Don't come in!"

I yeeped and looked around for my stuff, my boob bindings all loose around my waist. There was no time to rewrap. It had taken more than five minutes to get myself all squished down, so I just grabbed my robe and hoped for the best.

"Surgeon, please! A man is bleeding to death! He's lost a hand!"

Lhan looked back, wild-eyed, as I danced around in the middle of the room, trying to cover myself. The robe was twisted and sticking to my sweaty skin like a rubber sheet. Fighting into it was like trying climb into a bear skin with the bear still in it.

Lhan stepped to the door. "I am not at liberty! I am performing a delicate surgery!"

Whoever it was pounded harder on the door. "The barman said the only other surgeon is at the salt plant, and that's an iln away. You've got to come!"

"I cannot!" He rolled his eyes and muttered back at me. "And what would I do when I arrived? I've no skill with knife and brand."

Finally I got the robe on and buttoned up, pulled the pointy hood and ninja mask down over my head, grabbed the gloves, and gave Lhan a thumbs-up.

"Okay."

He groaned, then turned the latch. And that's when I realized that I was all dressed up but he wasn't.

"Lhan! Your hood! Your mask!"

He squeaked and looked back at the table, where the stork-face mask lay with his hood. He'd been so worried about covering up all my giant pinkness that he'd totally forgot himself.

It was too late. The door flew open and three purple guys pushed in, sweaty and out of breath. They looked like sailors, and smelled like a St. Patty's Day morning after.

"Surgeon! Thank you!" The first one was a thin guy with an adams apple like a golf ball. "Our mate, Zha, got in a fight at the Red Sails and took the worst of it. You've got to—" He stopped and squinted at Lhan's face. "Do I know you?"

Lhan shook his head and took a step back. "I know no one here. I have only stopped until my ship—"

Adams-Apple pointed a finger at Lhan. "I *do* know you." He looked around at his two pals. "Where do I know him from?"

The one on the left frowned. "He do look familiar, don't he?"

My sword was across the room, wrapped up with our gear to hide what it was. I started edging toward it, trying to look casual, while Lhan backed to the table and picked up his mask and hood, playing all high and mighty.

"Have you forgotten your friend so quickly? Did you not say he was bleeding to death? Come. Let us put aside these guessing games until I have saved his life, shall we?"

Adams-Apple nodded. "Aye, aye. Only, I know I've seen your face before. I just..."

At that second, my bindings decided to let go entirely, and flumped down to the floor around my feet. The noise turned Adams-Apple's head and he really looked at me for the first time—including the boob bulge the bindings shoulda been hiding.

"You—you're a woman?"

His pal on the left went all bug-eyed and started jumping up and down. "I have it! I have it! It's the ones from the poster! The ones who kidnapped the Aldhanan's daughter!"

Adams-Apple stared, gape-mouthed. "So it is! The ones with the ten thousand tolna price on their heads! I *knew* I knew 'im!"

Lhan jumped back to our gear, pulling on his mask. "Take your pack and sword, beloved. We must flee."

"Right there with ya."

I started throwing on all my stuff—pack and sword over one shoulder, satchel with the water tokens over the other, but the sailors didn't like this idea at all. They drew their swords and blocked the door.

Adams-Apple gave us a nasty smile. "And where do you think you're going, tolnas?"

I sneered at him—which was pointless behind my ninja mask, but oh well. "I thought you had a dying friend."

"Aye, and ten thousand will buy him a lot of doctoring. Now come quiet and we won't hurt you."

I threw the table at him, then kicked open the window. "Come on, Lhan!"

We jumped out together and landed side by side one floor down outside the front door of the inn, and right in the middle of seven more sailors, who were all standing beside a bench with another sailor on it, this one with a dirty cloth wrapped around the stump of his left wrist. Fuck! It was Adams-Apple's pals.

Adams-Apple leaned out the window and shouted down to them. "Get them, mess mates! There's a ten thousand tolna bounty on their heads!"

The sailors all turned and looked at us like we were the pot of gold at the end of the rainbow. And they weren't the only ones. Everybody on the goddamn street had heard Adams-Apple yell, and they all started toward us like a horde of greed zombies.

Lhan took my hand. "Make for the ship."

"But it doesn't leave for an hour."

"I can think of no other alternative."

Neither could I, but I didn't see how we were gonna do it. The crowd was starting to block the street between us and the docks, and more people were spilling outta every door along it as the word spread. We'd need to be able to fly to get beyond 'em all.

Duh. And I could fly, couldn't I? Well, sorta.

Lhan was drawing his sword. I stepped ahead of him and elbowed him back.

"Hang on, Lhan. I got a plan."

"Mistress, you mustn't—"

I peeled my hood and mask back to show my pink, alien face, then tore my wrapped-up sword outta my pack and jumped at the crowd, whooping and waving it around like a crazy person. They shrank back, gasping, and I grinned. The freak factor never failed—at least not the first time—and I wasn't gonna give 'em a second.

Before they could pull themselves together, I jumped back to Lhan and pulled him toward the inn, which was a two-story adobe with a flat roof—like every other building in town.

"Just like we did in Doshaan, remember? After the arena?"

Lhan swallowed. "Oh, gods."

But when I laced my fingers together and made a step with my hands he put his foot on 'em without flinching, and I lofted him like I was at a caber toss.

Seeing me heave a man two stories in the air stopped the crowd again, and I spidered up the front of the building while they just stood there with their faces hanging out. When I reached the top, Lhan was sitting up and holding his ribs where I'd sewn him up, but because of the red robes I couldn't tell if he was bleeding.

"All right, Lhan?"

"I will survive, but I fear we have only delayed the inevitable."

I looked over the edge. It didn't look good. The sailors were kicking their way into the building, while the crowd was starting to swarm around it, practically drooling with greed. Even from this distance I could see it in their eyes. Ten thousand tolnas? They weren't about to let us slip through their fingers. Imagine if they knew about the water tokens!

I stepped back, then looked toward ships, all floating at the ends of the docks. "Which one was ours again?"

Lhan nodded. "That with the blue canopy."

"Will they take wanted criminals?"

Lhan gave me a slanted smile. "The fortune you carry in that box would allow every man aboard to become a Dhanan. They would certainly take us—if we were able to reach them."

"Oh, we'll reach them."

I looked along the street. All we had to do was hop from roof to roof down the buildings that flanked the main drag and we were golden. It wasn't going to be a slam dunk, though. The gap between the inn we were on and the next building was about fifteen feet. Easy on my own. Not so easy weighed down with my sword and the satchel full of glass coins and Lhan, but I'd make it. I'd have to. By now every door along the main drag was spilling greedy yokels. As far as they were concerned it was free money day in Galok.

Under my feet, the inn was shaking with the footsteps of the sailors running up the inside stairs. Time to go.

I turned my back to Lhan. "Climb on. Let's get moving."

He stood straight and stuck his chin out. "Mistress, I cannot."

I scowled at him, confused. "What? Why not? Are you too hurt? Did I screw something up throwing you up here?"

"'Tis not that. But I can no longer—"

The roof door slammed open and the sailors bulled out, followed by a swarm of tag-alongs, all waving spears, swords and clubs. Some of 'em had crossbows.

There was no more time to talk. I grabbed Lhan, slung him over my shoulder, then bolted for the edge and leapt. A spear shot past me and banged into the side of the next building as I landed on the roof.

Lhan grunted at the impact. I kept running, and sprang for the next roof at full gallop. Crossbow bolts whizzed by on all sides. Down on the street, the crowd was running with us, cat-calling and shaking their sticks and swords. I risked a look back and saw the sailors all filing back into the stairs.

By the third building I was pulling ahead of the crowd. By the fifth, they were far behind.

I called over my shoulder. "Hang on, Lhan! We're gonna make it!"

Lhan only croaked. I ran on, aiming for the ship with the blue balloon. There were five docks sticking out from the quayside like fat stone fingers, and our ride was hanging off the ring finger, but like I'd said, they were nowhere near ready to leave. Guys were still humping loads up the gangplank while the rest of the crew was cleaning and making repairs. All we were gonna do was tree ourselves, but what else was there to do?

I reached the last roof and slowed down at the dockside edge. By myself, I coulda jumped, but a two-story drop woulda had Lhan puking blood from slamming into my shoulder. Instead, I looked over the edge. Below me was an outside stair leading up to a door into the second floor. Perfect. I lifted Lhan off my shoulder then lowered him over the side. At full stretch, it was only a two-foot drop to the top stair. He let go and stuck the landing, and I vaulted over to join him.

"Beloved, I must protest—"

The sound of the crowd stampeding down the street was getting louder. I threw him on my shoulder again and ran down the stairs, then raced across the quay for the ring-finger dock, just in time for another dozen sailors to run out from a ship and block our way, some of 'em with crossbows.

I skipped to the high hills as they fired, and the bolts zipped under my heels, then I came down right in front of them and jumped again, higher. Their leader screamed bloody murder as I bounced over their heads and kept sprinting for the ship.

"Turn about! After her! That bounty's ours!"

But before they could, the crowd flowed around them from the street like a river, and poured after me down the dock. I looked ahead and saw the sailors on our ship staring at all the chaos coming their way with with their jaws unhinged.

I ran straight at 'em, waving and shouting. "Go! Go! All aboard! Cast off!"

They just kept staring.

I looked back. The crowd was halfway down the dock, with Adams-Apple and his gang shoving into the lead. Adams-Apple was waving one of the wanted posters over his head and shoving everybody else back.

"They're ours! We claim the bounty!"

I bounded past the lookee-loos on the gangplank to the deck of the ship, then leaned Lhan against the rail and turned toward the captain, a balding, sun-purpled little pit-bull with an Abraham Lincoln beard.

"Take off! Let's go!"

He edged back, giving me an uneasy once over. "What are you? What do you want on my ship?"

"We bought a ticket! We're your passengers to Ormolu. Now get going!"

"Impossible. We are not to sail for half a crossing. Our cargo is but half loaded."

"We'll make it up to you. We got plenty of money. Plenty."

He rolled his eyes. I wanted to punch him in the mouth. Adams-Apple's boys were closing fast, and the rest of the crowd weren't far behind. There was no time for eye rolling.

"You could not possibly have enough money to make it worth my while. Now get off my ship and—"

Lhan lifted his head. "Open the satchel."

I yanked the strap and pulled it open, then held it out so Captain Pit-Bull could see all the orange glass.

He blinked once, then turned to his men, his sneering and eye rolling gone in a hot second.

"Ard! Gen! Cast off the lines! Bring in the plank! Forau, get your lazy waisters into those shrouds! Everyone else, prepare to repel boarders! Lively now!"

The crew didn't need much encouragement. They'd seen the church money too, and it had worked on 'em like a double espresso with a Red Bull chaser. They were zipping around the ship like monkeys on meth, hauling on ropes and climbing up to the sails that stuck out from the balloon like fins, while the rest of us waited for the crush.

It wasn't long in coming. Adams-Apple and his gang reached the end of the dock just as the sailors untied the mooring ropes, and they charged for the gangplank. The sailors ran up ahead of them and tried to pull it in, but they were trampled in the rush.

"No you don't!"

I jumped in front of Adams-Apple, seeing red and swinging for his head with my bundled sword. If it wasn't for him busting into our room we woulda walked out of Galok as peaceful as we'd come in. I cracked him over the ear with the flat of the blade and knocked him ass-up over the rail, then caught two of his gang with my follow through. They went skidding across the deck, out cold, and I plowed into the crowd that was following them up the gangplank.

The guy at the top was a big bastard, and sent the others flying back as I put a foot in his chest and kicked. Most of 'em fell back on the dock, but some went off the sides, falling past the long stone legs of the dock and hitting hard on the red dry sea bed and rolling down toward the salt mine and out of my sight. Their screams raised the hairs on the back of my neck.

Didn't seem to faze the rest of the crowd, though. They kept running up the gangplank like it was gonna get 'em somewhere, even as the ship was floating up and away from the dock, and more were leaping the gap and grabbing onto the ship's rail. They were insane—gold-crazed lemmings of greed.

I stood at the head of the gangplank, bashing and kicking them back, while Lhan and the crew beat on the heads and hands of the ones at the rail, and sent them pinwheeling to the slope below. Then, just as another dozen or so piled onto the gangplank, the ship floated out another inch and it fell away, taking them all with it.

I stepped back and caught a breath as Lhan and the crew peeled off the rest of the boarders. Then I noticed one last hanger-on clinging to the rail right beside me—Adams-Apple, and he was terrified. He was holding on one-handed and reaching up with the other, which still had our wanted poster in it. He looked up at me, eyes bulging.

"Help me! Gods, please, help me!"

After all he'd done, I had every right to kick him in the face and watch him fall, but my mad was fading, and he looked so pitiful I couldn't help myself. I started forward to grab him, but just as I stretched out my hand, his fingers slipped and he dropped out of sight, screaming, as the wanted poster blew over the rail and fluttered to the deck.

I stared after him, feeling guilty and helpless, then cringed and turned away when he hit, and a puff of dust rose up to join the thick cloud that was drifting across the salt mines.

"Mistress!" Lhan hissed in my ear.

"Huh?"

"The broadsheet. Get it."

"The what?"

"The broadsheet. Before the captain sees it."

I looked down. Oh. He meant the poster. I bent down to get it. Too late again. A puff of wind blew it out from under my fingers and it skittered across the deck right to the feet of Captain Pit-Bull.

We turned, holding our breath, hoping he would cross to us without noticing it. He started to, but on his first step he put his foot on the paper and looked down.

Lhan and I froze.

The captain bent closer, squinting at the poster, then looked up at us.

We smiled.

He smiled back, then motioned to his men. "Take them. It seems we will have their water tokens *and* a reward."

CHAPTER SEVENTEEN

CAPTURED!

Well, I probably coulda made a mess of Pit-Bull's crew and his ship, but before I got the chance, one of his guys put a knife to Lhan's neck from behind and that was that. Lhan was too wrecked and winded to fight, and I wasn't gonna risk him getting his throat cut while I tried any Bruce Willis horse-shit. I dropped my sword and raised my hands.

The crew swarmed me like wolves on a deer, and a few seconds later I was face down on the deck with my legs hobbled and my hands tied behind my back. Lhan was the same. I gave him a hopeful smile, but he didn't return it, just winced in pain as they hauled him to his feet. What was that about? Usually he was winks and saucy grins when things went to shit. Now he hadn't even looked at me. Was he more hurt than I thought?

They got me up and were pushing us both toward the belowdecks door when a voice shouted from the dock, which was still only about thirty feet off to the right of the ship.

"Ahoy the ship! If you wish to collect your reward, you will deliver the fugitives to me!"

Captain Pit-Bull looked over the rail, and we did too. There was a priest in dusty orange robes standing at the end of the dock, all by himself. The crowd was hanging back a good ten feet, which just proved to me how scared everybody was of the church, 'cause the priest himself wasn't the type to make anybody stand back. He mighta carried himself like he was ten feet tall and made of solid gold, but really he was just a roly-poly little goober with pudgy purple hands and a prissy mouth.

He raised a staff and pointed it at Pit-Bull. "You will return to your mooring and take me on board."

The captain chewed his lip for a second, then turned to his mate and whispered in his ear. I didn't hear what he said, but as the Pit-Bull started motioning his crew to go back to the dock, the mate picked up the bag of water tokens and went below with it.

A few minutes later, Brother Rollo waddled up a makeshift gangplank like he owned the place and crossed to where Pit-Bull and his crew were holding us for inspection. He gave a bored little sniff as he looked at Lhan, but took his time with me, giving me a long once over and curling his lip like he was looking at Waar's tallest pile of shit. I wanted to headbutt him right between his sleepy little eyes, but he never got close enough. Instead he turned to Pit-Bull and waved a hand.

"Take them below and lock them up. Then you will transport them and myself to the ancient city of Durgallah at once, where you will receive your—"

"Durgallah!" Captain Pit-Bull didn't like that one bit. "But I'm bound for Ormolu. I've a cargo due there in three days. I can't go hieing off to the desert with—"

"The church commands it. Will you disobey?"

"But can you not get another—?"

"I cannot, but worry not. You will be amply compensated for your service. Now lock them up and make sail."

Pit-Bull ground his teeth, but gave the orders, and the ship started rising from the dock again as a handful of sailors shoved us toward the underdeck door.

***

It was just a cargo ship, so they didn't have a brig. Instead they put us in a little store room stacked up with piles of spare sails and rope, untied us, and locked us in. I flopped down on the sails and gave Lhan another grin, hoping to joke him out of his funk.

"Alone at last, eh? Maybe now we can have that reunion we've been putting off."

But Lhan just kept facing the door, like he had been since they shut it. What the hell was up? I sat up.

"Lhan, are you alright? Are you hurt or—"

He turned, and looked me right in the eye. "Beloved, you will not do that again."

I blinked, clueless. "Uh, do what again?"

He snorted, angry, then crossed to a pile of coiled ropes and lowered himself onto it, holding his ribs. A chill went up my spine. The last time I'd seen Lhan this mad, it had been when Sai had been afraid to fight Kedac-Zir for Wen-Jhai's hand. What the hell had I done?

"Come on, Lhan. Don't keep me in suspense. What the fuck did I do? 'Cause I haven't got a goddamn clue."

"Truly?" He looked up at me at last. His eyes as hard and cold as a gun. "You do not then remember only three days ago, when I asked you for the honor of being your Dhan, and you pledged to be my Dhanshai."

Uh-oh. "I remember. What about it?"

"The pledge meant nothing to you? It was mere words?"

"Lhan, if you're pissed off about something, come out and fucking say it! Don't pull this twenty questions bullshit."

Lhan drew himself up. "Very well, I shall speak plainly. A dhanshai does not push her dhan aside and fight in his place. Indeed, a dhanshai does not fight at all. Nor does a dhanshai pick her dhan up and carry him about as if he were an infant. And she most particularly does not pick her dhan up and carry him like an infant *in the presence of others*!"

He'd started off cold as ice, but by the time he got to the end of it he was spitting mad and as red in the face as I'd ever seen him. I stared at him, dumbfounded. I couldn't believe what I was hearing.

"You—you're serious?"

"Can you doubt it?"

I flopped back on the sails, my head spinning, then looked up at him again. I felt like I was in a bad dream. "Lhan, I. . . ." I didn't know what to say. I tried again. "Where is this shit coming from all of a sudden? I was only tryin' to save your life. We've been saving each other's lives like that since we've known each other. It never bothered you before."

"You were not my dhanshai then. I was not your dhan. We were but companions."

"Well, fuck, if that's all there is to it, let's go back to being companions again! Easy peasy."

Lhan looked like I'd slapped him. "You would deny our love so glibly?"

"I'm not denying anything! Didn't I come all the way across the universe to be with you?"

"Then I fail to understand you."

I got up. He was making me so crazy I wanted to pace. Unfortunately there was no room. It was a closet. We were basically face to face no matter where we stood.

"You asked me to be your girlfriend and I said yes. I didn't say I'd give up being me. I didn't say I'd put down my sword and turn into Wen-Jhai."

Lhan's eyes went cold again. "I did not ask you to be my 'girl-friend,' whatever that might mean. I asked you to be my Dhanshai. I asked that you accept me as your Dhan."

"There's a difference?"

"A dhanshai is sworn to love, comfort and support her dhan, in sickness as in health, in lean times and fat, and be faithful to him all her days. A dhan is sworn to defend his dhanshai's honor and person against all dangers, provide for her in sickness and health, in lean times and fat, and be faithful to her all his days. These duties are the sacred principles of Oran chivalry, and the pledging of dhan to dhanshai the most binding vow a man or woman can make."

I threw up my hands and nearly broke my knuckles on the ceiling. Our new digs were as low as they were narrow. "And you think I knew all this? I'm from another planet, remember? I don't know all your mumbo-jumbo. I thought you were just asking me out."

For the first time, a little of the old Lhan showed under the glacier. A confused frown wrinkled his forehead. "That—that had not occurred to me. Though your ways are often strange, I assumed that *this* at least would be universal. Forgive me. If you wish to withdraw your pledge—"

I groaned and closed my eyes. "Lhan, I don't get you. You like both boys and girls. You like me, the big pink freak, who's not even the same species as you. Your friends are all weirdos and church haters. And now you come out with all this macho 'defend her person against all dangers' stuff? I thought you were more modern than that!"

But even as I said it I remembered again how he'd acted when Sai had tried to get out of fighting Kedac-Zir for Wen-Jhai's hand. Lhan had told Sai that if he didn't give Kedac an honorable challenge, he would be abandoning the path of honor and he'd be on his own. It'd seemed like he woulda rather seen Sai get killed in a fight he couldn't win than go behind the bad guy's back and sneak off with the girl.

Lhan raised his chin, offended. "A man may question the authority of his betters and still be a dhan, and as to my appetites, I...." He cleared his throat, then looked at his boots. "I admit I have sinned, and felt no shame in sinning, but that is because I knew I could not honorably be with he who I truly loved, and did not believe I would ever truly love another." He raised his gaze to mine. "That has changed."

Those purple eyes went right through me, and I got weak in the knees. Put down the sword? Wear a dress? Let Lhan protect me? It wouldn't be that bad, would it?

I massaged my forehead. "Lemme get this straight. You screwed around with all and sundry because you couldn't have Sai. And if you couldn't have Sai there was no point in being honorable."

He nodded. "That is essentially correct, yes."

"But now that you've met me, you wanna be a gentleman again."

"Precisely."

I groaned. "Fucking hell. I'm a bad influence."

"I beg your pardon?"

I flopped down on the sails again. "Lhan, you picked the wrong person to go straight for. I'm no lady. You know that. I'm bigger than you. I'm stronger than you. I'm almost as good with a sword. I don't need a knight in shining armor."

He looked down again. "Of that I am aware. I was fool enough to hope you would *want* one."

"Aw, Lhan. That's not fair. I *do* want you. You know that. I just... I can't...."

"You do not wish to abide by your vow."

Of course I didn't. It was a bunch of macho crap. Why would I want to do all the comforting and soothing and let him do all the defending and protecting? But, wait. On the other hand...

"No. No, the vow sounds pretty good to me, actually, but why can't it go both ways?"

"What do you mean?"

"I mean, I'll do just like the vow says. I'll love and comfort you when you're down, but then you'll do the same for me when *I'm* down. And the same for the other part. You'll defend my honor and person when I can't, and I'll defend your honor and person when you can't. How's that? Fair?"

Lhan paused like he was considering it, then sighed and shook his head. "As appealing as that might sound, it cannot be. You propose a vow of brothers, not lovers. The vow of lovers states that a dhan must protect his dhanshai. It matters not the weakness of the dhan, nor the strength of the dhanshai. The rule remains the same."

And there we were back to the beginning again. A dhan protected his dhanshai because a dhan protected his dhanshai because a dhan protected his dhanshai and that's all there was to it. I was too tired from all the running and fighting we'd done to go through it all again, and besides, we were alone, and his lips were *right there*!

"Okay, Lhan, listen. I can't say I won't fight if it comes to fighting. But I won't lead, okay? I'll let you give the orders. And I won't pick you up anymore."

I patted the sails. After a second, he sat down beside me, and I put a hand on his leg. "And if you want me to love, comfort and support you, you got it—in sickness and in health, in lean times and fat, forever and ever amen. I promise."

He frowned, thinking about it, his mouth hard, and I was worried he was gonna say no dice, but I gave his leg a squeeze and he shivered.

"Very well, mistress. In light of your martial nature, I suppose an allowance can be made. But you must abide by my orders. I must insist on that."

I kissed his neck. "Of course, Lhan. Absolutely."

"Thank you, beloved. I know it was not an easy decision. I am honored that you have allowed me to be your dhan."

I started untying his robes. "And I'm honored that you offered."

And after that it was on 'er and off 'er all night long.

***

Actually, that's just a cheap joke. It didn't go like that at all. Not even close. You know what happens. You blow something up so big in your head, nothing in real life can match it, and I remembered that lost last night with Lhan like it was something out of a romance novel, all soft-focus and slow motion and power ballad guitar solos. Reality was gonna have a tough time living up to that, right?

And, well, it didn't.

That first night was a disaster. It didn't work at all. The first time we tried,

Lhan popped his cork almost before we got started, and then spent an hour apologizing for letting me down, while I kept saying it didn't matter—and wishing I thought it didn't. The second time was no better. That time, he did fine, but I couldn't cum for love nor money, I'm not sure why. Maybe 'cause my head was going around and around, wondering about all that vow business and if it was all going to work out.

Afterwards we spent another awkward hour or so holding each other like we were afraid to be the first one to let go. Finally though, that pile of sails just got too small, so I kissed him good night and rolled off onto the floor. I lay awake for a long time, pretending to sleep, wondering if I'd made a huge mistake—and then thinking that maybe it wouldn't matter since Lhan and I were both going to be killed by the priests anyway, and maybe that was for the best. Yeah, I was feeling pretty sorry for myself right about then, but after a while it got me thinking about what we were heading into, and I asked the question I woulda asked if all that other stuff hadn'ta come up first.

"So what the hell is Durgallah, and why the fuck is this priest taking us there?"

Lhan answered right away, which told me he hadn't been asleep either. "Durgallah is an ancient city to the south of here, known now as the City of Black Glass. It too lies on the shores of the Vanished Sea, but it is a ruin—destroyed by the Church of the Seven for heresy thousands of years ago."

"Heresy?"

"Aye. The people of Durgallah turned from the Seven and worshiped false gods. The church rained the fire of heaven down upon them as punishment." He shook his head. "It is strange that the church would bring us there. The priests fear it like no other place on Waar."

"Why?"

"The ghosts of their victims. They are said to haunt the ruins still, held to this world by their hatred for the church. I have heard that no priest who has entered the ruins has left with his life or sanity intact."

I normally don't believe in ghosts, or any of that supernatural bullshit, but after everything I'd seen on this weird-ass planet it was a little harder to be all rational and modern.

"You—you think there are really ghosts there?"

He shrugged. "I think ghosts will be the least of our worries in Durgallah. Whatever the reason the Church wants us, I am certain it will not be pleasant. Indeed, it may be the death of us."

He looked so miserable that I reached up to him and squeezed his hand. "I'm sorry, Lhan. If I hadn't dropped into your life, none of this evil shit would have happened."

He squeezed back and looked down at me, and those purple eyes swallowed me whole. "And I would count that a tragedy, Mistress. Despite these troubles, I would choose any life that contained you over an easier one without."

Man, that boy could talk. I almost pulled him down to the floor and started lovin' on him again, but I was still too freaked out about how badly things had gone earlier, so I just stayed where I was.

***

After that, though, it gradually got better—even when it didn't. Once we started to realize that having a bad night one night didn't mean we were falling out of love, and that we were going to be there for each other every night, no matter how the sex went, we started to have more good nights.

It's funny. Well, sad really. I'd known all this stuff back when I was with Big Don—taking it as it came, being easy when it didn't. All that hard-won wisdom shoulda carried over, right? Not so much. I guess it's something you have to relearn with every new person you get with.

Anyway, by the time we got to Durgallah, we were laughing when it was good, we were laughing when it was bad, and some nights we blew the fucking roof off the place. Captain Pit-Bull and his crew musta had to sleep with their fingers in their ears, and I bet we gave Brother Rollo ulcers.

Yeah, we were locked up in jail and heading into deep shit, but still, it mighta just been my happiest time on Waar.

CHAPTER EIGHTEEN

SOLD!

"I don't get it. Why is it called the City of Black Glass? It looks like a bunch of sandcastles after a wave hit 'em."

Lhan and I were craning our necks to look out the tiny port-hole which was the only source of light in the sail closet, as the City of Black Glass appeared in the distance below us, silhouetted in the pink light of a desert dawn. There were towers and spires everywhere, but all half crumbled and rounded off and caved in. And I didn't see any black glass anywhere. Everything looked red and dead and dusty to me.

"We are not at quite the right angle. It is the north half of the city that—"

Then the ship turned and all of a sudden we *were* at the right angle, and Lhan and I flinched back as the city stabbed us in the eyes.

"There. You see?"

"Can't see a goddamned thing. Yikes."

When the spots faded I shielded my eyes and looked again. The whole north side, which had been hidden behind the hull of the ship, was spread out below us, shining like a freshly polished Mercedes and reflecting the morning sun right into our faces. In the middle of the glare was a huge crater, half a mile wide, and all around it a circle of glittery rubble that spread out to a ring of lumpy, half-melted buildings all leaning away from the center like they'd been frozen halfway through falling down.

I'd never seen anything like it. What the fuck had happened? Did these sword-swinging savages have an atom bomb? They didn't even have cannons yet! On the other hand, the priests had wands of blue fire and anti-gravity ski-doos, so I guessed anything was possible.

"The church did that?"

"Thousands of years ago, yes."

"Sheesh. No wonder they don't like to come back. That musta killed everybody within a hundred miles."

The ship turned away from the glare again, and we watched as we dropped toward the sandy part of the city, angling to land in the middle of what looked like the main drag, a freeway-wide boulevard with fancy buildings on both sides, all slumped and shattered, and neighborhoods of smaller buildings and skinnier streets behind them, all completely dead, deserted and knee-deep in sand.

A few minutes later we heard the pounding of sledgehammers below us, then the back and forth tug of the crew threading the lines through the mooring rings and tying them off. We pulled on our red robes and hoods, and few minutes after that, there was a key in the lock and our door swung open. Captain Pit-Bull wasn't taking any chances. He had two guys with crossbows covering us as another two guys came in and tied us up, then they all marched us up onto the deck where the prissy priest, Brother Rollo, was waiting and looking over the side like he was being stood up on his big date.

"Where are they?" he asked nobody in particular, then he turned to Captain Pit-Bull. "Lower the gangplank. We must descend."

"Where is my reward?"

"Those we are here to meet will have it. Now let us go."

Pit-Bull didn't look very happy about that, but had his guys let down the long plank anyway, and Rollo tip-toed down it while the sailors prodded us along behind and carried our weapons and gear all wrapped up in bundles.

We ended up in the middle of the street, with the wind moaning through the empty ruins all around us and dust blowing in our faces. There wasn't any other sound, or any other movement, just wind and sand and all those empty windows and doors looking at us like they were the eyes and mouths of giant skulls. The whole scene gave me the creeps.

I shot Rollo a look. "So, we here for a picnic?"

"Silence! We are waiting!"

So we waited—me and Lhan sagging against our ropes, our guards fidgeting, Rollo twitching and looking over his shoulder every five seconds, and Captain Pit-Bull with his arms crossed, grunting and glaring at the back of Rollo's head.

Finally, just as the sand was starting to bury my feet, a voice on my seven made us all jump out of our pants.

"What do you want here?"

Everybody spun around, gasping, and we saw a guy in head-to-toe black robes standing in the street and aiming a crossbow at us. Then we saw the dozen or so other crossbows pointing out of the dark windows of the building behind him, and we all did the gasp and jump out of our pants thing a second time. We couldn't see any men in there—just crossbows. And we couldn't see any face under Mr. Black-Robes' hood either—just black.

Rollo was shaking like someone'd shoved a jackhammer up his ass. "We—we seek a priest of Ormolu, who—"

"There are no priests here, fool. Who told you there were priests here?"

All the crossbows swung toward Rollo. He threw up his hands.

"It was in the edict! If we found the fugitives we were to bring them here to meet with a priest of the Temple!"

"Fugitives?"

Rollo motioned to us with a trembling hand. "The kidnappers! The outcast dhan and the outland giantess!"

At this, Black-Robes looked at us for the first time. "Pull back their hoods."

Rollo motioned to the sailors, and they yanked our hoods off.

Black-Robes stared, then lowered his crossbow and started to laugh. He pulled back his hood, grinning like a sideshow geek, and it was my turn to stare, 'cause it was the same Beak-Nosed asshole priest who'd threatened me with the wand of blue fire when I'd jumped on board the priest ship back at Toaga!

"Ormolu be praised! I had thought them lost!"

He started toward us and Rollo backed up, hands out. "Stay back! We are armed!"

This made Beak-Nose crack up even more. He pulled open his black robes to show orange and white beneath. "You squealing ruktug. I am the priest you are looking for."

Rollo let out a breath and slumped like an inflatable snowman with a bad leak. "Oh, my brother. I am so glad to see you. I feared—"

"Never mind. Never mind. You must sail away again at once. There can be no ships here when our play begins. Give them to us and go."

More guys in black robes stepped out of the nearby buildings and closed in on us, but Captain Pit-Bull stepped in front of us, chin out.

"There was a reward."

Beak-Nose looked annoyed, but then pasted on a smile. "It was you who captured them?"

Pit-Bull nodded. "I did."

Beak-Nose looked at Rollo.

He nodded. "He did."

"Very good. Will water tokens be acceptable?"

Pit-Bull licked his lips. "Certainly, your reverence."

I shot Lhan a questioning look. He nodded in agreement. We weren't about to let that happen. I raised my voice.

"Hey, Beak-Nose. Yeah, you. You shouldn't give the captain any more tokens. He already has plenty. He stole the ones we stole from you. They're in his cabin."

Beak-Nose turned on Pit-Bull, who was looking at me like he wanted to tear my lungs out with his bare hands.

"Is this true?"

Pit-Bull opened his mouth, but nothing came out.

Beak-Nose turned to his men. "Search the cabin."

Three of 'em trotted up the gangplank, then came back down again about five minutes later with the satchel. They opened it and showed it to Beak-Nose.

He nodded, then turned to Pit-Bull, cold. "I would kill you for stealing temple property, but your ship must be gone as soon as possible, so you are free to go, but there will be no reward for you, and no mercy if you cross the church again, do you understand?"

"Yes, your reverence."

"Good. Then go, and quickly."

I gave Pit-Bull a big smile as he turned to the gangplank. "Now you know how it feels, dick."

He gave me the death stare, but couldn't say anything in front of the priests, so he just walked on, stiff as week-old roadkill, with his men following up behind him.

"I think that guy wants to kill me."

Lhan chuckled. "I fear there are others who will beat him to it."

I looked around and found Beak-Nose standing in front of me. He grinned again, which was too bad. He was ugly to begin with. Smiling he was hideous.

"Truly, Ormolu blesses us. I did not expect my master's broadsheets to bear fruit in time for our little drama, and feared we would have to make do with bit players. But here you are. The cast is complete. The stage is set. We wait only for our audience to arrive."

"What the fuck are you talking about, Beak-Nose?"

His smile turned into a snarl, and he slapped me, hard.

"My name is Ru-Sul. *Your reverence* to filth like—"

"Your reverence! The skelshas are waking!"

Beak-Nose glanced at the priest who spoke, then scanned around the sky, suddenly tense. I followed his gaze and saw a few black-winged silhouettes wheeling over the rooftops off in the distance.

Beak-Nose turned back toward the ruins and waved a hand at us. "Paladins, bring them. We must retire."

***

Ru-Sul's paladins—which was apparently some kinda fancy name for temple guard—led us through a maze of broken-down buildings, climbing over mounds of rubble and slogging through knee-deep sand drifts as we walked under high, arched ceilings and by smashed statues whose heads and hands had been worn down to lumpy nubs by the blowing sand.

They tried to stay inside the buildings as much as possible, and took every covered passage and underground walkway they could find, but every now and then they had to cross a street or alley, and they'd all stop at the door and check the sky before hustling us across to the next building as quick as they could.

I gave Ru-Sul a look as they shoved us through a door into what looked like some kind of ancient lecture hall. "What's the matter? I figured you pricks would be all about feeding us to the birds."

He laughed. "We are not so wasteful. Your death will serve a far greater purpose than that of food for skelshas."

Lhan got a cagey look in his eye at that. "It must be a great purpose indeed to risk the wrath of the Aldhanan. Surely even the church cannot kill those upon who he has bestowed his favor with impunity."

Ru-Sul laughed again, louder this time, then stopped and looked at us. "You fools, the church won't kill you. It is the Aldhanan himself who will kill you. Indeed, he sails here as we speak to do that very thing."

CHAPTER NINETEEN

THE PIT!

I stared at him, and couldn't manage more than a stunned, "Uh, what?"

Lhan did better. "Do you tell me, then, that the Aldhanan has swallowed your pathetic lies and truly believes Mistress Jae-En and I have kidnapped his daughter and son-in-law?"

Ru-Sul looked smug. "How could he not, when you were seen taking them by a score of witnesses? One was even wounded trying to prevent your escape."

"*We* were seen? We were nowhere near—" I choked as I got it. "Wait a minute. You put some poor bastard in pink paint and a red wig and had him storm the Aldhanan's castle?"

Ru-Sul smirked. "The likeness was uncanny."

Lhan shook his head. "I fail to understand why you have gone to such trouble to defame us. Do you truly fear Mistress Jae-En that much?"

"This is hardly about the demoness. Not anymore." Ru-Sul turned and entered a dark hall at the back of the lecture hall, and our guards shoved us after him. "When she appeared, during the Kedac-Zir fiasco, we warned the Aldhanan in the strongest possible terms that she was a danger, and must be given over to us for the safety of Ora. Instead he gave her honors and rewards. He named her hero of the Empire."

"Hey! Asshole! How long are you gonna keep talking about me like I'm not here?"

He kept talking to Lhan. "Nor was this the first time the Aldhanan ignored our counsel. Indeed, since he ascended to the throne, Kor-Har has sided with the dhanans and 'the people,' and against the Church, more than any Aldhanan since his great-great-grandfather, Kor-Karan, he who is known to the histories as The Apostate."

Lhan curled his lip. "Aye, and the church had Kor-Karan… killed…" Lhan's eyes went wide. He stared at Ru-Sul. "This… this has been no trap for us. This is a trap for the Aldhanan! You have lured him here, telling him we hold his daughter in the ruins, and you mean to fall upon him in your black robes, priests pretending to be heretics. This is an assassination!"

Ru-Sul gave him a flat smile. "A shame you haven't the faith to match your mind. You would have made an excellent priest." He motioned ahead to where the dark hall opened out again. "We are here. I will introduce you to your fellow players."

We stepped out into a ginormous room, as big a cathedral, but with a creepy ocean theme going on. There were shell and seaweed designs studded into the marble floor like barnacles, and flaking gold leaf tentacles winding up the massive columns that held up what was left of the roof. A shaft of red sunlight angled through one of the holes up there and lit up a statue of some haughty-faced goddess with a shark-fin on her head at the far end. It made her look like she was covered in blood.

I leaned into Lhan. "Is this one of them false gods you were talking about?"

"Aye, a goddess of the depths. She demanded human sacrifice."

"She looks it."

Shabby tents were set up all around the edges of the room, and an area off to one side had been roped off as a corral for kraes. Disguised priests and paladins cooked their breakfast over campfires and watched us as Ru-Sul led us in. There was also some kind of magic circle painted on the floor in the middle of the chamber, with weird symbols and unlit candles on head-high iron candlesticks all around it.

"What the hell is all that for?"

Ru-Sul smiled. "Set dressing."

We tramped across the circle toward the shark lady, and I saw that the room had one more interesting feature—a big round hole in the floor right below the pedestal she was standing on. It was about twenty feet wide, and went down so far I couldn't see the bottom in the murky light. Two paladins with spears in their hands and crossbows on their backs were guarding it.

Ru-Sul turned at the edge and waved a hand like he was a real estate agent showing off a jacuzzi. "Your new home. Also your last." He motioned to the paladins. "Ready the hooks. Their friends await them."

Off to one side there were some coils of rope with grapples attached, tied off to various tentacle decorations. The paladins grabbed two of 'em and hooked 'em to the ropes tied around me and Lhan, then kicked us into the hole—no warning, no buildup, just hook, kick, boom.

I yelped like a stepped-on cat as I went into free fall, but the rope pulled tight a second later and I slammed against the side of the pit instead of the bottom. Lhan thudded next to me a second later, gasping, and then I felt the wall rubbing against my face as the paladins started lowering us down into the darkness inch by inch.

Ru-Sul's voice echoed from above. "You should feel glad it is not a thousand years ago. In that time, the pit was filled with water, and those thrown into it became sport for something known as the God of a Thousand Mouths. Fortunately, the Church of the Seven destroyed that horror, as it destroys all that threatens the security of Ora."

Lhan snarled. "The security of the Church, you mean."

"They are one and the same."

A couple seconds later my feet hit bottom and I toppled onto my side like a sack of laundry. The floor was a deep drift of sand and rocks and broken bones. Not real comfy. Then Lhan fell on top of me, and we just lay there, breathing and staring up at the top of the pit, until something moved in the darkness off to our left.

I raised my head and tried to shift around, but I was tied up tighter than butterfly in a cocoon, and the hook was still in the ropes. I could hardly move.

"Who the fuck is there? Come out where I can see you!"

A face emerged from the darkness, then another—zombie faces—hollow eyes and grimy skin and sunken cheeks. But I'd never heard of zombies with pouty lips or perfect jawlines before.

"Mistress Jae-En," said the one with the pouty lips. "Is this a dream? Are you but another priestly trick?"

"It is Jae-En!" said the one with the jawline. "And Lhan as well!"

"Get their hooks off," said the one with the lips.

Lhan and I gaped at them like the fish that probably used to swim in our pit before the sea dried up.

"Sai-Far! Wen-Jhai! You live!"

Yup, it was them, in the flesh, though a lot less flesh than I remembered. They were both as scrawny as Lhan had been when I found him on Toaga. Scrawnier even, but still ridiculously hot. Even covered in dirt and bruises and with their hair all ratty, the two of 'em looked like they coulda been centerfolds for Naughty Urchin magazine.

Sai got to work untying our ropes as Wen-Jhai gave us hugs and cried over us.

When we were free, Sai clutched our hands. "Mistress Jae-En. Dearest Lhan. I grieve that you have suffered the same miserable fate as we. I had hoped—no, prayed—that you had escaped the reach of the church and found your freedom."

Wen-Jhai wiped a tear from her eye. "And with you here, trapped, then all hope of rescue is gone, for surely there can be no other with the strength to defeat these villains."

Yeesh. I'd forgotten they talked that way. Even Lhan didn't get as Little Lord Fauntelroy as all that.

"Well, actually, your dad is coming."

Wen-Jhai gasped. "My father?"

"The Aldhanan?" Sai gasped too. "Then we are saved!"

Lhan shook his head. "It is a trap. The priests lure him here, saying that Jae-En and I hold you hostage. They mean, I fear, to kill him."

Wen-Jhai stared. "They—they will kill my father? But why? Is he not the most beloved Aldhanan of our age? What could he possibly have done to anger them?"

"Quite a lot, I fear." Lhan frowned. "If I recall, your father, early in his reign, discovered that priests in Pinau had falsely branded a Dhan a heretic in order to purchase his lands and holdings at a reduced price. The Aldhanan forced the Church to return the lands, and had the offending priests executed. There was also the case of the Temple in Hucarrah, which was selling water tokens at inflated prices and transferring the overage into private accounts. The temple of Ormolu denied this was happening, and your father was forced to expose them himself in order to get them to admit it. Indeed, the Aldhanan has been the most vigorous critic of the church and its corruptions since—"

Wen-Jhai moaned and finished his sentence for him. "Since my great-great-grandfather, Kor-Karan, who they also killed."

Sai slumped back against the wall. "By the Seven, we must get free. We must warn him. He cannot be allowed to come."

Wen-Jhai sobbed. "But it is impossible. We are trapped! Trapped!"

Sai looked up at me like a hopeful puppy. "Unless perhaps Mistress Jae-En could jump out of the pit?"

Wen-Jhai clasped her hands together like Rebbeca of Sunnybrook Farm. "Oh, but of course! Mistress Jae-En is magnificently strong. It will be nothing for her to escape the pit!"

Well, it was nice of her to say so, but it wasn't gonna happen. "Sorry, kids. That's about twice what I can jump. There's no way."

She pouted, crestfallen.

Sai was still hopeful. "Can you perhaps climb out?"

It was hard to see the walls down there in the dark, but I ran my hands over 'em. No good. They were made of close-fitted granite blocks, and though they were weathered and cracked, it wasn't enough. They were still too smooth. I woulda needed Spiderman powers.

"Nope. No can do."

He sagged too. "Then all is lost."

"Not necessarily." Lhan looked around at the rocks and bones. "We may have an opportunity when they pull us out. We must arm ourselves in anticipation of the moment."

"*Will* they pull us out?" Wen-Jhai looked doubtful. "If their aim is to kill my father—"

"It is more than that." Lhan glanced up at the top of the pit. "His reverence, Ru-Sul, spoke of drama, and set dressing. And then there are the elaborate disguises of the priests, all pretending to be heretics. Your father's murder will be a play, meant to be seen, the story of it brought back to Ormolu as truth by unassailable witnesses."

Sai nodded, getting it. "And we are all supposed to play parts in this play."

Wen-Jhai put her hands on her hips. "Ha! If they think I shall play a role in my own father's murder, they are quite mistaken! Do they expect me to say lines? Do they expect me to do as they ask?"

I hated to be the bearer of bad news, but… "I don't think you'll have many lines."

Wen-Jhai's eyes widened. "What do you mean?"

I jerked a thumb toward the surface. "They've got the whole place dressed up like a satanic ritual up there, and I think you and Sai are gonna be the sacrifices. I think they're gonna wait until your dad and whoever's with him bust through the door, then they'll 'perform the ceremony.'"

"Kill us, you mean."

"Yeah. That. Then your dad'll run in, trying to save you, and get jumped by all the disguised priests, and he'll die too."

Lhan raised a finger. "But someone will survive. Someone will return to Ormolu with the tale, and your bodies."

I pointed to my chest. "And ours. That'll be the proof that we kidnapped you like they said."

Sai threw up his hands. "But what is it all in aid of! What do they hope to accomplish with this murderous charade?"

"Other than ridding Ora of an Aldhanan the Church dislikes?" Lhan leaned back against the wall and crossed his arms. "My guess is that there will be, among the Aldhanan's party, a secret friend of the church whose part it will be to play the hero. It will be he who chases off the 'heretics' and 'saves' the witnesses. It will be he who 'slays' the kidnappers and returns to Ormolu clothed in glory. And it will be he whom the Church suggests as the next Aldhanan."

I raised my head, frowning. "And they're not gonna leave that slaying to chance, are they? They can't risk us blowing the game and warning the Aldhanan. I'm guessing we're gonna be pre-slayed, right before the old man gets here."

Lhan nodded. "Or perhaps drugged."

I groaned and lay back, looking up at the rim of the pit, so close, but yet so far. "We gotta get outta here."

"Aye."

But nobody had any ideas.

***

Half an hour later, I was still lying on my back, and nobody still had any ideas. Lhan was lying beside me, muttering under his breath as he tried to come up with something. Sai and Wen-Jhai were snoozing, so weak from starvation it was about all they could manage. I was half asleep too, watching the light from the hole in the temple ceiling crawling down the side of the pit as the sun got higher, and wondering if I'd live to see another sunrise, when suddenly Lhan jumped to his feet.

"Mistress!"

I jumped up, snapping out of my daydream, and went on guard. "What? What?"

Sai and Wen-Jhai raised their heads and looked around, blinking like newborn kittens.

Lhan pointed up the pit. "Look!"

I looked up. It had been too dark before, but now that the light was shining down, we could see, halfway up the wall, a smallish hole with the end of a clay pipe sticking out of it—for filling the pit with water, I guessed.

"Surely, beloved, that is within your reach."

I nodded. "Yeah. But then what? I got no way to kick up to the top. I'd just be hanging there."

"Er, forgive me, Mistress Jae-En." Wen-Jhai raised to her knees, trying to lift something that looked like a mastodon tusk, all curved and about five feet long. "But could you fit this into that hole?"

I grinned. "That's what my prom date said."

They didn't get it.

I shrugged and took the tusk, then looked up at the drain pipe. I couldn't tell exactly, but the diameters looked about the same.

"Well, we'll just have to try it and see."

And yeah, that's what I said to my prom date.

We cleared some running room, moving aside bones and rocks, then I got down into a linebacker crouch with the tusk in one hand.

"Here goes nothing."

I ran for the far side of the pit, sprang as hard as I could straight at the wall, then kicked off and ricocheted back toward the pipe. I was way too wide. I tried a stab at it with the tusk anyway, and missed, but at least I saw that it would fit.

Landing sucked. I crashed down in the middle of the bones and rocks and scraped up my knees and shins. At least I didn't twist anything.

A paladin looked over the side. "What is all this noise?"

Lhan grinned up at him. "We are building a ladder of bones, and will come up later to murder you in your sleep!"

The paladin sneered. "You may murder us in your dreams, heretic. But not in this life. Now be quiet."

He turned away from the lip and disappeared and Lhan helped me up.

"Are you ready to try again, beloved?"

"Yeah. But I'm gonna try a different way this time."

As Lhan and the gang watched, I got set like before, and launched like before. Running and jumping and kicking off the wall. This time, however, I changed my angle a little and got closer to the hole. I also didn't stab at it with the tusk again. That was like trying to take a flying fuck at a rolling donut. Instead I grabbed for it with my free hand and caught the rim.

It was full of sand, and I almost slipped, but I grabbed again and held on, hanging from my fingers. I waited to see if the paladin was going to show his face again, but he didn't, so I lifted the tusk with my other hand and slid the butt end of it into the hole. There was just enough room that it didn't crush my fingers, but it would as soon as I put any weight on it. I had to pull 'em out before I was sure it would hold my weight. It made my sphincter pucker just thinking about it, but it had to be done.

"One, two, three...."

I yanked my fingers out and the tusk dropped, then held. A little sand dribbled out of the hole and got in my face, but otherwise good. Whew! Now came the tricky part.

I did a chin-up on the tusk, then threw a leg over the curly end of it and pulled myself up until I was straddling it. Below me, Lhan, Sai and Wen-Jhai were all craning their necks to watch. I gave them a thumbs-up, then braced against the wall and used it to get into a standing position.

Damn. The top of the pit looked a lot farther away than I'd thought. I mighta been able to reach it with a running jump, but from standing on the tusk? It was gonna be close. I had one thing going for me. There was some ornamental moulding at the top of the wall that looked like tentacles rising up out of the pit and stretching over the lip. It was pretty worn away, but...

I crouched on the tusk, tensing, then sprang up and kicked off the wall at a glancing angle. It got me another ten feet and I was right at the base of the tentacles. I grabbed a sucker and it crumbled away in my fingers. Fuck! Falling! I grabbed another as I dropped. This one held, barely, and I grabbed for a third. It held too. Whew!

I wanted to hang there a minute and catch my breath, but the paladin looked over the edge again and stared right into my eyes.

"What in the name of the—"

Honestly, I'm not sure how I climbed that wall. I mean, I musta gone up hand over hand, using the tentacles as holds, but I don't remember that. All I remember is launching myself straight up at that guy and slamming him down on the floor on the lip of the hole. Fear makes spider monkeys of us all, I guess.

I bounced his head off a stone barnacle, then looked up as his lights went out. I froze. In all the excitement about figuring a way out of the pit I'd kinda forgot there was a whole crew of priests and paladins up here, all waiting around with nothing to do. Now they were standing from their cooking fires and stepping from their tents and staring at me like I was some kind of giant pink jack-in-the-box.

I swallowed and smiled and gave 'em a little salute.

"Uh, hi fellas."

CHAPTER TWENTY

SKELSHAS!

The other pit guard was the first guy to make a move. He started running around from the other side. I scooped up the first guard's spear and jumped at him, straight across the hole.

He stabbed at me as I came down, but I whacked his spear aside and shoulder-checked him into one of the iron candlesticks, sending them both to the floor.

One down. A couple dozen to go. And they were all coming now, closing in left, right and center.

I stepped back, on guard, and my back foot touched one of the coiled up grapple ropes. I kicked it into the pit.

"Grab it, Lhan! Hold tight!"

If he answered, I didn't hear, 'cause the priests and paladins were on me like flies on shit. I jumped over their heads as they tried to bulldoze me into the pit, then came down swinging in the middle of 'em, and knocked a bunch off the edge.

The rest ducked back as I whirled my spear around, and suddenly I had a clear shot at the rope. I hooked it with the spear and lifted. Somebody was definitely on the other end, 'cause I felt the weight as I hauled on it. I just hoped it was Lhan.

The priests and paladins were coming in again. I screamed and ran straight at them, spear held out like I was grabbing the handlebars of a Harley, and the rope rasping around the shaft between my hands like cable through a pulley.

A few went splat as I mowed 'em down, but most backed and stabbed for my hands and face. I blocked and parried like Robin Hood with a quarter staff when all of a sudden, the tension went outta the rope and I crashed into the guys with the spears, knocking three of 'em flat.

"Shit! Lhan!"

Had he fallen off the rope? Did somebody cut it?

I looked behind me as I fell and saw Lhan shooting up out of the pit like he'd been riding a piston, a giant thigh bone in one hand like a club, and the rope and grapple spinning free and smacking some priest in the back of the head. Then I was flat on my back in the middle of the circle and everybody was rushing in and stabbing at me. I blocked like crazy, but a few got through. Spear tips grazed my arms and legs, and I twisted like a yoga instructor to get out of the way of one that was heading straight for my belly button. It tore my side instead. Another stabbed the floor right next to my face and sprayed me with marble chips.

"Get off of me, you fucks!"

I swiped the spear around, aiming at ankles, and knocked a handful flat, but not enough. A guy with a face like a kung-fu assassin leapt over my swing and lanced down at me like I was a fish in a barrel, but just as his spear should have run me through, he staggered forward, yelping, and it glanced off the floor instead.

He fell across me, bleeding from a gash in his skull, and I saw Lhan behind him, bashing at the rest of the mob with the thigh bone.

"Unhand my beloved, you charlatans!"

I don't know how other gals woulda felt about it, but hearing that was like a magic elixir. I didn't feel my wounds any more. I wasn't exhausted. I didn't need to take a breather. All of a sudden I was right back on my feet again, fresh as a daisy, and back to back with Lhan like I coulda fought on for hours.

"Good to see ya, Lhan."

"And you, Mistress."

Of course fighting for hours wasn't actually gonna happen. In fact, we were seconds away from being dead meat. Now that they were over their panic, the priests and paladins were getting their act together and working like a team. The spear guys were forming up in a tight circle around us while the priests were fading back and readying crossbows. We were gonna get stuck six ways to Sunday.

"Uh-oh. Gotta go."

"Indeed, mistress."

I looked around. We were surrounded, but the crowd was thinnest toward the front of the temple, away from the hole.

"That way!"

I ducked a spear thrust and grabbed the robes of the kung-fu assassin, who was still face down on the floor, then threw him at the guys between us and the door. He flattened two, and Lhan and I charged after him, bashing back the rest as they tried to recover.

We were clear, but with a double-dozen shouting church assholes surging after us. Not to mention the crossbows.

"Go go go!"

I coulda made the door in about four steps, but I wasn't gonna leave Lhan behind—and I'd promised him I wouldn't pick him up anymore—so I paced him, waving my spear behind me like I was trying to fend off a swarm of buzzing bees. We got a swarm of whistling bolts instead, and Lhan got nicked just above the ankle, but after one volley, the guys who were chasing us got too close behind and the shooters couldn't shoot anymore.

They were less than two steps behind us as we reached the door, and I turned just outside it, ready to use it as a bottleneck to hold 'em in, but they skidded to a stop just inside it and didn't even try to come out.

I shook my spear at 'em. "Come on, you pussies! What are you afraid of?"

Fwump!

Somewhere above me, something made a sound like somebody opening an umbrella, and a shadow passed between me and the sun.

Lhan coughed. "Erm, 'tis most likely the skelshas they fear."

I looked up. A coupla shapes like evil kites were circling overhead, grinning down at me out of their pointy Woody Woodpecker heads.

"Oh, goddamn it."

Skelshas are Waar's answer to pterodactyls—big-ass, leather-winged, flying lizards with mouths like a crocodile's and a personality to match. The Oran navy uses 'em like fighter planes, with nut-job bird jockeys spurring them into loop-de-loops during air battles, but even fully tamed and trained they are ornery sons-of-bitches, and the two fuckers who were circling over us had never been anybody's ride.

As we stared up at them, they both folded their wings and dropped at us like a couple of living darts. I woulda grabbed Lhan and jumped back inside the temple. Unfortunately, the door was filled with paladins lowering spears at us, with priests standing behind them, aiming crossbows.

Lhan and I hit the dirt as the two skelshas swept in inches above us, wings wide and claws out—and as big as fucking horses! I swiped my spear after them as we rolled back to our feet, and one veered off, shrieking, with a gash across its chest and one of the little steering wings it had tucked under its bigger wings hanging limp.

"Ha! Fucker! Take that!"

Unfortunately, the other one was just fine, and whipped into a tight circle to come back snapping for my head. I hauled Lhan back, and we ended up behind a pillar near the door as it banked away.

"Damn it! I need my sword! I coulda cut that fucker in half with—"

A crossbow bolt hit the pillar right over my head. The priests were angling shots at us from the door. We ducked around the other side of the pillar, out of sight of the priests, but right back in the open again. I looked across the street for another hiding place, but none of the buildings over there seemed to have roofs. We'd be just as exposed inside as out.

"There! Jae-En! The red building!"

Lhan was pointing down the street toward a skinny place at the next intersection that looked like it shoulda been a law firm. The upper windows had sunlight behind 'em, but the ones on the bottom were dark. Cover!

"Yes!"

I took his hand and we ran as the wounded skelsha swooped down at us again. We dodged and kept going, but there were three more up there now. And more shrieks were echoing from behind the buildings all around. Fucking hell! The first two had rung the dinner bell, and now everybody was coming to the party!

Two more came diving in, slashing with claws and wings. We ducked and swiped behind us, and somehow I connected, snapping my spear and opening one up neck to nuts. It crashed down nose first, clipping us with a wing and spilling its intestines all over the ground. We ate pavement as the second one looped up for another try. I felt like I'd been hit across the shoulders with a baseball bat.

Lhan was up first and pulled me up, then winced as he put weight on his left foot.

"Lhan! You're hurt!"

"It is nothing. Now come—"

"Make way! Clear the door!"

We looked back at the shout and saw Ru-Sul charging out the temple door at the head of six paladins, every one of 'em mounted on a krae.

"Fuck!"

CHAPTER TWENTY-ONE

SKELETONS!

I threw down my snapped spear and we ran again, half a dozen skelshas banking after us and Ru-Sul's cavalry shaking the ground. It was bad. The red building was still a half a block away and Lhan was slowing, limping with every step. Then he shoved me ahead.

"Go on. Save yourself."

"Come on, Lhan. I'm not gonna—"

The kraes were almost on top of us. Ru-Sul was out in front, his spear tucked under his arm like a lance, and it was aiming right at Lhan.

Without thinking, I scooped Lhan up and leapt sideways as Ru-Sul and his riders thundered past us.

"Mistress! Did I not say—!"

I kept leaping, too busy to listen. The skelshas were dropping out of the sky like Stukas with teeth, and I zigged and zagged and bounced all over the fucking street dodging 'em as I ran toward the red building.

Ru-Sul and his paladins were pulling up right in front of me, turning for another pass. I jumped right through the middle of 'em and kept going. The red building still had a front door, but the windows on the first floor were wide open. I kicked up and jumped through one into the interior—which was a lot more exterior than I hoped it would be. I'd thought it was covered, but it turned out it only had half a ceiling—not much more than an overhang, and plenty of room for the skelshas to come down and get us. I backed under it and looked around for something better.

"Mistress. Put me down."

"Not now, Lhan. We gotta—"

"Put me down!"

I put him down. He stood, stiff as a board, and stared at me like I'd shit on his lawn.

"You promised not to carry me."

My guts clenched like a fist. Fuck. I'd been so panicked, I hadn't even thought about it.

"I—I'm sorry, Lhan. It was instinct. We weren't gonna make it, and—"

Skelsha shadows rippled over the rubble in the uncovered half of the room. The bastards were floating over the wall and smiling down at us.

Lhan sniffed and started limping for a door at the back. "We will discuss it later. Now is not the time."

Man, he coulda froze gasoline with that sniff. I shivered and followed, then shoved him forward as the skelshas started their dive.

"Faster, Lhan!"

We dove through the door inches ahead of a pair of 'em, and they crashed into the frame, cracking it, their wings too wide for the opening. Another one whumped down in the room in front of us—which had even less roof than the first—and started screeching and snapping. We split left and right, and a crossbow bolt whistled between us and punched the skelsha through the roof of its mouth. It screamed and flapped away. I looked back. Ru-Sul and his paladins were climbing into the first room, crossbows out.

We dodged through another archway and found some stairs going down. They were choked with rubble, and I thought it was a dead end, but Lhan pointed.

"A hole."

He started down, skidding on loose stones, and I followed. There *was* a hole—a tight black throat down through the rubble that I couldn't see the bottom of. It made me queasy just looking at it.

"Shit. Maybe we should find another—"

A skelsha shrieked right over head. The footsteps of the paladins were thudding closer. I couldn't move. My claustrophobia had a grip on my chest like a vise.

Lhan stepped to it. "I will guide you."

I grunted with relief as Lhan lowered himself into the hole, then beckoned me to follow. Alone? No way. With Lhan? Even angry Lhan? Okay. I swallowed, then started wriggling after him. Ru-Sul and his paladins appeared at the head of the stairs. Ru-Sul laughed as his guys raised their crossbows.

"Look! A kiv-kiv too fat for its burrow."

I grabbed the edges of the hole with both hands and crammed myself down into it like Santa down a chimney, scraping my hips and arms all to hell. Bolts thwacked into the junk all around me, and then I was through, and rolling down a slope of broken stairs to a low-ceilinged cellar.

I looked around as Lhan got to his feet beside me. Sunlight coming through cracks in the ceiling showed me we were in a cellar, all caved-in toward the front, with a black trench in the floor right under the collapsed part. It looked like a roof beam had snapped and punched through it into some kind of hidden pit. What the sunlight didn't show me was any other way back to the surface. We were trapped, and I could hear the priests kicking at the rubble on the stairs. The blockage was starting to crumble. Any second now it would fall in and they'd come down shooting.

Lhan looked down into the black trench. "Salvation. It is a sewer pipe."

That tripped me up. "Sal-salvation? A sewer pipe?"

Lhan started into it without answering. I crawled to the hole and looked after him, chewing my teeth. He was squeezing around the splintered end of the heavy beam and slipping into a broken clay sewer pipe, about a foot and a half in diameter which slanted down into complete darkness. Then he got past the beam and let go, and slid down the pipe like a kid on a water slide—except, you know, into complete darkness.

"Lhan!"

After a second, Lhan's voice came up to me, cold and echoey. "It is safe. Hurry."

Safe? For him maybe, with his skinny ass and boyish figure. Me, I was a bit bigger than him all around, and a little deeper in the chest, if you know what I mean. What if I got stuck halfway down? I looked back over my shoulder as more and more rubble was starting to roll down the stairs into the cellar, and more light was starting to show. I tried to tell myself I could take the paladins when they came down, even though I knew I couldn't—not with the crossbows.

"Okay. Here goes nothing."

I gritted my teeth and squeezed down into the pipe, feet first. With the roof beam jammed down into it like a two-by-four sticking out of a can of paint, it was way tight going in, and I had to squash my boobs almost flat and twist my headhalf way off getting under it, but after that it was smooth sailing. Too smooth. Once I got all the way into the pipe it was water park time, just like with Lhan. The inside was smooth and dry, and my shoulders actually had a quarter inch to spare.

Just as I was taking a couple of breaths to prepare myself, the last of the rubble on the stair caved in and Ru-Sul and his pals came swarming down into the cellar. Time to jet. I squeezed my arms together and shot down it like it was a Hot Wheels track.

Two seconds later I slid out of the bottom of the pipe into complete black, and a pile of what felt like pebbles and dry sticks. I looked around, heart pounding. I could see absolutely nothing. All I could hear was a moaning wind—at least I hoped it was wind.

"Lhan?"

"Wait. Be silent."

I shut up and listened. Up the pipe I could hear Ru-Sul and his boys moving around. Then a trickle of pebbles rattled down it and his voice came down to us.

"Demoness! Dhan Lhan Lar! This cowardly hiding will not avail you. You will starve. Or worse. Come up and fight."

I was gonna give him a snappy comeback, but Lhan put his hand on my arm and I held off. After a second Ru-Sul called down again.

"Dhan? Demoness?" Another wait, then, "Go down and see if they live."

"No, your reverence. I will not."

"It is an order."

"It is an order we will follow—if you will lead."

A longer wait this time, then finally, "I hear nothing. They must be dead or fled. In either case, we will not find them in the dark. Come, we must go and guard against their return."

I waited as I heard their footsteps fade, then chuckled. "Man, they really are afraid of this place, aren't they?"

"Is it any wonder? Look around you."

I was about to say I couldn't see anything in the dark, but then I realized my eyes had adjusted, and I could. There was just enough light coming down from cracks in the ceiling that I could see that we were in an arched stone sewer tunnel, bigger and older than the one I'd run through in Ormolu—and filled waist-high with human-looking skeletons.

I stared as I saw that they went on like that down the tunnel in both directions as far as the eye could see. There were mounds of them, all piled up against the side walls.

"What. The. Fuck."

"Those that escaped the fire from the sky took shelter here, but the fire stole all the air."

I looked around at all the bones again. I normally don't believe in ghosts, or any of that supernatural bullshit, but suddenly I could see 'em all down here like they were right in front of me, huddling up with their families, their kids, their pets, looking up at the ceiling and waiting for the all clear. And then the panic as the firestorms on the surface started to suck all the oxygen up and out, and they all tried to claw their way after it, tearing each other to pieces, climbing the walls as they tried to reach one last breath of fresh air.

I sucked in a huge breath and shivered like a wet dog. "Fuck."

"Indeed."

I turned to him and looked him in the eyes. "Listen, Lhan. I wanna apologize. About back there. About picking you—"

He stood and started limping down the tunnel. "Come. We must find a place where we may see the Aldhanan's arrival."

Well, okay then. If that's how he wanted to play it. I stomped along behind him, glaring at his back and thinking of snarky things to say, but then not saying them.

Finally, after a half-hour of tiptoing through the skeletons and searching for another way back to the surface, we found an intersection where a street had caved into the tunnels and sunlight was streaming down through the break onto the drifts of skeletons and making them look like bone snow. We crept up the side of a collapsed pillar and scanned the sky for skelshas. There were some off in the distance, but none above us.

The neighborhood we were in was a lot less fancy than the place where all the temples were, with lots of places that looked like they'd been shops and bars and apartment buildings. Lhan pointed to a nearly intact building with some shops in the bottom. We ran to it and ducked inside, then looked back out to make sure we hadn't attracted any attention. All good. The big bastards were still circling where they had been. They weren't turning our way.

Lhan found a flight of stairs and we went up to the top floor and looked out the windows of what musta been somebody's apartment once. They weren't high enough. We couldn't see over the other buildings.

"The roof?"

Lhan nodded and started limping for the stairs again. I made to join him, but he held up his hand, as cool as the other side of the pillow.

"Wait here."

"Huh? Why?"

He kept walking. "Because I do not require your assistance."

My teeth clenched. "Lhan, if this has to do with—"

"It has nothing to do with that. With the skelshas hunting, stealth is required, and—forgive me for saying so—but you are, by your very nature, stealth's antithesis."

"Are you kidding? I'm light as a feather on this planet. I can out-ninja a ninja. You've got a twisted knee."

He wasn't listening. "Please. Just wait for my return."

I stepped after him. "Come on, Lhan. It's dangerous out there."

He stopped at the stairs, but didn't look back. "Indeed. And in the face of such danger, a man must be able to trust his companions. He cannot fear that they will manhandle him without his consent, nor toss him about like a doll, nor break solemn vows as it pleases them."

And there is was, cold on a plate, no garnish.

I groaned. "Lhan, there were skelshas! That fucking priest was gonna *run you through*! I'm not gonna let a vow stand in the way of saving your life."

He turned, drawing himself up. "Then perhaps you should not have returned to Ora. Here, a man's honor is far more precious than his life."

And with that, he started up the stairs like an opera singer making his grand exit.

Well, it kinda took the wind outta me, and I stood there, huffing and puffing for a minute, then finally shouted up after him. "Yeah, well, maybe I shouldn't have, 'cause I sure as hell didn't come all the way back here to cry over your grave!"

He was already through the door at the top, and stepping out of sight onto the open roof. I didn't hear any answer.

"Dumbass motherfucker!"

I wanted to go after him, but I wasn't gonna give him the satisfaction. What the fuck was his problem, anyway? I stomped back into the thousand-year-old apartment, looking for something to kick, but before I did any damage, a shadow blocked out the sun coming through the windows. I raised my head, thinking, "That's one big-ass skelsha," and went to look out.

It wasn't a skelsha. It was a top of the line Oran Navy airship, and it was gliding right over the building!

CHAPTER TWENTY-TWO

SACRIFICE!

"Lhan!"

I ran up the stairs and bumped into him as he was limping in from the roof.

"Lhan. The Aldhanan. He's already—"

"I saw. Yes." He pushed past me and started down the stairs. "Come. We must hurry."

Still cold as ice, the fucker.

We headed for the temple as fast as we could, but we couldn't just go blazing through the streets like we wanted to. We woulda had every skelsha in the city after us in a hot second. Instead we went cover to cover and building to building, trying the whole time to see the airship through the ruins and praying we weren't too late, and it took fucking *forever*.

Finally we reached the big street with all the fancy buildings and looked toward the temple from the door of some place that mighta been a bank back in the day.

It was bad.

The ship was already down and tied off, and a troop of the Aldhanan's personal guard—maybe forty guys—were marching straight for the temple's front door, their red cloaks blowing in the breeze. There was an officer in a shiny helmet and a priest of Ormolu in a seriously fancy hat toward the head of the line, but the guy right out in front was a tall, silver-haired dude in fancy armor and a gold circlet on his head. Yup, the Aldhanan of the Oran Empire himself, walking right into Ru-Sul's trap, exactly as planned. Goddamn it! Why did he have to come do this hero shit himself? Wasn't that what the army was for?

I started ahead. "Come on, Lhan. We gotta warn him."

"Have a care. We are who they seek, remember?"

"Yeah, but if I start hollerin', then they'll come after me and they won't get jumped in the temple, right?"

"But you could be killed."

I gave him a look. "What was your line? A man's honor is more precious than his life, or some shit? That doesn't count for chicks?"

He made some answer, but I didn't hear him. I was already speeding down the street screaming bloody murder.

Unfortunately, what with the wind singing through the airship's rigging and all the boots marching and the armor jingling, nobody heard me until it was too late. The Aldhanan and his boys were already through the temple door before the crossbow guys who were guarding the ship saw me and started shouting.

"The demoness!"

"She's coming!"

"Shoot her!"

I hopped like a bunny and their bolts zinged under me to kick dust off the street.

"It's an ambush! Stop the Aldhanan! Call 'im back!"

They kept shooting, so I kept running, straight for the temple doors. They were closing! The fucking priests were locking out the reinforcements! Including Lhan, dammit. Oh well. I steamed ahead and bounded through the doors just before they boomed shut, and came down smack dab in the middle of Ru-Sul's little stage play. I gotta hand it to him. He'd really done it up right.

The Aldhanan was standing in the middle of the temple with his jaw hanging open and the captain and the priest and the rest of his posse all spread out around him, all staring at the scene going on in the middle of the magic circle, which looked like something out of a drive-in horror movie. The candles on the big candlesticks were lit up all around the circle, and green smoke was rising up from a wide, wok-shaped hibachi full of coals right in the center, where a tall guy in black robes was chanting some mumbo jumbo and holding up a gold dagger in the shape of a pointy tentacle. Laid out on the floor at his feet were Sai and Wen-Jhai, both naked and bound and gagged and painted with weird symbols, and held down by more guys in black robes.

I wondered for a second who these black robe guys were, 'cause they were about to take one for the team in the most permanent way possible. I mean, they might just be pretending to be evil heretics, but they were gonna get their playacting priest asses chopped into tiny little pieces by real live swords. Maybe they thought they'd get their reward in heaven. Whatever. It wasn't them I was worried about. It was my friends' asses I was here to save.

"Aldhanan! Watch out! It's an ambush! Behind you!"

The Aldhanan's guards spun around at my shout, but just then an army of black-robed guys exploded out of all the tents around the circle and charged them, stabbing and screaming, while more shot crossbows down at them from the tops of the pillars all around the room.

At least ten guards went down with bolts through their necks and chests as the Aldhanan and his crew faced out to meet the attack, and a bunch more died from spear thrusts before they got themselves together and dressed their lines. Shit! It was already a massacre, and it had only just started.

"Aldhanan! Turn! Your daughter is in peril!"

The voice was high and sharp. I looked around and saw the priest with the fancy hat standing behind the Aldhanan and pushing him toward the circle where Wen-Jhai was being menaced by the fake heretic with the tentacle knife. Was he in on it? Was he Ru-Sul's irrefutable witness? I didn't know, and couldn't worry about it right then. The guy with the knife didn't look like he was pretending, or waiting.

I leapt right over the Aldhanan's head and hit Tentacle-Knife with a flying tackle that sent us both rolling towards the pit. We stopped right at the edge with me on top, and he stabbed up at me with the dagger. Which is when I remembered I didn't have a weapon.

Fuck!

I cut my hand catching his wrist, then headbutted him in the nose and stripped the knife from his hand as he shrieked and grabbed his face.

"Sorry, bro. I need that."

I rolled off him and kicked him into the pit, then came up brandishing the dagger at the guys who were holding down my friends.

"Okay, you fuckers, now you're gonna—"

"She attacks my daughter! Drive her into the pit!"

The Aldhanan was shoving towards me through his men, screaming bloody murder. He looked like shit. The last time I'd seen him, he'd been as healthy and happy as one of those gray-haired triathletes you see in vitamin commercials for old people—trim, fit, with a big white smile, a chin beard, and a mane of silver hair that flowed down over his shoulders. Now he looked like Gary Busey on a bad day. His cheeks were hollowed out, his beard was all over his face, and his hair was greasy and limp. His eyes, however, were blazing at me like purple death rays. Which, okay, was understandable. I mean, I was standing over his daughter with a sacrificial knife in my hand, but, come on, we'd been buddies, hadn't we? Wasn't he gonna give me a chance to explain?

Not so much.

The captain of his guard came in first, a hard-faced motherfucker with an eye-patch who looked like he was made out of leather and leaf springs, cutting down the heretics who were holding Sai and Wen-Jhai, but when he charged me, the Aldhanan pushed past him and started swinging at me like a psycho with a chainsaw. I dropped the dagger and dodged away, inches ahead of his sword—and almost fell into the pit just like he wanted.

"Hey! Stop! I'm on your side!"

He just kept coming. Dammit, I didn't want to fight the Aldhanan! Maybe he'd get the idea if I fought the heretics. I ducked a swing from Captain Eye-Patch and snatched up one of the big-ass candlesticks, then jumped out of the circle and started laying into the fake heretics from behind. The thing made a good weapon—heavy duty wrought iron, lots of spikes, and as tall as me—and I cleaned house as I shouted over the fight to the Aldhanan.

"See! I'm fighting the bad guys!"

The Aldhanan looked confused for a second, but then Fancy Hat piped up again.

"Listen not to her unholy whispers! She seeks only to trick you into lowering your guard! 'Tis the same trick she used to steal your daughter!"

Okay, this guy was definitely in on the set-up. He was working way too hard to keep the Aldhanan fighting me, and unfortunately Sai and Wen-Jhai couldn't come to my defense. I saw them trying, struggling on the ground and shouting into their gags, but the Aldhanan and his dudes were too busy fighting to stop and free them.

The Aldhanan snarled at me. "You cannot fool me, demoness! Come near and you will die like the rest!"

Fine, then. I could fight the fake heretics from outside the circle just the same as I could from inside. Except, actually, I couldn't, 'cause the crossbow guys up on the tops of the columns were shooting at me now. In fact, the only reason they hadn't killed me yet was 'cause the half-dozen heretics I was fighting had me dodgin' and hoppin' around like a one-legged man in an ass-kicking contest. I had bolts zipping past my ears and spears stabbing at the rest of me, and I knew if I stopped dancing even for a second, one or the other was gonna make a pin-cushion out of me.

And it wasn't only me who was in a bad spot. The Aldhanan's boys were getting clobbered too. They were top-notch soldiers, and fighting smart and strong, but almost half of 'em had gone down in that first charge, and the rest were outnumbered two to one—and it was getting closer to three to one every second. Worse, it seemed like all the fire that wasn't coming my way was concentrated on the Aldhanan. Bolts were bouncing off the floor all around him like hail, and I saw one punch down through his shoulder armor so hard his knees buckled.

"Aldhanan!"

Eye-Patch and surged in and hauled him behind a pillar, then stood over him like a one-eyed monolith, swiping at the bolts that glanced down at him from above.

I had to get up there and take those crossbow guys out, but the damned columns were as high as the pit Ru-Sul had thrown us in was deep. No way I could jump that high. Maybe I could throw rocks at 'em. I started trying to back outta the scrum, but before I could, one of the crossbow guys screamed and pitched off his pillar to splat right in the middle of the guys I was fighting.

If you think I wasn't gonna take advantage of a gift like that you're nuts. I mowed down half a dozen of the fuckers before they had a chance to recover, and the whole time more crossbow guys were taking the high dive—one, two, three, and a fourth, bouncing off shark lady's finned head before disappearing down into the pit.

I looked around. The crossbow guys from the Aldhanan's ship were pouring through a break in the side wall of the temple, and Lhan was leading them. The little smarty had found them another way in, and they were going to town, peppering the tops of the columns like they had their pieces on autofire.

"Alright, Lhan!"

I raised my jumbo candlestick in a salute, then waded into the fake heretics again. Without having to worry about death from above, it all suddenly went much better, with me cleaning house on the outside of the ring and the Aldhanan and his crew chopping priests down in the middle—and, a couple seconds later, Lhan and the guys from the ship dropping their crossbows and lining up on either side of me with cutlasses swinging.

"Good work, Lhan! I think you saved the day."

He nodded, but wouldn't meet my eye. "I did what was required."

Still as chilly as a toilet seat in January, the punk. Before I could give him shit for it, though, the disguised priests' nerve finally broke and they started running for the exits, and we got separated chasing 'em down.

When we all came back, the Aldhanan was kneeling beside Wen-Jhai in the middle of the circle as Captain Eye-Patch cut her free and his men saw to Sai. Monsignor Fancy Hat was standing behind him, pretending to be concerned, but looking like he'd just eaten a lemon, skin and all.

I gave the Aldhanan a salute and a smile as I stepped to the edge of the circle. "Still want to kill me?"

He looked up at me and I noticed he still had the crossbow bolt sticking up out of his shoulder armor. Damn, that fucker was tough. He shook his head.

"Questions first. Seize her."

CHAPTER TWENTY-THREE

TREACHERY!

Before I knew what was going on, I had about six swords poking me in the neck and Captain Eye-Patch was knocking my candlestick out of my hands.

"Beloved!"

Lhan got in between me and the guards, sword up. "My Aldhanan! What is the meaning of this? Did we not just save your life?"

"Did you? Or did you fail to take it?" His eyes flashed. "Take him as well."

More swords poked at Lhan, and Eye-Patch knocked his sword to the ground too. But even though we were both disarmed and a few wrong answers away from being shish-kabobbed, all I could do was stare at Lhan. Was I hearing things? Had he just called me beloved?

The Aldhanan rose, wincing, and stepped towards us, crossbow bolt and all, but the priest put out a hand.

"Waste not your breath, my Aldhanan. They will tell you naught but lies. Kill them where they stand."

Lhan sneered. "It is the priest you should kill, my Aldhanan. For it was he and his brethren who led you into this trap."

I pointed at Wen-Jhai, who was being helped to her feet by Captain Eye-

Patch. "Ask your daughter about it. She'll—"

The Aldhanan shot up a hand. "Silence! All of you!"

Everybody shut up. He had that kind of voice.

"Now." He turned to me, burning into my eyes with those violet lasers of his. "Why did you kidnap my daughter?"

"Father, she did not." Wen-Jhai motioned toward all the corpses in black robes. "It was these villains, priests of Ormolu, disguised as heretics!"

Sai stood up beside her. "It is true, my father. The temple took us in order to lure you to your death!"

The Aldhanan turned to them, scowling with disbelief. "Daughter, son, how can this be? Why would—?"

Fancy Hat shook his head, sad. "It is as I told you, my Aldhanan. Their minds have been turned by the demoness's foul sorcery. They speak the lies she commands them to tell."

I'd had just about enough. "Oh, come on! Why don't y'all just look for yourselves!" I nodded toward the dead guys. "They're all priests under those black robes. Take a peek and see!"

Fancy Hat laughed and stepped to the nearest corpse. He threw back its hood to show a bald purple guy.

I pointed. "There! See! A priest!"

The Aldhanan folded his arms. "Many heretic cults also shave their heads. You will have to do better than that."

Fancy Hat pulled aside the dead guy's robe too, showing nothing but skin. "And I find no hidden orange. You see, Aldhanan? All lies."

Goddammit! What was I thinking? Of course the priests wouldn'ta been that stupid. They woulda disguised themselves all the way down to their undies. But wait a minute! Hadn't Ru-Sul shown us his orange robes under all his black? Yeah, but that was earlier. He woulda changed for the big show, just like everybody else, right? On the other hand, maybe not. The Aldhanan had shown up pretty damn quick. Maybe he'd been caught flat-footed. Maybe he hadn't had time to change.

I started looking around at the corpses, hoping to see his, not that I could turn around or move my head much. The guards still had their swords at my neck, but I did my best, searching for Ru-Sul's buzzard nose sticking out of a hood somewhere.

And then I saw it, but it wasn't on a corpse. It was behind a pillar on the far side of the room, poking up over the gunsight of a crossbow that was aimed straight at the Aldhanan's back!

"Aldhanan! Look out!"

I knocked away the blades at my neck—and cut the shit out of my forearm in the process—and kicked the Aldhanan aside just as Ru-Sul fired. The bolt whipped past his nose as everybody shouted at once and Captain Eye-Patch tried to stab me. I dodged 'im and bounded across the floor for Ru-Sul.

He saw me coming and tried to crank back his piece for another shot, then gave up and ran. I caught up in two steps and grabbed him by the neck. He tried to stab back at me with a dagger, but I tapped his noggin with my candlestick and he went all wobbly.

"Alright, fucker. Let's go."

I dragged him back to the circle and shoved him down as the guards swarmed me and Captain Eye-Patch put his sword to my neck again.

"You assaulted the Aldhanan! You will die for this!"

"Yeah yeah, fine. But just look at that guy first! He's the leader of these guys, and he's a priest. He showed me his orange robe this morning, I swear it!"

Fancy Hat was practically jumping out of his skin at this. "No! Do not touch him! He is another demon! Throw him into the pit or he will corrupt you with—"

Sai stepped forward and yanked Ru-Sul's hood and cloak down to the middle of his back, showing his chest and arms. I groaned. No orange robes. He was as naked underneath as the other guy. But the Aldhanan still gasped, and so did Captain Eye-Patch.

The Aldhanan turned on Fancy Hat. "Ru-Ranan, is this not your assistant, Ru-Sul? He who you said was ill and keeping to his bed?"

"By Ormolu, it is!" Fancy Hat pasted on a surprised look and backed toward the Aldhanan, pointing at Ru-Sul like he was seeing a ghost. "Deceiver! Pretending to be devout when all along you were a filthy heretic!" He turned to the Aldhanan. "My Aldhanan, forgive me. I did not—"

And all of a sudden he had a sharp little knife at the Aldhanan's throat and was hissing around at us all like a cornered cat.

"Drop your weapons! Drop them or the Aldhanan dies!"

The Aldhanan tried to elbow Fancy Hat in the nose, but the old priest was quicker than he looked and got behind him, gashing him good under the chin with the knife. It wasn't a killing cut, but it was deep enough to make the Aldhanan stay very very still.

He held up a hand as his guards started surging forward. "Stop! Do as he says! Lay down your arms!"

The guards and crossbow guys didn't look very happy about that, but did as they were told, and the place suddenly sounded like a slot machine paying off, as all their weapons cling-clanged off the stone floor.

Fancy Hat looked at me. "You too, demoness. Ru-Sul, throw the weapons into the pit. The plan can still be salvaged."

I snorted, disgusted, and was about to what he said, when I got an idea. We were all in the circle, and all standing around the wok-shaped hibachi thing, which was still full of smoking charcoal, and the Aldhanan and Fancy Hat were closer to it than the rest. Hmmm.

I tossed my weapon down like everybody else, but made sure it hit the lip of the hibachi as it fell. Crash! The wok flipped up and over and threw glowing charcoal all over Fancy Hat and the Aldhanan. As I'd hoped, they did the predictable thing, and threw their hands up as all that hot crap came flying at their eyes, and that's when I stepped past the Aldhanan and punched Fancy Hat square in the face.

He flew back like a broken kite and came down all splayed out and stunned. Behind me, all the guards were shouting again, but I ignored 'em and hauled Fancy Hat up by the neck till his feet were dangling.

"Alright, jack-hole, what's this all about?"

Captain Eye-Patch shouted in my ear and tried to turn me around, but then somebody else moved him away and stood beside me. It was the Aldhanan. He touched my shoulder, then turned those laser eyes on Fancy Hat.

"Now, Ru-Ranan, answer Mistress Jae-En's question. What is this about? Who is behind this?"

He choked and sneered. "I… say… nothing. You may… do your… worst!"

The Aldhanan motioned me forward, and I walked Fancy Hat over to the pit and held him out over the edge. "How 'bout now?"

"Never!"

"You sure?" I reached out and twisted his neck, forcing him to look down. "Ain't a high enough drop to kill you. You'll just break your legs, then sit there and starve to death."

"Aye," said the Aldhanan, smiling. "Alone in the pit at night, with the ghosts of Durgallah's dead rising from their bones, asking you why you burned them alive. Asking—"

Fancy Hat whimpered and started kicking. "Stop! I will… speak! I… will—"

"Coward! You will not!"

There was a confused shout from the guards and I looked back. Ru-Sul was charging through them, straight for us.

"You will not reveal the master's plan!"

Me and the Aldhanan dodged left and right to get out of his way, but he wasn't after us. Instead, he leapt at Fancy Hat and hit him right in the numbers, ripping him out of my grip. The two of 'em flew out over the pit like the instant replay of a QB sack, then bounced off the far wall and dropped to the bottom.

I'd been wrong about the fall not being high enough to kill you. It was plenty high enough, if you hit head first.

CHAPTER TWENTY-FOUR

BREAK-UP!

Everybody stood around the edge of the pit for a second, looking down at the bodies, then Wen-Jhai ran to the Aldhanan and started weeping on his chest.

"Oh, Father, it was horrible!"

That broke the moment, and we all looked up and let out a breath and realized it was over. Sai came over and gave me and Lhan a hug. There were tears in his pretty-boy eyes.

"Once again, friends, you have saved my worthless life, and more importantly, the life of my beloved Wen-Jhai, who is my whole world. Thank you. I will not forget."

I never know what to do when people get all weepy on me, so I just shrugged and looked at my feet. "Aw, come on, Sai. What else were we gonna do?"

"Still, you did it. And for that, I am—"

Right there in mid-sentence, he started swaying like a palm tree in a wind storm. Lhan and I caught him as he fell and set him down with his head between his legs.

Lhan patted his shoulder. "Easy, Sai. The worst is over."

"Yeah, we'll get some food in you. Everything'll be fine."

I wasn't feeling so good myself, what with all the running and getting knocked around by skelshas and cut up by swords, but as I was looking around for someplace to sit down that wasn't covered in blood or bodies, the Aldhanan crossed to us with Wen-Jhai at his side and Eye-Patch hovering behind like a terminator nursemaid.

The Aldhanan bowed. "Thank you, Lhan-Lar. Thank you, Mistress Jae-En. And allow me to offer you my most humble of apologies. Though in my heart I knew you to be the stoutest of heroes and best of friends, I allowed these knife-tongued priests to convince me otherwise." He shook his head. "Were it not for your quick wits here today, I would have slain you at their bidding, and then been slain by them in turn. Truly, I am a fool."

Wen-Jhai took my hand. "We owe you our lives, Mistress Jae-En. And our freedom. Thank you."

I let Lhan handle the thanks this time. He was way better at that shit than I would ever be.

"It was an honor to serve, my Aldhanan, though we only did what any friend would do in similar circumstance. Thank you."

The Aldhanan smiled. "Never-the-less, I owe you more than I can ever repay, and will reward you in time, but there is much yet to discuss." He nodded toward Eye-Patch. "Captain Anan will be dining with me in my cabin once we have sailed. Will you join us?"

"Of course, my Aldhanan."

I nodded. "Sure."

"Excellent. Then, rest. I have summoned the surgeons from the ship. Your wounds will be seen to. We leave as soon as all are ready."

Lhan bowed again. "Thank you, my Aldhanan."

After that he and Wen-Jhai helped Sai to his feet and led him off, and left me and Lhan standing alone together near the pit. I looked over at him, hoping he'd look back, but he was looking around at all the carnage and the guards like he didn't know I was there.

"Hey, uh, Lhan?"

He kept scanning around. "Where is the hero?"

"Huh? What hero?"

He lowered his voice. "The secret friend of the church. He who was to have 'avenged the Aldhanan' and brought back the news of his death. The *new Aldhanan*."

Oh yeah. I'd almost forgot. For Ru-Sul's plan to be complete, there was supposed to be witnesses and a hero. Well, there were plenty of witnesses. There were guards all over the place, but nobody had really stepped up to play the hero, had they? I looked back toward the Aldhanan, frowning. "Uh, Captain Anan, maybe?"

"No. He has no royal blood, nor noble either. He could never be Aldhanan." Lhan shook his head. "I was certain there would be someone, but…"

"The priest? Ru-whatever his name was?"

"A priest cannot be Aldhanan either. The people would not allow it." He stepped to the edge and looked down at the bodies of Fancy Hat and Ru-Sul, stroking his goatee. "Can it be the plan was not what I thought? What else could it be?"

He stood there thinking, and I stood there looking at him, my mind drifting away from Aldhanans and heroes. I cleared my throat. He didn't look around. Oh well, fuck it.

"Uh, you called me beloved back there, Lhan. Does—does that mean—?"

He raised his head, but didn't look around. "Forgive me. It was *instinct.* Think nothing of it."

Ouch.

He started picking his way through the bodies toward the tents. "Our clothes must be here. And the water tokens. Rest there. I will find them."

Not a chance. I wanted to have this out now. I followed him. "What do you want me to say, Lhan? I'm sorry. I'm sorry I picked you up."

"Are you?"

I sighed. "Are you saying you don't believe me? I really am sorry."

He looked at me for the first time. His eyes were like needles. They stabbed right through me. "I do believe you. I also believe that you will do it again—that in the heat of the moment your *instinct* will cause you to once again forget your vow to me, and you will catch me up against my will and at the expense of my dignity."

I tried to hold his gaze. I couldn't. I also tried to promise that I would keep my vow next time. I couldn't do that either. I looked away from him and hung my head.

"You're right. I would do it again. I'm sorry, but if I saw you were gonna die, I'd grab you every time, vow or no vow."

He nodded slowly, like he was thinking through a math problem, then spoke again, staring at the stone floor. "Then I think it best that I release you from your vow, and from our union. It was a great joy to be your Dhan, and to have you as my Dhanshai—one of the greatest of my life—but I believe we are better suited as companions."

I blinked, trying to sort though all that, then blinked again as I got it. "Wait a minute. Was that some kind of hoity-toity kiss off? Did you just break up with me?"

"Surely you can see 'tis for the best?"

"No, I can't, actually. I love you. You love me. Everything else is just bullshit rules made up by some jerks who think every woman is a precious little flower and every man is a knight in shining armor!"

Lhan looked over his shoulder at the Aldhanan's guards, who were doing clean-up behind us. "Jae-En, please. Lower your voice."

I balled my fists, a gnat's ass from punching his lights out. Instead I turned away from him.

"You know what? You're right. I've changed my mind. This is a great idea. Why would I want to be with a guy with a stick so far up his ass he can't bend for love. Go fuck yourself, Lhan."

"Jae-En, please don't be angry. I—"

I strode off without looking back, starting for the tents on the other side of the circle, but then I kept going, past the tents and straight for the hole in the wall. I was wound so tight I could barely keep myself on the ground. I wanted to run out into the streets and shout and smash things until all the skelshas in the ruins came looking, then punch every single one of 'em in the teeth.

Well, I got as far as the courtyard on the other side of the hole, then realized I didn't actually want to get eaten, so I just stomped around in the dust, flailing my arms and having a silent one-sided argument with a guy who wasn't there, until something through a door in a corner of the yard started winking at me and blinding me every time I stepped past it.

The third time I got a face full of glare I stopped and turned towards it, wanting to smash it and make it go away. What the hell was it anyway? Except for the black glass crater at the far end of town, everything I'd seen in Durgallah so far had been as dry and dull as sandstone. I stepped through the door into what might once have been a stables and saw something about the size of a washing machine hidden under a blanket at the back of a stone stall. It winked again as the never-ending wind blew up a corner of the blanket. I crossed to it and pulled the blanket off and found the stolen water tokens, all still neatly bundled in their satchel, but I only gave them a glance. What the coins were leaning on was way more interesting. It looked like an oversized ice cream maker, but with all the insides showing behind see-through walls. And it was humming like an electric clock.

I stared. The thing looked like it had been made by Westinghouse or Maytag. It was clean and smooth and plastic, and looked as out of place in the ruins as an AK-47 in a cowboy movie. What the fuck was it? And how had it got here?

Well, the second one was easy. The priests had brought it. It had Temple of Ormolu written all over it. The whole design of it, the shininess, the whiteness, all made it look like it came out of the same catalog as the wands of blue fire, and all the hallways and rooms I'd seen inside the temple.

It was more than that, though. The thing actually reminded me of the temple itself, though for a second I couldn't figure out why. I squatted down next to it, frowning through the glass panels at its innards. There were columns of little fans all around the interior wall of it, mounted behind vents in the plastic exterior, and they were all blowing on a ring of little silver slinkies that corkscrewed down through it from top to bottom. The slinkies kinda looked like the coils in an old electric heater, but cold instead of hot, because there was water condensing on them and running down the corkscrew in slow drips.

They also looked kinda like… Well, duh! This thing looked like a miniature version of that huge room with the turbines in the Temple of Ormolu where I'd run down the steps with all the guards chasing after me. Yes! That's exactly what it was. But… what was it? What did it do?

I peeked beyond the slinkies, deeper into the machine, and saw a clear tank in the center, half-filled with water. Was it just some kind of glorified water cooler? I looked at the outside of the thing again and sure enough, there was a spigot sticking out of it. I pushed it and took a drink from my hand. It was cool and good, and seemed like overkill. Crazy priests, they couldn't just carry water around in barrels like normal people. They had to keep it in some kind of space-aged super barrel that—

No. Wait a minute. It wasn't a barrel, was it? My heart was suddenly thudding so hard I felt it in my ears. I had to tell Lhan.

I stood up and turned back to the temple to find him, but he was already there, standing in the hole in the wall with a bundle on his back that had my sword sticking out of it.

"I have your things, Mistress."

"Yeah yeah, forget that. Come here."

"You wish to berate me again?"

"This doesn't have anything to do with you being an asshole. This is important. Come here!"

He gave me a flat look, then dropped my stuff and crossed to me. I stepped aside to show off the machine. His eyes went wide.

"The water tokens! Well spotted!"

"Not that, doofus! That! Look at it!"

He tore his eyes away from the satchel and looked at the machine.

"This... this is the work of the Seven. What is it?"

I gave him a grin. "It's a—a moisture gatherer! A dehumidifier! And so is the motherfucking Temple of Ormolu!"

Well, it didn't go over as big as I'd hoped. Lhan just blinked at me.

"The temple is a... a what?"

"Never mind, never mind." I slung the satchel of water tokens over my shoulder, then squatted down and tried to get my arms around the thing. It was a little too big to get a good grip on. "Just help me get it through the gap. We gotta show this to the Aldhanan."

CHAPTER TWENTY-FIVE

SECRETS!

"Father, we cannot let it go! They have hurt Sai and assaulted my person! By the Seven, they have attempted your assassination!"

The damn moisture gatherer had been too big to get through the little passageways on the Aldhanan's warship, so Lhan and I had left it on the deck and gone through to his cabin without it, and that's the scene we came in on—Wen-Jhai in the middle of the cabin, shouting at her dad with her hands on her hips while he sat, naked to the waist, at the head of a fancy dining table with Sai on one side and Captain Anan on the other, and a couple of surgeons pulling the crossbow bolt out of his shoulder. Even with blood dribbling down his chest, the old boy was trying to calm her down. She wasn't having it, though, and I was right there with her. Let it go? What the fuck? They'd just tried to cap his ass.

"Daughter. I promise you. I have no intention of letting it go, only..." He sighed. "Only it must be done with care. I cannot return to Ormolu shouting to the sky that the church has tried to murder me. That would be suicide. Indeed, as yet, I know not if it is true."

Wen-Jhai flailed her arms. "Of course it is true! You have a bolt in your shoulder to prove it! Ru-Manan admitted it."

Captain Anan held up a hand. "True, but he also spoke of some 'master.' This suggests the possibility that the plan was not the will of the church as a whole, but of some man within it."

"That is my most fervent hope." The Aldhanan gritted his teeth as the surgeons got busy with a pair of pliers. "For if it is one man, then my course is simple. I will have my spies discover his identity and destroy him. If, however, it is the church as a whole, that would mean war, and… and…."

He hung his head. I stared at him. The guy with the brass balls who'd marched into that abandoned temple to rescue his daughter was gone. He'd been replaced by a wet cardboard cutout of himself. And I wasn't the only one who thought so. Beside me, Lhan folded his arms and gave him the kind of look he'd been giving me lately.

"My Aldhanan, you deceive yourself if you do not believe that it is the church as a whole who stands against you. A scheme as elaborate as this could not have been perpetrated without the blessings of the Temple's highest ranks. It is no longer a question of deciding to go to war. This was the opening salvo. The war has already begun."

The Aldhanan looked up at him, then grimaced as the bolt finally popped out and the surgeons started to clean the wound. "And if it has? What strategy do you suggest that might win it? The church has weapons against which mortal armies cannot hope to stand. And even without them, they would win. They control the water that supplies the palace and the barracks of my army and navy just as surely as they control the water in the farmers' fields. Were I to declare this war, they would shut their taps, then tell the people I am the reason they die of thirst. I would be overthrown in a matter of days."

Wen-Jhai gaped. "So… so, you will do nothing? Father!"

Even Sai was shocked. "Forgive me, my Aldhanan, but they sought your life. You must do *something*!"

The Aldhanan eased back in his chair and let the surgeons start piling on the gauze. "It is easy for those who do not wear the crown to speak. They have not the welfare of an entire nation to think of. Aye, I have been attacked, and my daughter and son-in-law kidnapped and misused. And my honor demands that I let not these insults go unpunished. But if I anger the church, my people go thirsty. Their crops wither. Their animals die. The whole nation may die!"

Wen-Jhai looked at him, almost crying. "Are you saying then that you will do nothing? After all this?"

"War will be waged, I promise you, but not publicly." The Aldhanan's hands clenched. "Did we live in the golden age, when water was plentiful, I would not hesitate to declare open war, but we live in a dry time, daughter, and have no one to turn to but the priests, whose prayers to the Seven fill their temples with water when none falls from the sky. With that power they hold the rest of us, even your father, by the throat."

I raised my hand. "But—"

He kept talking. "Sometimes, however, their grip is less tight than others. There have been good high priests, benevolent and open-handed. High Priest Duru-Vau is not one of those, and he knows I have fought against him as he has tightened his fist. This, I believe, is why I was led here. So that he may be rid of me, and some more malleable man placed on the throne. Well, two can play at that game. He too can be removed, and another, more tractable priest put in his place."

I couldn't keep quiet any longer. "But, bro—sorry—Aldhanan, that's where you're wrong. It doesn't matter who runs that place. The temple isn't in the business of giving out water. It's in the business of taking it."

The Aldhanan frowned. "I do not understand you. What do you mean?"

"I mean the priests don't *make* water. They steal it. From you!"

Everybody turned toward me now.

Anan snorted. "The woman is mad."

Sai wrinkled his beautiful brow. "How can they steal water from us when we have none to steal?"

"But you do!" I held my hand out toward the door. "Come on, I'll show you. I found something."

The Aldhanan stared at me. "You certainly have! Where did you find it?"

At first I thought he was looking at my boobs and I checked to see if I'd had a nip slip, but then I realized he was staring at the satchel full of water tokens, which musta opened up while I was heaving around the moisture gatherer. Dammit! I shoulda stashed it before I came into the room.

"Oh, uh, this? Well, that wasn't what I…"

"The priests who came to kill us at Toaga carried it upon their ship." Lhan bowed. "We took it as spoils, but if you were to use it against the church, we would be honored to give it to you."

"W-we would?" So much for our all-expenses-paid trip around Waar.

The Aldhanan's eyes glittered. "A tempting offer, Dhan. Almost tempting enough to go to war with no reason, but keep it for now. You have certainly earned it this day."

I breathed a sigh of relief, then pointed to the door again. "That wasn't what I wanted to show you. It's out on the deck. I can prove to you that the priests are stealing water."

The Aldhanan looked skeptical. "Mistress Jae-En, as much as I value your generosity and your prowess in battle, you are new to this land, and know little of the church or our—"

"Yeah yeah, but who else here has been inside the Temple of Ormolu? Anybody? Right, well, I saw something in there that—"

"You have not been in the temple." Aldhanan stood up, which made his surgeons babble and ease him back down again. "Beside the priests, only the Aldhanan is permitted to enter, and only for the blessing of the high priest. The way is barred for all others."

"So you've been there! You know! Well, I got there by popping in on one of their 'living stone' thingies. And that's when I saw—"

"Describe it."

Geez. What was he getting his panties in a bunch for? He was keeping me from getting to the good part. "Uh, okay. Um, white walls, everything all smooth and round, automatic doors that slide open when you get near 'em, and a big tank with glass walls in the middle of it all, as big as your palace, filled with *water they stole from you*!"

"You... you *have* been inside." The Aldhanan blinked, then looked to the surgeons. They were just tying off his bandage. He nodded to them, then rose and stepped around the table. "Lead on. I will see what you have found."

"Finally! Come on."

We went out on deck with Lhan, Sai, Wen-Jhai and Captain Anan following, and I squatted down next to the moisture gatherer as they gathered around it. "Okay, lookit." I pressed the spigot and water spilled out on the deck. "If I let all the water out of this thing, a while later it would be full again 'cause it pulls water out of the air."

Wen-Jhai scowled. "There is no water in air!"

I gave her a look. "Sure there is. You know when you have a cold glass? And water beads on it? Where do you think that comes from?"

"Oh."

"So this machine does the same thing, only faster. Those fans blow air on those curly-cue things and water forms on 'em, then drips down and fills up the tank. Simple, right?"

The Aldhanan squinted through the glass. "Ingenious, but what has it to do with the priests?"

I groaned. "Don't you get it? The Temple of Ormolu isn't a temple. It's one of these things, only as big as a skyscraper! Uh, okay. Not a skyscraper. A mountain! Anyway, the only thing it does is steal water out of the air and store it in that huge tank in the middle. Why do you think it never rains around here?"

The Aldhanan didn't look convinced. "I saw no such fans."

"Then maybe you heard 'em then. They make the whole place hum like a bee hive."

"I know not what a bee hive is, but… but…." The Aldhanan frowned. "There was a tale my father told, of when *he* was Aldhanan. Once, on his yearly visit to the Temple, there was an accident, or an attack of some kind, a maddened slave, perhaps. In any event, his escort left him for a moment, and he opened a door into a…." He closed his eyes like he was trying to remember. "'A dark void of frigid air and howling winds,' he called it."

"That's it! That's where the fans are!" I pointed through the moisture gatherer's glass panels again. "See!"

The Aldhanan stared. "Can it be true? It cannot be true."

Wen-Jhai looked like she was going to cry. "But the priests say our land was a desert until the Seven brought to us the water of life, and the Seven withhold it when we sin. Do you say that is all a lie?"

Lhan stroked his chin beard. "Less a lie than an admission of blackmail and bribery I would say."

Captain Anan glared at him. "That is blasphemy."

"Perhaps, but I have read old texts which tell of a time before the war between the Seven and the One when Ora was a paradise, a lush land of plenty. Not until the towers were built did the droughts begin to come."

The Aldhanan was as grim as a prison door. "I still cannot believe it. Surely the church has not always been so self-serving. Surely they have not always been thieves."

I shrugged. "Hey, maybe there was a good reason for collecting the water back in the day. Holding some back for the lean times or whatever. But, Christ, how much leaner does it gotta get?"

The Aldhanan kept staring at the moisture gatherer like he still wasn't sure. I stood up and looked down at him.

"Bro, come on. You wanna help your people? There's a real simple way to make Ora a land of plenty again. Stand up to these assholes and shut their shit down. You turn off those fans, the rains will come. I guarantee it."

He still didn't look up, but Sai did.

"Mistress Jae-En, do you truly suggest open war? If you think the people suffer now, imagine the suffering when the armies march. There will be death on a grand scale."

Anan nodded. "Aye. We might never recover."

"So you'd rather just lie there and take it?" I thought back to all the dead fields and abandoned farms I'd seen between here and Ormolu. All the lives ruined by lack of water. "Fighting the church might suck in the short term, but it's gotta be better than taking it up the ass for eternity. These clowns gotta be stopped."

"And if the war cannot be won?" The Aldhanan lifted his head at last. "The palace has risen against the church before. Even the Wargod fought them, but the church still remains, while he is gone. Even were I certain you speak the truth, I know not if I would venture the fight. Blood and death in the short term may lead to nothing but defeat."

I blinked at him. Politicians didn't usually admit stuff like that. The rest were looking at him too.

He sighed, then smiled. "A father may choose to rescue his daughter on the spur of the moment, but an Aldhanan cannot decide to rescue his country in the same manner. I must think on this. Please, take your ease."

And with that, he headed back to his cabin with Captain Anan following, and left the rest of us staring after him. At least I was. Lhan was looking at me with a funny little smile on his face.

I met his eye. "What?"

"You are a wonder, mistress. A thousand years of theology, gone with a snap of your fingers."

I squirmed, embarrassed. "I didn't mean to rock any boats. I just—"

"Do not apologize. We of Ora have too long breathed the stultifying staleness of myth. The cold wind of truth is bracing, and welcome. Even if it makes us shiver."

I raised an eyebrow. "I thought you were all about tradition. Or have you changed your mind again about...?" I glanced at Sai and Wen-Jhai, and changed what I was gonna say. "Uh, about, you know?"

"That is an entirely different matter." He sniffed, cold again, then motioned toward the front of the ship, where the cook house was. "Come, there is food."

CHAPTER TWENTY-SIX

HEARTACHE!

The Aldhanan put us up in his officers' quarters—Sai and Wen-Jhai in one cabin, and me and Lhan in another, which was nice and open-minded of him, but kinda awkward too, since we didn't actually want to share a cabin, but also didn't wanna go into details about how we were broken up and all. So once again the two of us were crammed into a cramped closet without enough room to turn around in without elbowing each other in the face. At least this one had two cots, one over the other, bunk bed style.

Still it was kinda tough lying there in the dark with my feet hanging a foot off the end of the bed and all my bruises and cuts and scrapes screaming at me, wishing I had someone to hold me and kiss me and make it all go away—particularly when the someone I wanted was right under me, not wanting to be with me. That was the thing that was gnawing at me like a sack full of rats. I could deal with the pain, but this was really the first quiet minute I'd had since Lhan had told me to pack my bags, and thinking about that fucking hurt worse than all the rest of it.

Why had I come back to Waar? Why hadn't I realized how little I knew about Lhan? Because I'd been thinking with my cunt, is why. My brain had been scrambled by that romance novel night we'd had together before the priests had sent me back to Earth, and I'd jumped right back across the whole fucking universe to try to have it again. How was I supposed to guess he'd be a stupid, stiff-necked caveman who wanted me to play Snow White to his Prince Charming? How was I supposed to know he'd have a stick so far up his ass that he'd rather die than let a woman save him—even a woman who could bench press him for reps.

I'd fucked up. I'd made a mistake. I shouldn't have come back. I should have stayed on Earth and taken Eli up on his trip to Mexico. I coulda been alone there just as easy as here, and at least there I coulda drowned my sorrows in beers and Marlboros. At least there I wouldn't be rubbing elbows with Lhan every five minutes without bein' allowed to jump his bones.

Thinking about not being able to touch him flipped the switch, and all of a sudden all the pain and loneliness and anger I'd been tryin' to hold down just filled me up like a balloon and I started crying into my pillow. I tried to keep quiet about it, but it just kept getting worse, and after a minute of clenching and wiping my nose, a sob got away from me and I heard Lhan shift on the bottom bunk.

"Mistress? Is all well?"

"It's f-f-fine."

I heard him sit up. "Mistress, you are weeping."

"What if I am? Whadda you care!"

There was a pause from below, then, "Mistress, if it is I who have caused this unhappiness, then I apologize. If it is any consolation, the decision has hurt me as well. More than you can know."

"Oh yeah? I don't see you cryin'."

"Nevertheless. I assure you I am in pain."

"Whatever, dude."

This time the pause was even longer, but after a minute he spoke again.

"Mistress. Jae-En. I—I hope... I hope you do not intend to help the Aldhanan in his fight against the church—if indeed he chooses to fight."

I frowned, confused. Why were we talking about that all of a sudden? "Huh? I thought you hated those guys."

"With ever fiber of my being. They are a cancer in the breast of Ora. But... but it need not be your fight."

I frowned, then rolled over and looked down at him over the edge of the top bunk. "Of course it's my fight! After all they've done to me, and you, and

Sai and Wen-Jhai, I owe the whole fucking temple a swift kick up the—"

"What they did to you is precisely what gives me cause for concern, Mistress. You came close to death today, more times than I could count, and, just as often, I failed to protect you."

I gave him a look. "You don't have to protect me anymore. You broke up with me. Or don't you remember—"

I stopped as I noticed a little leather cord around his waist that disappeared into his loincloth. He twitched as he saw where I was looking, and tried to stop me as I reached down to him and pulled it out. It was the balurrah he'd made for me—the pink pebble with the crappy sketch of my sword scratched into it. I stared at it, heart hammering.

"Wh-what the hell, Lhan?"

He looked away. "Forgive me, Mistress. That our love is impossible does not make it easier to deny. I—I. . . ."

I clamped my hand around the thing, choking up. "Goddamn it, Lhan. You are tearing me in half!"

He touched my hand. "And myself as well, which is why I ask that you not participate in the conflict before us. I—I could not bear it if you were to fall in the fighting because of my failings. Indeed. . . Indeed. . ." He got stuck there, skipping like a broken record, then he jumped the groove and went on. "Indeed, I believe it would be for the best if. . . if you were to go home."

I blinked. "Go home? Whaddaya mean, go home? You mean go back to Earth?"

"Back to your lands. Yes."

I switched my grip to his throat, pinning him to his cot.

"First off, you dipstick, I don't have any more clue how to get back to Earth this time than I did last time. Second, why the fuck would I go back when you're still wearing my ballurah?"

There were tears in his eyes. "Because you cannot have me, and I cannot have you, and I would spare us both the torture of proximity."

Funny, I'd just been thinking the same thing, but coming out of his mouth I didn't like it. "You idiot! The only thing keeping you from having me is your goddamn Oran code. Look, you said before we were better suited as companions. Okay fine. Let's be companions—companions who fuck."

He stiffened up like I'd slapped him. "This is not a youthful fling. This is not the crude rutting of beasts. This is a grand passion, a noble meeting of hearts, a pure and—"

"And because of that we can't touch each other?" I let go of him and grabbed the balurrah again. The cord snapped. I held onto it and rolled back onto my bunk to face the wall. "Get out of here, Lhan. Go sleep in the hall. If you're gonna leave me alone, I'd rather be by myself."

He stood from his cot and looked at me. I could hear him breathing at my shoulder. "Mistress, you have my balurrah. You must return it to me."

"Why? We can't be together, right? So what's the point of you wearing it?"

"It speaks what my heart may not."

"Yeah, well, I think I'll just keep it. It'll make a nice little memento of that cute Lhan guy who couldn't make up his mind whether he loved me or not."

"I do love you, Mistress. You know that I do."

"Okay, then." I rolled over to face him, then slipped the thing into my loincloth and spread my legs. "So come get it."

He stared at me, quivering, for a long minute, then stepped back with as much dignity as a guy pitching a tent in his banana hammock can muster, and drew himself up. "You are cruel, Mistress, and I will take my leave, but not before you answer my question."

I closed my legs. "What question is that?"

"Will you keep out of the coming fight?"

He must have seen how I was going to answer, 'cause his cool broke and he stepped forward again. "Come, Jae-En. Did you not say you would only fight until Sai and Wen-Jh'ai were rescued? Well, you have done so. They are safe, and you have no personal stake in the conflict to come. Why risk your life?"

Well, he had me there. As mad as I was at the church for everything they'd done, I was also fed up with being stabbed at and shot at and running for my life every other second. But the original plan had been for me and Lhan to head out on the open road together once we'd saved the kids, and that didn't look like it was going to happen. What was I supposed to do by myself? Sit around in Ormolu and twiddle my thumbs while Lhan and everybody else went off and saved the world? Yeah, right. And what if they screwed up and the priests won?

I must have been staring off into space for a while, because Lhan cleared his throat. "Er, has my speech offended, Mistress?"

"Huh? No, no. It's not that. I'm sick of fighting, believe me."

"And yet?"

Yeah, there was an "and yet." I wished there wasn't, but there was. "I don't know, Lhan. If we were back on Earth, I'd be wishing you good luck and heading off to the bar, but...." I shook my head. "Back there, one person can't change anything. Not even the President of the United States. Nothing anybody does makes one damn bit of difference. The government, the corporations, poverty, hunger, they're like clouds. They're so big and so murky and so *everywhere*, you can't fight 'em. There's no one bad guy you can punch in the face to save the world. But here..."

I swept a hand at the porthole. "Things aren't so set on Waar, the way they are back home. Here, one person *can* make a difference. I already have, and so have you." I pointed to my sword, which was leaning against the bulkhead nearby. "You and me and that sword, we brought down Kedac-Zir, who was gonna kill the Aldhanan and take over the country. Just now we saved Sai and Wen-Jhai and the Aldhanan from a bunch of evil priests."

"We *did* have help, Mistress."

"Sure, but would they have won if we hadn't helped? And that's what I'm saying. This fight with the church? I could be the difference between the Aldhanan winning and losing. How can I turn my back and walk away when I know that?"

Lhan hung his head. "You shame me, Mistress, with your nobility. My thoughts have been only for my frustrations and fears, while you think of the good of the world."

"It ain't nobility, Lhan. It's guilt."

He gave me a sideways smile. "It is rare indeed when the two are not one and the same."

I looked up at him. "So, you're okay with it, then? Me coming along?"

His smile died. "You would not demur were I not, so it matters not." He bowed, then turned for the door. "Good night, Mistress."

He looked so forlorn that, even after everything he'd said, I wanted to pull him onto the bunk and comfort him, but I didn't. He would have brought his pride with him, and there wasn't enough room. The fucking thing was bigger than the both of us combined.

"Good night, Lhan."

When he was gone, I pulled the balurrah out of my loincloth, then wondered what I was gonna do with it. It felt a little weird to wear it. Who wears their own love-token, right? I stuffed it in my pack. I'd have to give it some more thought.

Whatever I did with it, I wanted to make sure it was something that would really piss off Lhan.

CHAPTER TWENTY-SEVEN

WAR!

Three days later, just after sunset, the whole gang walked down the airship's gangplank right onto the balcony of the Aldhanan's private apartments on the top floor of the palace—door-to-door service, just like rockstars—only Lhan and I were dressed up like guards so no church spies could see who we were.

And it was a good thing too, 'cause the church was waiting on us. Before the Aldhanan even had time to take off his cloak, one of his servants scurried up to him and bowed.

"My Aldhanan. The High Priest Duru-Vau wishes to speak with you on a matter of great urgency. He awaits without."

The Aldhanan glared at the guy like he was gonna kill him, then waved him away. "Have him wait. I will receive him in my bed chamber."

The servant bowed himself out and the Aldhanan turned to us. "It seems the battle is joined already."

Lhan stepped forward, his hand on his sword. "And we are ready, my Aldhanan."

The Aldhanan chuckled. "It will not come to blows yet. The first skirmish will be one of words, and I believe I have a way to win it." He grinned. "If you wish to listen, there is a screen in my room, behind which you will not be seen. Wen-Jhai knows the way."

He headed out one door with Captain Anan and his guards and Wen-Jhai led the rest of us out another, and brought us to a little room like a walk-in closet, except it had some benches in it and one wall was a fancy wooden lattice with black fabric tacked to the back of it. With the lamps lit in the room beyond we could see everything that went on, and with the no lights on our side, nobody could see us—at least I hoped not. There was a tiny door in the left-hand wall of the closet, but I didn't know what it was for. Maybe it was an actual closet.

Wen-Jhai motioned us all to sit down on the benches and be quiet while on the other side of the screen, the Aldhanan entered and his maids helped him into his bed clothes, then tucked him into the bed. The old fox lay back and did his best to look more wounded than he was, then motioned for them to go.

"Just like wide screen TV."

"Shhh!"

"Sorry."

After a second, a door opened and the servant bowed in a guard and a young, bookish-looking poindexter who woulda been kinda pretty except for his lack of chin. I looked behind him, expecting to see an older, scarier looking priest come in after him, but he was it. I was surprised. He looked too young to run the choir, let alone the whole temple.

But any doubts I had about whether he was the guy behind everything disappeared when I saw him look at the Aldhanan. He was truly surprised to see him, and blinked like he thought the bed would be empty if he looked again. After that, an angry look flashed across his face, but he managed to turn it into a look of concern as he approached the bed.

"Aldhanan. I grieve to see you so hurt. May the Seven grant that you recover quickly."

"My thanks, Duru-Vau. And I thank you for seeking me out so promptly. You are no doubt anxious to hear what occurred in Durgallah."

Duru-Vau bowed, but didn't cross his wrists. "Most anxious indeed, my Aldhanan. I... I feared when you left that the, the danger was too much, and am greatly relieved to see you safely returned."

The Aldhanan smiled. "No doubt. No doubt." He sighed like he was in pain and sank back into his pillows, holding his bandaged shoulder. "Well, your

Reverence, it was precisely as you said. The outcast Dhan and his outland giantess were holding my daughter and her consort in the heathen temple, lying in wait for us with an army of black-robed heretics at their backs."

Duru-Vau pretended to be surprised. "It must have been terrifying. Er, did… did all survive?"

The Aldhanan grinned. "The outcast and his giantess did not, that is for certain, nor did their followers. Despite the ambush, we killed them to a man."

Duru-Vau was starting to look a little sick. "And your daughter? Her consort? You rescued them?"

"Indeed. They had been starved and grievously abused, and were about to be sacrificed by the heretics in some unholy ceremony, but through luck and swiftness, we saved them from the heathen blade." He put on a sad face, though I could see him struggling to hold it. "We did lose some, however. Many good men fell in that battle, and your brother, his reverence Ru-Manan, as well. One of the heretics kicked him into the pit and he broke his neck. I beg your forgiveness that I was not able to protect him."

Duru-Vau's cheek twitched. He bowed his head to hide it. "I am certain you did your best, but am most grieved to hear it. He will be missed." Well, maybe, but his sadness disappeared a split second later, and he looked around the room as if he was hunting for somebody. "I am more pleased than I can say, however, that your daughter and her consort have survived their terrible ordeal. It would be an honor if you allowed me to pay my respects to them in person."

I bared my teeth. "And cut their throats, I bet, you weasel."

Lhan elbowed me in the ribs.

The Aldhanan gave Duru-Vau a fake smile. "I'm afraid they have retired. Their experiences were very wearying, and they have not yet been able to speak coherently of what had happened to them. When they recover, I will pass along your good wishes."

"You are most kind, but I am disturbed to hear that they have not recovered themselves enough to speak sense. Can—can you tell me anything of what they said?"

The Aldhanan frowned, like he was trying to decide how much to tell, then he shrugged. "It was very strange, your Reverence. Both claimed that it was not heretics that kidnapped them, but priests of Ormolu, and that it was the church who were their tormentors, and not the giantess and the degenerate."

He shook his head. "I dismissed this as confusion, of course, but it was still most disturbing."

Duru-Vau was clenching his fists so hard his knuckles were turning white. "My Aldhanan, I'm afraid it may be more dangerous than it is disturbing."

The Aldhanan looked at him. "How so?"

Duru-Vau bowed, and this time crossed his wrists. "Forgive me for what I am about to say, Aldhanan, and I mean no disrespect to the valor of yourself or your guards, but I fear that you were *allowed* to take back your daughter and son-in-law. That it was all part of the heretics' insidious master plan."

Down the bench to my right, Wen-Jhai was starting to breathe through her nose. Sai put a hand on her arm.

Out in the bedroom, the Aldhanan laughed. "Indeed? You say the heretics allowed themselves to be slaughtered to a man? What sort of plan is that?"

"Their leaders put no value on the lives of their followers. So that their goal was achieved, they—"

"You led me to understand that the degenerate and the giantess were the leaders. Was it part of their plan to die as well?"

Duru-Vau covered like a pro. "Obviously not, but there must then be some even more sinister figure who pulled their strings."

"Yeah," I muttered. "You."

Duru-Vau looked at the Aldhanan like a doctor giving the bad news. "Forgive me, my Aldhanan, but I fear your daughter and her consort have been brainwashed by these fiends, made into automatons designed to betray you when you are most vulnerable. The gift of their return may in truth a poison dagger, that will turn in your hand and cut—"

"Liar!"

Everybody in the little room whipped around. Wen-Jhai was on her feet, glaring at the screen, while out in the room, Duru-Vau and his guard were looking right at the screen and reaching for weapons.

Sai put a hand on Wen-Jhai's arm. "Beloved. Quiet yourself. We mustn't—"

She shook him off and stepped to the tiny door, then stormed through it with Sai stumbling after her. A second later she was in the bedroom stabbing a finger at Duru-Vau and spattering him with spit as she shouted at him.

"You know very well Lhan-Lar and Mistress Jae-En did not kidnap us, for it was your own minions who brought us to Durgallah as a ruse to trick my father to his doom. And by the Seven, you would have succeeded were it not for—"

"Wen-Jhai!" The Aldhanan looked like he was going to jump out of bed and clap a hand over her mouth. "How dare you attack our guest in this fashion! You say far too much!"

Wen-Jhai went white as she realized she'd almost spilled the beans on me and Lhan—and Dad too. She stammered for a second, then turned up her nose and sniffed. "Then I will only say, Father, that I pray you never again fall for the underhanded tricks of priests."

Duru-Vau gave her a sad smile, then turned to the Aldhanan. "You see? She believes all they told her. The monsters have made themselves out the heroes and we the villains."

I could see the Aldhanan's jaw clenching under his beard. "Yes," he said through his teeth. "It is impossible that they could have been kidnapped by priests. Unthinkable."

"Indeed." Duru-Vau let out a breath. "Now. As you understand that, then you will understand also that it is imperative I take the poor things to the temple now, so that my brothers and I can use the gifts of the Seven to cleanse their minds of this vile poison and return them to you the innocent, untroubled children they were before they were kidnapped."

"No!" Sai and Wen-Jhai shouted it in stereo and backed away from the priest like he'd just turned into a vampire.

The Aldhanan pushed himself up in his bed. "That—that will not be necessary, Duru-Vau. Armed with your warning, I will keep a cautious eye on Wen-Jhai and Sai-Far. But I would see what a father's love and the comfort of familiar surroundings can do before I give them into your tender care."

Duru-Vau stood. "I am afraid I must insist, Aldhanan. The safety of your person, and that of the nation—"

"And I must insist, High Priest, that the welfare of my family is my affair, and if the church wishes to contest this, they should send more than a single guard and a single priest."

I hadn't seen any signals passed, or heard any alarms rung, but just then Captain Anan and his men entered the room and took up positions around the walls. They kept their swords sheathed and their hands behind their backs, but the threat couldn't have been more obvious if ol' Captain Eye-Patch had put his dagger to Duru-Vau's throat.

Duru-Vau stiffened. "I see. So, you believe the lies your daughter has been taught."

The Aldhanan's face looked like a storm cloud about to spit lightning.

"No I do not. I saw the bodies of those killed, and their identity was beyond question. Nevertheless, my daughter and her consort remain with me. Now, leave me, please. I find I am growing tired."

Duru-Vau bowed. "As the Aldhanan commands. I will return when you are recovered."

Man, these Waarians and their saying-shit-without-saying-shit. Back home, the Aldhanan woulda said, "Get outta my face, asshole. You're making me sick." And Duru-Vau woulda said, "Yeah, I'm leaving. But when I've got some back-up, I'm comin' back to kick your ass." Here it was all snarky jabs and double talk. I preferred the up-front method myself, which is why I was glad I was in the little closet and not out with the Aldhanan. That little weasel in the orange robe would have been spitting teeth—and that would have spoiled the whole thing.

Because I saw the Aldhanan's game the way Wen-Jhai almost hadn't. He'd had to admit that Sai and Wen-Jhai thought it was priests who'd kidnapped them. If he hadn't, Duru-Vau might have guessed he was lying, but if the Aldhanan had admitted we were still alive, and that *he* knew the heretics had been priests in disguise, it would have been war with the church right then and there, and no time to get his shit together.

I'm not sure he coulda kept from punching Duru-Vau's lights out for another five minutes though. By the time the door had closed on the high priest's ass and Lhan and I filed out of the closet into the room, he was out of his bed and pacing around like a tweaker, his face as purple as a bruise. Then he stopped and looked around at us all, his eyes hot and cold at the same time.

"He wishes to take my daughter again? He tries to turn me against my own blood? Friends, my past hesitations have been burned to nothing in the fire of my rage. We will go to war, and we will win!"

Sai went whiter than I thought a purple man could.

Wen-Jhai clasped her hands together like something out of a bad melodrama. "Father! At last!"

Lhan squared his shoulders. "Right and brave, my Aldhanan. I commend you for making such a bold move."

The Aldhanan waved that aside. "It will not yet be so very bold. Not for a while. I will need the support of my Dhanans and their armies before I can reveal my hand, and that of the people as well, and I must win it in secret."

Sai looked like he was going to pee himself. "How is that possible? The church has spies everywhere."

"Not everywhere." He started to pace again. "I gave this much thought as we sailed, wondering, if I were to do it, how it might be done, and I believe I have a way, but there is much to be done first, and many people to speak with, the first of which I go to now, while you two…." He turned to me and Lhan as he grabbed a robe and started pulling it on. "…will go and speak to some others."

Lhan and I looked at each other.

"Uh, us? But aren't we supposed to be dead?"

The Aldhanan grinned. "That will only add to your glamour."

Lhan coughed. "My Aldhanan, we will of course do anything you require, but I know not who we could talk to who would help—"

"You are a heretic, are you not, Lhan-Lar? An unbeliever? You believe the Seven are less than gods?" The Aldhanan's eyes were blazing like blow torches.

Lhan swallowed and stepped back. "My Aldhanan, I…"

"Do not bother to deny it. Do you think I did not look deeply into the past of my daughter's future husband—and that of his greatest friends—before I allowed her to marry him? I know all."

Lhan opened and closed his mouth like a muppet, but nothing came out. I was afraid I was gonna have to give him the Heimlich Manuever.

The Aldhanan laughed. "Fear not, Dhan. Had I believed you a threat, you would have been dead long ago. Put it aside and listen. You were once a member of a group known as the Flames of Truth, or some such. Dedicated to the overthrow of the church and all its works, yes?"

"O-only for a short while. A passing phase while I was at university. I—"

"And I know from recent reports that they still exist—still meet and plot in secret, and are still highly regarded among the underground of malcontents."

"I really could not say. I have not spoken with them in—"

"Well, you will speak to them again now. This very night! And you will tell them that the time of reckoning they have worked so long to bring about is finally at hand! The firebrands must be lit. The word must be spread. It is time for them to rise and the church to fall!"

Lhan looked like he'd rather go skinny-dipping in a swimming pool full of piranhas, but he only bowed and crossed his wrists.

"At your command, my Aldhanan."

CHAPTER TWENTY-EIGHT

ORMOLU!

And that's the problem with being friends with someone like the Aldhanan. Nice as he is, personal friend and all that, he's still the fucking Aldhanan, and he still woulda thrown us in jail if we'd told him to go take a hike. So about half an hour later we were back in our surgeon's duds, masks and all, sneaking out a back door of the palace and heading down into the city to go see about recruiting Lhan's old college buddies to the Aldhanan's crazy fucking plan—which he'd given us the lowdown on before he sent us on our way.

Lhan was hating it. I couldn't see his face behind his pointy mask, but I didn't have to. Everything about him, the way he walked, the set of his shoulders, the never-ending string of Waarian swears, all told me he was less than happy.

I cleared my throat. "So, who are these guys?"

Lhan didn't look around.

"Lhan?"

"What *is* it?"

Jeez. Snap much? "Uh, I just wanted to know who these Flame guys were."

Lhan sighed. "You recall after our rescue of Wen-Jhai from Kedac-Zir? Our picnic on the hillside above the palace? Sai and I spoke of our old tutor."

I frowned, remembering. That had been right before we'd gone to hide at Rian-Gi's place. Sai and Lhan had told me about some guy who'd been a "collector of forbidden knowledge." Rian-Gi had mentioned him too. "Oh right. He was supposed to bring us a map to a living stone so I could go home, but I got grabbed by the priests before he had a chance."

"Yes. Preceptor Shal-Hau, a teacher of the classics at the Aldhanan's College—and the secret leader of the Flame of Truth. In my idealistic youth, I was one of them, until… until…."

I waited for him to finish the sentence, but he'd disappeared back inside of himself, and was walking along more clenched up than ever.

"So, uh, y'all had a falling out or something?"

"That would be an understatement."

"What happened?"

"Nothing that need concern you."

And that was about all I got out of him for about a half hour. At least I got to see more of Ormolu.

***

The last time I'd been here, all I'd really seen was the inside of a navy base and a coupla temples and palaces. I hadn't really been to any of the places where people actually lived. Now we were walking through the heart of it, and there was a lot to look at. It wasn't my first taste of Oran city life. I'd been to a place called Kalnah before, which was where most of Ora's flying ships were built, but Kalnah was to Ormolu like Gary, Indiana was to New York City—two completely different animals.

We started in the government district, which was all ministries and temples and colleges, which Lhan said were for teaching bureaucrats how to be bureaucrats and priests how to be priests, and with the sun down it was as deserted as the City of Black Glass—a bunch of huge dark buildings with our wanted posters all over the walls. Kinda creepy.

After that was a ritzy area filled with the offices of trading companies, wholesalers and slave dealers, every one of 'em trying to outdo each other with the biggest tower, the fanciest entrance, the flashiest statues and curlicues. Next came an industrial district, with streets full of workshops and warehouses. This was deserted too, mostly, but a little bit further west and we were in a much livelier neighborhood—all tight streets with colorful three-story tenements squeezed together on either side, lots of people walking around, lots of open shops, and lots of folks with carts selling street food—and singing about it. This was where Lhan had been leading us. He called it the Academy District, 'cause the *real* colleges—the ones that didn't get you into government or temple service—were there. He listed off colleges of philosophy, history, science, math, music, art, even a cooking school if you can believe it—and just like every college town I'd ever been in, there were bars and coffee houses—well, it wasn't coffee, but you know what I mean—on every corner, and crowds of young guys in stupid clothes and funny hats hanging out and arguing about everything under the sun, and fighting about everything else. What was different from back home was that it was *only* guys. I mean, there were gals around, but only as waitresses, singers, or hookers. There were no female students.

Yeah, I know I should have left it alone, but it bugged me. I leaned in to Lhan as we passed a bunch of guys all arguing about whether Arrurrh had souls.

"So gals don't go to school here?"

One of Lhan's eyebrows raised up over the top of his mask. "Women in school?"

My hackles started to rise. "Something funny about that?"

Lhan frowned. "No. But it isn't done."

"Why not?"

"It is for a man to study, so that his wife may live a life free of toil or taxing thought."

I was about to say something about, "What if she didn't want to live a life free of toil or taxing thought?" but then I looked around at all the waitresses cleaning up spilled booze and puke as drunk students staggered past them arm in arm, and I stopped short. "So, those women? Their men didn't study hard enough?"

Lhan shrugged. "Those women are servants. Their men are undoubtedly the same. They would not be allowed into the colleges regardless. Only men of good birth may enroll here."

He said it so matter-of-fact that I blinked. Another Waarian slap in the face, though really, how different was that from back home? We had scholarships on Earth, sure. But mostly you didn't get into Harvard without some serious green. Still…

"So, you're saying the the rules of the Seven only apply if you're a Dhan? A poor guy doesn't have to make his wife's life easier?"

"He should certainly try, but it is the lot of the poor to struggle. All they can do is pray to be born into a better station in their next life."

Now he was really making me mad. "Hang on. The only way to be upwardly mobile around here is to die?"

"Upwardly mobile? I don't know the term."

"Lhan, don't be an idiot. It's the great American dream. You work hard, make money, buy your way out of the slums, and get to rub elbows with kings and queens. That doesn't happen here?"

He scowled behind his mask. "Poor men occasionally get rich, but one could never become a Dhan. Nobility is an honor conferred by birth."

I stopped, then turned to him, my face getting all tight. "Is that what you believe?"

Lhan looked nervous, like a puppy who knows his owner is mad, but isn't sure why. "Mistress, we have had this conversation before. All souls are returned to the great sea in death. When it is time for them to be reborn, Majdu the Life Giver judges them and chooses their birth. A poor man who has led a blameless life may come back a Dhan, or even the Aldhanan. But a poor man cannot become noble in the course of one life. It is—"

"How can you say all that shit when you know what I am?"

He stared, completely confused. "I do not understand you, Mistress. Though we have parted ways, I still consider you the most noble, honorable—"

"Is that what you think? You think I'm some kind of space royalty or something? You think I'm fucking Princess Leia?"

"I know not this princess you speak of, but in my eyes—"

I cut him off with my hand. "Don't. Please. Listen, I—I think we better clear this shit up right here. I don't want you saying later on that I conned you into palling around with me on false pretenses or something."

"Mistress, I would never—"

"Just listen!" I pointed to one of the waitresses, bending over as she served a tray of drinks so the college boys could get a good look at her cleavage. "My mom did *that* for a living." Then I pointed to a whore, standing in the mouth of an alley. "Sometimes she did *that*. My dad worked in an orchard when he wasn't in jail. He was a field hand. Your fucking Life Giver judged my soul and decided it was the lowest of the fucking low. So maybe…" I was glad he couldn't see my face behind my ninja mask thingy. My eyes were leaking like a bad seal. "So maybe you wanna rethink calling me "Mistress," 'cause I ain't no noble. I never will be. There ain't enough spins of the wheel left."

Lhan laughed, and I nearly punched his lights out, but then he touched my shoulder and looked through my veil into my eyes. "Mistress, you misunderstand me. I only meant to explain that title cannot be given to those that do not already have it. That is only law, though some fools think it nature." He sighed. "It is true that most on Waar are blind to the difference between nobility and noble birth, but I cannot help but see it, for I have known too many who were born noble, but have no nobility, and many more who have inner nobility but no title. Certainly I know that *I* will be a dung hauler or a slave when next I rise from the sea, and I pray that my dear father will be born into worse than that."

"Oh, come on, Lhan. You—"

"Jae-En, by your actions, you are more noble than any man on this street. It is *I* who, despite my birth, am not worthy of the appellation. I who, despite privilege and education, wasted my youth to license and debauchery in these holes you see around you."

I shook my head. "Lhan. I know you. Maybe you fucked around some. Everybody does that in college. But you couldn't have been that bad. You've got too big a heart. You'd never hurt anybody. Not on purpose."

He drew himself up. "And do you count inaction as 'on purpose?' What say you of cowardice?"

Before I could put together an answer, he turned away from me, as cold as he had been warm ten seconds ago.

"Come. The Dusty Tome is this way."

***

Lhan led me down the noisy street to an open-fronted place that had a big leather-bound book nailed over its door for a sign, and tables and chairs spilling out in the street, all filled with intense, robe-wearing bookworm-types shouting over each other's arguments, or sitting by themselves and trying to look tortured while they wrote in their journals.

He paused in front of it, then stayed paused, like somebody'd glued his feet to the ground.

I took a wild guess. "So, this act of cowardice you were talking about. Your, uh, inaction. Is that why you're all weirded out about coming to see these guys again?"

"Aye. Preceptor Shal-Hau has forgiven me, but the others…" Lhan hung his head.

I cracked my knuckles. "Well, fuck 'em. If they give you any trouble, I'll—"

Lhan paled. "Please, Jae-En. Be not impulsive. They have every right. What I did was…. inexcusable."

I shrugged. "All right, but if you want somebody slapped, just say the word."

"I will not fail to speak. I promise you."

We stepped through the crowded tables and pushed inside. It was hot as a sauna in there, and smelled like distilled nerd—book mold, B.O., and unwashed clothes. Back home it would have been a Starbucks, or actually one of those coffee houses that hates Starbucks and serves organic coffee from someplace you've never heard of. Not the kind of place I'd usually be caught dead in. I tend to favor places where the coffee comes in regular and decaf, and you can get a bowl of chili and a side of fries.

They weren't drinking coffee here. Lhan said it was called halga, and it looked to me like steaming cups of milk and smelled like hot, over-ripe banana. Whatever it was, it was hyping the hell out of those school-boys. They were all talking a mile a minute, and didn't seem to be able to sit still.

Lhan pulled his hood down low as we edged through the press, which I thought was overkill. His mask hid pretty much everything but his eyes already.

"Try not to look *too* guilty, Lhan."

"Forgive me, but this was an old haunt during my school days, and some may still remember me."

He pushed toward a little archway in the back wall. It had a curtain across it and a sign hanging in front of it that said, "Reserved."

"Good. They are in session."

Lhan stepped past the sign and ducked through the curtain. I followed him into a dark hallway with a crack of light coming out from under a door at the end. It was a lot quieter in here, quiet enough that I heard somebody draw a blade ahead of us.

"Who's that?" came a man's voice.

I reached over my shoulder for my bundled sword but Lhan stopped me.

"One who is a friend."

"A true friend?"

Lhan pulled off his mask. "A friend of truth."

The guy with the knife stepped forward. He was another student type, though a bit older. Grad student maybe? He lowered the blade, but didn't put it away.

"Lhan, it is you?"

"Well met, Mio."

Mio didn't seem to think so. "Is it? After the trouble at Rian-Gi's and your past villainies, I know some among us who would consider you well met only if they could cut your—" He broke off as he noticed me, then did a double take at my height. "Wh-who's this?"

"I'm the cause of the trouble," I said.

Mio looked at Lhan. "Not…?"

"The same. Worry not. She is a friend. But you mentioned Rian-Gi. Is he…?"

"They watch him, hoping to catch the rest of us. He lives."

Lhan breathed a sigh of relief, and so did I. He mighta been a bit of a drama queen, but the guy'd done right by me when he didn't have to. I was glad he was okay.

Lhan looked at the door. "Is the tutor instructing tonight?"

Mio was having a hard time peeling his eyes off me, but he turned back to Lhan at last. "I know not why I should tell you anything of us."

"Please, Mio. It is a matter of great urgency. I must speak with him."

Mio gave him the stone face for a long moment, then shrugged. "I'll ask."

He cracked the door, letting light and voices spill out, then slipped through. Over his shoulder, I could see a little private dining room with a table in the middle, chairs all around, and benches along the walls. Every seat was taken with more student types, all laughing and jabbering away with each other, and all facing toward a balding old purple guy with a big nose and bigger ears who sat at the head of the table, smiling like the world's ugliest buddha. Then the door closed and it was all dark again.

"That's your secret society?"

Lhan looked around. "This? No. Nothing more than an informal debating club, moderated by Master Shal-Hau, all correct and approved by the college. But young men who attend here, and show a certain fervor and slant, are invited to attend more exclusive gatherings, which are—"

"The secret society."

"Precisely."

After another minute of waiting in the dark hall, Mio slipped back out the door and gave Lhan a nod. "The Master's house, in half a crossing." He looked down the hall toward the noisy main room, then opened another door just to the left of the first one. This one was dark.

"Best if you went out the back."

CHAPTER TWENTY-NINE

HERETICS!

Half a crossing later—I'd say about an hour and a half Earth time—Lhan lead me up the creaky stairs of an old three-story tenement on the edge of the Academy District. It had a lot of fancy tile work around the doors and windows, and mighta been a swanky address back in the day, but it was a bit shabby at the edges now.

On the third floor Lhan stopped outside an apartment, and I could hear voices arguing behind the door. Lhan took off his mask, then took a breath—and another. Finally he pulled himself together and knocked. The voices cut off, and a few seconds later the door swung open and the ugly Buddha guy stood there in slippers and a green silk robe, smiling like a happy grandpa.

"Lhan-Lar, you live!"

Lhan bowed and crossed his wrists. "Only by greatest good fortune and the efforts of my companion, Mistress Jae-En." He turned to me. "Mistress Jae-En, may I present my tutor and friend, Master Shal-Hau of Ormolu."

Shal-Hau bowed. "Thank you, Mistress, for returning to me so dear a student. Please, welcome to my home."

I waved, embarrassed, and ducked through the door, which was a little low. "Uh, thanks. Hi."

He took our cloaks and masks and weapons and put them on hooks, then turned back and stared at Lhan's belly wound, which still looked pretty raw.

"By the One, pupil, *do* you live? It seems impossible."

Lhan shrugged, embarrassed. "'Tis due almost entirely to my own foolishness. A tale for another time."

"Of course, of course. Come in. The others are waiting."

Knowing he was a professor, I'd kinda expected Shal-Hau's place to be like Rian-Gi's study—all stacks of scrolls and piles of papers and dirty cups and saucers everywhere, but it was more like something out of the Waar edition of House Beautiful. There were wide, low couches all around, piled with tasseled pillows and bookended with little tables with vases on them. Greenish bronze lamps with patterns punched in their sides shined patterns of light on weird old masks and musical instruments that were hung on the walls as art. It was as spotless and neat as a model home, but at the same time felt as warm and welcoming as Shal-Hau's smile.

I couldn't say the same for the dudes that were filling the couches.

There were seven of them, all dressed in dark students' robes like the guys in the back room at the Dusty Tome, but these guys weren't laughing. As Shal-Hau stepped out to fetch drinks and snacks, they all stared at me and Lhan like we'd run over their cat, and I heard some whispering in the ranks.

"By the One, she *is* a demon."

"The Church's broadsheets did not exaggerate after all."

I was kinda feeling like something Lhan had brought in for show and tell, and it was making me a little hot under the collar. Lhan wasn't doing anything about it, either. He was just standing there, as stiff as a kid meeting his girlfriend's parents for the first time. So it was almost a relief when one of the guys, a dignified beanpole with a samurai topknot and the cheekbones of a hungry elf, broke the ice and spoke up, even though he didn't have anything nice to say.

"I am surprised to see you, Lhan. I hadn't thought you would have the courage to show your face. Unless perhaps you have come to betray us to the priests as you did Bedu-Bas."

I had no idea what he was talking about, but I coulda punched him in the nose on attitude alone. Lhan just crossed his wrists and bowed.

"In truth, Sei-Sien, I feared to come, knowing the reception I would receive. I hope it speaks to the urgency of my message that I conquered that fear."

A little butterball with a droopy mohawk folded his arms. "And what message is this?"

Lhan bowed to him too. "Thank you, Gaer-Zhau. It is this. That it is time at last to strike the church as you have always meant to."

Cheekbones curled his lip. "Really? With Rian-Gi under surveillance? With you and your companion accused of kidnapping the Aldhanan's daughter? With the church looking everywhere for you? I cannot think of a worse time."

"And yet, in truth, there has never been a better time." Lhan took a step forward. "Though you know it not, we are stronger now, and better allied than ever before. And when I tell you—"

"What do you know of our strength?" Cheekbones flicked a hand at him. "Did someone speak of it in a brothel? You haven't—"

"Let him speak, Sei." Shal-Hau trundled back in with a tray of crunchies and some kind of wine in a clay jug, then motioned for us to take a couch across from Sei-Sien and his pals. I felt like I was sitting down at the defendant's table in a courtroom, and shivered. The last time I'd felt like that I'd done a year in county for assault.

Shal-Hua helped himself to the vino, poured some for me and Lhan, then crossed to another couch and sat down.

"Go on, Lhan."

Lhan nodded thanks to Shal-Hau, then licked his lips and turned to the others. "First you must know that it was not Mistress Jae-En and I who kidnapped Wen-Jhai and Sai-Far, but the church itself."

Gaer-Zhau raised an eyebrow. "And why would they do that?"

"As bait."

Sei-Sien laughed. "To catch what fish? You? They wouldn't waste the effort."

Shal-Hau gave him a warning look.

Lhan shrugged. "At first, I admit, we thought their aim was to lure Mistress Jae-En into their clutches, but soon we learned the truth. It was the Aldhanan they wanted."

That perked up everybody's ears.

"The Aldhanan?"

Lhan leaned forward. "The church told the Aldhanan that Mistress Jae-En and I held his daughter and her consort in Durgallah, and meant to sacrifice them to the ancient gods of the sea. In reality, a large group of priests disguised as heretics waited there in ambush, intending to kill him."

"What!"

They were all staring now.

"Mistress Jae-En and I were to have been named the Aldhanan's assassins, and used as an excuse for a *new Aldhanan*, a puppet fully under the control of the church, to wage war against true heretics such as yourselves and further tighten the Temple's control of Ora and its water."

Shal-Hau put down his cup. "You—you speak of these things as if they have already happened. Do you say that the Aldhanan is dead?"

Lhan smiled. "If not for the courage and strength of Mistress Jae-En, I believe he would be. Fortunately, she warned him in time, and the false heretics were defeated and exposed, and the Aldhanan's daughter and her consort rescued as well."

Sei-Sien coughed. "Forgive me, do you say that the Aldhanan is aware that his daughter was kidnapped by the church? That he knows they meant to kill him?"

"He knows worse than that."

"What could be worse than that?"

Lhan looked at me, then back to them, then coughed. "This is the second thing you must know, a secret that could destroy the church if it was revealed."

Sei-Sien didn't look impressed. "There have been so many of those over the years. All failures. What might this one be?"

Lhan smiled. "One of your main complaints against the church is that, though it creates water using the gifts of the Seven, it distributes it only to the rich, leaving the poor to die when the droughts come, correct?"

Sei-Sien and the others said nothing, but Shal-Hau played along.

"Correct, Lhan. It is the greatest of their crimes."

"Not so. There is one greater, for, despite their claims, they do not in truth create water. They steal it, from us. The Temple of Ormolu and the six others are not temples at all, but immense moisture gatherers. They suck the moisture from the air and store it in great tanks. The only thing the priests of the Seven create is drought."

Gaer-Zhau's eyes bulged out of his head. "By the One, is this true? This is what we have waited for since—"

"I do not believe it." Sei-Sien sat back. "How could anyone know this? One would have to enter a temple to see it, and no one enters the—"

I tapped my chest. "I have. I've been in the Temple of Ormolu. I saw the machines."

Then it wasn't just Sei-Sien rolling his eyes. It was everybody.

"She is a liar like her friend."

"None enters the temple!"

"And those that do never come out again!"

"Only the priests can go in and out."

Shal-Hau held up a hand and everybody shut up. He looked me in the eyes. "Describe it."

This again? "Yeah, okay. Fine. Uh, white walls, sliding doors, elevators—ah, I mean rooms that move up and down between floors—a big tank of water in the middle with see-through walls, and, uh, 'living stones' that let you pop in and out without going through the walls. There's also big fans and condenser coils behind the scenes, but…"

I trailed off as Shal-Hau blinked. It was the first time since I'd met him that he looked like anything had surprised him.

"She is correct."

His posse all started babbling at him at once. He cut 'em off again.

"There is one other man besides a priest who can return from the temple. Once each year the current Aldhanan is brought within to confer with the high priests and receive their blessing. It is said the priests swear the Aldhanans to secrecy with such terrible vows that they fear to speak of what they saw, but there have been one or two who have written of it in private correspondence, and I have been privileged to read two such accounts." He smiled at me. "Both match Mistress Jae-En's description in nearly every detail."

Sei-Sien stared at me. "And you told your tale of moisture gatherers to the Aldhanan?"

Gaer-Zhau did too. "And he believed you?"

I shrugged. "Well, I had to go through the same rigmarole with him, but once he realized I'd been in the temple too, yeah. He believed me. He knows the priests are stealing water and causing drought, and he's mad as hell about it."

Lhan nodded and looked around at them all. "You see? For the first time since the reign of his grandfather, Kor-Karan, Ora has an Aldhanan who understands the true nature of the church, and is prepared to fight it with all the resources at his command. But unlike Kor-Karan, he has the ammunition that will bring them down. The secret of the stolen water." He stabbed the little coffee table in front of him with a finger. "That is why I am here. The Aldhanan will soon go on a covert journey to beg his Dhanans for their support in the coming war, but he knows that even all their money and troops will not be enough. Without the people behind him, he will not win. And to win the hearts of the people, he needs you. As he travels from city to city, visiting the Dhanans in their castles, the Flames of Truth will travel with him, meeting in secret with other far-flung heretic groups and urging them to spread the word in the tap rooms and halga houses of their—"

All of a sudden everybody—well, everybody except Shal-Hau—was on their feet, shouting at once.

"You come from the Aldhanan?"

"You have told him of us?"

"You have *led* him to us?"

Gaer-Zhau was looking for the exit. "We've been trapped!"

Sei-Sien had turned red in the face, which, since he'd started off kinda blueberry yogurt, meant he was now more of a blackberry sorbet. "You have betrayed us! Given our names to our enemies! We are ended. The Flame is extinguished!"

I stood up and punched the ceiling, which shook the room and rained plaster dust down on everybody. It did the trick, they clammed up like I'd fired a gun.

"What the fuck is wrong with you fucks? Lhan told me that all you've ever wanted was to bring down the church, and now you're gonna chicken out when you've finally got the chance?"

"There is no chance," said Sei-Sien. "I see it now. You have come here with a lie—a finely crafted lie, I admit—fed to you by the Aldhanan, and designed to make us walk into his dungeons of our own free will. You will forgive me if I do not take the bait."

"You are a fool, Sei-Sien." Lhan stood too. "If the Aldhanan wished to arrest you, he would arrest you. He would need no lie, nor would he send someone you hate and mistrust to try to trick you into some snare."

Gaer-Zhau curled his lip. "So why would he send someone we hate and mistrust to try to win our support? That makes even less sense."

"Because I was witness to the ambush that nearly killed him. Because Jae-En knows the truth of the water. Because I know you. Because he has *no one else*!"

Sei-Sien waved all that away. "More lies, but let us pretend for a moment it is true. Why should we agree to help? Even if the church were somehow defeated, *we* certainly would not live to see it. We will not even live to see the beginning! You tell us the Aldhanan would woo his Dhanans—his personal friends—in their castles, but we would be seeking out unknown conspirators, never knowing if we spoke instead to a Temple spy, and risking arrest and torture at every turn. Did you truly think we would fall all over ourselves to volunteer for that?"

Lhan snarled. "You see, Mistress Jae-En? This is why the church still stands. Because these dilletante demagogues see the great cause only as a diverting thing to discuss over wine and issae. They may talk blood and fire, but they have always been more interested in saving their own skin than risking it out in the wider world."

"As were you, if I recall," sneered Sei-Sien.

Lhan blushed at that, but didn't look away. "At least I had the decency to leave the society when I realized my cowardice. You aspire to lead it, and yet you will not—"

Old Shal-Hau stood at last. He didn't look like anybody's grandfather anymore. "There is none here without fault! We have all let our ease and comfort keep us from taking the steps that might win us what we talk of so fervently." He turned to Lhan. "Well no more. If the offer you make is real, if the Aldhanan wants our help against the church, if our voices might turn the tide, then I will gladly—"

"If." Sei-Sien spit it out like it was a cockroach he'd found in his salad. "If! We still have not one shred of proof that any of this is true. You line up for the slaughterhouse, Shal-Hau. I will not follow. Not without proof."

Lhan threw up his hands. "And what proof would suffice? Had the Aldhanan himself come to you, you would have said it was but another ruse. I—"

I'd had enough. "You know what, Lhan? Fuck these guys." I kneed past the coffee table, then stomped for the door. "Why would you want 'em anyways? Who would listen to 'em? They're all just a bunch of whining pussies. Let's get out of here."

I looked back and saw Lhan trying to hide a smile behind a snotty look as he started after me. "Yes, Mistress. An excellent idea. The Aldhanan has no need of limp weeds such as these. There are other heretics in Ormolu, younger, more stout-hearted fellows—the Third Moon, the Rain Makers, the Voice of Dead. We will see what they say."

Well, I hadn't meant it as a trick. I'd really wanted to get out of there. Those guys were making me sick. But if Lhan thought it would work, fine.

We went into the entry hall and started pulling on our cloaks and masks, and I thought we weren't gonna get any takers after all, but then, just as we were reaching for the door, Shal-Hau came in.

"I will go with you, pupil. Perhaps Sei-Sien is correct, and you lie, but the chance to finally see an end to the church—I cannot turn away from it."

And once the boss said yes, pretty soon the rest of 'em trickled in and said they'd come too, even Gaer-Zhau, until it was just Sei-Sien standing all by himself in the living room, trying to look dignified, but shaking like a dog shitting a peach pit.

Finally he came too. "Very well, I will come. How could I bear to be free knowing all my fellows were in chains?"

I opened the door. "Whatever you gotta tell yourself, dude."

CHAPTER THIRTY

PREPARATIONS!

We slipped back into the palace the same way we'd slipped out, and one of the Aldhanan's servants led us up a lot of back stairs and passages until we ended up right where we'd started, in the Aldhanan's private suite, twiddling our thumbs in some kind of fancy waiting room with chairs all around.

Lhan gave Sei-Sien a smug smile. "Not the dungeons after all, eh, brother?"

Sei-Sien shrugged. "Not yet."

Finally, after a half-hour or so, the Aldhanan strode in with Sai, Wen-Jhai, Captain Anan, and two guys I didn't recognize. The first one was a big, beefy bastard with a hard jaw and harder eyes. He was dressed like a civilian, but had ex-military written all over him, mostly in scars. The other guy was the Don Knotts to his Andy Griffith, a goggle-eyed little goop who looked like he'd shit himself if you looked at him hard. I didn't want to look at him at all. He kept licking his lips. They were red from it. Made me kind of queasy.

The Aldhanan was something to look at too. He'd had an extreme makeover. His beard was gone, his hair was shorter and died black, and he was dressed in a navy uniform. He looked like a completely different person.

"Welcome, friends, I am very pleased to see you. Your help in this endeavor may be the saving of Ora." He rubbed his hands together like an excited gameshow host. "You have heard what we intend to do from Lhan-Lar and Mistess Jae-En? Good. Good. Now let me tell you how we will accomplish it. As you know, I mean to visit each of my Dhanans personally to enlist their support. This, of course, must be done in secret, or the church will move against us before we are ready. So I have asked the help of my old comrade Aur-Aun."

He motioned to the military guy, who gave us a tight-lipped nod.

"Aur-Aun was once my standard bearer in battle, as brave and fierce as a kiten, but is now a tax collector for my treasury. With the help of his assistant, Yal-Faen—" He indicated the nebbish with the red lips, who twitched at the mention of his name. "He twice yearly visits my Dhanans, and takes from them the tithes they have gathered from their people. Now, to protect his person and the tithes, Aur-Aun is accompanied by an armed retinue. I and my guards will become this retinue and travel with him, allowing us to make a complete tour of Ora without the church any wiser."

Lhan raised his hand. "Will you not be missed, my Aldhanan? Such a trip will take more than a moon. Surely the church will begin to wonder if you do not appear in public."

The Aldhanan looked at Sai and Wen-Jhai. "I will put it about that the wounds I took fighting in Durgallah have sickened me and sent me to my bed, and that my daughter and her consort will rule in my stead until I recover."

I had to bite the inside of my cheek at that. I mean, Sai and Wen-Jhai were good kids at heart, but they were about as qualified to run a country as I was. It was like giving the keys to Fort Knox to a couple of third graders and telling 'em to keep the bad guys out.

I could see that Lhan felt the same, but with Sai and Wen-Jhai standing right there, what could he say. He just bowed. "Very good, my Aldhanan."

But Shal-Hau had a question too.

"Forgive me, my Aldhanan, but do you think that in a ship full of sailors and marines there will not be one set of lips that will not slip? Your secret will be out in one stop."

The Aldhanan smiled. "That is why the secret will not leave this room. Even the captain of our ship will not know who I am. To all but you who hear me now, I will be nothing more than the captain of Aur-Aun's retinue. You will address me as Captain Zhiu, and you will dispense with all the formalities due an Aldhanan."

"It won't be enough."

At first I didn't know who'd spoken, but the Aldhanan turned to Aur-Aun. "You still fear I will be recognized?"

The tax man shook his head. "I know we spoke of this before, my Aldhanan, and I will of course obey your commands, but I must speak again."

Holy shit! I suddenly realized why I hadn't known who was talking. Aur-Aun was like a Schwartzenegger action figure. He could talk without unclenching his jaw or moving his lips.

"The church is too powerful, my Aldhanan, and too rich. Even the most loyal of your subjects might betray you if the church offered them unlimited amounts of water. Every Dhanan you take into your confidence adds to your risk of betrayal. Someone will speak, and ruin will follow. You must abandon this plan now."

The Aldhanan put a hand on Aur-Aun's shoulder. "I thank you for your concern, Aun, but it is precisely because the church inspires such fear that I must do this. And also, thanks to Dhan Lhan-Lar and Mistress Jae-En, we can offer water of our own."

He motioned to Anan, and the Captain lifted a satchel off his shoulder and opened it up. It was the water tokens! I shot a hard look at Lhan. So he'd donated our honeymoon money to the cause after all. Thanks a bunch, pal.

The tax collector's eyes bugged out when he saw all the orange glass, but then he shook his head. "It is indeed a fortune, my Aldhanan, but not even a sixtieth of what the church can put on the scales."

"We must still try. We must break their hold on us, or die."

Aur-Aun looked like a bullfrog who'd swallowed a football. He was fighting so hard to keep his opinions to himself that he was shaking, but at last he lowered his head. "Then I will die at your side, my Aldhanan. And gladly."

Wen-Jhai choked up a little at that, and looked at him with glistening eyes. Sai wasn't so impressed. He shot the guy a dirty look, then looked at the floor. Something going on there?

Shal-Hau broke the moment with a cough. "My apologies, Aldhanan. This is, I think, for the most part a wise and well thought-out plan, but might I ask how you expect the heretic leaders you wish us to meet with to believe we are fellow dissidents when we travel as companions of the Imperial tax collector?"

The Aldhanan smiled. "It is simple. You will tell them you travel under false pretenses, that the Imperial tax collector is unwittingly helping you spread the word."

Sei-Sien scowled. “But who else travels with the tax collector except his retinue? Will you disguise us as sailors? Some of us have not the correct physique.” He looked at me. “Nor gender.”

“Worry not. We have devised the perfect disguise.”

Oh hell. Not again. What the fuck was with Waarians and their fucking disguises. I couldn’t wait to see what they’d cooked up for me this time—robot? Sack of laundry? Dancing bear?

The Aldhanan grinned. “Mistress Jae-En shall be a priestess of Laef, while Lhan-Lar and two others will be her escorts.”

Sei-Sien had a coughing fit at this, and Shal-Hau and Gaer-Zhau burst out laughing. I shot them a hard look and turned to Lhan. He was as pink as a guy with purple skin can get. He couldn’t look me in the eye.

“What? What are y’all laughing about?”

The Aldhanan harrumphed. “If they find humor in it, Mistress, it is entirely their juvenile natures to blame, not your disguise. Laef is one of the Seven—the Goddess of Fertility, prayed to both by farmers hoping for bountiful crops, and couples hoping for children. More importantly for our purposes, her priestesses often travel with the Imperial tax collectors so that they might have their protection when they collect their own tithes from her outlying shrines. It will therefore be entirely natural for you to travel with us.”

I didn’t get it. It didn’t sound very funny to me, but when I slid a glance over at Shal-Hau, he was still tittering like a schoolgirl. Sei-Sien looked like he’d been kicked in the stomach. Lhan was still red in the face.

“Yeah, okay. So? Am I gonna have to do some kinda funny dance or pretend to be a wise woman or something? What’s the gag?”

The Aldhanan shrugged. “It is a baseless rumor, but priestesses of Laef, because of their connection with fertility, have a certain reputation among the unsophisticated. They believe them to be, how shall I put this....”

I put up a hand. “Don’t bother. I get it. You’re dressing me up as some kind of super hooker.”

The Aldhanan raised his eyebrow. “A-a what, Mistress?”

“A pro, a whore, a prostitute.”

He grimaced. “As I said, the rumors are baseless. The priestesses are highly respected women.”

Shal-Hau burst out laughing again. “They are also rumored to practice fertility rites with their escorts at every opportunity.”

Sei-Sien pounded his leg and stood up. “I—I refuse this disguise! I will not be thought of as the... plaything of some gargantuan love priestess! It is beneath my dignity!"

The Aldhanan shrugged. "Then you need not go. Besides Mistress Jae-En and Lhan-Lar, there is room on board for only two more. The rest of your society will stay behind and spread the word here in Ormolu. I would hope that you send your best orator, he who can stir hearts and minds to action, but you may decide that among yourselves."

"I will go, for one," said Shal-Hau, putting a hand to his chest. "I have done naught but sit and talk for too many years. Before I die, I wish for once to act. As to the other..."

He and the other heretics looked at Sei-Sien, who squirmed under their gaze like a three-year-old in church.

"What do you look at? Did I not say I would not go? I will rouse Ormolu, as someone must."

Gaer-Zhau laughed like a rusty gate. "Come, Sei-Sien. How many times have we heard you say that you wished to bring our message to the rest of Ora? The disparate cells of discontent must unite, you said. A rebellion against the church will not work, you said, unless all rise up as one."

"Yes, but—but this...."

"This is the most perfect opportunity you will ever be given." Shal-Hau patted Sei's arm. "You claim great skills as an orator, pupil. Here is your chance to test them. Here is your chance to shine."

Sei-Sien opened his mouth like he was going to whine some more, but then he stopped and his eyes went all dreamy and far away. "Yes. Yes. Shine."

It was like watching Dr. Evil as a teenager, suddenly having the idea that he could be a super villain. Holy crap, Shal-Hau had just created a monster and he didn't even know it. It made me realize why all revolutions end up being just as bad as the governments they replace. 'Cause guys like Sei-Sien are always at the head of them, and they like hearing the sound of their own voice way too much.

Lhan turned to the Aldhanan. "We have our four, my Aldhanan. We are ready."

"Excellent." The Aldhanan clapped his hands like a camp counselor getting everybody out of bed for calisthenics. "Now come. Don your disguises. Aur-Aun's ship is to sail within the hour."

CHAPTER THIRTY-ONE

SUSPICIONS!

Considering the luck I'd had with disguises on this stupid planet, I was afraid that dressing up like a priestess of Laef was gonna mean climbing into some kinda burlap gunny sack with a Darth Vader helmet stuck on my head. But no, once we split up and the Aldhanan's maids brought me to some kind of dressing room, they handed me something that actually looked half-human—and all female!

Of course, I still had to get painted up so I didn't stick out like the big pink freak that I am, but the Aldhanan had thought ahead, and the maids had already whipped up all the fixings they needed to turn me purple. So, after a half-hour getting sluiced and splashed and massaged, I was the color of a ninth-grader's fingernail polish from head to toe. Even my hair got the treatment—my white-trash red hidden under a coat of goth-chick black. After that came the priestess's duds, and I have to admit they looked better than anything else I'd worn so far on Waar. The bottom half was the usual loincloth bikini thing in a dark maroon, which the maid said was the Waarian color of love, and which draped all the way to the ground in the front and back. The matching top had long sleeves, but was cropped just under the boobs like those sari tops Indian gals wear, and laced up the front like a ren-faire bustier. It pushed everything up, together and out, which was kinda overkill in my case, but why not? At least nobody would remember my face.

Actually, they wouldn't anyway, 'cause I also wore a headdress and a flimsy pink veil, like a nun and a harem dancer all wrapped up in one—which I guess it what a priestess of Laef was supposed to be, right? The other thing I wore… well, let's just say I finally figured what to do with Lhan's balurrah. I tied it around my neck and wore it like a necklace, right in the cleavage where he was sure to look.

And he did. In fact everybody did. Well, Shal-Hau giggled, but everybody else absolutely unhinged their jaws as we all stepped out of our dressing rooms.

Lhan swallowed. "Y-you look… magnificent, Mistress."

I gave him a look. "Is that some kind of code word for large?"

"Not at all. You—you are the very image of Laef. You—" He saw it, right between my tits, and his face went lavender white. "Is that…?"

I gave him an innocent look. "Is that what?"

He flushed as maroon as he had been white a second before, then turned away. "Nothing, Mistress. Nothing."

Shal-Hau didn't seem to have noticed the exchange. He clapped his hands. "You will have men falling over themselves in the streets."

"Thanks, professor. But, uh, is that a good thing? I'm still six-one. Even with all this on, ain't people gonna recognize me as 'The Giantess' from all the wanted posters?"

Shal-Hau coughed. "It is possible, but priestesses of Laef are known for being… How shall I put this."

"Fat?"

"Er, strapping, I think, is the word I would have chosen. They are outsize women with outsize appetites. Your height may cause comment, but taken with the rest of your, er, attributes… I… I…."

Fortunately for him, the Aldhanan and Aur-Aun entered just then and said it was time to go, and Sai and Wen-Jhai came to wish us luck and say their goodbyes.

Wen-Jhai gave Lhan and I a hug and a kiss each. There were tears in her eyes. "Bring my father back safely."

Lhan bowed to her. "We will guard him with our lives."

Sai gave us a formal bow with crossed wrists. "And protect each other as well. You are both as dear to me as my own heart."

Lhan and I gave each other uncomfortable looks.

Lhan nodded. "But of course."

I gave him a little salute. "Sure, bro. And you guys take care of yourselves too. It might get rough here with your dad away."

Sai raised his chin. "We will be strong. We promise."

As they went to say goodbye to the Aldhanan and Aur-Aun, I saw Aur-Aun take Wen-Jhai's hand and kiss it, which Sai didn't seem to take well at all.

I leaned in to Lhan. "What's up between Wen-Jhai and old Iron-Jaw over there? Some kind of love triangle thing going on?"

Lhan smiled sadly. "Aur-Aun has been part of the Aldhanan's household for thirty years, and has known the Aldhanshai since her birth. I believe he has always loved her, and she him, though unfortunately, she loves him as an uncle, while he...."

"Yeah, got it. Though I guess Sai didn't get the message about the Uncle part."

Lhan shrugged. "Aur-Aun has known Sai since his birth as well—as Sai's father has always been at court—and seen him grown from child to... what he is now. He does not think Sai worthy of Wen-Jhai's hand."

I looked at Sai, with his long hair and slim hips, looking more like Wen-Jhai's sister than her husband. "Now that you mention it, I'm kinda surprised the Aldhanan did."

"He let Wen-Jhai follow her heart."

I smiled. "He's a good guy, the Aldhanan."

"Aye. An Oran gentleman of the finest sort."

***

An hour later at the Imperial Naval Base, Lhan, Shal-Hau, Sei-Sien and me walked up the gangplank of Aur-Aun's warship with the Aldhanan and Captain Anan and their men, just as the sun peeked over the mountains to the east, and a chilly morning wind flapped the guide sails on the balloon. We upped anchor soon after, and what a lift off! We seemed to rise up at the same speed as the sun, and got to see it spread its gold and pink and orange all over the roofs of the city below us. It looked like it was pouring honey over the world. Everything glinted and gleamed and looked as fake and pretty as something on TV. The only thing that ruined it was the Tower of Ormolu sticking up out of the middle of the city. Its gigantic shadow cut across all the golden goodness like a big black "Censored" bar across the good parts of a girly mag. Or maybe I was just biased.

When I finally turned around from watching the sun rise I saw that everybody on the deck was staring at me, just like they had in the Aldhanan's apartments. Being the big pink freak on a planet of shrimpy purple types, I was pretty used to lookee-loos by now, but this was a different kind of staring. Before it had been like, "What *is* that?" This was more like, "Who is *she*?"

That I wasn't used to. Even back home it took a special kind of man to find me attractive. Usually it was either big burly guys like Big Don who wanted a woman they wouldn't break in half, or it was little squirrelly guys with some kind of amazon fetish, who wanted me to crush their heads between my thighs or some other ick. Average, ordinary guys didn't usually give me the time of day. They either ignored me completely, or turned away and made gagging motions when they thought I wasn't looking. That's what I was used to.

These guys were looking at me like I was Christina Hendricks and Beyonce all rolled into one. It was a weird feeling. On one hand it felt pretty hot knowing that everybody on board wanted to fuck me. On the other hand it felt kinda terrifying. I felt like a rabbit at a wolf convention. It looked like they might tear me apart any second. And pretty girls got this all the time! Christ! How did they stand it? No wonder they all came off like such cold bitches.

I could hear Lhan growling beside me, like he was about to challenge the whole ship to a duel to defend my honor. I whispered to him out of the corner of my mouth.

"Do we all have a private cabin downstairs somewhere?"

It broke his attention. He took a breath. "I certainly hope so, Mistress. Or there will be dead sailors before our next port of call."

We started for the door to the cabins, but one of the staring guys broke from the pack and crossed to intercept. He was pretty nondescript—bland face, wispy hair, chin beard—and didn't look any older or wiser than the rest, but he had a fancier uniform so I guessed he was important.

"Priestess." He bowed and crossed his wrists to me. "I am Ku-Rho, your captain. We are honored to be allowed to carry you on your holy rounds. Please, if there is anything that I can do to make your time aboard more comfortable, do not hesitate to ask. And I and my officers would welcome your company at our table for dinner if you would deign to sit with us."

We'd already arranged it so that I wouldn't talk. One word out of me with my Dixie accent and the the gig was up. Lhan knew what to do.

"The Priestess Le-Cir has taken a vow of silence until the rains come once more and the land awakes. It is her personal supplication to Laef. She thanks you for your hospitality, but regrets that she must keep to her cabin and maintain her regimen of meditation."

"Meditating on your cock, most likely," said somebody in the background. "Lucky bastard."

The captain shot the speaker a vicious look and turned maroon around the ears. "Of course, Priestess. We understand completely. But as I say, if there is anything you need."

Lhan bowed for me. "You are most kind."

We stepped around the captain as he bowed again, and Sei-Sien and Shal-Hau followed us below decks. Our cabin was a four-bunk job, which meant that, even if Lhan and I had still been hooked up, we still couldn'ta hooked up, since the two Flames would've been hanging around cluttering up the place. I wanted to scream. Here I was the living embodiment of an honest-to-god love goddess, and I wasn't going to be getting any! Irony sucks.

Just as I was pulling off my headdress and veil a knock came on the door, and I scrambled to put 'em back on, but it was just the Aldhanan, popping his head in.

"All well?"

Shal-Hau laughed before Lhan could speak. He really was a merry old fucker. "Mistress Jae-En has enraptured the whole crew. I fear no trouble on that score."

I rolled my eyes. "Captain Ku was drooling on his gold braid."

The Aldhanan grinned. "I fancied it would pass thus. Excellent. Well, it should not appear we know each other, so I will take my leave. Good voyage to you. We will meet again just before Rivi to discuss plans, aye?"

"Aye, Aldhanan," said Lhan.

The Aldhanan scowled at him. "That is not my title."

"Er, forgive me, Captain Zhiu. Until Rivi."

It wasn't until he closed the door and Lhan, Sei-Sien, Shal-Hau and I all looked around at each other that it really hit me that I was going to be spending more than a Waarian month shut up in this cabin with these guys. And no TV or iTunes to distract me. Not even a magazine.

"So, any of you guys know Twenty Questions?"

***

It wasn't as bad as I thought it would be. It was worse! All day every day in a room the size of a walk-in closet with a pompous ass and an old man who giggled and hummed to himself twenty-four hours a day, even in his sleep! And the whole time Lhan's just sitting there all delicious and untouchable on the opposite bunk? It was torture. And I don't even want to go into how much I learned about the personal grooming habits—or lack thereof—of middle-aged professor types on Waar. Actually, you know what? I won't. I'd rather forget that part anyway.

What made it even more fantastic was the fact that Lhan and Sei-Sien kept sniping at each other. They may have teamed up to fight the church and take the message to the people, but they did not like each other—at all.

One morning we were all sitting around in the room, eating our breakfast mush and trying to come up with a plan B in case it all went wrong, and Lhan was saying we could lay low at his father's estate if we were caught in Rivi or Lamgan, which were the first two stops on the tax tour.

"He may be a villain in many things, but he would never betray his family or friends to the church. He—"

Sei-Sien cut in. "Unlike his son."

Lhan looked down into his bowl of slop. "Thank you, Sei-Sien, for bringing my cowardice up once again. Master Shal-Hau and Mistress Jae-En no doubt find the stating of it just as edifying and illuminating this thirtieth time as they did the first."

Sei-Sien sneered. "Sarcasm, Lhan? Do you then suggest I should say something new this time? Perhaps tell your Mistress Jae-En the facts of your cowardice? Would that be more illuminating?"

Shal-Hau looked up. "Enough, Sei. Enough."

I was ready to smash Sei in the distinguished profile, but before I could do anything rash, Lhan put down his bowl.

"No, Master, Sei-Sien is right. Out of shame I have kept from Mistress Jae-En the most shameful episode of my life, and I would not have our friendship built on any false perceptions she might have of me. It is time I told the truth of it." He raised his eyes to Elf-Cheeks. "And I am sure Sei-Sien will be kind enough to correct me if I leave out any details."

Sei bowed from his seat. "It would be my pleasure."

I sighed. "Come on, Lhan. You don't have to do this."

"No, Mistress. I must. Indeed, I have left it too long."

"And you leave it longer every second." Sei waved a hand. "Begin!"

Lhan swallowed, then nodded and looked up at me. "It was when I was with the Flame of Truth. I—I allowed a fellow Flame named Bedu-Bas to be arrested. I might have saved him, but was afraid, and did nothing. He died."

"Aw, Lhan."

"We had found a man willing to sell us a rare, forbidden volume of church history, and so went to buy it, wearing masks to hide our identities. There was no book. It was a trap, set by the priests. We escaped, but Bedu-Bas was wounded, and we hid within a nearby sword school, splitting up and disguising ourselves as students."

Sei-Sien raised his voice. "Now tell her what you did when the priests entered and noticed Bedu's blood seeping through his fencing jacket."

Lhan hung his head. "Nothing. I did nothing. I might have attacked the priests and freed him. I wore a sparring mask, so they would not have seen my face, but… but I was known at that school, and feared the masters would recognize me, and so, though the priests beat Bedu-Bas and asked him where I was, I—I only stood and watched, even when they dragged him away."

Sei-Sien folded his arms. "If we had only had Lhan-Lar's courage to rely on, we would have all been exposed, but Bedu-Bas showed true bravery, and, rather than betray us under torture, he threw himself under a cart as the priests led him through the streets. *He* did not let his friends die to save himself."

I stared. "He killed himself?"

Lhan covered his face in his hands. "As I should have done. You see now, Mistress? I will never forgive myself for my cowardice."

Sei-Sien was giving me a smug look, like he was expecting me to join him in the "Let's all hate Lhan" club. It just made me want to punch him in the face even more. I turned to Lhan.

"You think I'm any better? I've done shit that eats at me every day. I killed a man for touching me. If you think this is gonna make me change my mind about you, you got another think coming. I don't care, Lhan. I—"

"You should care!" Lhan jolted up and stepped to the door. "I am without honor! If you had any of your own, that would matter to you!"

And with that, he slammed out of the cabin and left me staring at the door, feeling like the gal who didn't know it was loaded. I had to check my fingers to make sure he hadn't bitten any off.

Sei gave an "I told you so" look, but Shal-Hau patted my knee.

"I hope you can forgive him. He is a good man at heart."

"I do forgive him! I want *him* to forgive him!"

Shal-Hau pursed his lips. "You may wait a long while for that, I'm afraid. Regret is a very large rock. Lhan has been pinned under it for many years."

Sei-Sien snorted. "If only it had crushed him."

I jumped up and pulled back a fist, and he curled up like a pill bug, arms up in front of his face.

"No! Please!"

I just sneered at him. "Now who's the coward, asshole?"

I shoved out of the room and headed up to the deck, looking for Lhan.

***

I found him leaning on the rail, and looking like he was thinking of throwing himself over it. I leaned next to him.

"Lhan, listen. I—"

"You forget yourself, Priestess. Have you not taken a vow of silence?"

I looked around at the crew. They were all looking at me like they always did when I came out on deck, but I was wearing my veil, and they were all far away, so…

"Yeah, but I never took a vow of not throwing you over the side."

That at least got him smiling. "Then do it, and free me from my misery."

"Come on, Lhan. All I was trying to say down there was nobody's perfect. You're not perfect. I'm not perfect. Not even the Aldhanan's perfect. That's why you gotta give everybody a break—even yourself."

He shook his head. "But without honor—"

"Hey, I'm not saying honor isn't a good thing to shoot for. It is. But if you think you gotta be perfect to be loved, or—ha!—you think I gotta be perfect to be your lover, well, you're gonna be lonely a long damn time."

Lhan looked over the side again, chewing his lip. "It is a lovely sentiment, Mistress, but… but I must think."

"Take your time."

I leaned back on the rail and looked around, just happy to be out in the fresh air instead of our stuffy little cabin, but then I saw something that made me cock my head. There were some barrels under a little awning behind the cookhouse, which was up at the front of the ship near where we were leaning, and as I glanced past them I saw a balding head bob up behind them, then disappear again. At first I thought it was somebody cleaning up a spill, but then the head came up again and I saw it was the bean counter, Yal-Faen.

His head disappeared behind the barrels again, then came up again a second later. Was he looking for a contact? Was he shooting craps? Then I noticed that he kept crossing his wrists in front of his mopey, red-lipped face and whispering to himself.

I nudged Lhan. "Ain't that Aur-Aun's bookkeeper?"

He looked around, then frowned. "So it is."

"What the hell is he doing?"

"It appears he is praying, Mistress."

"Oh. Uh, to the Seven?"

"I would presume so."

"So, should we be worried?"

"Worried?"

"Well, we're kinda fighting the Seven right now, right? So isn't it a little weird for one of our gang to be praying to them?"

He shrugged. "I think you will find the Aldhanan and his men still worship the Seven. They do not see this as a war against the gods, only the church, which they believe has corrupted the original teaching of the Seven."

"Okay. So why is he praying behind those barrels? I mean if you wanted to pray in private, wouldn't you pray in your cabin?"

"But he shares a cabin with Aur-Aun. He—" Lhan stopped, blinking. "Oh."

"Yeah. Oh. Maybe he's praying for something he doesn't want Aur-Aun to know about."

Lhan nodded. "You make an excellent point, Mistress. I shall warn the Aldhanan."

"Good plan. Meanwhile, I'm gonna watch that little dish-rag like a hawk."

"Aye, Mistress. I as well. Er, what is a hawk?"

CHAPTER THIRTY-TWO

RIOT!

After my fourth day in the stateroom from hell, I finally heard the magic words I'd been waiting for. Up on the deck Captain Ku-Rho was calling for gas to be let out of the bag, and for the crew to pull in the sails and clear the deck for landing.

Thank god!

It was after dark when we went up on deck to wait for touch down, but both moons were up and full so I got a good look at Rivi as we came down over it, all picturesque with its rooftops frosted in the moonlight. It was built in a little bowl of a valley, with the market square and the temples down in the middle, and all these little round-topped houses climbing up the sides of the surrounding hills like six-sided bee-hives. At the top of the highest hill was a sturdy little hexagonal castle with sandy walls, a couple of fat towers sticking up, and dome roofs on all the structures inside. That's where we were heading.

It was all so pretty from up there it should have been a travel poster, but while we'd all been cooped up in our stateroom, Master Shal-Hau had told us—in way too much detail—that the place was hurting bad. It was an agricultural town. All the hillsides that didn't have houses on them had been cut into steps like rice paddies, and they grew a kind of vegetable called an

Uehl Bean. At least they did when there was any rain, but over the past few years the rains had been coming less and less often, and the farmers had had to buy water from the Temple, which had cut their profits down to nothing. Half the step-farms on the hills had gone out of business in the last two years and were just sitting there dry. The town was becoming a ghost town, and also, Sei-Sien said, a hotbed for anti-church heretics, who held their secret meetings—according to his sources—in the back room of the farmer's guild hall. He was all excited to have a enthusiastic audience. I was just excited to be out of the funk of unwashed heretic and old-man farts I'd been living in. I wanted to breathe and stretch my legs.

We came down onto a leveled off landing area right outside the castle gate, while a ground crew with lanterns waved us down to the mooring rings.

I looked over at the Aldhanan, who was standing at attention behind Aur-Aun like the guard captain he was supposed to be, the satchel full of water tokens slung over one shoulder.

I gave him a nod. He returned it.

Then the landing crew caught our lines, threaded 'em through the rings and winched us down. It was showtime. The sailors trundled out the gang-plank, then stood aside as we all walked down to meet the welcoming party that was marching out of the castle gate—a bunch of guards and nobles with a big, grizzled guy up front. He had long hair and scars, and he was barking at us before we got halfway to him.

"Back again, Aur-Aun? Was it not only yesterday you cut my heart out and called it six percent? This time it'll have to be my head, for there's no other way I'll let you take what I don't have."

Aur-Aun gave him a quarter-inch smile. "The same complaint, Gura? And yet you always pay in the end."

"Aye. It is my end that pays, that is certain." He crossed his wrists and bowed to Aur-Aun, then clapped him on the shoulder. "It is bad, though, brother. This year worse than ever."

Up close he looked like half a dozen old bikers I've known in my time—weathered face, easy-going eyes, drinker's nose, hard arms and a beer gut. Except for the purple skin he woulda fit in at any road house in America. He turned back toward the castle and motioned for us to follow.

"Come in. Come in. I can at least give you a drink to wash away the disappointment my coffers will—"

"Gura-Nan."

"Eh?" The Dhanan turned, and frowned around. "Who spoke?"

The Aldhanan pulled back the hood of his cloak a little, and smiled at him. "Do not speak my name."

Gura sputtered like he'd swallowed his tongue. "My—my..."

"I am but a captain, friend. And a thirsty one. You mentioned wine?"

Gura reeled in his eyes, which had been bugging out like a Boston terrier's, then laughed. "Aye, Captain. Wine. And stories, I've no doubt. Come then. *I* need a drink now, that's certain."

As Aur-Aun and his men followed the Dhanan into the castle, the Aldhanan looked back at us and bowed.

"Best of luck with your tithe gathering, Priestess."

"Likewise, Captain."

Little red-lipped Yal-Faen took a last leery look back at us as he scurried after his boss, then vanished into the castle with the rest of 'em.

"He's gonna try something, I know it."

"He will be in the presence of the Aldhanan and Aur-Aun, Mistress. And they have been warned to watch him. What can he do?"

"I don't know. But I wish I was gonna be around to stop him doing it."

***

Rivi was as bad as Sei-Sien had painted it. Worse, actually. I'd seen towns like this back home—Carolina textile towns that had dried up into bitter little husks when all the jobs moved overseas, dust bowl cow towns after drought had wiped out the local ranches. The farmers were still here, too stuck in their ways to move on, but they were like zombies, wandering around like they were in town on business just like the old days, except all the stores were closed down, and they had nothing to sell at the exchanges. The only places open were the bars.

As we got closer to the center of town I started to see them on every corner, ratty little places with leathery red-necks—maroon-necks?—sitting outside or standing in the doorways, all with the thousand-yard stares of men who were putting as much hard work into their drinking as they used to put into their farms. The bars were as quiet as funeral homes. No laughter. No singing. Just, every now and then, the occasional shout and smash of a fight, but even those sounded tired.

This, it turned out, was a bad place to be a priestess of Laef. Well, it was a bad place to be a *fake* priestess of Laef. A real one woulda cleaned up.

It started as we were passing the third bar. One of those poor dead-eyed bastards looked up and stared after me as we walked by, then he nudged his buddy. A second later they were standing up and calling after me.

"Priestess! Come back!"

"A blessing. Please! For a farmer down on his luck."

We kept walking, but now everybody was standing, and more were coming out of the bars and crowding the porches. A guy got in front of us and crossed his wrists to me.

"I beg you, Priestess. We have not seen rain this season."

"Nor the last," said another guy.

A woman caught my arm. "I have nothing to feed my children. If you could grant us only enough to live on."

They were all around me now, pulling on me, holding their hands out to me, looking at me like I was their last hope. I couldn't deal with it. I started to sweat.

"I—I'm not— I can't—"

Lhan and Shal-Hau spread their arms, trying to shield me. Sei-Sien, the dumb-ass, started shoving guys away.

"Back, layabouts! Let us through! We are on important business!"

Lhan pulled him back, but it was too late. In a split second the crowd went from pleading to pissed. They started surging around, grabbing and pushing and shouting. I was starting to wish I had my sword, but it was back on the ship. Didn't go with the costume.

"What is more important than saving our lives!"

"Stuck up bitch!"

"Too busy fucking your escorts to help honest farmers?"

"Why don't you give *us* a fuck?"

"Won't make up for dead beans, but at least we'll get laid."

Shal-Hau was covering his head and Lhan was doing his best to protect me, but Sei-Sien was swatting and shouting at them, and I could feel a rage coming on too. I tried to hold it down. I didn't want to hurt these people. They had a right to be pissed. But if one more of 'em grabbed for my tits…

"Goddamn it, I can't help you! I'm not—"

Lhan cut me off with a shove, then stepped in front of me and raised his arms. "Friends! Friends, listen! We are here to help, I promise you! Please! Listen!"

The crowd quieted down and waited, like a ring of wolves.

I gave Lhan a sidelong glance. "Hope you know what you're doing, bro."

"As do I." He spread his hands. "Friends, forgive us. Priestess Le-Cir cannot bless you individually, but we go now to the farmer's guild hall where she will bless all of Rivi and its residents collectively."

I practically did a spit take. I hissed in his ear. "What are you doing? You said I wouldn't have to do any of that—"

He ignored me. "Please, friends! Follow us now to the guild hall and you will all receive Laef's blessing!"

The crowd cheered and started down the street, pulling us along with them like we were driftwood on a river. Shal-Hau and Sei-Sien were giving Lhan looks just as dirty as I was.

"You call me fool?" Sei hissed. "At least out here we might have run. In the guild hall we will be trapped."

Shal-Hau nodded. "Truly, Lhan. I see no good outcome here."

I motioned around at the crowd. "Whaddaya expect me to do for these guys? Tell jokes?"

Lhan grimaced and gave me an uneasy look. "Er, well, the traditional blessing is given in the form of a seductive dance, I don't suppose...?"

"No fucking way, Lhan. Not without a bottle of Jim Beam first, and even then, unless you think the Texas Two Step is seductive, I'm fresh out. I ain't never been a stripper."

They all looked at me like I'd started talking Swahili.

"Right. Sorry. Short answer. No. I don't dance."

Shal-Hau cleared his throat. "There is another traditional ceremony, but it, er, involves a partner."

I didn't know what he meant until I saw Lhan go from lavender to mauve.

CHAPTER THIRTY-THREE

CEREMONY!

I turned on Shal-Hau, ready to slap the shit out of him, even if he was an old man. "Are you out of your mind? You think I'm going to say yes to live sex on stage when I said no to the hoochie-koo? No way!"

"Indeed," said Lhan. "I refuse to share so intimate an act before a crowd. Besides, we are not—"

Sei-Sien clutched his arm, angry. "You must do something! If you reneg on your promise they will tear us apart!"

"And whose fault is that? It was you who angered them in the first place!"

Shal-Hau separated them. "Easy, friends. We are here."

I looked up. We were being carried up the steps of a big hexagonal building with a decorative band of curly-cue vines and stylized fruits and veggies running around the top just under the eaves. A statue of a chick who looked a hell of a lot like me in my current get-up stood out front on a pedestal, holding a basket of fruit on her hip and a wine bottle in her other hand. Shal-Hau had been right, Laef was a strapping gal.

A trio of older guys in robes that had the same curly-cues and vegetables on their collars and cuffs stood at the top of the steps looking down at everybody with confused frowns on their faces.

The guy in the middle stepped forward. Even in his robes of office, he still looked like a farmer—a sun-blasted face and big, hard hands. "What is this?"

One of the crowd bowed to him. "Guild-master, a priestess of Laef comes to bless us. She invited us to the hall."

The guild master looked at us, eyebrow raised. "And to what do we owe this unexpected honor?"

Lhan was going to say something, but Sei-Sien stepped ahead of him and made a funny sign with his left hand while hiding it from the crowd. It was like he was giving the guild-master the finger, except he was using the ring finger instead of the middle finger.

"I can explain everything, brother."

The guild-master looked from Sei-Sien to his finger to me, and then the crowd. Then shrugged and bowed.

"Welcome then, Priestess. We'll not say nay to what we so badly need. Please, enter."

Him and his pals turned and led us into the guild hall, which was a high-ceilinged room that was half the hexagon, with a big stage on the dividing wall and wedges of church pews angling in toward the center.

As we walked down the aisle the crowd filled into the pews and Sei-Sien whispered to the guild master.

"We did not intend this, brother. We meant to come in secret, on matters pertaining to the church."

The guild-master laughed. "You have failed at secrecy, brother, but this makes a good cover. We will speak after your priestess gives her blessing."

I coughed. "Yeah. About that."

But we were already going up the steps to the stage, and the guild-master was turning to the crowd and raising his hands.

"Guild-brothers! Friends! Silence please! We are fortunate to be visited by a most beauteous, bountiful priestess of Laef, who has graciously agreed to bless us and our beleaguered fields. Please join me in prayer as she petitions the goddess on our behalf."

The room went quiet and everybody looked at me as the guild-master backed off. My heart was hammering in my chest. What the fuck was I going to do? I looked over at Lhan. He looked back, licking his lips. There was a gleam in his eye and a bulge in his loincloth that even the people in the cheap seats musta been able to see.

I rolled my eyes and whispered out of the side of my mouth. "Lhan. Are you kidding?"

"I—I am sorry, Mistress. I know it is wrong. I know we have parted, but for some reason...."

I flushed. The thought of him being turned on by this was turning me on too, and I looked around. There was a kind of altar table on the stage. It looked a little small for getting down on, but...

But I couldn't. Even turned on, I couldn't. I know people think all biker chicks are crazy-ass free-love extrovert sluts who will show their tits at the drop of a hat and don't think twice about having sex on a pool table in front of a whole bar, and sure, some of them are. But that ain't me. Sure I sleep around, and I've been with girls and guys and couples too once or twice, but wild as I am, that stuff is private for me. I ain't interested in putting on a show for anybody, so, as much as I wanted to pull Lhan's loincloth off and go to town, I wasn't gonna do it here.

Which was a problem, because I had a hundred people waiting for me to do something, and we weren't going to be able to talk to Sei-Sien's heretic pals unless I did. Hell, we probably wouldn't be walking out of here alive unless I did. To buy time, I put my hands together like I was praying, then turned away like I was building up to something.

Lhan raised an eyebrow. "Have you thought of something, Mistress?"

"Sorry, I'm fresh outta— No, wait!" I had it. Thinking about the heretics had given me the way. "Okay, listen. You're going to announce that I'm taking a few lucky winners to the back for a ceremonial gang bang. I'll point 'em out to you, okay?"

He looked horrified. "Mistress!"

"I'm not really going to do it, Lhan. It's a trick."

I turned and beckoned to the guild-master, trying to be as grand and priestessy with my movements as I could.

"Here. Come to me."

He looked behind him, like he thought I was pointing to someone else. Then realized I meant him, and he swallowed.

"Not me, priestess. I—"

"Not for that, you idiot!" I whispered. "Come here!"

He shuffled out like a kid in a school play and I spoke out of the side of my mouth. "Stand beside me and tell me who the heretics in the crowd are. I'm going to point 'em out and bring them in the back."

He his eyes bulged for a second, then he smiled. "Ah, I understand. Very well."

I turned back toward the crowd and raised my arms. "Now, Lhan."

Lhan stepped forward, smiling nervously. "Friends, the Priestess has determined that woes of Rivi are too deep, too grievous, to be banished by a simple blessing. To heal your wounded town and bring her fields back to their proper fruiting glory, she must perform her most private and intense rituals. For these rituals to work, she must perform them with those who tend this land, and suffer from its privations."

A gasp went up from the guys in the crowd and about half of them started to stand. Lhan waved them down.

"Stay in your seats! Please. The priestess will chose those she will commune with."

"Okay, guild-master. Tell me."

And so for the next five minutes, the guild-master stood at my side and whispered in my ear. "Front row, left. Red hat. Long hair. Third row, center. Bald. Heavy. Fifth row, right. Skinny. Crest of hair. Missing left hand." And I turned and pointed to them one after the other like I was in a trance. I felt like some stage magician, pulling people out a crowd for a trick—like I was going to make them all bark like dogs or dance the funky-chicken or something.

The first couple guys looked like they didn't want to play along—like maybe they had wives or girlfriends—but then, once the third guy I called up was also a heretic, they started to catch on, and the rest of them all came up smiling. Finally, when I had eleven guys up on stage, the guild-master told me that was all she wrote. I sent Lhan out again and he told the crowd to go home and pray that our ceremonies would be a success, and that we would now retire to the back to begin.

The crowd seemed a little bummed at this—*ahem*—"anti-climax," but they shuffled out of the hall without saying anything, and me, Lhan, Sei-Sien and Shal-Hau went into the back with the heretics. They us led down a couple hallways and into an office, then closed the door behind us, drew their knives from their belts, and put them to our necks.

CHAPTER THIRTY-FOUR

BETRAYED!

"Now then," said the guild-master, stepping up in front of me. "Who are you, truly?"

I swallowed, and the blade of the guy behind me pressed into my jugular. I decided I wouldn't swallow again.

Shal-Hau goggled. Sei-Sien looked like he was gonna faint.

Lhan coughed. "I—I know not what you mean. We are heretics like yourselves."

"Are you?"

Sei-Sien looked indignant. "Did we not make the secret sign?"

The guild-master folded his arms. "Aye, you did, but you also arrived in Rivi aboard a navy warship, in the company of the Aldhanan's tax collector. Not the sort of company a heretic usually keeps."

Well, we'd already had this argument, and we had the answer down pat.

Shal-Hau gave it. "True. But what better a ruse than that of a priestess of Laef to visit our brothers all over Ora."

The guild-master nodded. "Just the sort of ruse a spy would concoct, to root out heretics. We feared something like this was coming."

"Something like what?" asked Lhan.

The guild-master turned on him. "Word came to us a day ago. The entire Ormolu cell had been rounded up and put to the question by the Aldhanan. Now here you are from Ormolu, saying you wish to speak to us on matters pertaining to the church? Ha! Subtler spies would have waited a crossing or two before coming to us."

"But we are the Ormolu cell!" Sei-Sien pointed to himself. "I am Sei-Sien, noted pamphleteer and heretic philosopher. That is Shal-Hau, leader of our brotherhood. That is Lhan-Lhar of Herva and that is the outland giantess Mistress Jae-En, both wanted by—"

The guild-master snorted. "You betray yourselves out of your own mouths. Lhan-Lar and the giantess were killed by the Aldhanan in the City of Black Glass when he rescued his daughter. That too we heard. Besides, the giantess is an albino—a pink-skinned freak."

Lhan laughed. "Do you think we would come to you undisguised when all Ora thinks us dead? Her skin is dyed."

The guy who had his knife to my throat wet the finger of his off hand and rubbed it across my arm. Nothing happened except that he let his knife stray outta position a little bit. I sighed.

"It's gonna take more than that, doofus, but I got proof if you want it."

The guild-master raised his eyebrow. "What proof?"

"If you heard of me, maybe you also heard I can lift a man over my head with one hand and jump as high as two men?"

The guild-master laughed. "And you say you can do that?"

"I don't say it. I—"

I elbowed the knife guy in the face, then threw him across my shoulder and jumped up to the sill of a grilled window that was built high up in the outside wall. I caught a crossbar and held on, then took doofus off my shoulder and pressed him up over my head with my free hand as he shrieked and struggled.

"Stop squirming, asshole, or I'm gonna drop you."

He stopped, whimpering, and I looked down at the guild guys. They were all staring up at me with their jaws on the floor.

"It is her."

The guild-master stepped forward. "Mistress, forgive us. I believe you now, but… please come down. You are scaring poor Ghin to death."

I lowered Ghin back to my shoulder, then jumped down and set him in a chair. He was hyperventilating. The rest of them took their knives from my pals' throats, but they didn't look any more welcoming. The guild-master was looking at us like we had the plague.

"You have proved yourself enemies of the church, but I cannot see how we might count you as friends."

Shal-Hau turned to him. "Why might that be?"

The guild-master threw out his hand toward me and Lhan. "They kidnapped the Aldhanan's daughter and her consort! How did that help the cause? You have turned the whole empire against us!"

Lhan held up his hand. "We did not kidnap the Aldhanan's daughter and her consort. It was the church."

There was a big gasp at that. Sei-Sien shouted over it.

"Aye brothers. A ruse to blacken our names! And it would have been worse had not the noble Lhan-Lar and his stalwart companion Mistress Jae-En not saved the day, for their target was the Aldhanan himself!"

Lhan and I exchanged a look as the guild members goggled and shouted questions. The noble Lhan-Lar and his stalwart companion Mistress Jae-En? Since when had Sei-Sien become our best bud? Anything for the cause, I guess.

Sei-Sien was going like a TV evangelist now. "Yes, friends. The church meant to assassinate the Aldhanan and pin the blame on us! A two-fold strike that would silence their most outspoken critics and rid the Empire of a leader who thought too much for himself. That is why we are here! The church has at last taken a step too far, and we must strike while they are weak and exposed!"

He had 'em in the palm of his hand now. The crisis was over. I let out a breath and leaned against the wall, glad to not have a knife to my throat anymore. Lhan leaned beside me and whispered in my ear.

"I thank you, Mistress. Once again, you prove that actions speak louder than words."

And so did his loincloth. He was still sporting wood, and it was speaking to me loud and clear. I looked over at our pals and the guild guys, who were all gabbing at each other now a mile a minute, then back at the door that led to the main hall.

I gave Lhan a dirty smile. "You know, I'd hate to cheat these people."

Lhan raised an eyebrow. "Cheat them? What do you mean?"

I leaned in so our shoulders touched and let my lips brush his ear. "Well, we did promise them that the priestess of Laef would perform a ceremony of blessing for them, didn't we? What did you call it? A private and intense ritual? The altar table is just behind that door. . . ."

Lhan's eyes widened. He went beet red. He groaned. "Mistress, do not take advantage of my weakness. We are companions now, nothing more. I cannot... I cannot...."

"It sure looks like you could."

"But it would not be right. It would make a mockery of my vow as a Dhan, and—"

You know, if I'd touched him then, I bet he woulda melted, and we woulda been riding that table like a mechanical bull in under a minute, and I was damn tempted, but I knew what would happen after. Lhan would be mad at himself for breaking his vow and mad at me for tempting him, and things would be all awkward and ugly, so...

"Okay, okay, forget it. Never mind."

Most grown-up thing I've ever done.

***

When we got back to the Dhanan's castle, the sailors were carrying iron-bound chests full of tax money out to the landing field and the Aldhanan was all smiles. Even Aur-Aun looked happy—well, less grim anyway.

"Gura-Nan has signed on with a will," said the Aldhanan as we stood off to one side and watched the cash boxes being weighed on a big scale. "He has pledged troops and money to the cause, and awaits only our command."

"Well done, Ald— er, Captain." Lhan motioned down the hill toward Rivi. "And we have had success too. The heretics have agreed to spread the word and have given us their blessing."

"Excellent. And Mistress Jae-En's impersonation of a priestess of Laef? That went well?"

Lhan looked at his boots. "Er, very well indeed. Yes."

I gave him a sideways look. "I only wish I could have done more."

Lhan blushed, but the Aldhanan didn't seem to notice. He just patted us on the backs, then stepped back as the sailors carried the first chest up the gangplank and the next one was heaved up onto the scale.

As I turned to watch, I suddenly found myself eye-locked with Yal-Faen. He was standing by the scale, ledger and pen at the ready, but he wasn't watching his assistants weigh the chests like he was supposed to be. He was watching us. At least he was until he we caught each others' eyes, then he turned away.

I leaned into the Aldhanan. "And what about Yal-Faen, er, Captain. Did you keep an eye on him?"

The Aldhanan nodded, his face hard. "Aye. And when I withdrew to talk to Gura-Nan, Aur-Aun instructed his men to watch him. He never spoke to anyone."

"Good. That little weasel worries me."

"Fear not, Mistress Jae-En. Thanks to your observant eye, he will never be left alone. I promise you."

A few minutes later, all the gold was packed in the hold and we were off again. Which meant I was crammed back into the little closet again with Lhan, Shal-Hau and Sei-Sien.

It was worse than ever. That old thing about always wanting what you can't have was in full effect, and Lhan and I lay on our bunks, trying to pretend we weren't noticing each other, but both completely aware of every move the other one was making. Every twist of his torso, every stretch of his arms or legs, had me thinking bad thoughts, and I was squirming around like I had ants in my pants. Which was making him squirm too. I'm surprised our loincloths didn't catch fire.

***

The next town we dropped anchor in was called Lamgan, and everything there went down pretty much the same way as Rivi had, only with less craziness. Aur-Aun got his taxes, the Aldhanan got the local Dhanan to sign on the dotted line, Yal-Faen never slipped his leash, and me and my escort learned from our past mistakes and managed to recruit the local heretics without causing a riot or having anybody pull a knife on us. It all went as smooth as glass, and had us thinking that the rest of the trip would be a breeze.

Yeah. Not so much.

The town after Lamgan was called Modgalu, and I got a bad feeling about it even before we landed. First off, there was a temple there—another gigantic white rocketship skyscraper sticking up out of the middle of it just like back in Ormolu, only a little bit shorter and fatter—a pudgy little prick instead a John Holmes hammer. Second, the place reeked. It was a cattle town, a river port at the edge of an endless prairie where all the ranchers brought their meat on the hoof to be shipped off to markets downstream. Even from a thousand feet up I could smell the shit and piss-mud of the maku pens, and the blood and death of the slaughterhouses. It wafted up to us in a red-brown smog that almost hid the sand-colored houses and yellow brick buildings. Third, Yal-Faen went all quiet the minute the place appeared on the horizon—like he knew something we didn't. I didn't like it. As much as I hated his suspicious glances and nervous praying, having it all stop was worse. It was like that moment when the fuse on the firecracker you've lit seems to go out and you don't know if you should go look to see if it needs to be lit again, or if you should stay back in case it's gonna blow up in your face.

So, when we tied off on the dusty private shipfield between the Dhanan's yellow brick castle and the yellow brick arena beside it I wasn't exactly surprised to see a ring of crossbowmen all around the field and the Dhanan waiting for us at the bottom of the gangplank with a dozen armed guards.

At Aur-Aun's back, the Aldhanan coughed. "Does he always welcome you in this way?"

Aur-Aun shook his head, then called down to the welcoming party. "Dhanan Paar-Il! Greetings! Is all well?"

Paar-Il, who was a stooped, stringy sad-sack with a bald head and a fu-manchu mustache, shielded his eyes against the sun and peered up at us. "Aur-Aun, is that you?"

"Aye, Dhanan. Is… Is something amiss?"

Paar-Il hesitated, then had a little conference with his guard captain. The captain was shaking his head no, and pointing back toward the castle, but finally Paar-Il blew him off and stomped up the gangplank alone, then stopped in front of us, puffing. He didn't look any better up close. His skin was as parched as his town, all crusty and dead looking, and his mustache looked like dry string. The only thing wet about him were his eyes, which were red and runny and sad.

Aur-Aun bowed. "Welcome, Dhanan. I—"

But Paar-Il wasn't looking at him. He was scanning over his shoulders, then looked right at the Aldhanan. He crossed his wrists.

"Aldhanan, I was told of your coming. I was told you had gone against the church and that I was to arrest you as soon as you arrived."

CHAPTER THIRTY-FIVE

LOCKDOWN!

Everybody dropped their hands to their weapons. Sei-Sien whimpered like a whipped dog. Captain Anan motioned his men to move the sailors on the deck out of earshot, and I was once again wishing my sword was on my back where it should have been, instead of down in our cabin being useless.

When the sailors were all backed up, the Aldhanan looked Paar-Il square in the eye. "And do you intend to obey this order?"

"Would I have come to you alone were that my intent? No, my Aldhanan. We have had our differences in the past, but I would not obey such an order. And I killed the man who gave it me. You are my leader, not those orange-robed thieves."

The Aldhanan let out a breath. "Relieved I am to hear it, Paar-Il, and I thank you for your loyalty. But I could have wished that you had not killed this man. I would have given much to speak to him."

Paar-Il waved that away. "He had little to say, even under the knife. All I could get out of him was that he was a fervent follower of the church, and that another such had approached him in Rivi and given him water tokens to warn me of your supposed treason."

"Rivi?" The Aldhanan hung his head. "We have been betrayed from the beginning."

Shal-Hau sighed. Sei-Sien groaned.

"I knew there would be traitors. I knew it."

Aur-Aun opened his jaw a sixteenth of an inch. "Did he describe the man who paid him?"

"Only that he was cloaked and masked. Nothing more."

Everybody suddenly looked at each other like they were wondering what they'd look like behind a ninja hood. Yal-Faen wasn't calm anymore. He was shaking in his sandals.

The Aldhanan glanced around the ship, then turned back to Paar-Il. "We should speak of this in private."

Paar-Il looked uneasily toward the castle. There was an awful lot of hustle and bustle going on around it and the arena beside it—a lot of armored men going in and out, a lot of wagons and coaches and people herding animals around, a lot of crowds.

"You have picked an awkward time to visit. My dhans have come in from the prairies to pay their tithes and trade livestock—our annual spring gathering. My house is full. There will be blood games at the arena later."

Aur-Aun coughed. "Still, you have set aside time to go over your accounts with me in private, yes?"

"Oh, aye."

"Then my guards—and my *guard captain*—shall accompany me."

Paar-Il smiled. It didn't improve his looks. His teeth looked like kandy korn. "Of course. Then come." He started down the gangplank.

"Wait." The Aldhanan turned to Anan and his guards. "Stay on the ship and inform Captain Ku-Rho that he and his crew are not to leave it for any reason. You will make sure they obey the order."

Anan didn't like it. "Ald... er, Captain, we cannot leave you unprotected."

"Paar-Il's men will be at hand. Protecting our secret is more important. We must not let the traitor off the ship."

Anan gave a reluctant salute. "Aye, Captain."

The Aldhanan looked at me and the heretics. "Nor will there be any recruitment here. You too will stay here."

Sei-Sien looked offended. "You think us traitors?"

"It is for your protection. And I wish you to watch the crew." He turned to Yal-Faen, but gave me a significant look over his head. "And you as well, bookkeeper. Remain in your cabin."

Aur-Aun turned. "Forgive me, Aldhanan. But we must keep Yal-Faen at his work, if only to keep up appearances. I will make sure he is returned to the ship under armed guard."

The Aldhanan grunted, then motioned them all ahead. "Very well. After you, Dhans."

I felt a little funny letting the Aldhanan walk into that castle all by his lonesome. Maybe Paar-Il was lulling us all into a false sense of security and he meant to cut the Aldhanan's throat as soon as he got him in the door, but there was nothing we could do. The Aldhanan was giving the orders. At least he had Aur-Aun with him, and Aur-Aun looked like he could take care of himself.

***

Sei-Sien was looking around at us all like we were crazy. "How can you sit there? The plan is discovered. The church knows all! We must leave!"

Shal-Hau waved a finger. "No, I do not believe the church knows."

It was a few hours later, and me and my "escort" were still in our cabin, talking everything over. Well, actually, I was out in the hallway with the door open, while Sei-Sien paced like a caged cat, and Lhan and Shal-Hau sat on their bunks.

Why was I in the hall? Three reasons. One, it smelled better out there. Two, I didn't want anybody sneaking up and listening at the door. And three, Yal-Faen's cabin was just down the passageway. He'd been marched back to it by two of Paar-Il's finest about a half-hour before, and they'd left him there without a guard. That seemed a bit slipshod to me, so I decided I'd be the guard. That little weasel wouldn't be sneaking past me.

"But they must." Sei-Sien's hands were clenching and unclenching. "Who else would give such an order?"

"Anyone *but* the church," said Lhan. "If the church knew, they would not have sent a single messenger. We would have been met here with temple guards and wands of blue fire."

Shal-Hau nodded. "Precisely. Whoever he is, our betrayer does not want to inform the church. Not yet. I believe instead, that he wishes to bring the Aldhanan to them in chains. He wants to have the credit of exposing him and capturing him all to himself."

Sei-Sien held out pleading hands. "But with that fool Dhanan Paar-Il speaking for all the world to hear, the traitor must know he is exposed, and will go to the Temple now! He is likely already there! We must escape before the hammer falls!"

"Easy, Sei. None can leave the ship. No one will come. Now let us cease this arguing and spend our time trying to discover our traitor's identity." Lhan sat back, thinking. "Who was it? Was it one of our company? One of the crew? Or have we betrayed ourselves? Did we somehow let slip that we traveled with the Aldhanan when we were in Rivi?"

Sei-Sien glared. "I said nothing of the kind!"

"Nor did any of us," said Shal-Hau. "We would have scared our heretic brothers to death with such talk."

"It still might have been us." Lhan shook his head. "We might have spoke too loudly here in the cabin and been overheard by some zealot sailor who saw a chance for advancement."

I looked down the hallway. "Or it might have been that red-lipped little Don Knotts down there like I've been saying all along."

Shal-Hau frowned. "Dhan who?"

"Sheesh. Sorry. Yal-Faen, I mean."

"Ah, yes. But he has always been under guard. How can he have slipped away to warn anyone?"

"Are you kidding?" I waved my hand around to indicate the ship. "There's no reason he had to slip away. He's got a ship full of accomplices right here. He finds one sailor who's as much of a fanatic as he is, and he tells him about the Aldhanan. The sailor slips off the ship, and tells a pal to send word to Paar-Il."

Sei-Sien went as pale as a corpse. He grabbed his pack from under his cot and slung the strap over his shoulder. "Then it is certain. The church knows. They are coming. We must flee!"

And this guy had been accusing Lhan of cowardice? "Dude. Nobody can get off the ship, remember? Anan's up there keeping watch. It doesn't matter if liver-lips tells anybody. Everybody's just as trapped as we are."

Sei looked at me with eyes like ping-pong balls. "You think Anan is enough to stop a determined sailor? They know the ship! They will have sixty ways out!"

Down the hall I saw Yal-Faen pop his head out his door and look toward the noise. I whispered out of the side of my mouth. "Dude, shut up. You woke the baby."

"Sei-Sien, calm yourself!" Shal-Hau stood and put a hand on nervous nelly's arm. "We will relay our concerns to the Aldhanan when he returns, but until then we must—"

"No!" Sei-Sien shoved Shal-Hau back and tried to push past him toward the door. "I cannot be taken! I must be free to spread the word. My voice must not be allowed to be silenced! Let me by!"

I stepped forward, but Lhan was quicker. He grabbed Sei by the arm and pulled him back. "Sit down, Sei! You embarrass your—"

Sei snarled and threw a punch, which caught Lhan over the eye. That was it. Great orator or not, I'd had enough of this jackass. I ducked through the door and pulled him off Lhan, then threw him against the bulkhead hard enough to drop him. Only he didn't drop. Fear had made a wolverine outta him and he bounced back swinging. Fortunately, his punches were as wild as his eyes. I backed up, then slapped him on the ear so hard he hit the floor like a flapjack that missed the pan, then curled up and covered the side of his head with trembling hands. The handprint of my slap was dark purple on his violet face.

I put a foot on his neck. "You gonna ease up now, goof ball? Or do you want another—"

I cut off as a sound from the passageway made me turn my head. I stepped off Sei and crossed to the door. The passage looked the same as it had. Yal-Faen's door was closed. There was nobody in sight. All the same…

"Keep quiet. I'll be right back."

I tiptoed down the hall and listened at Yal's door.

Nothing.

I knocked.

"Yal-Faen? Are you in there?"

No answer. I pushed open the door. The cabin was empty.

CHAPTER THIRTY-SIX

MAN HUNT!

"Shit. Lhan! Guys! He flew the coop!"

I pounded back down to our cabin and grabbed my sword from under my bunk, then ran out again, strapping it on as I went. Lhan did the same and followed me. Shal-Hau was helping Sei-Sien to his feet. Sei wailed after us.

"Did I not tell you he would?"

I wanted to slap him again, but no time. We ran to the stairs and up to where the captain and his officers had their quarters. I tried all the doors. Locked.

Lhan pointed past me. "To the deck."

We burst out and looked around. It was late afternoon, and quiet except for faint cheers coming from the arena next to the palace. Paar-Il's blood games sounded like they were in full swing. The crew looked back at us, sullen. We were the ones who'd canceled their shore leave. Captain Anan and his men were there too, on guard at the rails, looking sleepy and bored. Had Yal-Faen slipped by them?

Captain Ku-Rho came down from the poop deck, goggling at my sword—which was a change. "Ah, Priestess? Is something wrong?"

"Yal-Faen. The bookkeeper. Did he come out here?"

"He is in the latrine."

"Crap."

I bounded to the prow where the poop hole was as the crew gasped and Captain Anan shouted a question. I pulled aside the curtain. The shitter was empty.

"Crap!"

With the ship winched to its mooring rings, the deck was more than twenty feet above the ground. A hell of a jump for a wimp like Yal-Faen, but then I saw the rope—right down through the hole. I scanned over the rail. The landing area was empty except for a few guards patrolling the edges, but they were few and far between. The shifty little bastard coulda slipped through them easy. I turned back. Sei-Sien was staggering out onto the deck behind Lhan, a sword in one hand and the other still holding his ear. I shouted to them both.

"Yal-Faen took off! We gotta go find him! Come on!"

Sei-Sien hesitated, but Lhan and I started for the rail. The crew all cheered and followed. I guess they figured helping was their chance to slip off and go raise some hell in town.

Captain Anan must have figured the same way. "Stand down! All of you!"

Everybody turned as he stepped to the center of the deck. "No one is to leave the ship. Aur-Aun's orders!"

The sailors groaned and turned back, but I was hopping mad.

"But Yal-Faen's the spy! We've gotta catch him before he betrays the—"

"Silence!"

I clapped my hand over my mouth. I'd almost betrayed him myself. "Okay, okay! But we still have to catch him! He could be going to the you-know-who!"

Anan nodded, then turned to his guards. "Hou-Doan, go look for the bookkeeper."

The guard saluted and ran down the gangplank. I stared at Anan.

"One guy? You're sending one guy? He could have gone anywhere."

"The ship must be watched. I can spare no more."

"Then let us go. I can cover more ground, and Lhan—"

"No-one is to leave the ship."

"Oh, come on! You know us. We were with you when—well you know."

"I only know my orders. No one is to leave the ship!"

I stood in front of him, trying really hard not to smash him in the nose. "You know, I'd shove a spear up your ass, but that'd just be redundant."

He didn't bat an eye.

I turned away with a snort, then started for the rail. "Come on, Lhan. I'll catch you."

Anan started after me. "Where are you going?"

"To look for Yal-Faen."

He tried to grab me, but I shoved him back and hopped up onto the rail. His men converged on me, but way too late. I jumped down to the ground and turned. Lhan was on the rail above me, kicking free of the guards, then he fell backwards like the guy in that iced tea commercial. Didn't even look. Fuck. I wondered if I trusted *him* that much.

I caught him and set him down, but just as we turned to run, Sei-Sien slid down the rope from the shitter and waved us on.

"Hurry! Find him or we are all dead!"

I shot Lhan a look. He shrugged.

"We cannot send him back without being caught ourselves."

With a sigh, we started for the city after our fearless leader, while Captain Anan shouted for us to return. He didn't follow though. Like he said, he couldn't spare the men.

***

The area around the Dhanan's palace was all massive temples, government buildings and plazas, all kinda run down and covered in the same red-brown grime that coated the whole city. And it was a ghost town. The buildings were dark and the streets empty except for a few people hurrying in the direction of the arena. It should have been easy to spot Yal-Faen, but it wasn't. Like most buildings on Waar, the temples and government offices were all hexagons, and that made the streets in between them all crooked and zig-zag. All the intersections had three arms, and you could never see any further than the next one. There were no lines of sight.

While Lhan and Sei-Sien checked doors and courtyards, I ran around like a maniac, bounding from intersection to intersection, trying to see down as many streets as I could. But it was Sei-Sien who finally found our man, drawing his sword as I bounced over his head to look over the wall of a temple.

"Ha! I have him! The dirty traitor!"

I dropped down in beside him and looked around. "Where?"

He pointed down the north arm of the intersection we were in and I caught a glimpse of a stoop-shouldered shadow limping around a corner. Fortunately, it didn't look like he'd heard Sei-Sien shouting.

I frowned. "You sure it's him? Yal doesn't have a limp."

"It is he. I saw his face. Now hurry before he flees!"

"Wait!"

We turned. Lhan was running up to us. "Let us see where he goes, and who he visits. Spy on him as he has spied on us."

Sei-Sien's eyes bulged. "Are you mad? He might go to the temple! We must kill him now!"

I exchanged a look with Lhan. The guy needed a Valium. Lhan patted his arm. "If he nears it, we will act, but I would follow first. After you, Mistress."

I didn't wait to see how Sei took it. Instead I ran to the end of the alley, then looked around the corner. Yal-Faen was still in sight, and now I could see that it was him, though he was limping like a dog had bit him. Maybe he'd hurt his leg sliding down the rope.

Lhan and Sei-Sien caught up to me, and we followed him. I kept expecting him to do what Sei had said, and turn toward the Temple of Modgalu, which loomed off to our right the whole time, but he didn't. He kept going south, into a market area, which was all closed up at this time of night, then through a rowdy, red-light district where the streets seemed to be paved in shit. The place was like something out of a cowboy movie—streets lined with taverns, drunk prairie-men staggering around arm in arm, hitching posts full of krae, and hookers leaning over the balconies of the tenements above.

Yal-Faen limped on until he got to a little hexagonal building right in the middle of it all. Then he stopped and looked over his shoulder.

Lhan ducked back. "A chapel of the Seven."

Sei-Sien growled and drew his sword. "I knew it. Come, before he betrays us all."

We tip-toed toward the church as Yal-Faen slipped inside. Sei-Sien was ready to charge in after him, but I stepped in his way and we listened at the door. There were muffled sounds of low talking inside, and another sound I couldn't quite figure out.

I drew my sword, then turned to Sei-Sien and put a finger to my lips. "Easy, alright?"

He bared his teeth, but finally nodded, and Lhan opened the door as quietly as he could. We slipped in, ready for anything. It was dark in there, but a light from below showed me a little six-sided amphitheater with paintings of six noble-looking guys and gals on the walls, all looking down toward a crude statue of an even nobler-looking guy on a pedestal down in the middle of the pit. There were two figures down by the statue. An old priest held a lamp over Yal-Faen, who was on his knees in front of the statue, his shoulders shaking. Sei-Sien tensed like he was gonna charge, but I held him back.

"Is he crying? What the fuck is he crying for?"

"I know not, Mistress."

The priest looked up, peering in our direction. "Who is there?"

Sei-Sien tore outta my hand and jumped down into the pit, howling and swinging his sword like a four-year-old pretending to be he-man. "Justice is here, traitor! And it brings you death!"

"Goddamn it!"

I leapt after him as he slashed at the priest, and kicked him in the back before he could take a second swing. Fortunately, the priest had ducked the first one, and was cowering back against the statue as Yal-Faen shrieked and tried to get in front of him.

"Stop! Do not kill him, I beg you!"

Sei-Sien staggered up again and was raising his sword for more, but Lhan held him back as I grabbed Yal by the front of his robe and shook him. I woulda rather eavesdropped on him and the priest, but since Sei-Sien had started with the "death from above" routine, I decided to run with it. I put my sword to his neck. "Fine. I'll start with you first, you two-faced fuck! Talk or die!"

The priest caught at my sword arm. "Please, Mistress! Stop!"

I elbowed him to the floor, then put my foot on him. He didn't shut up. He raised his hands, begging. "Yal-Faen is no traitor to you. That is the reason he sought me out!"

"Lies!" Sei-Sien tried to squirm past Lhan. "You protect your spy!"

I looked to Lhan. He shrugged. I dug my heel into the priest's ribs. "What the fuck are you talking about?"

It was Yal-Faen that answered. "Do not harm him, Priestess, please. Modgalu is my home, Ru-Zhera my family's priest. Who else should I turn to when… when…."

Sei-Sien bared his teeth. "When what?"

The priest, Ru-Zhera, took a breath under my foot. "Yal-Faen was confessing a crisis of faith when you entered. He is torn between his loyalty to his Aldhanan and to his church."

Yal-Faen clutched my wrist. "They mean to kill him, Priestess! The Aldhanan! They will kill him within the hour!"

CHAPTER THIRTY-SEVEN

CONFESSION!

I set Yal-Faen down with a thump and stepped off Ru-Zhera. "What! How? Where?"

Yal slumped against the statue and buried his face in his hands, sobbing again. "It is all my fault. I should have acted, but how could I dare go against the church?"

Sei-Sien pointed his sword. "How could you dare go against your Aldhanan? Traitor!"

The priest pushed to his feet. "Calm yourself, my son. Tell us what has happened."

"Fuck what happened!" I shook Yal-Faen so hard his teeth rattled. "What about now! Who's going to kill the Aldhanan? Where?"

"Aur-Aun," he squeaked. "At the arena. Paar-Il has taken the Aldhanan there to introduce him to his most trusted Dhans and—"

"Aur-Aun you say?" Lhan let go of Sei-Sien. "Now I know you for a liar! Aur-Aun has been the Aldhanan's most loyal servant since he was his banner guard. He has saved the Aldhanan's life!"

"Aye," said Yal-Faen. "And the Aldhanan repaid him by giving Wen-Jhai to another, when he feels she should have been his."

Lhan stared, stunned. "I cannot believe it. To allow jealousy to turn him against the man who has been his friend and benefactor all these years?"

Yal-Faen shook his head. "It is ambition as well. He believes the church will make him Aldhanan when he shows them the Aldhanan is plotting war against them."

Lhan looked at me. "Then has it been Aur-Aun all along? Is it he with whom the church wished to replace the Aldhanan? But he was not at Durgallah. How—?"

I cut him off. "Not now, Lhan! We gotta go!" I started up the steps. "Come on!"

Sei-Sien was right beside me, but Lhan was still hanging back.

"Wait. We must take them with us."

I turned. "Are you nuts? They'll slow us down! Poindexter was slow even before he hurt his leg."

Lhan pointed at Yal-Faen. "We will need him to speak against Aur-Aun, and..." He pointed at Ru-Zhera. "We cannot let a priest free when he knows so much."

Sei-Sien snarled. "Then kill him!"

Lhan looked at him, disgusted. "You have a blade. Kill him yourself."

Now that it was cold blood, Sei hesitated, eyes wide. Lhan snorted and grabbed both Yal-Faen and the priest.

"Come. We must hurry."

We hustled them up the stairs and out into the street as Sei-Sien followed behind. I started back the way we'd come, but Lhan stopped and looked around, then pointed to a couple of burly guys unloading a wagon full of wine jars in the alley beside a tavern.

"That is what we need." He turned to Yal-Faen. "You have coin?"

"Y-yes."

"Give it to me. All of it."

Yal-Faen reached for the pouch on his belt. He was too slow. Lhan ripped it from him and hurried into the alley with the rest of us coming after.

"Brothers, we have need of your wagon."

Lhan hopped up on the back of the cart and dumped the last jars of wine off the tail gate and the dudes gaped, then tossed them the pouch. "For your troubles."

He pulled Yal-Faen and Ru-Zhera up onto the back, then sat down on the bench like he thought everything was a-okay. The carters didn't agree. They started to climb up onto the cart.

"Your troubles are just beginning, 'brothers.'"

I was pretty much on their side. Lhan was pulling some high-handed shit here, and a little bag of coins wasn't gonna make up for them stealing their cart and fucking up their night. At the same time, we needed to go, like five minutes ago. I hefted Sei-Sien on the cart as it started to roll, then hopped up in front of the carters and shoved them back.

"Sorry, dudes. This is bullshit. I know."

They flew backwards off the cart and landed on their asses in a puddle of wine mud and we were gone, picking up speed as we took the corner into the street, scattering drunks in every direction. I caught my balance and sat behind Lhan.

"That shit woulda got you shot in Texas, bro."

He looked grim. "Forgive me, Mistress. Expediency makes churls of us all. I only hope Yal-Faen's purse was well filled. Now, on to the arena!"

Sei-Sien's head snapped around. "The arena? We go to the ship! We must warn Captain Anan of the Aldhanan's peril!"

"There is no time for that. We must warn the Aldhanan himself."

Sei-Sien turned the color of hand cream. "But… but…."

Lhan looked around at him, his face as snarky as I'd ever seen it. "Come, Sei-Sien. Surely you would not abandon the Aldhanan to his fate? Surely you would not allow cowardice to turn you from your duty?"

Sei-Sien swallowed, but shook his head. "Surely not."

As we rattled on through the slum, I grabbed Yal-Faen and shook him. "So, what's supposed to happen at the arena? Aur-Aun can't be crazy enough to just shank the Aldhanan with Paar-Il and all his guards around. He'd be dead in seconds flat."

Yal-Faen shook his head. "Aur-Aun wanted desperately to apprehend the Aldhanan himself, but with Paar-Il's warning, he knew he would not succeed, so he has gone to the church for assistance. While I was at my books, and the Aldhanan talked to Paar-Il, Aur-Aun slipped away to the Temple of Modgalu. It will be the priests who kill him."

"Fuck! But what are they going to do?"

He shrugged. "I know not, but Aur-Aun warned me it would be during the final event of the blood games."

Sei-Sien turned, suspicious, as we took a corner. "He *warned* you? Why?"

"I—I was to wait until that moment to set the canopy of the Ku-Rho's airship alight, so he and Captain Anan would be either dead or too busy to come to the Aldhanan's aid, and to prevent his escape if somehow he managed to—"

I stared at him. "Wait a minute. You were part of all this? This isn't just stuff you overheard?"

He looked like he was going to cry again. "Aur-Aun convinced me we did the will of the Seven! He said the Aldhanan had been corrupted by heresy and must be stopped." Yal hung his head. "It was I who sent the messenger to Paar-Il to arrest the Aldhanan. I sent other messages as well, to other Dhanans."

Sei-Sien whipped around, reaching for his sword again. "Betrayer! I knew it! It was you!"

I shoved him back as Lhan looked around.

"Which Dhanans did you warn? Speak! Ah! One curse it!"

A carriage veered into our path. Lhan swerved around it and we hit a bump that had us bouncing around like frogs on a hot skillet. I caught Yal-Faen as he was about to pitch over the side and he answered.

"There were many. I—I have their names in my journal. I—"

Sei-Sien shook his fist. "You villain! You have wrecked us!"

Yal wailed. "Think you I do not know it? Why else have I been so miserable?"

"So what changed your mind?"

Yal frowned. "I am a tax collector. By their tithes, I know how poorly the farmers fare. It has been getting worse every year. It made me begin to believe your story of the church stealing water from the air."

I looked at Ru-Zhera. "What about it, priest? Is stealing water church policy?"

Ru-Zhera frowned. "My superiors have always denied it, but the rumors of such practices persist."

Yal-Faen clutched at the sideboard as we skidded around a corner. "Even knowing this I might have continued to side with the church. The priests might have had some plan for the greater good that required collecting the water. But today Aur-Aun did not say he would have the Aldhanan arrested and held for trial, as he had always said before. Today he said that he would call upon the priests to assassinate him." He looked off into the middle distance, staring at nothing. "That I could not abide."

***

We heard the arena before we saw it—cheers and boos and singing echoing through the empty streets of the temple quarter—which made me breathe a sigh of relief. If everybody was still into games, shit probably hadn't gone down yet. Unless of course they'd been subtle about it—put a knife in the Aldhanan's back and carried him out like he was some drunk bodyguard. Suddenly I wasn't so relieved.

The kraes swung our wagon around another corner and the place came into sight at last. It was about the size of a minor league baseball stadium—and just like stadiums back home, it was surrounded by vendors selling cheap snacks and knick-knacks and people drinking more than was good for them. There were big open arches on every side, and uniformed guards standing in them taking coin from the people going in.

Lhan reined to a stop at the edge of the plaza and jumped down.

"Come. Quickly."

I frowned, confused. So did Sei.

"Ride on! To the gate!"

"No. It will make a scene, which will delay us."

Sei saw his point and so did I. We helped Yal-Faen and Ru-Zhera down, then steamed them across the plaza like we were power-walking.

Lhan laughed and put on a big smile as we neared the guards. "Have we missed it, Dhans? The Priestess wants to see the vurlaks fighting. Their virility excites her."

The guards gave Lhan a dirty chuckle and me a leering look, and took his coins without batting an eyelash. We didn't even have to slow down, and charged up the ramp to the arch that led to the bleachers almost at a run.

The smell of blood hit me first. It was like an iron hammer shoved up my nose. I nearly gagged. Then we stepped out to the bleachers and I did gag. I don't know what I was expecting to see. Maybe gladiator fights like the ones Lhan and I had fought in down in Doshaan? Maybe wild beasts tearing apart condemned men, which had also been on the card down there?

This was neither of those. Instead it seemed to be some kind of cross between bullfighting and a butcher shop. The arena floor was divided into six wedges, with a naked matador guy in each one, armed only with what looked like a giant skinning knife. In the middle of the arena was a big six-gated corral full of terrified maku, and every few seconds, one of the cage doors would open and one of the big bastards would charge into a wedge, heading straight for the matador.

Then the matador killed it.

There were no fancy dance moves or cape flapping. The guy just dodged and ducked until he could get behind the maku's head and cut its throat.

But the fun wasn't over yet. As soon as the thing was dead—and sometimes even sooner—he started skinning it and cutting it up into its various parts, all of which got thrown into various piles—legs over here, head over there, carcasses in the middle, guts behind, skins to the side—blood everywhere. There were huge, six-foot mounds of steaming, bleeding meat behind each of the matadors, and they were rising higher every second. As soon as a guy finished sorting his meat, he gave a signal and the guys in the middle let another one out. It looked like they were counting which guy slaughtered the most in the shortest amount of time.

It was so horrible it was hard to tear my eyes away. I mean, I know that's pretty much what goes into making my bacon cheeseburgers, but making a sport out of it, hearing everybody cheer when another one of those big dumb beasts went down gushing out its life blood? It made my stomach curdle.

"There they are!"

With a grunt of relief, I turned and looked where Lhan was pointing, and saw Paar-Il and some other hick Dhans sitting in a private box with the Aldhanan way at the top on the other side of the arena. The Adhanan was dressed like a Dhan now too, only with a domino mask to hide his face, but there was no way you could miss that jaw.

I sized up the guards standing at the foot of the stairs that led up to the boxes. They were tough-looking hombres, and we weren't going to get by them with a laugh and dirty joke, but maybe we could sneak up to another box and—

"Priests!" Beside me, Sei-Sien was suddenly pointing like a bird dog at a duck hunt. "And disguised as Flames! Infamy!"

Lhan and I turned. Sei was staring at the box to the right of Paar-Il's, where a bunch of guys were pulling up the hoods of their cloaks. One of 'em had a face I knew.

"The high priest! Duru-Vau!"

Lhan glanced at the box on the left left of Paar-Il's. It was packed too. "And more on the opposite side!" He edged back. "Come, we must find a way to warn the Aldhanan before they—"

"Murderers! False priests! This is not the church I love! I will slay you all!"

Lhan and I froze as the little poindexter Yal-Faen ripped Sei-Sien's sword from his hand and started running full tilt around the arena with it, screaming at the top of his lungs.

CHAPTER THIRTY-EIGHT

ASSASSINS!

The crowd was too busy watching animals being skinned alive to notice Yal-Faen, but that beady-eyed little fucker Duru-Vau saw him right away. Then he saw me and Lhan. Then he waved to his men.

The disguised priests moved like they were one big, multi-legged animal, swarming over the railing and swinging around the little dividing walls into Paar-Il's box, swords out, while more kicked in the door at the back and poured in that way.

"Yal! You dumb-ass!"

I charged after the accountant, rage rising and heart sinking. The stupid goober had ruined everything! Somewhere behind me, I heard Lhan shouting.

"Sei-Sien, take the priest back to the cart! Go!"

I didn't hear Sei complaining, and I didn't wait for Lhan to catch up. There was no time. I kicked off Yal-Faen's back and launched into the bleachers, sending spectators diving every which way.

Up in the VIP box it was dire. There had been about ten guys standing guard around the bigwigs, and they had at least kept Paar-Il and his guests from dying in the priests' first wave, but they hadn't lasted long, and now it was Paar-Il and his Dhans and the Aldhanan who were fighting the fake heretics. They were doing a fuck of a lot better than any politicians back home woulda done, but it wasn't enough. They were still outnumbered three to one.

I leapt a rail to the next bank of bleachers and kept going. Three more jumps and I'd be there.

"Stop her! It is the giantess who kidnapped the Aldhanan's daughter. Now she's helping the heretics kill Paar-Il!"

I looked around in mid-leap. Aur-Aun was running out from a ramp to my left and pointing at me, a gang of priests—for once dressed like priests—at his back.

With all the cheering and the shrieking of butchered maku, it had taken the arena until now to realize something was happening up in the boxes, but what with my human flea routine and Aur-Aun's shouting, they were catching on fast. All of a sudden, people weren't diving out of my way anymore. Instead, they were all screaming bloody murder and grabbing for me. I felt like the beach ball at a rock concert.

I shoved at a beefy guy who had a hold of my left calf. "Get off! I'm the good guy! I gotta go save them!"

He wasn't listening, and neither were the rest of them. There were twenty hands grabbing at me now. I was swamped, and Aur-Aun and his little orange buddies were closing in. Goddamn it! I didn't want to hurt these people, but I had to get through. The Aldhanan was fighting for his life up there. I could see blood on his arms, and under his mask.

I grabbed Beefy by the belt and swung him around at everybody else, smashing them back like meat bowling pins. I was in the clear, but just for good measure I heaved the fat fuck at Aur-Aun and his pet priests, then took off again without bothering to see if I'd connected.

Two more leaps and I vaulted over the rail into Paar-Il's box, slashing around like a weed wacker. The fake heretics were busy butchering the Dhans and went down like—well—weeds. I cut the legs out from under three guys on my first slash, then beheaded another guy on the backhand. The rest turned to face me, and I tore into 'em like a steel tornado, snapping swords, chopping off hands, smashing rib cages as, behind them, I saw Paar-Il and the Aldhanan fighting back to back.

"Hang on! I'm coming!"

But then I wasn't.

As I hacked down another two priests, I saw a movement out of the corner of my eye and glanced around just in time to see Duru-Vau step over the rail from the box to the right and stare right at me with his mild little eyes. He didn't have a weapon and he was fifteen feet away, so I put him on the back burner and was turning back to my fight, when the little pip-squeak thrust his palm at me like something out of Five Fingers of Death and I flew backwards across the box like I'd taken a cannonball to the tits. It felt like it too. My skin was tingling and my heart was hammering like I'd touched a live wire. I couldn't breathe. I couldn't feel my hands or feet.

My mind hurt worse than all that combined. The little fucker hadn't touched me, and yet he'd knocked me on my ass and fried all my circuits. How the fuck do you do that? I'd seen a lot of weird-ass shit since I'd showed up on Waar, but I'd always been able to put it into the science fiction category—alien technology, super science, whatever. This was straight up wizards and witches shit! He'd hit me with a fucking death spell!

Then I had some more down-to-earth death to worry about. All the guys I'd been chopping up started charging forward, ready to chop me up, and I was a long way from doing anything more than remembering how to breathe. I felt like I'd been tazed. Fortunately, Lhan chose that moment to throw himself over the railing and drive 'em back.

"Mistress, can you stand?"

I tried. I felt like I was made out of rubber chickens. "What the fuck wuzzat?" Even my tongue was rubber. "Little prick jus' hit me with a lightnin' bolt."

"A Gift of the Seven." Lhan blocked another stab, but they were forcing him back now. "Divine power granted by the gods to their most devout."

"Shure packs a helluva whallop."

I made it to my feet, though I felt like I was standin' in a rowboat on a stormy sea, and saw Duru-Vau cocking back for another death strike. I beat him to it. Somebody's helmet was on the ground, with a lot of blood and hair still sticking to it; I scooped it up and hurled it at him over Lhan's head.

It was a sucky throw, and didn't come within a foot of him, but he was balanced on the railing and jerked back when he saw it coming, and next thing I saw was his sandals kicking up in the air as he took a header into the cheap seats.

I was still moving like the Vicodin had just kicked in, but at least I was moving, and plowed into the guys who were driving Lhan back. I couldn't swing in a straight line, but a six-foot sword doesn't have to be precise to be scary, and I had 'em ducking and blocking while Lhan took care of the actually hitting them part.

Five seconds and five corpses later they'd had enough and broke for the exits, and Lhan and I charged for the Aldhanan—way too fucking late.

Paar-Il was face-down in his own blood. The Aldhanan had a sword through his guts, and a cut on his neck that was never going to heal. He was still up, still hacking at four last priests, but he was weaving like a two AM drunk.

The guys he was fighting were trying to pull the water token satchel from his shoulder. Lhan and I hacked two of 'em down and the other two fled, diving over the rail, and it was just the three of us. The Aldhanan turned on me, snarling and slashing, so much blood in his eyes he couldn't see. I blocked the cut and backed up.

"Aldhanan, it's us! Jane and Lhan!"

He checked his swing and stumbled against me, wheezing through the hole in his throat. "Mistress Jae-En, we are betrayed. We..."

I caught him before he fell, then sobbed as his knees buckled and he clutched at me. "Oh, god, Lhan, this can't— We... I shoulda run faster. I shoulda—"

The Aldhanan's sword dropped from his hand. I lowered him to the ground. The world was all swimmy and blurred. Tears were splashing on his face as I leaned over him, making little holes in the blood.

"Hold on, sir. Please don't die. I'll find somebody who can fix you up."

But I knew it was a lie as I said it. There was no fixing all that. Not on this stupid fucking backwards planet. Not without EMTs and a medevac. Goddamn it! Why did I ever come back to this shit hole? I—

The Aldhanan gripped my hand. "Mistress, Lhan, listen to me."

I wiped my eyes and leaned in. "We're here. What is it?"

"Protect my daughter. And her... f-fool of a consort. It will not go... well for them, now I am... gone."

I wanted to tell him he should find somebody who hadn't just failed to save his life, that I was the wrong person for the job, that I sucked in every way possible, but he was fading fast, so I just squeezed his hand. Lhan did too.

"We'll do our best, sir. I promise."

"Aye, Aldhanan. Of course."

He was dead before we'd finished.

My throat closed up like a giant was choking me. "Goddamn it, Lhan. Goddamn it all to hell." My lip started to quiver and the tears came again, I was shaking so hard. "I fucked up. I didn't save him. I should have—"

Then Yal-Faen pulled himself over the rail and looked around. My grief turned to rage in a hot second. I grabbed for my sword and stood up, staring at him like a can of Raid stares at a roach.

"You little puke. You did this."

I started toward him, sword raised, but behind me, Lhan gasped, then grabbed my arm and pulled me back, pointing to the stairs at the back of the box.

"No, Mistress. The priests come, with a wand. We must fly. Hurry! To the roof!"

I pulled away, snarling, and raised my sword, but Yal-Faen was staring past me at the body of the Aldhanan, a look of horror on his face.

"What have I done? What have I done?"

"You killed him. And now I'm gonna kill—"

A blue-white light stabbed out from the stairwell.

Lhan jerked me aside. "Forget him, Mistress! Go!"

I staggered back as orange shadows swarmed in the stairwell and another blue bolt sizzled into the box. I didn't want to go. I wanted to cut Yal-Faen in half, then chop through the priests until they gunned me down, but then Yal-Faen looked up at me, and his eyes were more steady than I'd ever seen them.

"There is no need to kill me. I am already dead."

And with that he turned and charged, howling and hacking like a berserker with the sword he'd stolen from Sei-Sien, just as the priests spilled into the box.

Lhan tugged my arm. "Now, Mistress! The roof!"

I backed to the rail as Yal-Faen went down swinging and bleeding like a fountain, then looked up. There was a tile roof overhanging the box. It was an easy one-hand vault. I pulled myself up, then reached down, but Lhan was looking back at the Aldhanan.

"Lhan! What are you doing?"

He dodged back to the corpse, snatching up the box with the water tokens, then charged back to the rail and leapt up.

"Stop them!" Aur-Aun's voice.

I heaved Lhan up just as a blue beam passed through where he'd been standing and crackled out across the arena. I wanted to shake him.

"What the fuck?"

He slung the token box over his shoulder, his face like granite. "We cannot allow his cause to die with him."

The last thing we heard as we raced up the slant of the roof and over the peak was Aur-Aun shouting like the hero in a bad play.

"By the Seven, it is the Aldhanan! In disguise! Those heretic assassins have killed the Aldhanan! After them!"

CHAPTER THIRTY-NINE

OUTLAWS!

I kinda thought Sei-Sien woulda got while the getting was good, but he was waiting with Ru-Zhera at the cart just like Lhan had told him. Unfortunately, the dumb-ass hadn't had the foresight to turn the fucking thing around, so we were gonna have to cut a tight turn to make a run for the street. And the timing was gonna be tight too. As we jumped on and Lhan grabbed the reins, the entire arena flowed out after us like a tsunami wave.

"Go go go!"

"But, wait!" Ru-Zhera grabbed Lhan's arm. "Where is Yal-Faen!"

"Dead. Killed by the priests."

The old priest choked, but Sei-Sien only had eyes for the crowd. There were priests in the middle of it now. "By the One, what happened?"

"The—the Al—the Ald—" I couldn't get it out.

Lhan took over. "The Aldhanan is dead. We were not in time."

Sei-Sien stared. "The—the Aldhanan is dead?"

"Impossible." The old priest was shaking his head. "Impossible."

I felt the same. How could a guy so alive be dead? It didn't make sense! If only I'd insisted that Lhan leave Yal-Faen and the priest behind. If only I hadn't let those spectators slow me down. If... if... IF!

Goddamn it! What the fuck was I going to tell Wen-Jhai!

Sei-Sien snapped me out of it by screaming like a schoolgirl. "Faster, Lhan! Drive them faster!"

I looked around. We weren't out of our turn yet and already the crowd was halfway across the plaza and closing fast, and there were flashes of orange mixed in with them, pushing to the front. Priests! And I saw the white tube of the wand of blue fire at the back. We weren't gonna make it. The crowd was gonna close around us before the kraes got up to speed.

Unless…

"Lhan! Gimme the water tokens!"

He looked around at me as he finally got the krae straightened out. "For what, Mistress?"

"We're not getting outta here without 'em."

"But—but they are needed. Without coin, the Aldhanan's dream of bringing down the church will die!"

"And without a distraction *we're* gonna die! Now give 'em up and get going!"

He looked sick about it, but let me pull the satchel off his shoulder as he cracked the whip over the kraes' heads and we jolted forward. Sei-Sien, on the other hand, stared as I opened up the flap like he'd just seen the face of Jesus in a tortilla. He grabbed at me as I stepped to the back of the cart.

"You mustn't! The cause needs this money! By the One, the things we could do! The campaigns we could—"

I shoved him down. "You ain't gonna do any of 'em dead."

He reached after me, wailing, as I raised the satchel over my head. "But you're wasting it! You're giving it away!"

"I thought your whole deal was to take water from the church and give it to the people. Ain't that what I'm doin'?" I turned to the crowd, which was spreading out like an amoeba behind us, getting ready to swallow us whole. "The blessings of Laef be upon you! Water for everyone!"

And with that I grabbed the satchel by the bottom and swung it wide. The tokens flew out of it like an orange rainbow, glinting bright in the last of the sun, and the guys at the front stopped like they'd run into a wall as they realized what was raining down around them.

Well, that caused the mother of all pile-ups, as the rest of the crowd barreled into 'em and fell flat on their faces, and then the mother of all brawls as everybody and their grandmother started scrabbling in the dust, trying to snatch up as many coins as they could. Then the priests got into it and shit got really nasty. They started kicking and punching and cracking heads and shouting, "Touch not those tokens! They are tainted!"

Yeah. Like that was gonna work.

With nobody in our way, Lhan drove the kraes hard down the wide street that curved around the palace and headed for the ship at a gallop. I breathed a sigh of relief, but Sei-Sien was staring out over the backboard like we'd left his firstborn to the wolves.

"Wasted… wasted…"

Unfortunately, we weren't in the clear yet. Not by a Texas mile. As we rode onto the ship field, I saw half a dozen airships rising into the sky and more orange and white robes swarming around our navy cutter. We had as much trouble ahead of us as we did behind.

A whole squadron of temple paladins and priests was attacking the ship, climbing up the sides, killing the sailors who were trying to cut the mooring ropes, shooting crossbows into the canopy, while the ships around it were heading for the high ground as fast as their balloons would take them. There were dead sailors all over the ground, and more were falling over the rail every second. I didn't get it.

"Wh-what are they doing?"

"Killing them." Lhan's mouth was as thin as a razor blade. "All of them."

"But why? We didn't tell the crew anything. Not even Captain Ku-Rho knew what we were doing."

Ru-Zhera shouted over the rumble of the cart wheels. "The temple cannot allow the contagion of your heresy to spread!"

Lhan snorted. "Also, we have a hold full of tithes."

He aimed our cart straight for the ship, full tilt.

Sei-Sien cringed back. "'Ware, Lhan! Do you intend to crash us?"

"Yes."

I got into a crouch on the bench and drew my sword. Our kraes started to balk as we raced toward the crowd, but Lhan cracked the reins over their backs and they skittered on, squawking in protest. At the last second, the paladins under the ship heard us coming and turned, just in time to get a face full of beak. About half a dozen guys went down under claws and cart wheels as we bounced and bucked over their bodies. I used the jolt to launch myself toward a clump of priests who were fighting a gang of the sailors, just under the curve of the ship's belly.

I hit 'em like a wrecking ball, sending 'em flying in all directions, then helicoptered around with my sword, chopping meat and splintering bone at every point of the compass. Some of 'em died. Most scattered, and I started charging from rope to rope, hacking through them as behind me, Lhan rallied the sailors and Sei-Sien and Ru-Zhera picked themselves up, and the krae cart rattled off for the edge of the field with no one at the reins.

One rope at a time was not how you were supposed to unmoor an airship. You were supposed to let all the lines go at once so there would be a smooth liftoff. The way I was doing it, the ship was jerking up at different angles with every rope I cut, and I heard people shouting and falling above me. Oops.

I had to stop as the Paladins came in again, spears stabbing, and I ended up leaving the boat tilted above me like a jaunty hat as I beat 'em back. Then I ducked under the keel of the ship with Lhan and the sailors following after me and swung for the ropes on that side. I couldn't reach 'em. The paladins drove us back until I was ducking to keep from knocking my head on the hull, and more were coming from all over the field to stop us. Then a rope off to the right twanged. The guards looked around. Sei-Sien was stumbling back, a sword held in both hands, as the ship jerked up above him. Old Ru-Zhera stood in front of him, holding out his arms like he was trying to protect him.

"Brothers. Put up your spears. These men have done nothing."

A guard smashed him in the mouth with a spear butt, and he went down hard, his head bouncing off a mooring ring. Sei-Sien went batshit, screeching and slashing at them like a spastic hummingbird.

"You kill your own? You kill old men? Where is the mercy of the Seven? Where is it!"

Sei gutted the first guard by sheer force of crazy, but the second smashed him back, and there were more behind him. Before they could kill him, however, Lhan jumped in and drove them back.

"Bravely done, Sei, but attack the ropes and leave the spears to us. On your left, Jae-En!"

I spun left. Three guards had overrun our sailors and were stabbing for me with their spears. I bashed the points aside, then chopped at the guards. Two went down, almost cut in half. The other staggered away, holding his face, and I ended up fighting next to Lhan, and almost stepped on Ru-Zhera, who was staggering to his feet with a gushing head wound. I steadied him and looked around.

"Last three ropes behind us, Lhan."

He nodded, and we started circling that way, but then Sei stopped between us and almost caught a backhand in the mush.

"Aur-Aun!"

Ru-Zhera narrowed his eyes. "And Duru-Vau. The shame of the church."

I followed their gaze and saw the taxman and the chinless high priest striding onto the ship field with the priests from the arena behind them. And they still had that goddamn wand of blue fire.

"Fuck. Faster, Lhan. We gotta go."

I surged for the last three ropes, clearing a path with my sword, and Lhan came after, protecting my back. The guards scattered and died and we made it to the ropes, slipping on blood and entrails.

"Lhan! Sei! Grab a rope! You too, padre. I'll cut 'em and we'll…" I looked around. The priest wasn't with us. I looked back. I didn't see him there either, or on the ground with the dead.

"Where'd he go?"

"I know not. Ru-Zhera!"

The sailors on the ground were dead and the guards were closing in on us, with Aur-Aun and the fresh troops running in behind. There was no time to go looking for him. We were dead if we didn't go now.

"Goddamn it! Grab on!"

Lhan snarled something that didn't translate and grabbed a rope. I chopped through it under his feet, then slashed through Sei's to my left. The one I was holding creaked and stretched under my hand as it took the whole pull of the ship by itself.

The guards were feet away now, spears stabbing. I lashed out in a sweeping circle, then looped down, lifted my legs and cut through the rope beneath me.

The ship jerked up so fast I almost didn't go with it. The rope zipped through my hand like sandpaper, and I had to clamp down with my thighs and ankles to keep from slipping off it altogether.

"So long, suckers!"

Below me I saw Aur-Aun and Duru-Vau screaming up at me and shaking their fists. It was a beautiful sight, but then I saw an ugly one. The paladin with the wand of blue fire was aiming it at the gas canopy. He was going to blow us out of the sky.

"Oh fuck."

But just as he had us in his sights, a skinny little figure in orange robes burst through the paladins and chopped at the wand with a sword. The white tube cracked in the middle, and in the split second before the sizzling white flash that exploded from it knocked everybody back and filled my eyes with floating black spots, I saw that the guy in the orange robes was Ru-Zhera, screaming like an angry rabbit.

The blast turned the guard with the wand into a human candle, and I don't just mean he was on fire. He was melting too, like something out of one of those House of Wax movies.

Lhan gaped as we rose, but not at the melting guy. "Astonishing. To have seen the destruction of a sacred weapon of the Seven.

Sei-Sien nodded. "And at the hands of a priest."

"Crazy motherfucker, he's commiting suicide."

Actually, I was surprised he wasn't dead already, but amazingly, although all the priests and paladins around the melting guy were screaming and rolling around on fire, but, Ru-Zhera had only been singed. He was flat on his back about twenty feet back, his robes and hair smoldering and his sword half melted, whatever rage had pushed him over the edge was still firing on all cylinders. He hopped up again like somebody half his age and charged at Duru-Vau, who had caught the edge of the blast and was still stunned and smoking.

"Yes! Get that fucker!"

Unfortunately, shit that good only happens in the movies. Ru-Zhera took a running swipe, then went stumbling past when Duru-Vau ducked, and by the time he turned for another attack, the high priest was thrusting his palm at him, and Ru-Zhera flew back and slammed to the ground. It made my hair stand on end.

"How the fuck does he do that? It can't be magic. It can't!"

As the old priest lay there twitching, Aur-Aun crossed to him and stabbed him through the heart like somebody stepping on a bug.

I turned my head as we kept lifting higher. "Poor old guy."

Lhan lowered his eyes. "It is a brave man who stands up to his superiors when they are wrong. Would that the church had more like him."

Sei-Sien grunted. "Sadly, his bravery has not bought us much respite." He pointed down and left. "Look."

Lhan and I followed his gaze. The priests and paladins were running to the last few airships that were still on the ground and shouting at their captains. The fuckers were coming after us. It wasn't gonna be a clean getaway.

We climbed the ropes as our ship drifted over the palace and out of sight of the shipfield, then started up the side of the hull. At the rail, sailors hauled us over and set us on the deck, then shoved us to the center where Captain Ku-Rho and his first mate had Shal-Hau on his knees. The sailors made us kneel beside him.

Ku-Rho and the mate put their swords to me and Lhan's necks. Ku-Rho looked like he was about to blow a gasket.

"Your friend has been telling me the true purpose of this voyage, and why the priests were attacking us."

I swallowed. Uh-oh.

"What I fail to understand is why you cast us off when the Aldhanan was not on board."

I tried to tell him, but I still couldn't get it out. My throat still closed up every time I thought about it. "The Aldhanan… He…."

Lhan hung his head. "The Aldhanan is dead. Assassinated by the priests. We failed to stop them."

"It isn't true. It can't be true."

We all looked around. Captain Anan was sitting up from where he lay on the deck, cut to ribbons. He was shaking.

"The Aldhanan cannot be dead."

Lhan bowed to him and crossed his wrists. "I am sorry, Captain. It is true."

Anan's face, which had always been as calm and cold as a statue's, twisted up like an angry lion's. "Then you are at fault! You killed him!"

Lhan nodded. "It is true. We failed to reach him in time. We failed to see Aur-Aun's treachery before it was too late. Had we not—"

"Aur-Aun is a traitor?" Captain Ku-Rho looked shocked.

"You didn't see him down there with the priests?" I jerked a thumb over the rail. "He's the one who ratted us out. He wanted the Aldhanan's job. And his daughter."

"The villain!" Anan was standing now, though he shouldn't have. It looked like he'd left half his blood on the deck, and the rest was still leaking out of him. "I have long noted his lust for the Aldhanshai, but I did not think…"

"And there is more." Lhan edged back from Ku-Rho's sword point and stood. The captain didn't do anything to stop him. "Aur-Aun and the priests have named us the Aldhanan's assassins, and will stop at nothing to kill any who know the truth of this voyage." He looked around at Ku-Rho, Anan, the heretics and the crew. "Friends, we are now outlaw. All of us."

CHAPTER FORTY

AIR BATTLE!

We should have beat the three ships that were following us by a country mile. We were on an Oran warship, for fuck's sake. Unfortunately, the ship was pretty wrecked. Half the crew were dead or wounded, the canopy was leaking like a sieve from all the crossbow bolts the priests had shot at it, the sails were full o' holes, and the hold was full of gold. We were wallowing around like a walrus in quicksand, while slowly but surely, the priests' balloons got closer and clearer behind us in the moonlight.

Captain Ku sent his crew scrambling to make us ready to fight. Dead sailors were given sketchy last rights and then stuffed into the ballast. Leaks in the canopy were patched up. Sails were taken down and replaced by fresh ones. The blood on the deck was mopped up and sand was sprinkled around so it wouldn't be slippery. The surgeons went to work too, patching up everybody who could still fight, then seeing to the guys who were down for the count.

They patched Lhan and me up too, and we joined the rest of the crew at the rail, staring back at the oncoming ships. Shal-Hau and Sei-Sien stood with us.

Shal-Hau sighed. "So ends our brave rebellion."

Lhan stuck out his lip. "There is still hope."

Sei-Sien laughed at him. "Where? The Aldhanan is dead. The church knows our plans. This fool giantess threw away the only chance of salvaging things. And we shall die here on this ship, leaving no one to spread the truth of what happened."

"There are still the Aldhanan's daughter and her consort, Sai-Far. She will inherit the throne and he will help her rule, and having first-hand experience of the church's hospitality, they will continue the fight."

Shal-Hau stared over the side. "If they are not killed first."

I clenched my fists. "That's not going to happen. I promised the Aldhanan I wouldn't let anything happen to them."

Sei-Sien raised an eyebrow. "And how will you do this when you are dead?"

I wanted to punch him in the mouth for being a doomsayer, but I couldn't disagree with him. There was no way to escape the bastards who were trying to catch us, and we weren't gonna survive when they did. No amount of hopping around and kicking ass was going to beat six-to-one odds.

"Then I'll just take as many with me as I can."

Lhan looked at me like he wanted to say something personal, but then looked around at the others and kept quiet.

We all just went back to looking over the rail.

***

I've never been so bored and so tense at the same time in my life. Airship chases are like watching the minute hand catch up with the hour hand on a clock. You know it's going to get there eventually, but it's about as exciting as watching paint dry. At the same time, I was straining the whole time like I was trying to pull our ship through the air all by myself. It was exhausting. And pointless too. We all knew they were going to catch us. What was the point of running?

Amazingly, Captain Ku-Rho had an answer for that when I asked him.

"You see the moons through the clouds? Both will be down in two hours. And we may be able to slip away when they cannot see us."

Yeah, well. It was a nice thought.

Unfortunately, after an hour, the priests' ships were so close that they were never going to lose us, no matter how dark it got. Ku-Rho started throwing everything that wasn't nailed down over the side, trying to take us higher and make us faster. It was no use. In another half-hour they'd caught up and two of the priests' commandeered ships split left and right and started paralleling us just out of bowshot, while the third one inched up on our rear. Then, a horn trumpeted from the ship on the left and they swooped in.

This was where an Oran ship of the line had the advantage—in those few short seconds when they were in range but hadn't managed to hook onto us yet. There were five massive bolt throwers on either side of our ship, all loaded with what looked like pointy-tipped fence posts.

The gun crews cranked the elevation as the priests' ships came in, and Ku-Rho watched left and right, his hand raised.

"Prime!"

The crews doused the fence posts in lamp oil and set 'em on fire.

"Fire!"

The bolt throwers twanged like an out-of-tune guitar and the bolts shot straight at the balloons. It was too soon, at least on the left. Those bolts ripped across the deck of the left-hand ship, killing priests and sailors, but missing the balloon. The ship on the right, though, took two where it hurt the most. They punched through the skin of the balloon like harpoons through a whale, and that was all she wrote.

Christ, it was bad… Hindenberg bad. The balloon didn't explode like I thought it was gonna, but it burned so fast it was like somebody had sped up the film. I mean, one second, there's a little patch of fire along the flank of the thing, the next second, all the ribs are showing and there's a huge fireball rising up off it and everybody on the deck is screaming and running around with their clothes on fire.

The second after that, the ship dropped like a rock, burning all the way down and leaving drifting flags of black char coming over our rail and making us cough. The other two ships, however, kept closing, and there was no time to crank back the bolt throwers for another volley.

Arrows with lines attached to them zipped out from the priests' ships and stuck in our sides. I grabbed a hatch cover for a shield and jumped to the rail to chop through them as they reeled themselves in and arrows thudded into the hatch. I couldn't cut enough. There were too many. The ships kept closing, one along the side, one side-on to the stern.

I threw the shield across the gap and clocked a few guys, then ducked behind the rail with the others as bolts whiffed above us. Lhan, Sei-Sien and Shal-Hau knelt with the sailors, swords out and heads down, all waiting now for the ships to come together and the boarding to start. Sei-Sien's knees were knocking. I couldn't give a shit about him, but Shal-Hau was looking sick too.

I gave him a nudge. "Better go below, professor."

He shook his head. "They will kill me in my bunk just surely as they will here.

Better to die fighting for the cause."

"If you say so." I turned to Lhan. "Soon as you engage, I'm goin' over their heads and attacking from the rear."

"No. Make the crossbowmen your first target. They can kill us from afar."

"Got it."

He squeezed my hand. "Be careful, belove— er, Mistress."

I shot him a sideways look. He was blushing.

"Forgive me. I did not mean—"

I caught him around the back of the neck and kissed him hard. He pulled back, fighting it, then gave in and kissed back, and for a second the world went away, until a jolting double bump woke us to everybody shouting and the paladins pouring over the rail like an orange wave.

Lhan looked away as we broke off, his face hard, then tore after the others, stabbing and slashing like a lunatic as the two lines smacked together like a car wreck. It looked like he was trying to kill himself.

"Lhan! Goddamn it!"

I wanted to run in after him and pull him out of trouble, but I knew he'd hate me for it. Besides, the priests' crossbows were tearing our back ranks apart. If I didn't do something, we'd be done before we got started.

I jumped over the fight and launched straight at a guy in the rigging who was firing down with one leg hooked through the ropes. He yelped and tried to get off a shot, but I chopped through his crossbow, then through his neck. He flopped down, swinging from his hooked leg, and I kicked off his back for the foredeck, where three more were aiming for me. I swung my sword out hard and jerked sideways in the air.

The bolts whumped past me and I landed in the middle of 'em, and cut 'em all off at the knees—literally. It really was sick what that sword could do, and it made me a little sick using it sometimes, particularly when I was scrambling to my feet in a pick-up sticks pile of severed legs and screaming amputees. That's the thing they never show in those comic book movies—Superman, Wolverine, the Hulk—when you've got super strength or razor sharp blades, or both, you don't just knock guys out, or poke polite little holes in them. You chop them to fucking pieces. There is blood and flying arms everywhere. You're not a hero. You're a fucking monster.

And the worst thing is—it's not all bad.

A bolt punched through my sleeve and into my arm and I looked around, hissing. There was another guy in the rigging, cranking back his piece for another shot. I picked up one of the legless bodies at my feet and hurled it at him. It knocked him to the deck. There were four more on the aft deck. I hoisted up another dying guy by the arm strap and bounded toward them, holding him in front of me.

He jerked as bolts thudded into him, and his arms went slack. At least he stopped screaming. I whipped him at the crossbow guys as I bounced over the rail and knocked two of them off their feet. The other two scattered, but my sword was six feet long. I hamstrung 'em before they took two steps, then finished off the two guys I'd knocked down.

By this time I was drunk on slaughter and feeling pretty good. Nobody could hurt me. Nobody could stand against me. I was the fucking goddess of war. Time to do some real killing. I jumped down to the lower deck, right in the middle of the scrimmage at the rail—and promptly got a spear upside the head.

It was more a bash than a cut, but it rang my bell and hurt like living fuck, and popped my red rage balloon like a pin. All of a sudden I was human again and there were a lot of swords coming at me and everything was blurred and too bright. I must have slipped too, because the next thing I knew Lhan was catching my arm and holding me upright as I swung at the bad guys. He was bleeding from a cut across the chest.

"Thanks."

"Think nothing of it… ah, Mistress."

Three guards stabbed at me. I knocked 'em back. "You can call me beloved if you want, Lhan. I won't mind."

Lhan said nothing, just kept fighting.

I rolled my eyes. "I mean we're all gonna die here anyway, right?"

And we were. There was no way out. As I'd predicted, all my hopping around hadn't mattered one bit. Me and my gang and the sailors were still being driven back from the left rail by the temple guards, and the paladins who had swarmed over the stern were pushing Captain Ku-Rho and his men down off the aft deck and into the waist of the ship. We were all getting squeezed together and surrounded, and more troops were coming. Behind the guys we were fighting a whole new mob was charging across the deck of the priests' ship and leaping onto ours.

"Oh, come on! How can there be more? Where the fuck are they coming from?"

I groaned, really wishing I hadn't already been in two fights today, and got ready to have a whole new crop of spears stabbing my way, but as I tried to drive the dude in front of me back so I could get myself a little swinging room, a foot of sharp steel ripped out of his belly from behind, and he fell at my feet.

All along the line the same thing was happening. The temple guards were dying like flies, stabbed and bashed and chopped down from behind. I stared, then looked beyond them and saw that the guys who were pouring over the rail weren't reinforcements after all. There wasn't an orange robe among them, but there were a hell of a lot of earrings and wild clothes and second-hand armor. There was also a red-ballooned warship hanging off the right-hand rail that hadn't been there five minutes ago.

"Pirates!" shouted a sailor.

"We're flanked! Turn about!" shouted a paladin.

I joined the shouting. "Kill the priests! Kill 'em!"

Between us and the pirates the orangecicles were dead in half a minute. Surprised and trapped, between us they didn't stand a chance. What had been a slow slaughter with me and my pals as the slaughtered, became a quick massacre. No matter where they turned, the priests were getting stabbed in the back, and we didn't take mercy on them. Not a single one.

When it was all done, Captain Ku-Rho saluted the leader of the pirates, a big burly guy who I gaped at as he stepped forward. Was my vision still wonky, or…?

"Thank you, friend. You have saved us from certain death."

The burly guy put his sword to Ku-Rho's neck. "I wouldn't say saved, Captain. Not exactly."

A little woman in red swaggered out from behind the big guy's bulk and gave Ku-Rho a jaunty salute. "Postponed your death is more like it. But you can postpone it indefinitely if you hand over what you have in your hold with no—"

"Kai-La!"

I whooped with relief and pushed forward grinning and waving my sword.

"Kai-La! Where the hell—?"

Burly swung his sword at me, wild-eyed, and Kai-La backed up, drawing hers. Another pirate with a braided beard lunged at me, murder in his eyes. I was so surprised I almost didn't block in time, and Burly's sword came within an inch of chopping through my ear and into my brain. The guy with the braid grazed me, and I fell back with a gash across my abs. I knew him too—Lo-Zhar, the guy I'd called Braid Face. He didn't seem to know me.

"Wait! Wait!" I threw down my sword and put my hands up like I'd just been pulled over for a traffic stop. "It's Jane! Remember? I saved your asses at Toaga!"

CHAPTER FORTY-ONE

PIRATES!

Burly checked his swing, and pulled Lo-Zhar back.

Kai-La stared, frowning. "Jae-En? Is it truly you? Where is your pink skin? Your flame-colored hair?"

I shrugged. "Disguised again."

Lhan stepped forward, smiling. "And again in disreputable company."

Kai-La gave him the once-over, then grinned. "The dandy! So it *is* you. Well met!" She clapped me on the shoulder, then turned to her crew and raised her voice. "Hold a moment, friends! We will parley. See to your wounded, and let the Orans see to theirs!"

Lo-Zhar looked disgusted, and turned away.

I shook my head, still staggered, as she faced me again and the two crews started picking up their dead and maimed. "How are you even here? I though you were headed for the border and not looking back. What an insane coincidence."

Kai-La laughed. "Do you call it coincidence that the greatest pirate in all Ora should raid the fattest prize in all Ora? We have been following the tax ship since Rivi. Indeed, we would have waited for it to get fatter still but for fear these priests would make off with—"

"You know these villains?" Captain Ku-Rho was giving me and Lhan the fish eye all over again. I felt for him. First he thinks we're a priestess of Laef and her escorts, then he finds out we're heretics helping the Aldhanan defeat the Church of the Seven, then he finds out the Aldhanan is dead and the church thinks we did it, and now we're best friends with the pirates who are robbing his ship.

Well, I could ease his mind there. "This is Kai-La, who helped the Aldhanan stop Kedac-Zir in his tracks a few months back. She's one of the good guys, remember?"

Ku-Rho curled his lip. "I do remember. She was given a pardon and a rich reward for her brave actions, and now she is back robbing ships?"

Oh.

Yeah.

I'd been so surprised to see her again that I'd forgot about that part. Kai-La seemed to take it in stride. She laughed.

"Worry not, Captain. I will retire again once we bank these tithes—at least for a time. Now, open your hatches."

Ku-Rho drew himself up. "I am sworn to protect the imperial tithes against all thieves. You will not—"

"You're in no condition to protect anything, Captain. Besides, the Aldhanan won't miss it. He has plenty more where this came from."

Ku-Rho was getting hotter and hotter as she spoke. I was afraid he was going to pop. I stepped between them.

"Kai-La. The Aldhanan is dead."

That made her blink. She turned to Lhan like she was expecting him to say it was a joke. He didn't. She stared.

"Dead? What do you mean, dead?"

I swallowed. "Dead dead. Laid out on a slab dead. The priests killed him. He was traveling with us in disguise. They found out and—" The images of him lying there ambushed me again and I choked up. I pulled my thumb across my neck instead of talking. "Now—now they're after us 'cause we know they did it."

Lhan nodded. "They have named us his assassins."

Burly whistled. "I wondered why priests attacked an imperial ship."

Kai-La was frowning. "So, this has to do with the kidnapping of the Aldhanan's daughter and that fool Sai-Far? He went to war over it?"

"Not that alone." Lhan stepped forward. "He discovered that the priests were guilty of worse crimes, not just against his family, but against all Ora."

"He asked us to help take 'em down." I motioned to myself, Lhan, and Shal-Hau and Sei-Sien, who were sitting with the wounded and helping patch each other up. "We hitched a ride on the tax ship so we could go to each of his Dhanans in secret and tell 'em to get ready for war."

Kai-La smirked sadly. "But there was a spy. You were betrayed."

I nodded.

She sighed. "I am sorry. He was a good man, as far as Aldhanans go, and did right by us where others would have hanged us."

"And yet you repay his mercy by robbing him of his gold?" Ku-Rho sneered.

Kai-La gave him a sharp look. "It is his people's gold. And we will spend it more freely than he ever would have. Instead of sitting in some treasury for a hundred years, it will go right back into the purses of the poor wretches your tax collectors twisted it from."

Ku-Rho rolled his eyes. "The rationalizations of an outlaw."

Kai-La grinned. "Then you had best learn them, Captain."

"What?"

"Come, do we not both sail the same side of the wind now?" She looked around at us all, suddenly serious. "Friends, I have often before offered men the choice between ransom, death, or life as a pirate, but this is the first time fate has made the offer before I, and she has narrowed the choices to only two—death or piracy."

She grabbed a rope and stepped up on the rail so everybody could see her. "If you have angered the church, if you are accused of killing the Aldhanan, then there is only death behind you. No one will ransom enemies of the Empire—except of course the Empire itself, but they will care not whether you are dead or alive."

There was a lot of murmuring at that. She waved it down.

"Fear not. Fear not. I'll not turn you in. They would hang me beside you. What I say is, as you are already outlaw, what objection can you have to joining me? Ora is no longer your home, and the church has a long reach. Fly with me and you will be beyond it. Freedom and chance for vengeance will always be yours. With a ship such as this and the gold it carries, it would be we who were rulers of the air, and the Oran navy who were mere pretenders to our throne." She threw out a hand. "So what say you, will you sign the articles?"

A lot of the crew looked tempted. Even Captain Ku-Rho was thinking about it. So was I. I'd wanted to sign on with Kai-La and her gang from the first time I'd met 'em. Me and Lhan riding the sky, flying free, living outside of Ora's stuffy, medieval society—I couldn't think of a better life. The only reason I hadn't taken her up on her offer the last time was 'cause they were slaving, criminal fucks. Now, however, they were starting to look like the good guys. I couldn't think of a single reason why we shouldn't…

Goddamn it. Yes I could. Two reasons, in fact.

I caught Lhan's eye. He nodded. I sighed and picked up my sword, then looked up at Kai-La on the rail.

"I'm sorry. We gotta go back."

She stared at me like I was talking pig latin. "Sister, you are mad. You were born to sail the skies. Why continue to deny it?"

"I swore to the Aldhanan as he was dying that I'd protect Wen-Jhai. I can't break that promise."

Lhan stepped up beside me. "Nor can I. Nor abandon Sai-Far. With the Aldhanan dead, I cannot think but that they will be next."

"But what do you think you can do against the might of the church?" Kai-La was really angry. "You would have died here had I not intervened, and this miserable flotilla was nothing compared to what they can bring to bear. You won't save your friends. You will only die beside them."

"Then they will not die alone." Captain Ku-Rho fell in with Lhan and me. "For I will go with them, and any of my crew who will follow me. I will not allow the church to go unpunished for this assassination, nor allow them another."

From the rail, Lo-Zhar sneered. "Good riddance."

Kai-La shook her head. "And what use will you be, though your whole crew goes with you, when I have taken your ship and your gold? You will walk into Ormolu a moon from now to find your friends dead and the church waiting for you."

I shrugged. "So come with us."

Kai-La whipped around, eyes bulging. "What?"

"Why not? You don't like the church any more than we do. Shit, after Toaga, you should hate 'em! And you'd be doing the Empire another solid. They'll probably pay you twice what you've got now if you help us get Sai and Wen-Jhai to safety."

Lo-Zhar barked a laugh. "Pay us? They'd kill us!"

Kai-La snorted in agreement. "Stick my hand in a vurlak's mouth to pull its tongue? My thanks, but no. I may hate the church, but I am not ready to sacrifice myself for their destruction. If you wish to fight them I'll set you down and you may go to your deaths, and good luck to you."

I tried to think of something to say that would change her mind, but nothing was coming. She was right. She'd have to be an idiot to come with us. It was certain death. I looked at Lhan and Ku-Rho and Sei-Sien. They didn't have anything either. Then old Shal-Hau shuffled forward, holding a bandaged arm. He coughed.

"Mistress Captain, by your accent I suspect you are from Liaovan?"

She looked at him like he was a bug that had fallen in her coffee. "Aye. What of it?"

"Your parents were perhaps farmers there?"

Kai-La snarled and slapped her flat chest. "*I* was a farmer there. Until it dried up and blew away."

"Ah. Yes. I thought so. The Great Drought of Liaovan turned many honest farmers outlaw. And what if I were to tell you that the drought was the church's fault?"

She laughed, as bitter as chewing an aspirin. "Of course it was the church's fault! They drove the price of water tokens so high none could pay for irrigation. My… My…." She swallowed, then continued. "We could do nothing but watch our ruktugs die and curse the bone-dry sky. Do you think you will change my mind with things I already know?"

Shal-Hau smiled and ducked his head like he was afraid he was going to get hit, but he kept going. "Forgive me, Mistress, but I did not mean the church's practice of raising prices during a drought, though that of course was a crime as well. What I thought you might perhaps not know, what Mistress Jae-En has only recently brought to light, was that the church caused the drought in the first place. It was they who stole the rain. And, though you did not know it, it was they you cursed when you cursed the sky."

Kai-La blinked at him. "What? What are you saying?" She looked around at Lhan and me. "Who is this old fool? I know first-hand the power of the church, but they are not gods, no matter what they think themselves. They cannot steal the rain."

"They can, though." I leaned on the pommel of my sword. "I saw it. I was inside the Temple of Ormolu, and you know what it was? A big fucking water tank. The whole thing. They use fans and, uh, gifts of the Seven, to suck the moisture out of the air and fill the tank. That's why Ora is so dry all the time. All seven temples, Ormolu, Modgalu, all the rest, they're moisture traps.

They're stealing the water from the land and selling it back to you." I laughed. "You think you're the greatest pirate in all Ora? You're not a patch on these fuckers. They're holding a whole country for ransom."

Kai-La's knuckles were white on the rope. She looked me in the eye. I couldn't look away.

"Do you lie to me? Is this some trick to make me join you?" She pointed at Shal-Hau without looking at him. "Is he a mind reader? Does he know my life? My past?"

I had no clue. "I—I don't think so. He's just a professor. He teaches at the university in—"

"My—my husband *died* in that drought. He would not leave the farm. Just kept praying to the Seven to bring the clouds. They never came, so one day he went with some others to steal water from the Dhan." She fisted her eyes. "They brought his body back and I buried him in the field with the lassi roots that never grew, then I went with the others when the Dhan's men came for us."

She raised her head like she was coming out of a dream, then snarled around at us. "But what has that to do with this? You ask me to save a pair of foolish children. In what way will this win me vengeance against the church?"

Shal-Hau bowed again. "It is the first step. Once the Aldhanshai and her consort are out of reach of the church, we can act without fear for their safety. We will be free to plan something more substantial than just stealing their hostages out from under their noses."

Was he talking rebellion again? I hadn't promised the Aldhanan anything like that. Or maybe I had. When exactly would Wen-Jhai be safe? Would she ever be safe with the church around? What the hell had I signed up for?

Kai-La was still standing on the rail. Still gripping the rope and staring at nothing. Then a sob choked out of her and she looked over at Burly. "Halan. He was your brother. What say you? What would he have had me do?"

There were tears in Burly's eyes too. "You know already, sister. All he ever wanted was for the rain to come."

Kai-La closed her eyes and hung her head, nodding, but before she had a chance to think it out one way or the other, Lo-Zhar pushed forward, snarling like a badger.

"No, Kai-La! You cannot be considering this! We are pirates, not rebels! Listen to these fools and it will Toaga all over again. Let us take their gold and throw them over the side!"

Kai-La gave him a cold look. "You are no crew of mine, Lo-Zhar. You may do as you like. Take a ship, take your share of the spoils, take as many as will go with you. But on my ship, I will make my own decisions, and this is my ship."

Lo-Zhar glared at her, then shot a glance at her red-ballooned warship, which I suddenly recognized as the church ship she'd taken at Toaga with a new coat of paint. "As always, Skelsha, you claim the best for yourself. Our association cannot end soon enough." He gave her a tight bow, then turned on his heel and faced the crew. "Well, brothers, will you stay and die for nothing? Or will come with me and live for gold!"

A substantial chunk of the pirates followed him as he strode toward the ship at the back rail, but more stayed, waiting for Kai-La to make a decision.

It was a long wait. She stood there, staring out at the horizon for so long I thought she mighta fallen asleep or died or something, but finally she turned back and looked at Ku-Rho.

"I return your ship to you, Captain. But you are under my command, aye?"

"It depends, mistress, upon your orders."

Kai-La smiled like a shark. "All sails for Ormolu."

Ku-Rho squared his shoulders and snapped off a salute that woulda made a drill sergeant come. "With a will, Captain!"

CHAPTER FORTY-TWO

BLIND-SIDED!

We came in at night, in the full dark, and even then, Kai-La and her remaining ships stayed just the other side of the hills on Ormolu's west side. The spotters of the Oran Navy weren't gonna miss a whole fleet coming over the skyline, but one lonely navy ship? Coming in toward the navy base? Nothing out of the ordinary about that, right? It wouldn't even be too weird if we stopped over the palace. I mean, we'd done exactly the same thing when the Aldhanan had brought us back home after Durgallah.

I still kept my fingers crossed as we sailed in, even though I couldn't imagine how they'd know what had happened in Modgalu yet.

Ku-Rho kept his ship on the correct flight path until the last possible minute, then drifted west toward the palace and started dropping down. Lhan, Shal-Hau, Sei-Sien and I looked over the palace as we got lower. It all looked pretty normal at first. Quiet, calm, the guards going on their rounds as usual, but then I noticed a lot of orange happening, and my heart seized up.

"Hey, are those paladins?"

Lhan looked closer. "Indeed. There seem to be as many of them as there are palace guards."

I swallowed. "Does this mean Sai and Wen-Jhai are already—"

"Do not speculate, Mistress. We will know soon enough."

Ku-Rho trimmed sails and brought us to a stop just over the Aldhanan's balcony, then dropped a rope ladder.

Shal-Hau bowed to us and crossed his wrists.

"Return swiftly, pupil, Mistress."

Sei-Sien bowed too, then lifted his chin and looked noble. "And if you do not, be sure that we spread the tale of your bravery to all corners of Ora. You martyrdom will inspire us all."

Lhan returned their bows, but I shivered and turned away. "Jinxing bastard. Fuck off. We'll be back in five minutes."

I had a weird little deja-vu moment as we started down when I realized that this was almost exactly like when we had gone to rescue Wen-Jhai in Doshaan and Kedac-Zir had swung through the window and snatched her out from under our noses, only this time it was us doing Kedac-Zir's rope ladder trick.

Unfortunately for us, the palace was a little better guarded than the house of the guy we'd rescued Wen-Jhai from, and we didn't get halfway down the ladder before we heard guards shouting and lanterns started to swarm around in the courtyards below.

"Hurry, Mistress."

"Yeah, yeah."

I gave up taking it one rung at a time and slid down like a pirate. Skinned the hell out of my hands and thighs, but what the fuck else were we going to do.

There wasn't any time for sneaking around when we reached the balcony either. The fuckers already knew we were there. I kicked through the door into the Aldhanan's suite and we looked around. The lights were on, but nobody was home.

"Fuck. Where are they? Check the side rooms."

Lhan raised his voice as we crossed toward the doors. "Wen-Jhai? Sai-Far? Are you here?"

There was a shuffling noise behind the bedroom door and it opened. Wen-Jhai stepped out, dressed all in see-through white and looking like she'd been crying. Her top heavy maid, Shae-Vai, stood behind her, peeking over her shoulder.

"Sai, did you call? Have you returned to your senses at—" She stopped and gasped when she saw us, hand over her mouth, eyes wide, the whole thing.

She looked like something out of a silent movie.

"You!"

Lhan stepped to her, bowing, as Shae-Vai kept her from falling. "My Aldhanshai, where is Sai-Far? We are here to save you from the priests."

She backed into Shae-Vai's arms, still doing her damsel in distress routine. "No! I cannot! And you must leave! The priests say you have killed my father!"

"They told you already?"

Fucking priests and their fucking teleporters. It didn't matter how fast we flew. They were always gonna beat us home with the news. I felt like a Cherokee looking at a telegraph pole.

"We did not kill your father," said Lhan. "Though I count our failure to prevent his death as great a crime. But it was the priests who assassinated him."

"Think you I do not know it?" Wen-Jhai was pushing at us now, trying to get us to go back to the balcony. "You would never have betrayed him. But it matters not what I know. The priests will kill you for it just the same. You must go!"

"And you gotta come with us. Both of you." I took her arm and beckoned to Shae-Vai. "Come on. Show us where Sai is."

"You don't understand! Sai will not go! And if he does not, I cannot!"

Lhan and I stopped and looked at her.

"Sai will not go?"

"Why the hell not?"

"Because he—"

The door to the Aldhanan's study opened and Sai stepped out, looking around.

"Beloved? Who is it you speak to? You are interrupting my studies with—" He stopped dead when he saw us, and stared, then called back into the room behind him.

"The assassins! Master, the assassins are here!"

A guy in orange robes stepped out of the study and stood at his shoulder. It was Duru-Vau. He smiled a chinless smile.

"I wondered if they would arrive. Fear not, my Aldhanan. The guards are already on their way."

***

I stared at Sai, gobsmacked. "Sai, what the fuck is the matter with you? Kick that sleezebag the junk and let's go."

Sai looked at me like he didn't know me. "You killed the Aldhanan, my beloved father-in-law. You tricked him into rebelling against the Seven. You are heretics in the eyes of the church and traitors in the eyes of all loyal Orans."

I blinked, stunned, then turned to Lhan. "What the fuck? What's wrong with him?"

Wen-Jhai moaned behind us. "I told you. I told you."

Lhan shook his head. "Sai, what is this? How can you believe that Mistress Jae-En, who helped return you to your beloved Wen-Jhai, and who saved the life of the Aldhanan not two moons ago, could wish to harm him or threaten Ora?"

I stepped forward. "Sai, the church kidnapped you, remember? They tortured you and threw you in a hole! How the fuck are you on their side now?"

"They drove your evil influence from my body. I am purified now. I—"

"Evil influence? What the fuck did I ever do to you except save your ass every five minutes? Who's been feeding you this crap?"

Well, actually, that was pretty obvious. He was standing right there behind him, simpering him like a smug fish.

Beside me, Lhan choked. "By the One, it was Sai. The church's replacement for the Aldhanan. It was Sai all along!"

I gaped at him. "Oh fuck!"

Sai just kept talking and pointing. "You are a demoness. A disruptive entity from a nether hell, sent here to overthrow all that is good and decent in this world. You corrupted my wife, making of her a harlot, and turned my father-in-law into a heretic before you—"

I spread my hands, pleading. "Sai. Come on, dude. You know that's bullshit. I—"

"No. It has all been a ruse, from the beginning—befriending me, helping me. All just a trick to get close to the Aldhanan and win his confidence so that you could turn him from the church."

Wen-Jhai balled her fists. "Sai! Stop!"

He ignored her. "And when he began to rebel against you, when the Aldhanan's true nature began to reassert itself and he wanted to break from you, you killed him."

I rolled my eyes. "What the fuck, Sai? You sound like that mouth-breathing pencil-neck has his hand up your ass and he's movin' your lips for you. You're the one who needs to reassert yourself. Wake the fuck up!"

Lhan looked toward the stairs. "'Ware, Mistress. They come."

"I hear 'em."

I turned to the door, hefting my sword. The sound of running boots boomed from behind it, then it exploded open and the room flooded with paladins, spears out. They surrounded us and started to close in as we turned this way and that, braced to fight.

"Call 'em off, Sai. You're the Aldhanan now. Call 'em off!"

Sai didn't say a word, but Duru-Vau stepped forward, slipping through the ring of guards. "No need, brothers. I have a clear shot."

And before I could figure out what he was talking about, he thrust his hand at me and Lhan, just like he had the last time—only this time he was closer, and it was worse. We flew back like we'd been hit by a fire hose and crashed through the guards to slam against the far wall. I slumped to the ground like my bones had been turned to oatmeal. I could see Lhan twitching beside me out of the corner of my eye, but I couldn't turn to look at him. I couldn't move a muscle. My heart hurt like somebody was squeezing it in a trash compactor. I couldn't breathe, and my vision was starting to get dark and fuzzy around the edges.

The guards moved in, raising their spears like they were gonna finish the job, but Duru-Vau waved them off.

"No. To the temple with them. They are to be questioned first."

We couldn't do a thing to stop 'em. They just grabbed our ankles and wrists and walked us toward the door like we were hog carcasses. I could still hear and see, though, and heard Wen-Jhai going to town on Sai.

"Stop them, husband! Do not let them take our friends into the temple! They will never be seen again! Have you no honor? Have you no courage?"

Sai turned on her, as cold and dead as before. "You would defend those that killed your father? It is you who have no honor."

Wen-Jhai backed away from him, weeping. "Perhaps not, but at least I have courage."

And with that she turned and ran for the balcony, reaching for the rope ladder to Ku-Rho's warship, with Shae-Vai following right on her heels. That's last thing I saw before they carried Lhan and me out the door, but I could hear Duru-Vau shouting all the way down the stairs.

"Stop her! Bring her down! Bring her back!"

***

I must have passed out completely at some point after that, 'cause the next thing I knew, I woke up butt naked in a closet-sized room with one glass wall.

My head hurt so much that it took me a while to recognize the smooth white architecture and figure out where I must be—a jail cell somewhere inside the Temple of Ormolu.

This was so thrilling I threw up. Then I just sat there for a while, watching the little pool of puke spread out on the metal floor. My head throbbed. My heart throbbed. My everything throbbed. I felt like some miniature stereo freak had set up a boomin' system deep down in my guts, and had turned the bass up to eleven. The pulse made all the cuts and bruises I'd got over the past few weeks hurt worse than they already did. I ached from head to foot.

Then I noticed I was pink again, and my hair was its natural red, and damp. The fucking priests musta washed all my purple off while I was knocked out. The thought of all those priest hands soaping me up was so creepy I threw up again. Then I panicked and felt for Lhan's balurrah around my neck.

It was gone!

For some reason that was the worst thing that had ever happened to me, and I bawled like a baby until I ran out out of tears.

Sometime later a guard came by with a plate of food and a mug. I tensed, waiting for the doors to whoosh open so I could jump him, even though I knew I probably couldn't even stand. The doors didn't whoosh. Instead, they hissed and raised up together, less than three inches, and he slid the plate and mug under. Then they hissed down again and he went away. Didn't offer to clean up the mess I'd made. Didn't seem to notice I'd made it.

Watching him leave drew my attention to the outside of the cell for the first time, not that there was much to see. The hallway beyond the glass was blank and dark, and when I crawled to the door I couldn't see another cell in either direction. So where had they put Lhan?

"Lhan! Lhan, are you here? Can you hear me?"

No answer. Of course, I don't know how loud I shouted. It sounded plenty loud to me, but for all I know I coulda been whispering. Pretty soon I gave up and crawled back to the food.

It took me a while to remember how to sit up straight and pick things up with my hands, but eventually I got the hang of it, and ate what was in the bowl. I didn't know what it was. It didn't taste like anything I'd eaten on Waar before, but that's 'cause it didn't taste like anything, period. Still, I ate it. If there's one thing I've learned in my many stays inside, it's that you should eat every chance you get. You never know when you're gonna get another meal, and you never know when you're gonna need your strength.

I fell asleep again sometime after that, my aches and pains not quite enough to counter the sick, wiped-out feeling that was dragging me down, but I woke up again after what felt like only an hour or so to the sounds of bootheels clicking slowly down the hall.

I pulled myself up to a crouch and tested my arms and legs. The sleep hadn't been much, but at least I felt like I could move a bit now, and my head wasn't spinning. I wouldn't fall over if I stood up—at least I hoped not. If it was the guard, asking for the plate and cup back, I'd see if he would open the door to clean up my puke. If not, I'd figure something else out. Maybe I could grab his hand and pull him under the three-inch gap. It'd sure be fun to try.

It wasn't the guard.

The boots stopped in front of the cell and I looked up. The guy giving me the once-over from the other side of the glass was old, seriously old, with a mop of white hair, a stringy neck and blue veins as thick as licorice snaking under his skin. But for all that he didn't look one bit frail or weak. He was more than six feet tall, and had probably been taller back before he started to stoop, and the harness and loincloth he wore showed me that he was as wiry and ripped as a greyhound. He looked like Clint Eastwood on his hundredth birthday.

It took me a full ten seconds to realize he wasn't purple. His skin was a pinkish tan—just like mine.

He shook his head and sighed. "You have been a burr in my britches, missy. You surely have."

CHAPTER FORTY-THREE

THE WARGOD!

I stared at the guy, and if my mouth was hanging open I wouldn't be a damned bit surprised. Not only was he speaking English, he was talking in an accent I hadn't heard since the last time me and Big Don had ridden our bikes through Alabama. It took me a couple of tries to get any words out—and they weren't much when they came.

"You—I—how… Who the fuck are you?"

He gave me a disapproving look. "Language of that nature is not proper for young ladies. Particularly not southern young ladies like yourself. Show some decorum."

Well, I was still shocked, but that pissed me off. Decorum woulda been not throwing me in a cell. I snorted. "Let me out of here and I'll show you all the decorum you want. Otherwise, go fuck yourself."

He looked like he was gonna get mad, but then he just sat down on a bench built into the wall opposite the cell. He took what looked like a Sherlock Holmes pipe outta a pouch at his belt and pointed it at me. "Duru-Vau was right. You got some fire in you. That's good. Fire's what's needed."

"You still haven't told me who the fuck you are."

He sighed like I was some potty-mouthed granddaughter, then looked at the pipe. "You know the worst thing about coming to this place? I never did find a good substitute for tobaccy. Couldn't rid myself o'the habit of suckin' on the stem though."

I don't know why that did it, but that did it. All of a sudden I knew who he was. "Wait a minute! You're the guy from the book! *Savages of the Red Planet*! You're Captain Jack Wainwright!"

He raised a shaggy white eyebrow. "So you read my nephew's little piece of trash? Godawful thing, that book. Turns the hardest work a white man ever done into a cheap romance for pimply adolescents. Woulda sued him for slander if I'da stayed home."

"But—but how are you even alive! You fought in the Civil War! You must be two hundred years old!"

"A hundred and seventy-two, thank you very much. And as to how, well the fellas that built this here rocket ship got a little rejuvenation machine upstairs that I been using since I took over. Kept me young and fit for nigh on fifty years. Now it just keeps me old."

"So Lhan was right. You've been running things from behind the scenes since you disappeared."

He scratched his thatch of white hair. "Yeah, well, I learned a lesson back then. People don't like it when their gods stick around too long. They want 'em gone, up in the sky, where they can pray to 'em, but don't feel like they're pushin' 'em around all the time. At the end there, I had all the Dhanans in Ora after my hide. Figured it was time to take my bows and go. Make it seem like the church was running things."

"Well now you've got the Dhanans rising up against the church. And killing off the Aldhanan ain't gonna stop that. They know who really did it."

Wainwright sighed and sucked his pipe. "Y'see, this is what comes of gettin' old. I don't tend to the day-to-day o' the church so much anymore. I spend most of my time up in the machine, sleepin' and dreamin' o' times gone by. That Duru-Vau, damned smart boy. Proved he could handle himself time and time again, so I let him start running things while I just... supervised." He went through the motions of cleaning and filling the bowl of the pipe even though there was nothing in it, then took a draw and continued. "Didn't realize how greedy he was until it was way too late. I'd seen from the beginning that the water could be used as a tool to shape Waar how I wanted, but he uses it like a weapon. He wants the church to own every goddamned thing on the planet."

I curled my lip. "If you don't like 'im, why don't you take 'im out? You're the Wargod, ain't you?"

"I was, girl. I was. But now? That pole-cat's got half the priesthood under his sway. If I were to make an open move against him, they'd kill me in my sleep. Fact, I been expecting that any day now."

"So, what are you gonna do about it?"

He smiled and cupped the pipe between his big knuckly hands. "Well now, that's why you and me are having this little tete-a-tete."

"Whaddaya mean?"

"What I mean is, I want you to be my successor."

If he had asked me to referee a basketball game between oompa-loompas and unicorns, I wouldn'ta been more surprised. In fact, that would have made a whole lot more sense.

"Wh-what? Wait. Aren't we enemies? Haven't you been fucking with me since I got here?"

He held up his hands. "Now now, settle yourself. I admit I didn't see it at first. That's why I had my boys send you back to Earth. I didn't want to kill you. I don't hold with doing violence to ladies, and it didn't feel right hurting another Earthman—er, woman—but you were a goddamn nuisance, pardon my French, and since you'd been talking so eager about goin' back, I figured you'd stay once you got there."

"You coulda asked."

He went on like I hadn't said anything. "It was when you came back that I started to realize how much gumption you had, and I went to a hell of a lot of trouble tryin' to get you to come see me."

"Like I just said. You coulda asked."

He still wasn't listening to me. Instead he was frowning and looking somewhere over my shoulder. I looked back. There was nothing back there but wall and cot.

"Y'see, I been keepin' an eye on you, and despite our differences, I believe you and I are kindred spirits under the skin. We ain't neither of us the type to just sit back and wish for a better world. We don't wait for no politician or preacher to do what's right. We get up outta our rockers and we do it ourselves. That's the way I've led this world for the past hundred and fifty years. That's the way I want it led for the next hundred and fifty." He finally looked at me, right in the eyes. "That's why it's you. You believe in honor. You believe in courage. You understand how important it is to live in a world where strength and valor can still solve problems. Well, that's the world I've worked so hard to make here, and I know, from the way you fight, from the way you think, from the way you live, that you're the one who'll keep it just the way it is."

"I—I am?" Did he really think that? Did he really think I wanted Waar to stay a place where a church and a bunch of rich slave owners lorded it over everybody else, and where rich kids pretended that defending their girlfriends by hacking each other to pieces meant they were more honorable than everybody else?

He did.

He leaned forward, his eyes all googily just thinking about it. "Right now, Waar is a perfect little gem, a world of chivalry. A place where honor and courage matter. A place where men of noble blood protect the weak and the weak are grateful."

I snorted. "Yeah. Wouldn't want 'em talking back or anything."

"Exactly. And that is why I have trapped it in amber. So it will never grow ugly and modern and corrupt." He clenched his fists. "You know, I went back to Earth a few times. To visit my nephew. I saw what they'd done to the south, with their factories, and their motor cars, and their negros in fancy suits. They ruined it. They murdered the finest place that ever was. Well, that won't happen here. *That's* what the water's for. Not to buy up everything lock, stock and barrel, like Duru-Vau thinks, but as a carrot and a stick, all wrapped up in one."

I was starting to think that living for a hundred and seventy-five years wasn't so good for the brain. I didn't know what he was talking about anymore.

"That's what I've done since I took over the church. I give water to the folk that are doin' it right, living a life of chivalry and honor, and being good stewards of the land and the people. For them, rain and water tokens—anything they want. But I keep it from anybody who starts getting ideas, anybody who talks about wanting a vote, or better pay, or equality under the law." He made a twisting motion with his left hand. "For them, off goes the tap. And anybody who invents any kind of labor-saving device, or manufacturing process, or anything even remotely like a gun?" He twisted with his right hand. "No water for them either."

He jerked his thumb over his shoulder. "There's a little room way at the top of this roman candle where can I control all the moisture gatherers in all the temple cities all by myself, and I've used 'em to play this world like an instrument. I keep it just dry enough that water is a blessing that they thank the church for, but not so dry that they curse us. At least I did until Duru-Vau got ahold of the switch. Shoulda known better than to let any o' these purple monkeys mess with the machinery."

He trailed off, his face glum, and I almost spoke, but then he started again. "I—I wanted to have an heir, a son, but it just don't work with the local squaws. Lord knows I tried often enough, but we're like cats and dogs. Close, but not the same. You'll never make any younguns with your fella there. Hate to be the one to tell you."

Well, I coulda told him I'd had my tubes tied when I was twenty-three, but I let it go. He was still talking anyway.

"Like I said, I thought it would be Duru-Vau, but he keeps talkin' about making Ora into a war machine, figuring out how the Seven made all their nasty toys and using 'em to take over the planet. He thinks that's what I want. Thinks that's what the Wargod *should* want. But that kind of war brings all the things I hate. Factories, smoke stacks, businessmen, agitators, a world where peasants have guns and men of honor are no longer safe in their homes. He just doesn't understand, but you do."

He looked me in the eye again. "It takes someone who's seen the mess modern men have made of the world to understand how beautiful this place is, and to wanna keep it that way. Someone like you."

You know, if I was a smart girl, I woulda kissed his ass and pretended to go along with him, then clobbered him when he let me out of the cell, but anger makes me stupid, and right then he'd made me so angry I probably couldn't have added up one plus one. I was so mad the walls of the cell were turning red around the edges. I stood up and stepped up to the glass.

"Who the fuck are you to play god with these people, you creep? Who gave you the right to decide who's doin' it right and who's doin' it wrong? You're just some jumped-up peckerwood jackhole who still thinks it's okay for people to own other people." I spat. I had to. "You know what, I'm proud to be a southern girl. I grew up on RC Cola, moon pies and 'Sweet Home Alabama,' and my neck's redder than yours ever was, but the world you lost, the world you've tried to remake out here in the middle of wherever the fuck we are, that world was so poisonous that a hundred and fifty years later I still gotta prove I'm not a racist every time somebody figures out I'm from south of the Mason-Dixon."

I stabbed a finger at him and stoved it on the glass. I was too mad to feel the pain. "You did that, you motherfucker. You gave every generation of redneck that's come after you a case of the ku klux clap. We can only ever hold our heads so high, 'cause we know everybody that meets us still sees you standing behind us, holding a goddamn whip. Well fuck you. Fuck you if you think I'm gonna keep the grand old traditions of the 'land o' cotton' alive for you after you've gone."

His face had gone cold and hard on the other side of the glass, and he was standing up, but I wasn't done.

"And if you think this place is so beautiful, you haven't been looking where I've been looking. It's nice in the palace, alright. I'll give you that. And the Dhanans have it pretty good. But all those weak people who you think should be so grateful to you? Their lives suck! They're dying of thirst. They're starving to death. They're getting sick on diseases we figured out cures for back on Earth a hundred years ago. Yeah, factories ain't pretty. And modern life can be kinda ugly sometimes, but the things that come with all that ugly make life better for most people. They don't die from the plague anymore. They don't have to work eighty hours a week just to get by. They don't have to lower their eyes to anybody or call anybody master. But you don't care about 'most people,' do you? You just care about your 'men of honor.'" I stopped as something hit me, and I looked right in his eyes, fist balled like I was going to punch right through the unbreakable glass. "You know what you are? You're a kid playing with dolls. You took a living breathing world and you turned it into a pretty little stage for all your pretty little knights and ladies so they could play out their soap operas of chivalry on it. Everybody else is just extras and spear carriers to you, ain't they? Jesus fuck, you make me sick!"

Wainwright looked at me like a father who just found cigarettes in his daughter's purse. He sighed. "Well, that's too bad. I thought you understood. I truly did."

"I do understand, you cancerous old cracker. You wanna remake the world in your own image. Well, your image blows."

I don't think he heard me. He hung his head and made a sad little motion with one hand. "I do not care to kill women, but in your case I fear I have no choice. You are too strong and strong-willed to leave here alive. You and your pretty-boy friend will be executed publicly tomorrow to remind the people of the power of the church and to unite them behind Sai-Far, who will be the next Aldhanan."

"You mean the next *puppet*. I already saw Duru-Vau making his lips move."

Wainwright shook his head. "It should have been you pullin' the strings. I'm too tired these days to bring Duru-Vau to heel like he should be, but I guess it'll have to be done. So long, missy. Sorry it worked out this way."

He turned away and started down the hall, looking older and sadder than when he showed up.

I hoped it killed him.

CHAPTER FORTY-FOUR

CONDEMNED!

So they were gonna kill us tomorrow. I could see Wainwright's reasons. One, he'd be getting rid of the troublemaking bitch with the sword. Two, he'd be giving Sai a public relations boost. The new Aldhanan announces that he's captured the old Aldhanan's killers and makes a big song and dance outta putting 'em to death. The crowd goes wild and thinks the new Aldhanan is a swell guy. Works the same way back home. DAs run for mayor after they've solved a big murder case. Generals run for president after they've won a war. But as much as I liked Sai, I wasn't ready to die to help his election campaign. I had to get out, and I had to take Lhan with me. The question was, how? I'd had a hard enough time getting outta here the first time, and I hadn't been locked in a cell. Also, what did we do once we were free? Did we take another whack at rescuing Sai? Did we hunt down Wainwright and Duru-Vau? Did we join Kai-La and go be pirates? Did we say fuck it and just head for the border like we'd wanted to do from the beginning?

I didn't like any of those ideas. I'd given up on running away a long time ago, and I wasn't about to change my mind now, not after meeting 'ol Foghorn Leghorn and hearing his plans, but killing him, or Duru-Vau, or any of the priests wasn't really going to change anything. Neither was rescuing Sai. The church would just find another puppet, and no matter how many priests we killed, more would rise up to take their place, and the whole corrupt system would just keep rolling along, sucking the water out of the sky and selling it back to the people at oil company prices. There had to be a way to kill the system itself, not just the guys who ran it.

And, duh! There was—right upstairs!

I smacked myself in the forehead as I thought of it. Hadn't Wainwright just said there was a control room upstairs which controlled all seven moisture collectors? All we had to do was get up there, shut 'em all down and smash the controls. Problem solved. It might take a while, but once the machines stopped drying out the atmosphere, the weather would return to normal, right?

Well, shit, I ain't no scientist. I had no idea if it would work, but taking away Wainwright's carrot and stick sure *sounded* like a step in the right direction. So, step one....

Yeah.

I sighed and sank back. I'd fought one of these doors before and I hadn't been able to budge it. Actually that had been an elevator door. A jail cell door would probably be even tougher. Locked even.

I stood up and pushed on the glass anyway. It was like pushing a building. There was no give at all. I tried to get my fingers between the halves. Not even a fingernail. They fit together like a glued joint. What about that three-inch gap on the bottom when the guard brought the food? Could I lift it up?

I knelt and looked. The bottom of the door was a chisel-shaped wedge that slotted into a little groove in the floor. Anything under it when it dropped would be chopped in two—cups, plates, fingers, toes. I got a little spine shudder just thinking about it. Next?

I looked around the little room. There was just nothing. The cot was molded into the wall. It had no sheets, pillows or blankets. The toilet was a hole in the floor. There were no pipes or cables I could pull out and use as a weapon, and the damn place was so narrow I wouldn't have had room to swing 'em even if there were.

Wait.

Maybe that was it.

I looked up at the ceiling. It went up a good three feet higher than the top of the door.

That was it. That was all I needed.

***

I tried to sleep for a bit, but I couldn't, so I exercised instead, stretching and doing push-ups to try and work out the weird stiffness that Duru-Vau's mind blast had knocked into me. Then I just sat there and strained my ears for the guard.

Instead, I finally heard Lhan. He was far off, or behind a lot of walls, or both, and I wouldn't have heard him if I hadn't been sitting completely still.

"Jae-En! Are you here! Do you live? Jae-En, answer if you hear!"

I jumped up and stepped to the door, then put my hands together like a megaphone. "Lhan! I'm here! Stay put! I'm gonna… Well, just stay put!"

His voice echoed to me again. "I will, beloved. But only because you ask."

I laughed. Good old Lhan. Even FUBARed all to hell, he still had his sense of humor. Kinda choked me up a bit.

I settled in to wait again, and this time I guess I did doze, because suddenly there were footsteps coming and I was jerking my chin up off my chest. Fuck! I had to get into position!

I stood and put my palms on one wall like I was assuming the position, then reached back with my feet and put them one at a time on the other wall. An average Waarian probably couldn'ta done it. Most of them weren't taller than five-ten or so, but at six-one, I just made it. I started to spider up the walls, hands walking up one, feet walking up the other.

And just in time too. I only just cleared the top of the door when the guard stepped in front of it with another mug and plate. I kept climbing, wedging myself as close to the ceiling and front wall as possible so I'd be out of his line of sight.

He stood there, looking into the empty cell for a long second, like if he stared long enough I'd suddenly appear. Then he stepped back until all I could see from my angle were his feet. Was he going to call for help? Was he drawing his weapon?

He stepped forward again without the plate and mug and pressed himself against the glass, looking left, right and up. I squeezed closer to the wall, hoping that, since I could see just the tip of his nose, but not his eyes, that he couldn't see me. I guess he couldn't, because I heard him draw his sword, then the doors whooshed open and he stepped in.

A hidden speaker squawked just as I dropped. "Mar-Gan, do not go into the cell! She hides above!"

Fuck! They had cameras in the cells! Fortunately poor old Mar-Gan had been too stupid to call back to the desk for a remote check, the dumb fuck. He yelped and tried to back out, but I squashed him flat, half in, half out of the doors, then rolled into the hall. The doors whooshed in again and pinched him at the ribs—hard. I heard bones snap as he shrieked.

"Open it! Open it!"

The doors opened again and I pulled him out, then stripped his sword from his hand. He was in too much pain to resist. The voice came over the speaker as I grabbed the guard by his harness and started dragging him down the hall in the direction he and Wainwright had come.

"Return to your cell, demoness. There can be no escape for you."

I raised my head. "You want me to go back, come in and put me back. Meanwhile I'm just gonna sit by the door and eat poor Mar-Gan."

"E-eat him?"

"What else do you expect from a demon?"

Mar-Gan started wailing as I pulled him along. "Captain, please! Save me! Seven protect me from all unholies!"

There were two more cells along the right-hand side of the hall, but both were dark. No Lhan. Then it ended in another glass door with some kinda central guard room beyond it. I lifted Mar-Gan to his feet and set him in front of it.

"Open it."

"I—"

Mr. Voice squawked again. "It will not open, Demoness. I control it from here."

Of course he did. Dammit! Why did these fuckers have to live in a space ship? Breaking outta shit was so much harder when it was high tech. If this was a typical Waar castle all I'd have had to worry about was deadbolts, bowmen and guys with swords. Sci-fi sucked. Maybe I could cut my way out. Well, not with this toothpick. Where was my sword? And my clothes? Had they thrown them away?

I glanced back down the hall. There were no doors in it except the cell doors. How about in the guard room? Bingo! There were lockers in the far wall, and I saw the long hilt of my sword sticking up out of one of them. The damn thing was so big the door couldn't completely close. Of course, it was useless to me out there. Hmmm.

I raised my voice. "Hey! Buddy! You wanna save your friend's life? Open the—"

A door on the far side of the guard room whooshed before I could finish, and a bunch of guards and a priest ran in. It closed behind them again as they crossed to my door and stared at me through it. One of the guards had a wand of blue fire. I gave him the finger as he aimed it at me.

Then the priest raised his voice. "Ru-Kol, be ready to open solitary door one at my order."

The speaker crackled. "Ready."

I pulled poor Mar-Gan in front of me and shouted. "Now, Ru-Kol! Open it now!"

The door whooshed open. I laughed, amazed that had worked, and charged through, shoving my hostage at the wand guy and slashing at the others with my stolen sword as the priest backpedaled, wide-eyed and screaming.

"That wasn't me, you fool! That was her!"

I bashed through the guards without doing much damage, then threw the little blade aside and ran to the half-open locker as they regrouped behind me. There was no time to mess with the trying to open the fucking thing. I just grabbed the hilt of my sword and pulled as hard as I could as they came in. The locker wanged open and I whipped the big bastard around behind me. Unfortunately it was still in its scabbard, so I didn't cut anybody in half, only cracked heads and slapped aside spears.

It still drove 'em back, and I bashed through them again toward the door, shouting, "Open solitary door two!"

"I can see you speaking this time, demoness! You will not fool me twice!"

I ripped my sword from its sheath and put it to the priest's neck. "Okay, how about straight up threats? Open it or I kill his reverence!"

"I—I must not."

The priest swallowed, shaking like a leaf. "Open the door, Ru-Kol!"

"I'm sorry, your reverence. Have you not told me that the rules are not to be—"

"Damn the rules! Open the door!"

"I—I'm sorry, your reverence. I will not."

Well, fuck. Just my luck Ru-Kol was a fucking by-the-book weenie. How the fuck was I gonna do this?

Then I saw the answer right in front of me. The wand guy was on his feet again, aiming at me.

"Ha! You're the guy I want."

I whipped the priest at him and knocked him flat, then stepped to him and ripped the wand from his hands.

"Actually, I just want this."

I held it out and raised my sword over it like I was a butcher and it was a salami. "Open the door or the wand gets it!"

The whole room gasped, and I heard Ru-Kol suck in a breath on the intercom. The priest held out a hand.

"Demoness, you must not. It is a holy relic."

"Oh yeah? What's this one's name? Slave Killer? Love Truncheon? Doom Cock?"

"That is Beast Queller, and you must not—"

I lowered my sword to it and started sawing, grooving the plastic. Ru-Kol shrieked in the speakers and solitary door two opened. I ran for it and it started to whoosh closed again as soon as I reached it. If I'd been wearing my usual loincloth getup it woulda got caught. Lucky I was naked.

"Nice try, Ru-Kol."

Lhan was standing at the door as I reached his cell. He was naked too.

"Jae-En! Again you perform miracles."

"Don't call it that until we're free. Now, stand back."

I leaned my sword against the wall and aimed the wand of blue fire at the door. Lhan's eyes widened and he backed to the side of the cell. I squeezed the trigger. Nothing happened.

"Goddamn it! Is it out of juice? What's wrong?"

I glanced back down the hall. The paladins were staring at me through the closed door, and I could hear the priest shouting at the intercom guy.

"No, fool! Do not sound the alarm! Do you not recall the punishments after her last escape? *We* will handle this!"

Ha! Good to know.

I looked at the gun. It really wasn't much more than a white plastic tube. There was a trigger—more like a big button—on the underside of it, and a row of three smaller buttons and lights further up the barrel on the side.

"Hmmm. Maybe that's some kinda safety. Maybe the trigger doesn't work unless I'm holding down one of these."

I aimed again and held down the first button. Nothing. Second. Nothing. Third. Nothing.

"Fucking thing! How do you work?"

In frustration, I jammed down all the buttons at once, then jumped like a spooked rabbit as a beam of blue white light shot out of the thing and carved a smoking black trench in the wall and the glass. I dropped it, squeaking like a chew toy, and it clattered to the floor, the beam snapping off as soon as my fingers came off the buttons.

"Mistress! Are you injured?"

It was hard to talk. My heart was going a mile a minute. "It's okay. I got it now. Jesus."

I picked up the wand again and aimed it at the door, depressed the three buttons on the side, then pulled the trigger. The blue fire erupted from the barrel and instantly started melting a line in the glass. I was expecting some kind of kick or push back, like a gun or a fire hose, but there wasn't any. Only a humming vibration, like an air conditioner on high. Fifteen seconds later I'd cut a square in the left-hand door and kicked it out. The wand was ticking like a cooling engine block.

Lhan ducked out, looking at the smoking edges of the glass in awe. "Neatly done, Mistress. I would not have had the courage to touch such an instrument."

"Better behind it than in front of it. Come on."

"Know you a way out?"

"We're not going out."

He looked a little uneasy at that. "Oh?"

"Got something to do first."

"Would you care to enlighten me?"

I gave him a look. "I don't know. You might think it's too dangerous for a Dhanshai."

He grunted, annoyed. "Jae-En, there is no option open to us which is not dangerous. Tell me."

I stopped at the guard room door and leveled the gun again. Behind it, the priest and the wand guy scattered. I hit the buttons and started blowtorching it just like before, then glanced at Lhan.

"I met the Wargod. He came to my cell."

Lhan blinked. "Truly? He still lives?"

"Well, he's getting on some, that's for sure, and...." Did I want to tell Lhan all about Wainwright offering me his job? Later maybe. Now was not the time. I finished my horizontal cut, and started the vertical one. "Well, he was bragging that he ran all the moisture gatherers in Ora from right here in the temple. Some control room upstairs. If we can get up there we can shut 'em all down and end all this water stealing shit once and for all."

Lhan's eyes went wide, then he tightened up his jaw and straightened his shoulders. "Yours is the noblest heart that beats upon Waar, Mistress. You head to certain death for the good of a world not your own. I will be proud to die at your side."

I swallowed. "I, uh, was actually hoping to escape afterwards."

Lhan nodded. "One must always hope, though the outcome be inevitable."

"Cut it out, Lhan! You're gonna make me change my mind!"

He laughed like I was kidding, but before he could say anything more, another squad of guards ran into the guard room, then scattered out of line of sight as they saw the blue beam cutting through the door.

Two seconds more and it was done. I lowered the wand. "Ready?"

"I could wish I had a weapon, but I am ready."

I held the wand out to him. "Here."

He edged back. "A wand is the holiest of holies. It is death for a layman even to touch one. Besides, I know not its use."

"It's just a gun, Lhan. They just put the hoodoo on it so nobody tries stealing one. Here, it's easy. Aim that end at the bad guys, hold down these three buttons, then push that one to fire. How's your aim?"

"I have been told I have a good eye."

"Good, then lay down some covering fire. I'll take care of the close-up work."

He looked like I'd handed him a live cobra. "I shall do my best, Mistress."

"Right. Here we go. No, wait." I turned to him. "When we get out there, say something out loud about going to the, uh, the nineteenth floor. Got it?"

"The nineteenth floor. Aye, Mistress. But why?"

"Because we're not going to the nineteenth floor."

"Ah. Misdirection. Of course."

"Okay. Let's go. No, sorry. One more thing."

I kissed him, just like I had back on Ku-Rho's airship. And just like then, he stiffened, then gave in.

I pulled back. He was looking at me, his eyes bright.

"Mistress, I—"

"Save it 'til we get out. Come on."

CHAPTER FORTY-FIVE

JAILBREAK!

I kicked out the square of glass and dove through the door, tucking and rolling as I hit the guard room floor, then came up near the door to the outer hallway. Everybody turned my way, swords and spears out. One guy had another wand of blue fire. Fuck! I thought these things were supposed to be rare!

"Wand on your left, Lhan!"

Lhan ducked out of Solitary Two with the wand at his shoulder like he'd been doing commando raids all his life. He fired at the guy with the wand and melted his head off. Yikes! I was thinking more along the lines of winging the guy, but okay.

The priests and the paladins cringed back as the guard's headless body hit the ground, neck stump smoking, and Lhan covered them. They really were not used to being on the business end of those wands. I was feeling pretty sick about it too, but maybe it was a good thing. I raised my head.

"See that, Ru-Kol? You want the rest of these guys to die just the same? No? Then open the door, and keep opening 'em all the way out!"

There was a pause, then Ru-Kol's voice fritzed on. "We are assured a better birth if we die in service to the Seven."

I groaned, and I wasn't the only one. A lot of the paladins were glaring at the ceiling and muttering under their breath.

"Okay, fine, then I guess I'm just gonna have to threaten a holy relic again."

I stepped to the headless corpse, then kicked the second wand over toward where the priest and paladins all huddled together.

"Lhan, aim at the wand."

The paladins all backed away as he got a bead on it, but Lhan had caught the gist now, and raised his wand at them.

"Back where you were!"

They inched back. Lhan aimed at the wand again. I looked up at the ceiling.

"Okay, Ru-Kol, ready to open the door now?"

"I do not believe you will do this. The blast will kill you too."

"Do you think I care at this point?"

"Perhaps not. But your lover will not kill you. I see it in his eyes."

Lhan laughed. "You misread me, friend. I am ready to die if my mistress and I cannot be together. Will you test me?"

Sheesh! Was he bluffing? Or was he gonna kill us if this didn't work out? I couldn't tell, but if it was a game, I wasn't gonna spoil it. I raised my voice again.

"Okay, Ru-Kol, here we go. If that door don't open by the time I count to five, that relic is history!"

No answer.

I swallowed. "One. Two. Three. Four—"

It wasn't Ru-Kol who blinked.

All of a sudden the priest broke for the door and slapped his hand against the circle beside it. It slid open. The motherfucker had some kind of override!

I jumped after him and hauled him back just as he was running through. The door whooshed closed again, but I didn't care. I had my ticket out.

Ru-Kol was wailing on the intercom. "Reverence Ru-Vas! You should not have done that!"

The priest was maroon with rage. "And you should not have left us here to die!"

I bonked him on the head with the flat of my blade, then turned back to the paladins as he wilted, waving them away from the gun.

"Back off!"

They did, and I snatched it up, slung it over my shoulder, then hauled up the wobbly priest and put my sword to his neck.

"Alright, Lhan, keep 'em covered. Let's—"

I stopped as I saw a string on the floor below the locker I'd ripped open—Lhan's balurrah! I hesitated, afraid somebody would make a move if I stooped for it, but I had to get it. I took my sword from the priest's neck, stepped out, reaching with the sword, and hooked the balurrah with the tip, then lifted. It dangled from the tip as I brought it to me. I pulled it off and looped it over my neck, then shoved Ru-Vas toward the door. Lhan had been covering the other guys. He hadn't seen a thing.

"Okay, pal. Open sesame."

Ru-Vas didn't get it, but he got it, and put his hand to the circle. I held my breath, afraid old Ru-Kol had some kinda override for his override, but it whooshed open just like it should.

"Hallelujah. Let's go."

And that's how we did it the rest of the way through the jail, door by door, hallway by hallway, until we entered a hallway with a big metal door at the end instead of a glass one, and two normal white sliding doors on each wall.

I nodded ahead. "What's through there?"

Ru-Vas swallowed. "That is the entry chamber."

"The way out?"

"Yes."

And probably a welcoming committee. "Right. Lhan, stay behind me, and be ready to shoot if I drop."

"Aye, Mistress."

"Okay. Let's go."

I put Ru-Vas more in front of me, afraid of what we might find when we opened the door, and we started forward again, but before we got halfway down the hall, I heard a "whoosh whoosh" behind me, then another pair of whooshes ahead. I hit the deck shouting.

"Lhan! Down!"

He dropped like a pro and four crossbow bolts whistled over our heads to thud into the one guy still standing, Ru-Vas. Then there were four paladins charging us out of the four open doors, shortswords raised.

Lhan rolled and fired and the two guys behind us died shrieking and burning. I sprang at the guys in front and sheared through their swords before crashing into them and knocking them flat. They came up again quick and reaching for daggers, but I slashed behind me and they collapsed, howling, their backs opened to the ribs. Lhan finished 'em off with a couple of quick bursts and we stood there panting and choking on the smell of cooked meat.

I looked down at Ru-Vas, who had toppled over, dead, with two bolts through the chest, and one in the gut. The last one was in the wall. Lhan's jaw clenched.

"It seems we need another escort."

"Maybe not."

I grabbed the priest by collar and dragged him to the steel door, then looked back at Lhan. "Get ready, but don't go crazy. We gotta leave one alive."

"We do?"

"Misdirection, remember?"

"Ah, yes."

Lhan raised the gun, and I raised Ru-Vas's arm. Then I noticed a big silver bracelet around the priest's wrist. I looked back at the guys we'd just killed. They had some too, but Ru-Vas had more bands on his. Was it that simple? I grabbed the bracelet and tried to pull it off. It was too tight, like it had been shrink-wrapped to him.

"Sorry, pal."

I chopped his hand off at the wrist, then pulled the bracelet off his bloody stump and waved it in front of the circle.

Whoosh.

The door opened onto a dim, metal-walled room that looked like every prisoner induction center I'd ever been processed through, except for the sad-faced priest cowering behind the table with some kind of hologram of the whole jail on it like a doll house made of light. No wonder the little fucker had been able to see us so well! His hand was hovering over a panel covered with glowing white circles. Lhan aimed his wand at him. I checked around to make sure there was nobody else in the room, then gave him a smile.

"Hello, Ru-Kol. Wanna back away from that thing, or are you ready for that better birth in service to the Seven?"

Ru-Kol cringed back from the panel, whimpering, and we started working our way around him toward the main doors, which were thick steel bastards, like on a safe. Lhan was snarling. His finger tightened on the trigger.

"So you are willing to sacrifice the lives of others but not your own? You are contemptable, even for a priest."

I whispered outta the side of my mouth. "Easy, Lhan. Remember?"

Lhan took a breath, then nodded. "Open the front door, you filthy shike. And if you betray us, you will not live long enough to regret it."

Ru-Kol edged back to the table and pushed a button with a shaking finger. The main doors whooshed open behind us. We started to back up, Lhan's wand still trained on Ru-Vas.

I gave him another side whisper. "Okay, now. Loud."

"Was it the nineteenth floor, Mistress?"

"Shut up, you idiot! Do you want him to hear?"

I shoved Lhan out the door, then ran after him. It slammed closed behind us and we sprinted down an empty corridor. Lhan shot a sideways glance at me.

"Did I do well, Mistress?"

WHOOP WHOOP WHOOP WHOOP!

I shouted over the alarm. "Perfect! I just hoped it worked, or we're gonna have the whole temple on our asses."

The hall ended in an intersection with a wide curving corridor just like the one that surrounded the water tank in the other hallways I'd been in, but this one didn't have any fancy glass walls. It looked like it belonged on a submarine, all metal bulkheads and exposed pipes. There was a lot more noise and traffic down here too—slaves and guards and priests, all looking up at the alarm and trying to decide where to run, and any second they were gonna look our way.

There was an elevator right across the hall, but who knew how long it would take to come, and with both of us naked and one of us pink we'd probably be spotted pretty damn fast. No time for disguises either.

"I think we gotta just run for it. Come on. This way! I think."

I took Lhan's hand and ran left down the hall, looking for the little service corridor that led to the turbine chamber. People started shouting as soon as they saw us, but we just kept running. Finally I saw a little door that looked right and veered toward it. It didn't open like the ones upstairs had.

"Damn it! They're locking down!"

Then I remembered I still had Ru-Vas's bracelet in my hand. I waved it at the circle beside the door.

Whoosh.

Yes! We ran in and it closed again after us—same service corridor as all the other levels. Somebody started banging on the door behind us. Ha! Guess they didn't have my clearance. I kicked through the door at the end and led Lhan into the freezing turbine chamber to the spiral staircase. I looked up. Nobody. Not yet. Good. This was the other part of my plan. The turbine chamber was dark, huge, god know how many stories high, filled with scaffolding and struts, and as noisy as a Nascar race. We could hide there all day and nobody would find us. We could also climb it without anybody seeing us.

At the end of the catwalk, I went over the railing and beckoned Lhan after me. We clambered across the scaffolding until we were hidden from the stairs behind one of the massive turbine shafts, then we started climbing. It was easy going, like climbing an endless jungle-gym. There was always another hand hold, and another place to put our feet. The worst part was the constant cold wind and the deafening noise. I felt like I was on the side of a mountain in the middle of a norwester, and I was beginning to regret not stopping to put on some clothes—not that a bikini and a metal-covered leather sleeve woulda made much of a difference.

A few minutes later a pack of guards came down the stairs, looking all around, and we held still, peeking through the whirling blur of the turbine blades. Before they passed us, another pack came up and met 'em in the middle. We couldn't hear 'em, but we saw 'em waving their arms at each other and pointing in every direction. Finally they split up and went back the way they'd come, one up, one down.

We gave 'em a minute to get out of sight, then kept climbing. It probably took ten minutes to reach the nineteenth floor, and by then even I was starting to feel it, while Lhan was lagging hard. It wasn't so much the climb, but the cold was stiffening our finger joints, and it made gripping hard.

We took a breather on a broad steel beam and looked through the scaffolding to the army of guards that were crowded onto the nineteenth floor landing, guarding the door to the service corridor.

I gave Lhan a tired grin. "See? It worked."

He saluted me. "All hail the Mistress of Misdirection."

We climbed on, staying tight behind the turbine shaft until they were out of sight beneath us. I was in unknown territory now, and wasn't sure where to go. Wainwright had said the control room was right at the top of the temple, but was that just a figure of speech? Was it really on the top floor, or just somewhere near the top? And how were we gonna know it when we found it. A lot of places in here looked like control rooms—the front desk of the jail for instance.

"I guess we just climb as far as we can go, then see what happens."

"As far as we can go," turned out to be farther than I expected. Way farther. I swear we climbed three times as long *after* the nineteenth floor as we had climbing *to* it. Eventually, though, we found the ceiling at last, as well as the huge superstructure of mega-thick beams and struts that held the tops of all the turbine columns and cooling coils in place. There were also more guards, about a dozen, all standing on a wide platform outside a pair of big double doors in the inner wall of the chamber. That door was all she wrote, the topmost door at the last landing of the endless spiral stairs. If we wanted to keep going up, we'd have to go through it. Unfortunately, four of the guys in front of it had wands of blue fire. Damn it, the fucking things were getting less rare by the second!

"A considerable defense, Mistress."

"Only if they get to use it. Listen up. I got a plan."

Lhan stiffened. "If it entails you charging into danger without me at your side—"

"Don't worry, sweet cheeks. You're the one they're gonna be shooting at."

CHAPTER FORTY-SIX

FIRE!

Five minutes later I'd ninjaed my way across the beams until I was above the platform, and right over the heads of the guards. I drew my sword as quiet as I could, then looked back toward Lhan, who was peeking around the dark side of the turbine column, and gave him the high sign. He waved back, then aimed the wand and fired twice.

The two guards closest to the catwalk went down screaming as blue-white bolts went through 'em like hot pokers. All the rest of ducked and shouted, raising their wands and scanning for the shooter.

"Where is he?"

"By the turbine!"

"I see him!"

That's when I dropped in.

The poor bastards didn't have a chance. They were all crowded up to the rail, pointing or aiming into the dark around the turbine. I butchered five of them before they even knew I was there, and the rest died trying to bring their weapons to bear. My sword cut through raised arms and spear shafts and white plastic barrels like they were so many corn stalks.

One of the wands fritzed and sizzled.

"Oh fuck!"

I backed up, heart pounding, and jumped straight up to the rafters just in time to miss being engulfed in a deafening blue-white explosion. Images of flying bodies were burned into the backs of my eyes, and every part of me that I didn't manage to hide behind an I-beam felt like I'd got a third-degree sunburn. Smoke choked me. It smelled like porkchops and burning plastic.

When I could see again, I saw that the platform was cleared—and a little melted. There were a few bodies mashed up against the twisted railings, but the rest had either been vaporized or taken the long fall. I felt a little queasy as I looked at the shreds of burnt meat that were sticking to the warped gratings of the catwalk.

Lhan shook his head as he clambered to me through the struts. "Mistress, you are terrible in your wrath."

I swallowed. "More terrible than I meant to be. Fuck."

Lhan and I dropped down to the catwalk, then hunted through the mangled meat. Lhan found a captain—or most of one—and pulled the bracelet off his wrist. I doubted it would work, and I was right. Nothing happened when I waved the bracelet in front of the circle by the door. Ru-Vas's didn't work either. The whole place was on total lock-down now.

Lhan hefted his gun. "Can we cut through it, as we did those downstairs?"

I frowned. "These doors look a lot tougher than that. I don't think it'll work. But you're giving me an idea. Look for more wands."

There were two more among the bodies, partially melted but still whole. I took 'em and laid 'em against the door like wood in a fireplace, then added the one I had slung across my back.

"There. Now back to where we were."

We climbed back into the scaffolding and took cover behind the turbine before I gave him the nod.

"You shoot better than I do. Go for it."

Lhan braced himself between two beams, raised the wand, and squeezed off a shot. Nothing. I could see it hit the guns, but it didn't do shit.

"Try again."

He took another shot. Again he hit the guns, and again, nothing.

"Goddamn it. Just pour it on. Let 'em have it."

Lhan took a third shot and leaned on the trigger button so that it shot a long stream of energy at the guns.

For a second I thought all he was going to do was melt them into a puddle, and

I started to curse, but then there was a pop, and a flash, and an arc of blue like a spark jumping the gap of a spark-plug.

"Back! Back!"

I grabbed Lhan around the waist and dragged him behind the turbine just as the turbine chamber went from black as night to bright as day in a split second. The sound was like a couple of sledgehammers to the ears, and the shock wave knocked us sideways, even behind the turbine. I had to grab a cable to keep from falling, and I could barely hold it. My brain was spinning so hard inside my head I didn't know where my hands were.

Bits of hot plastic flew past, glowing, on either side of us, and the echo of the explosion bounced up and down the shaft like a ball bearing in a paint mixer. We stayed where we were for a while, coughing out smoke that smelled like a car-fire and getting our balance back, then looked around the curve of the turbine. The door wasn't there anymore. Neither was the platform. The catwalk was just hanging in space at the top of the stairs, its severed end twisted like a tin foil gum wrapper. Part of the wall near where the door had been was on fire. I didn't know steel could burn.

"Holy shit."

Lhan looked aghast. "Holy indeed. What horrible power the Seven wielded."

"At least it worked."

We picked our way back across the superstructure. The part above the door was bent and almost too hot to step on or touch—not so good for a couple of naked people. Down below was even worse. The hallway beyond the obliterated door was filled with smoke and I saw that the walls were on fire, and sparks were spitting out of the fixtures.

From somewhere below a new alarm started going off. This one went, YEEN YEEN YEEN YEEN!

Lhan pointed. "There. A safe landing."

I looked down. The floor just inside the door was all scraped up, but not on fire. We jumped down one after the other, then looked into the smoking corridor.

The broken door lay halfway down the hall, all crumpled up like a used Kleenex, and bits and pieces of smoking rubble and circuitry were strewn all over. The worst part, though, was the fire, which was climbing up both walls to the ceiling and melting all that smooth white plastic like it was wax.

I could hear things shorting and popping behind the panels, and a second later, weird doohickies that looked like tiny chrome pineapples popped out of holes in the ceiling and started spinning. A few of 'em started spraying water around, but most of them didn't.

I hissed through my teeth. "What the hell? Why aren't they working? This shit's going to get out of control."

"What are they, Mistress?"

"A sprinkler system, I think. It goes off automatically when there's a fire. At least its supposed to."

Lhan stared. "Truly, the wonders of the Seven are limitless."

And there was my answer. The sprinkler system didn't work because these backwards nimrods didn't know what it was, and it hadn't been serviced in a thousand years. Doors, security systems, water collection systems—those were things the priests woulda had to figure out early. Fire prevention? They wouldn't even have known to look, and neither had Jack Wainwright. The last time he was on Earth, fire prevention was an axe and a bucket of sand. I might have just fucked this place up way worse than I meant to, and I had no idea how to fix it.

I hissed, uneasy. "All that water in the tank, and who knows how to get it to the fire? This might get serious."

Lhan started ahead. "Then we had best act quickly."

"Right."

I followed after him, and we walked into the flames.

***

Twenty yards on and the fire was behind us, except for the smoke, which followed us down the hall, making everything hazy and red. This area felt fancier and more enclosed than the other levels, more like an office than an airport. The floor was carpeted with some kind of orange spongey stuff, and the walls were closer together.

A few priests were hurrying in our direction, I guess to check on what had happened, but when they saw us coming, they turned and ran like the devil was after them. I jumped ahead, trying to stop them before they told anybody we were coming, but the smoke was so thick I only managed to grab one. I shook him.

"Where is the control room? Where does the Wargod control the temples?"

"Kill me, demoness! I care not! Though you burn us alive, I will never betray Ormolu to the devils of the One!"

Goddamn fanatics. "Fine, I'll find it myself."

I shoved him head first into the wall and we kept going as he slumped to the floor.

A few seconds later footsteps thudded in a corridor off to our left and we whipped around, peering through the smoke and ready to fight, but it was some guy running away from us, shouting into a side room. "Summon the guards from below! Have them bring water! Hurry!"

Twenty feet more, and another intersection appeared out of the haze. A line of priests was forming up to block the left arm of it and peering around like nervous rabbits. Two of 'em had wands of blue fire.

Lhan edged back. "It appears the others raised the alarm. Should we see if we might avoid them by going right?"

I chewed my lip. "I wish, but I'm guessing whichever way they're trying to stop us from going, that's the way we need to go."

"Astutely reasoned, Mistress." Lhan coughed and raised the wand toward the priests' line. "The same as before?"

I coughed too. The fucking smoke was going to kill us before the priests did. At least it gave us some cover. "Yeah. Just remember not to hit me when I drop—"

Lhan turned and looked back the way we'd come. "More."

I looked around. Priest-shaped shadows were coming through the smoke. Around ten of 'em, all armed.

"Fuck." My plan of having Lhan fire from cover while I went in like a weed whacker stuck its legs up in the air and died. The reinforcements would overrun him in a hot second.

I looked back and forth, heart thudding. There was a way, but… I cleared my throat. "I think we can make this, Lhan, but… but I'm gonna have to pick you up."

His jaw tightened. "You may not."

"Aw, come on, Lhan. You'd rather die?"

"I value my honor more than my life."

I was starting to see red. "Okay, then. How 'bout your people? How 'bout your country? If we don't make it upstairs, they're screwed! Seems kinda selfish to let a whole world die of thirst so you can save your goddamn dignity!"

Lhan's eyes blazed, and he opened his mouth, then shut it again, his jaw flexing. I looked over my shoulder. I was seeing faces through the smoke now, and they were seeing us. They started to shout and run forward.

Lhan closed his eyes and spread his arms. "Once again, Mistress, you show me where true honor lies—and true shame. Do as you will."

"Halle-fucking-lujah."

I scooped him up and threw him over my shoulder, then ran for the intersection. Just as the line of priests saw us coming, I jumped over their heads, then landed behind them and sprinted down the hall as they shouted and turned and fired. There was a stairwell on the left-hand wall. I dodged into it as blue fire scorched the walls behind me, then bounded up the stairs five at a time.

There was an archway at the top. I stumbled through, then stared as I put Lhan down. Had I gone the wrong way? This was no control room. It was a hangar—high-roofed and shaped like a bundt cake pan like the turbine chamber—with strange flying-car looking thingies like the one Ru-Sul had flown off on back at Toaga parked all over, and big submarine-hatch doors going around the outside wall. It was also filling with smoke.

"Goddamn it! How did the fire get up here?"

Lhan pointed to some kind of junction box on the inner wall of the bundt pan. It was smoking like an orange grove smudge pot, and all the pipes and ducts around it were leaking smoke too. The fire must be traveling from floor to floor through the air conditioning system. Bet they hadn't cleaned that out in centuries either.

I turned back to the stairs, wondering if we should go down again and look for the control room down there, but it was booming with running footsteps. The guys we'd blown past were coming up fast.

"Damn it. Onward and upward."

I looked around and saw the opening to another stairwell at the base of the central column.

"There."

We sprinted for it, dodging around the parked vehicles. Some of 'em were the same model as I'd seen before, flat-bottomed ski-doos, but others looked like futuristic city buses, long and sleek and shaped like a bar of soap, and some were the size of yachts, but with guns sticking out all over the place and what looked like bombs slung underneath. Man, if I coulda figured out how to fly one of those we woulda really evened the odds. But there was no time. The priests were spilling out of the stairwell behind and started blasting at us with everything they had.

We dodged behind one of the bus thingies and made it to the stairwell before they could get line of sight again. Unfortunately there were more priests waiting for us at the top of the steps. Two blue bolts lanced down at us as we came around the last curve, melting the walls.

I shoved Lhan back and launched straight at the shooters, screaming like a death-metal singer. Crazy, yeah. But with more guys coming up behind us, there wasn't any time to come up with some kind of fancy strategy.

Fortunately, being big, pink and loud worked its usual magic, and they freaked, flinching back instead of zapping me, with their beams zig-zagging all over the place. That wasn't much better. I nearly got diced into bite-sized pieces as they wrote lite-brite hieroglyphics into the air, but I flinched too—fortunately in the right direction—and only got an inch of hair singed off as I smashed, slashing and shouting, into their line.

"Blood! Death! Kill!"

Yes. I really said that.

What I'd meant to say was something scary about being a demon of the One who had come to kill them and use their blood as a sacrament for my unholy rites, but "Blood! Death! Kill!" is what actually came out of my mouth.

Anyway, it worked. Or maybe it was the giant blade cutting everybody to pieces, or Lhan shooting past me with his wand and torching guys left and right. Whichever, they turned and ran, and Lhan and I ran after 'em, cutting down the slow ones as we went, and the priests behind us pounding up after.

We came out into another curving hallway, as high as the other inner circles, but with a much tighter curve, like it was closer to the center of the temple. It was also hazy with smoke, just like below, and there were flames in the distance—lots of flames.

"Fuck. This is really getting out of hand."

The priests we'd chased outta the stairwell were falling back to a bigger group who were surging up the curved hall from the left, and the ones behind us on the stairs were coming up fast. We backed to the right of the door so we wouldn't be caught in the middle, then pulled ourselves together as the priests from the stairs spilled out and merged with the rest. Like before, since they were guarding that direction, I figured that direction was where we wanted to go.

I swallowed and shook out my arms. "Come on. We gotta hit 'em now before they get themselves set."

Lhan lifted the wand. "I am ready."

But just as I was psyching myself up to go all viking on their asses, a little robed figure pushed through them, backed up by four temple guards, all with blue wands.

"Do not fight, brothers! Rescue the holy artifacts and sacred texts and escape! I will deal with these heretics!"

Even shouting, that voice was as limp and wet as a used rubber, and I knew it as soon as I heard it.

I smiled. "Chinless. Just the man I wanted to see."

CHAPTER FORTY-SEVEN

DURU-VAU!

The priests looked relieved to be let off the hook and ran off like frightened chickens as Duru-Vau strode toward us with his escort. The hall behind him was deserted in seconds.

"I know what you want, demoness. You want my death. Come forward, and you may try to take it."

I sneered and shouted back. "Actually, I could give a rat's ass if you live or die, punk. All I want is to stop you from stealing everybody's water."

"One cannot steal what one already owns, but if you wish to stop the turbines, their controls are behind me. I wish you luck learning their use."

"I got a better idea. I'm gonna make you use 'em. Right after I slap the living shit out of—"

Before I could finish, the guards with the wands started firing, and these guys knew what they were doing. Two of them shot directly at us, while the other two started sweeping theirs back and forth like machine gunners, trying to cover the whole hall.

I squeaked and grabbed Lhan and jumped back thirty feet in a single second, then took another bounce to get back behind the curve of the hallway out of the line of fire. There wasn't gonna be any charging these guys, and no way to get in the middle of them so they couldn't fire without hitting each other. There wasn't any cover in these smooth-ass circular hallways either. All my usual tricks were useless.

Or were they?

I put Lhan down and turned to him as we kept backing up.

"You gotta slow 'em down. Back up, but keep firing every time you see one show even just a shoulder around the curve."

"Aye, Mistress. You have a plan?"

"If you can call running around in circles a plan." I gave him a kiss on the cheek. "Stay alive."

He fired past me, shaving a smoking slice out of the curve of the wall. "As long as you do the same, beloved. Luck be with you."

I went.

I pounded down the hall away from Duru-Vau and his gunners as the crackle of wand fire echoed from behind me. I clenched my teeth, praying it was Lhan fanning back the guards, and not the guards lasering him to pieces. At least the firing kept going. That was a good sign, right?

It was easy going at first. I was taking twenty-foot strides and loving getting to stretch my legs to the limit, but halfway around the circumference of the circle, things got hairy. The fire was really spreading on this side, and the hall was filled with smoke and flame. There was burning junk all over the floor, the walls and ceiling were buckling and melting, and I was, you know, naked.

I tightened my strides and bunched up, then sprang long and low, leaping through it all like Evel Knievel jumping a bike through a hoop of flame. Only trouble was, this was more like a tube of flame, and I couldn't see well enough to tell if I had a good landing place or not.

As it turned out, there *was* a spot to land, but I wasn't heading for it. Some big air-conditioner looking thing had dropped through the ceiling, and was laying there like an island in a sea of flame, but I was angling away from it, right toward the burning wall. With a wild-ass swipe of my sword, I swerved sideways in mid-air and managed to catch the very edge of it with one foot. It was a sharp edge, though, and I could feel the ball of my foot slice open as I kicked off.

At least it got me clear of the fire. I landed on spongy carpet again and kept going, leaving bloody prints with my right foot at every step and bounding past priests carrying books and crates toward the stairs. They didn't even have time to react before I was past 'em.

Another ten strides and I started hearing wand fire ahead of me instead of behind me. I breathed a sigh of relief. Lhan was still holding. Ten more strides and I saw the blue flashes ahead of me through the smoke. I poured it on, and the scene came into view around the curve of the hall—the four wand guys inching forward and firing ahead, Duru-Vau following behind, but keeping well back from Lhan's return fire.

I took one last big stride, kicking high and raising my sword as I arced up behind them. My plan was to come down with my feet between Duru-Vau's shoulder blades, then chop up the gunners while the little fucker was picking his teeth out of the carpet. It only half worked.

I don't know if he had eyes in the back of his head or whether he was just naturally nervous, but Duru-Vau looked over his shoulder just as I was coming down and managed to scoot out from under me like a stepped-on bar of soap.

He screeched a warning to the wand guys, but it was way too late. They turned around just in time to catch my blade right where they needed it most. I caught the first guy between the teeth, came out the back of his head, chopped through the next guy's neck, cut the third guy in two at the waist, and got jammed up halfway though the last guy's pelvis.

I cleared the blade with a kick, and turned to grab Duru-Vau, but the slippery little bastard was already disappearing around the curve of the hall.

"Mistress!" Lhan was charging forward, wand at the ready.

"Good job, Lhan! Come on."

I didn't wait. If Duru-Vau knew how to operate the turbine controls, I needed him. I sprang after him, skimming close to the wall and cocking my sword back, ready to hit him with the flat, but just as my feet left the ground he spun and unloaded at me with his palm.

In a panic, I kicked at the wall and veered left, but not quite fast enough. The spell rippled past my legs and even though I only caught the very edge of it, it turned them to jelly. I hit the ground feet first, but my knees couldn't hold me, and I crashed down tits first and slid into the wall.

Duru-Vau looked like he was going to stop and finish the job, but then a bolt of blue fire grazed his leg and he jumped back, screaming, and started limping away.

Lhan ran to me as the little priest vanished into the smoke. "Mistress, are you wounded? Can you—"

"Help me up. We can't let that little fuck get away. But don't kill him,

Lhan. We need him."

Lhan took my arm and pulled me up. My legs were all pins and needles, but my knees held, kinda. Lhan caught me as I tottered.

"Jae-En, perhaps you should—"

"Just gotta walk it off. Come on."

We started down the hall, me wobbling, Lhan propping me up. Ahead of us I could see Duru-Vau's silhouette limping away through the smoke, as slow as an arthritic turtle. Another of the world's most exciting chase scenes.

Ten yards later, he angled for a pair of big double doors on the outer curve of the hall.

"Faster!"

Lhan and I picked up our pace as he reached the doors and held up his bracelet in front of the circle. I thought we were gonna be way too far away, but these doors didn't whoosh open, they rumbled open, slowly. Even through the smoke I could see they were twice as thick as the other doors in the temple, with all kinds of deadbolts and meshing gears behind the smooth white plastic. Heavy duty security.

Duru-Vau stumbled through them as soon as the gap was wide enough, but the doors kept opening. I pulled Lhan ahead, my pins and needles starting to wear off. The doors thudded open, paused, then began closing again. We weren't going to make it.

"Goddamn it!"

I whipped Lhan ahead of me, through the doors, then powered forward like a drunk fullback and fell through them just as they boomed closed behind me. I could feel the the rumble of gears and the jolt of bolts slamming home as I struggled to my feet. Wherever we were, it was dark and filled with smoke, with a weird sea-green glow coming from somewhere deeper in the haze. My ears were filled with the hum of electronic equipment.

I looked around, then stared. Curving off into the smoke to the left and right of me was a line of tall silver statues standing in narrow alcoves in the walls. They were as smooth and polished and bland as everything else in the temple, but they still made me uneasy. Either they were supposed to be deliberately arty, or whoever made them didn't know shit about anatomy. They looked like 3D versions of some kid's stick figure drawing of a deep sea diver—heads like snail shells sitting on top of skinny, stretched out bodies, Popeye arms, and legs that bent the wrong way.

And weirder than their looks was that they were there at all. The rest of the temple didn't have any art. It had all been as bland as an airport lounge. Why suddenly go crazy with the ornamentation? Was this place some kind of chapel, like the one Ru-Zhera ran in Modgalu? If so, they needed to fire their sculptor. He made every single one of their gods look exactly the same.

Duru-Vau was backing away from us, hate all over his ratty little face. "You think you have me trapped now? It is you who are trapped. You will die here!"

He was pulling back for another palm strike. I stabbed my sword into the floor, trying to use it to pull myself up and feeling like I was made of tin cans tied together with string. He was gonna beat me to the punch.

"Priest."

Duru-Vau turned. Lhan was raising his wand.

Duru-Vau was faster. He shot his palm out and the air flexed in front of it. Lhan slammed back against the wall, neck and shoulders first, and slumped to the ground, the wand slipping from his hands.

"Lhan! Are you alright?"

No answer. He didn't even move.

I levered myself up and staggered forward, roaring and rage-blind, my sword dragging behind me. "You're dead, motherfucker! Dead!"

Duru-Vau edged away, looking at his wrist like he was checking a watch. Was he late for a date? Did people on Waar even have watches? Why wasn't he aiming another palm strike at me? He started backing up the stairs of a circular platform in the center of the room. Tall columns of light glowed though the smoke all around it.

"You cannot kill me here, demoness. This is my sanctuary. This is where *I* am the powerful one."

"I thought you were the powerful one everywhere, big shot." Anything to keep him talking and not shooting death spells at me.

"Soon enough, demoness. Soon enough."

As I pushed through the smoke I started to see that the glowing columns around Duru-Vau weren't actually columns. The platform he was on was in the middle of a ring of consoles covered in displays and flashing lights, and surrounding the consoles were six pedestals, on top of which were six see-through skyscraper shapes, each twelve feet high or more, and each with its guts exposed like a schematic. They were holograms, just like the one down in the jail, except these were the temples of the Seven, all glowing like ghosts in old movies!

Third from the left I recognized the stubby Temple of Modgalu, and there was a seventh one in the middle of the platform, bigger than all the rest—home sweet Temple of Ormolu. Little wisps of holographic smoke were trailing from its top floors like it was a guttering candle. I bet if I looked close enough, I'd be able to see myself up there, limping toward Duru-Vau with murder in my eyes.

I started up the stairs to the platform, stamping my feet to get the feeling back into my legs. Duru-Vau checked his wrist again, then cursed and started limping for the other side of the platform as fast as he could. I was grateful he wasn't killing me and all, but what the fuck was he waiting for?

"Where's all this power you were telling me about, jackass?"

"Doubt me at your peril, hellspawn!"

He dodged around the base of the Ormolu hologram's pedestal, then kept going as I staggered onto the platform and started hop-running after him. I was gaining. My legs were coming back, but the burn he'd got from Lhan's wand shot wasn't gonna wear off. In fact he seemed to be limping worse now.

I snatched at him and missed as he threw himself at the furthest away console, slapping one of the glowing circles that covered its face. He spun to face me, a crazed smile on his face.

"Now you will understand!"

I rolled my eyes and raised my sword at him, but a metallic clicking stopped me. It sounded like a bunch of revolvers all being cocked at once all over the room. I looked around, waiting for secret doors to open and ninjas to come flooding out, or gun turrets to pop up out of nowhere. That didn't happen. Actually, for a second it looked like nothing had happened, then I saw a movement out of the corner of my eye and turned my head. It looked like one of the big silver statues was falling forward, but at the last second, it threw out one of its legs and caught itself, then stood straight and looked around. One by one, the rest of 'em did the same.

CHAPTER FORTY-EIGHT

ROBOTS!

"Jesus fuck. They're robots!"

"They are the Servants of the Seven. And they are mine to command." Duru-Vau pointed at me and raised his voice, shouting in a language the universal translator in my brain couldn't make head nor tail of. That was okay. I translated it myself. He was saying, "Hey, robots! Kill the big redhead!"

There were seven of 'em, just like the seven temples, and they all turned their heads toward me at once, which was creepy, because they didn't have any eyes that I could see, just the blank snail shell helmets, with little openings underneath where the snail's head and neck woulda stuck out.

What actually stuck out was scarier. As they walked toward me with their weird backwards legs, black cables like electrical tape octopus tentacles snaked out and pointed at me, the tips of each tentacle glowing the same color as the wands of blue fire.

"Oh shit!"

You know, I thought my legs were all weak and wobbly. Turns out they were just fine. I jumped like a goddamn jackrabbit as those things shot at me. All the beams criss-crossed in the spot where I'd been a second ago and scorched the hell out of the platform and some of the consoles.

Duru-Vau shrieked again and threw himself in front of the machines. "No! Not the interface!" Then he repeated himself in robot lingo.

The robots paused and I kicked for the wall, trying to get behind one of 'em. It turned its head completely around and unloaded. Goddamn it! It didn't have a behind! I dove between its legs, slashing at them backhanded as blue fire lit up the wall behind me. My blade shivered as I hit, and my hand stung like I'd swung a baseball bat at a fire hydrant, but my cut didn't even leave a mark on those skinny metal legs.

Fuck!

I leapt for another one before it could turn and aimed for its head, hoping it would be more fragile than its legs.

Not so much.

The head rang like a bell and the robot staggered sideways as I bounced off and hit the ground, but just like before, the attack hadn't done a damn thing. I'd cut through four guys at once with a swing like that. The robot didn't have a scratch.

"Goddamn it."

The other robots were turning toward me. I dove for the platform and saw for the first time that it was made of wood, and was just posts and crossbeams underneath. The priests musta built it so they could reach the controls of the consoles. All I cared about was it would give me a breather. I rolled under it as blue fire burned black marks into the floor behind me. Course I couldn't stay down here for long. Fucking robots would smoke me out like a possum under the floorboards.

"Who the hell woke up my steel centurions? And what in tarnation is goin' on down there? I got alarms going off all over the place!"

Wainwright's voice boomed through the room, loud and harsh. I stopped, heart thudding. He was here too? I could kill 'em both! Then I realized he was talking over a speaker.

"Your prisoner has escaped, Wargod!" called Duru-Vau. "She has set the temple aflame!"

"Dang it all! I go to sleep for five minutes and all hell breaks loose. Round her up again!"

"No, I will not, Wargod! She must die!"

"What are you sayin' to me, boy?"

"I say that your senility has cost us the greatest temple of Ora! Had you killed her as I suggested, we would not be burning!"

Well, I loved that mom and dad were fighting, but the robots weren't one bit distracted. They were crouching down like skeletal spiders and bending their snail heads down so they could fry me. I had to move, like now!

I rolled out between two of 'em and vaulted on top of the platform in one motion, then launched straight at Duru-Vau, who was shaking his fists at the ceiling like he was shouting at god—which I guess he was, kinda.

"Your time is through, Wargod! It is my time now! I will be—Yie!"

That last yelp was him seeing me coming, sword high. He dove between two consoles and I chopped deep into a glowing plastic panel, smashing it, as he cowered from me.

"Get her! Get her!"

Wainwright bellowed over the intercom. "What was that? Goddamn it, boy! Stop what you're doin' right now! I'm comin' down there and showin' you the back of my hand."

I pulled back for another stab at Duru-Vau, but the robots were rising again and snaking their tentacles toward me. As quick as I'd come up I jumped back down and rolled under the platform again. I felt like a mole in one of those Whack-A-Mole games, but no plan is ridiculous if it works, as my old Captain used to say.

The robots, being robots, did exactly the same thing they'd done the last time I'd gone to ground, but this time, as they folded their legs to look under the platform, I noticed something. I'd thought the skinny bastards were like the T1000, all smooth metal with no joints, but now that they were squatting, those backwards-facing legs were showing black cable at the knee joint.

"Okay, you tin-foil Achilles!"

Quick as a badger, I darted out and hacked at the nearest one's exposed knee—and sheared straight through the black cable. Sparks spit and the robot twitched like it had touched a live wire, then crashed to the ground. But it still kept turning its head toward me. I howled and jumped on it, slashing down just as its tentacles slithered out of its hole. They sheared off too, and the blue light in their tips died.

Duru-Vau screeched at the robots as he tried to un-wedge himself from between the two consoles. "Kill her! Quickly! Hurry!"

I rolled back under the platform as they tried, inches ahead of the blue fire, then dove for the one that was closest to squatting down. Its head ducked under just as I scooted behind it, and I slashed left and right, severing both legs at the knee.

Its torso fell face first under the platform, but its head started to revolve toward me, just like the other one. I snarled and jumped on its chest, then jammed my sword up its face-hole before the tentacles could come out. There was a loud pop and a fizzle and its limbs went limp.

Just like before, the other robots turned toward me and it was Whack-A-Mole time again, but then a blue bolt shot out of the darkness and hit the nearest one in the head, burning a bubbling black hole in its silver skin.

It was Lhan, leaning against the door like it had taken all his strength to stand, and firing from the hip.

"No, Lhan! They'll kill you!"

Even as I shouted, I heard Duru-Vau shouting too. "Kill him! Take that wand! Stop him!"

As he repeated it in the other language, the robots stood and turned toward Lhan, forgetting me entirely now that they had new orders. I coulda dove out and attacked their joints, but by the time I'd cut down the first one, the rest woulda burned Lhan to a crisp. Instead I kicked past 'em to the door, slung him over my shoulder, then jumped for the platform as a couple dozen bolts of blue fire cut a tic-tac-toe into the door behind us.

The beams followed us as I sailed across the room, but cut off as soon as I got close to the consoles. Unfortunately, Duru-Vau was waiting for us at the far side of the platform—and he had his hand cocked back and ready to fire.

I did the only thing I could think of. I heaved Lhan like a shot put, and he hit the priest right in the numbers. They slammed against the consoles like a pair of rag-dolls and Lhan's wand went spinning off the platform to the floor beyond. I sprang to them and rolled Lhan aside, then hauled Duru-Vau up and put my sword to his throat.

"Turn 'em off! Turn 'em off or I kill you!"

He sneered at me. "I am ready to meet my god."

I grunted. More fucking fanatics. I swear. "Okay, well how about I don't kill you." I grabbed his hand, the one he shot the death spells with, and started twisting. "How about I just tear your fuckin' hand off? How about I—?"

I stopped. He had something on his arm, under his sleeve. Something smooth. I looked at it. It looked like a strip of blue metallic tape, running down the underside of his arm to a glowing white gem on the inside of his wrist, and then continuing on to end in a transparent circle on his palm. I pulled back the sleeve. The tape went all the way up his arm to his shoulder.

"What the hell is this?"

"Jae-En! The metal men!" Lhan was pointing from the floor.

I spun around and saw they were all aiming at me. I jerked Duru-Vau up in front of me like a human shield, then stepped in front of Lhan. They stopped.

"Ha! Ready to die with us, asshole?"

I shook him again, and as I did, his hood fell back. It was the first time I'd ever seen his bald head. Lines of blue tape snaked all over it, each one ending in a miniature version of the clear plastic circle that was on his hand. It looked like printed circuits on a circuit board.

"So *that's* how you do it! Well, son-of-a—"

I cut off as the robots spread left and right, looking for an angle to shoot me without hitting him. No more time to think about it. I squeezed his neck.

"Turn 'em off, you fuck!"

"Never!"

I grabbed for the line of tape that ran up the back of his skull and started to peel it off. It was really on there—like fused with his skin or something. He started screaming.

"No! You mustn't! You mustn't!"

"Then turn 'em off!"

"I will! I will!" He pointed right. "Take me to that panel."

I lugged him to the panel, keeping him between me and the robots, and he reached for one particular circle. The panels were as white as everything else in the temple, and as bland. Just rows and rows of glowing white on white circles, like the world's most boring touch-screen display. But then I saw something I'd been too busy jumping around to notice before. Near some of the buttons were little strips of paper. It looked like someone had stuck bits of cash register tape all over the panel, but when I looked closer I saw there were words written on them. English words.

"What the…?"

Duru-Vau was fumbling for a circle about halfway up the panel. There was a piece of paper next to it that said, in a flowery old-fashioned script, "Centurions—Wake—Sleep."

I stared, then looked across all the other strips on the console, my eyes flicking over random words—"Ventilation" "Master Lock" "Alarm" "Observation" and a fuckload more. My heart started going pitter-pat.

"Holy. Shit."

CHAPTER FORTY-NINE

SUB-MENUS!

In a finger snap, I knew exactly what I was looking at. These were Wainwright's notes on how everything on the panel worked. It must have taken him ages of trial and error to figure it all out, and he'd labeled it all so he wouldn't forget. And he hadn't had to put it all in code to keep it secret. Nobody else on Waar read English. Until now.

In another split second I realized I didn't need Duru-Vau's brain anymore. With everything labeled neat as you please, I could work the panel without his help. I also realized that he was stalling, reaching for the wrong button on purpose so that the robots would have time to get a clean shot on me. He didn't think I couldn't read it. Ha!

I knocked his fumbling hand away and stabbed the white circle marked "Sleep." Instantly, the robots turned away from me and started walking back to their niches.

Duru-Vau stared up at me, stunned. "How... How did you...?"

I lifted my sword, ready to finish off the little fuck once and for all. He squealed and pulled out of my grip with crazy-person strength, then backed away, cocking his hand back like he was going to death strike me again.

"No you don't, asshole."

I slashed at his hand. He jerked back, but not quite fast enough. I sliced his wrist open with the very tip of the blade, spraying blood everywhere. He seemed more worried about the blue tape gizmo. He stared at the gem on the inside of his wrist, his eyes going wide as it got brighter and brighter.

"The reservoir. You cracked the—"

There was a noise that didn't make a sound—the kind of thud you feel in your chest when some car with a boomin' system drives by, but without the music—and the air in front of the gem shivered like water in a glass when somebody bumps the table—and Duru-Vau's head imploded.

Literally.

His face caved in and squished his brain up against the back of his skull. Blood and bits of grey muck went everywhere and Lhan and I flinched back, gagging.

His body stood there for a full ten seconds before it finally realized it was dead, then it dropped to the ground like a bag of dirty laundry and lay there oozing stuff out its neck.

I looked away, a half-inch away from tossing my lunch, as Lhan picked himself up and wiped bits of priest off his shoulders and chest.

"It seems the gifts of the Seven are not entirely without risk."

"I wouldn't call a goddamn single one of 'em a gift. Christ."

I turned to the console and started reading all the little scraps of paper, trying to find one that said anything about shutting down the turbines. Lhan leaned wearily beside me.

"Can I assist in anyway, Mistress?"

"I really wish you could, Lhan, but unless you can read English, I'm—"

There was a banging on the door and the intercom squawked. "Duru-Vau! Open this door! You hear me?"

I raised my head. "Duru-Vau's dead, Wainwright! But don't worry, I turned off your 'steel centurions.'"

"You what?" For a second it sounded like the Wargod was gargling broken glass, then he came on again. "Don't you touch them controls, missy! You don't know what yer doin'!"

I bent over the console again. "Sure I do. Everything's labeled nice and clear."

"Get away from there! I'm warnin' you! Those things can't be fixed!"

"You don't like it, come in and stop me!"

"Don't think I won't! You'll pay for this, you hoyden!"

The intercom shut off with another squawk, and Lhan raised an eyebrow. "Forgive me, Mistress, but what was said?"

I hadn't even realized we'd been speaking English. "Heh. He told me to stop messing with the buttons, and I told him to go fuck himself."

"It did not sound as if he took kindly to the suggestion."

"He's a little steamed, alright. Hey! Here we go."

I pointed at a circle that looked like all the rest. This one, though, had a little bit of paper next to it that said "M.G."

"That's either machine gun or moisture gatherer, and I'm betting on number two."

Lhan nodded politely. "Ah."

I stabbed the circle. All the circles around it on the console disappeared, and new ones showed up in a different configuration. I stared, panicked. What the fuck had I done? Everything had changed. Was it some kind of sub-menu?

I pushed the same circle again and it went back to the way it was. I breathed a sigh of relief about that, but what the fuck did I do now? The new buttons that appeared weren't labeled. How the hell was I going to figure out what I was supposed to do?

I looked around the platform, searching for anything that looked like a notebook. There had to be one here. There's no way Wainwright woulda been able to remember all the steps for all the different things the console did with a bunch of blank buttons. If he could have, he wouldn'ta labeled the buttons in the first place.

"Lhan. Look around for a book or a bunch of paper, written in the same language as those labels."

"Aye, Mistress."

We started searching everywhere, on the consoles, under the consoles, between the consoles, but before we got far, a noise like a blast furnace started coming from the door. We looked up. I couldn't see anything, but I started to smell the stink of burning plastic, getting stronger over all the other burning smells.

Lhan's jaw clenched. "The Wargod is cutting through the door."

"He's got a long way to go. Keep searching."

Lhan finally found the thing in a place I would never have looked. It was lying on the pedestal of the hologram of the Temple of Ormolu—*inside* the hologram—hidden behind the illusion of walls and rooms. If he hadn't swept his hands through the walls, he wouldn't have found it.

He held up a book as big as a family bible. "Is this what you seek, Mistress?"

"Lhan, you're a genius!"

I snatched the book out of his hand and started flipping through it. Jackpot! Each page was another layout of circles, all with labels, and numbered one-through-whatever for however many sub-menus there were. The only trouble was, he hadn't organized it alphabetically, or in any way that I could figure out. It kinda looked like he just started on one end of the console and worked his way around. I was going to have to go through the fucking thing page by page.

I looked over at the door. There was a smoking black line about five inches long near the middle of the two doors, and I could see sparks and flame behind it. Wainwright musta gone and got himself an industrial grade wand of blue fire. I had to work fast.

I paged through the book as quick as I could, flipping past directions on how to operate the intercom, how to use the holograms, how to how to communicate with the other towers, how to use the teleporters, how to service the sprinkler system—guess Wainwright had never bothered to follow through on that—how to open the hangar doors—I dog-eared that page—and all kinds of other stuff. Finally, more than halfway through the book, I found it—"Moisture Gatherer Operation."

I breathed a sigh of relief, then squinted at the layout. There were about twenty buttons, each with a handwritten label below it. Some of 'em were related to the turbines, some were related to the cooling coils, some were related to the tank itself, but they weren't in any order, so I had to read them all.

"Turbine speed, coil maintenance, coil temperature, turbine shut down! Okay! No, wait, that's for individual turbines. I want to shut 'em all down. Uh, tank maintenance. No. Coil shut down. No. System flush. No. Turbine— Wait. What the fuck is system flush?"

My heart started beating like a drum. Was there a way to give back the water? That would be a fuck of lot better than just stopping the turbines. A lot of people in Ora needed water so bad they were gonna die before the weather got back to normal, but what was gonna happen if I just pulled the plug out? Was it all just going to go down the drain? That wouldn't help anybody.

I flipped to the page that showed what happened when you pushed the System Flush button. Wainwright had drawn it out like a little flow chart, showing the various options and the 'how to' steps. Sure enough, on the left-hand side of the page, there was a procedure called Emergency Flush that showed how to dump all the water into the sewers under Ormolu, but on the right side of the page was something that made me gape.

Wainwright had called it Atmospheric Dispersal Flush, and had scribbled beside it—*Drought Reduction/Spring Rains/Answered Prayers. Only use at night, full dark.* Even better, part of the procedure involved shutting down the turbines in order to reroute power to the pumps.

"Holy fuck. This is it. This is what we need."

"What is it, Mistress?"

"Look!" I tapped the page. "It looks like there's a way to put all the water in the tank back into the air." I pointed to the page. "This says spring rains and answered prayers. It looks like the Wargod used it to make it rain when he needed it to."

Lhan blinked like I'd punched him in the forehead.

I raised an eyebrow. "What?"

He shook his head, a look of wonder on his face. "One of the great proofs of the divinity of the Seven has always been that their priests could invoke their names and cause the rains to fall. But you say this was done with this machine?"

I grinned. "Whaddaya say we give it a try and find out?"

Lhan blinked again, then mirrored my grin. "Mistress, if you can do this… I…." He looked like he was going to cry.

"Alright. Lemme see."

I took the book over to the console and spread it open beside the M.G. circle, then pressed it again. The second layout of circles appeared, and I checked the book, then pressed the one that Wainwright had marked System Flush, and from there followed the procedure that he had written down, which had me going through a lot more sub-menus and failsafes and, "Are you sure you want to do this?" buttons, including a screen that asked me how much of the tank I wanted to blow off. I chose "All."

But then, just as I got to the bottom of the list, a screen popped up that wasn't on his chart. It was a screen with six buttons in a circle around a seventh, with two circles below which by now I recognized as the forward and back buttons that were on every screen. I checked the page in Wainwright's book again. There was nothing like the screen anywhere on it. My scalp started to prickle with anxiety.

"What the fuck? Why isn't this here? What is it? It's not in the book!"

Lhan leaned over my shoulder, then looked around. "It looks quite like the layout of the representations of the temples."

I looked at him, then smacked my forehead. "Outta the mouths of babes! Of course. That's exactly what it is! But what am I supposed to do with it? Wait. Is it to select which one I want to flush? Well that's easy. All of them."

I pushed one of the circles. It lit up. I pushed another one. It lit too, and the other one stayed lit. A tingle went up my spine. "Holy shit. Is it gonna be this easy?" I pushed all the rest, so that all seven circles were lit, then hit the "next" button.

Yes! The final screen. There were only two circles on it, and Wainwright's book said they were Execute and Cancel. With one push of a button, Wainwright's hold on the people of Ora would be gone. His priests wouldn't be able to tell 'em what to do, or starve 'em if they went against his view of the world. They wouldn't be able to punish them for trying new things. The people would be out from under the thumb of the church for the first time in thousands of years. They would be free.

I took a deep breath and held my finger over the Execute circle. "Here goes nothin'."

CHAPTER FIFTY

SHOW DOWN!

But then I stopped. My hand just hovered over the button, frozen, because all of a sudden, my brain had started churning. Wainwright and the church had been greedy bastards. They'd only used the water to hold onto power, but right now, this very second, that power was mine. I had all the water the church had stolen, and I could do whatever I wanted to with it. And if I was smart, I could use it to make things better.

Visions of what I could do started whirling in front of my eyes. I could dole out the water more equally, so poor farmers got as much of it as the rich bastards did. I could use it to encourage people to do the right thing. If you freed your slaves, boom. You get some water. If you stopped treating your wife like shit and let your daughter go to school, boom boom. More water. Shit, I could make the Aldhanan pass new laws, even if it was Sai. Fuck. *Especially* if it was Sai. He could make women equal to men. He could make slavery illegal. He could make a treaty with the Arrurrh and give them back some of their land. He could get rid of the fucking nobles and Aldhanans and have elections. He could have equal rights for gays so Lhan's pals wouldn't have to hide in the closet anymore. And if he didn't, no water for him. He'd be sitting in his big fancy castle, dying of thirst because he didn't have anything to drink. Ha!

My god, it was perfect. I could drag this backward hellhole into the twenty-first century and make it into a fair modern society like it was supposed to be, with equality for everyone and responsible government and no more honor-killings and wars, and… and… and a big, red-headed dictator at the top of it all, manipulating everything behind the scenes and taking naps in her rejuvenation machine so she could hold onto it all forever.

I snapped out of my trance to find Lhan looking at me, concerned.

"Mistress, are you well? Why do you hesitate?"

"Because I'm a fucking idiot, that's why."

Man, that absolute power stuff was bad shit. One sniff and I went from being ready to give the water back to the people to wanting to keep it all for myself so I could make them do what I wanted. I'd become Wainwright in four seconds flat. Oh, sure, my Waar would be different from his. It would be a lot more about taking care of the common folk than his was, and makin' sure the women didn't have to kiss ass to their men folk anymore, but it would be just as much of a snow globe as his was. I'd use the water to set it how I wanted it, then I'd try to freeze it that way, forever, killing or starving anybody who disagreed with me or tried to change it, and never able to let go of the power, because I couldn't trust anybody else to use it like I did.

I felt sick just thinking about it, but I knew myself too well. If I started down that road, I wouldn't be able to help it. I'd become the bad guy. No question about it. The only way to stop it was to put it out of reach, like leaving my Marlboros back on Earth.

I stabbed the Execute circle.

Lhan said something, but the temple started to shake and roar like the world's biggest air compressor, and I couldn't hear him. It felt like an earthquake. Was it the turbines shutting down? Was it supposed to feel like that?

I stepped back, heart pounding. What had I done? I'd already set the place on fire. Was I gonna shake it apart too? I backed into Lhan and we held each other, eyes going everywhere, wondering what was going to happen next.

The booming and shaking kept getting louder, and Lhan and I had to grab the consoles to stop from falling over. Then all at once, everything smoothed out into a deep vibration and the booming became a deafening roar, like a rocket blasting off.

Fuck! Was that it? Had I somehow hit all the wrong buttons and caused the temple to take off into outer space?

It was Lhan who saw what I'd really done.

"Mistress, look!" He pointed to the holograms.

I looked, then gaped, then laughed my ass off. Apparently, "Atmospheric Dispersal Flush" meant squirting all the water in the tank into the sky, 'cause all seven temples were going off like the money shot from a gang-bang porn movie. Huge jets of water were shooting out of the tops of them and going straight up into the air further than the hologram could show.

"Jesus Christ on a vibratin' bed! It's a mega-temple circle jerk!"

"A—a what, Mistress?"

"Uh, never mind. Doesn't matter. What matters is, we did it! We stole back the water!"

I gave Lhan a hug that had him gasping, then kissed him harder than that. It was a pretty sexy moment, actually, holding and kissing each other in the middle of the seven temples all going off like Old Faithful. I think, if we hadn't been interrupted, we might have patched up our difference and done our own Old Faithful impersonation, but Wainwright chose that moment to break through the door and run in, sword out, with a handful of guards at his back.

Halfway to the platform he just stopped dead and stared at the seven ejaculating towers. "Damn fool girl. What have you done?"

I laughed at him. "I broke your ant-farm, Jack. The experiment's over. The ants can do what they want now."

There were literally tears in his eyes. I didn't expect that. You kinda expect the super-villain to know he's the super-villain, but I guess Mad Jack thought he was the hero.

"You ruined it. You evil white trash jezebel. Everything I've done. All my work. You ruined it!"

And with that he raised his sword and sprang up to the platform. And when I say sprang, I mean he went from the bottom of the stairs to the top in one leap, then kicked straight at me. Suddenly I knew what it was like for everybody else when I did it. It was scary as shit!

I blocked his slash and nearly dropped my sword. He hit like a pile driver! Shit! I woulda thought being a hundred and fifty years old woulda weakened him a bit, but no. He was as hard as his robots. Or maybe he *had* weakened. Maybe this was him being feeble. What the hell had he been like when he was twenty-five? Holy hell! No wonder he'd conquered the planet!

I staggered back, blocking like crazy as he hacked at me with a sword almost as long as mine. It was shaped like the traditional Waarian sword—curved blade, rounded knuckle-duster, curliques around the hilt—but about a foot longer and a lot heavier—a sword for a guy with the strength to swing it. And he was good too, as good as Lhan. There was no way I was going to win this fight by makin' like a helicopter.

Lhan saw I was in trouble and came at Wainwright from behind, thrusting for his spine, but the old man had eyes in the back of his head. He whipped his sword back without looking, and Lhan parried with about an inch to spare. That only saved his neck, though. The hit smashed him back and he crashed to the floor, stunned.

"No, you fucker!"

I swung for Wainwright's ribs as he exposed his side, but his sword was back in front of him before I could connect, and then snaking for my face the next second.

I backflipped off the platform on the far side, trying to buy myself some breathing room, but as soon as I did, Wainwright's guards started blasting at me with their wands and, just like I'd guessed, one of 'em was a fucking cannon. It shot out a stream of blue-white energy as big around as a fire hose, and I had to do my hide under the platform thing again to keep from getting barbequed.

Fortunately, Wainwright didn't like it anymore than I did.

"Leave off, you monkeys! No fire in the control room! I done told you! And nobody kills the hellion hussy but me, hear?" He leapt down after me as they held their fire, then pointed back at Lhan. "You wanna kill something, kill the pantywaist."

"No!"

I leapt out at Wainwright, fanning him back, then zigged left and up, hopping back onto the platform just as the old man's goons were coming up the stairs and starting toward Lhan, who was still shaking it off. They scattered back down as I hacked at 'em, but Wainwright was sticking to me like a wet shirt. I couldn't finish 'em off. I had to face him or he'd stab me in the back.

I kicked off a console and spun, hoping to catch him as he jumped after me. He turned my blade in mid-air, then came down swinging as we landed by the far wall.

Lhan's voice came to me through the clang and clash as Wainwright drove me back. "Fear not, Mistress. I have them."

I hoped he wasn't lyin', 'cause Captain Jack was taking all my concentration. He mighta looked like the mummy, but he moved like a cobra. I couldn't get a hit in on him for love nor money. Then something he'd just said came back to me. No fire in the control room? How 'bout some steel?

On his next attack, I jumped back like I was caving, then leapt for the platform again. Lhan was at the top of the stairs, fencing the four guards—actually only three now—like he was Errol Flynn.

I landed inside the hologram Temple of Ormolu and turned. The whole top of the thing was burning like a torch. I had no idea why we weren't on fire too. The control room must have been extra protected or something.

Wainwright came after me, sailing high over the consoles to come down at me like a thunderbolt. I didn't stay and fight. Instead, I dodged right and slashed, not at him, but at the console. The glowing face of it shattered, sending shards and sparks everywhere. Its lights fizzled and died.

Wainwright charged, foaming at the mouth. "What d'you think yer doin', you trollop? Leave off!"

I ducked another attack and bashed another console. "I'm already burning the place down. Whadda you care?"

"The fire's goin' out as soon as you're dead! But I can't replace these controls! Now get away!"

I skipped back again and raised my sword to smash through the face of the console that controlled the moisture gatherers.

"No!"

Wainwright took the bait. He lunged forward to block my strike on the machine and left himself wide open. I turned my blade and hacked for his side instead. Even fully extended, he was quicker than a cat. He twisted himself aside and I missed caving in his ribs by a gnat's ass. It wasn't a total miss, though. He flung a leg wide to keep his balance and my sword bit deep, just above the knee. He barked like a kicked dog and went down on top of the guards Lhan had killed, bleeding like a stuck pig.

I kicked his sword out of his hand and raised mine to cut him in half, but just then I heard Lhan grunt and turned to see him falling back before the last two guards, his sword up, but a ragged gash on the side of his head.

"Lhan!"

I jumped forward, shouldering him aside and bulldozed the two guards off the platform. They crashed hard at the bottom of the stairs and I hacked down at 'em like I was chopping wood. Two whacks and they were both dead, chests caved in and blood leaking up through their crushed armor like lava coming up through a crack in the earth.

I turned. Lhan was laid out on the stairs, trying to push himself up. Blood was streaming down past his ear like a red curtain. I got an arm under him.

"Can you stand?"

"With some assistance, I believe so. Thank you, Mistress." He was slurring his S's like he'd had half a bottle of Jim Beam.

I set him on his feet and aimed us at the door. "Then let's get the fuck outta here."

"You ain't goin' nowhere, missy."

I looked around. Wainwright was leaning against one of the consoles and raising that ten-gauge wand of blue fire to his shoulder.

"'Cept back to the hell you came from."

CHAPTER FIFTY-ONE

INFERNO!

I froze. Wainwright had us dead to rights. He mighta been weaving like a tree in a windstorm, but that wand had a big enough bore that all he had to do was fire it in our general direction and he'd get a piece of us.

He shook his head as he aimed. "A damn shame, missy. A damn shame."

"Yeah? Well, it's a damn shame you're a piece of shit cracker prick." I raised my hand and flipped him off. "Go fuck yourself."

And just as I jerked that bird up to give it a little more emphasis, there was a muffled boom from somewhere down below and the whole temple rocked like it had been hit by an earthquake. Things in the ceiling cracked and groaned, and the console panel next to Wainwright popped like a overamped fuse, showering him in sparks. Lhan and I staggered a little at the impact, but with his butchered leg Wainwright fell against the console and had to take one hand off the wand to catch himself.

That was all I needed.

I grabbed Lhan around the waist and bounded for the door as fast as I could. Halfway there, the room lit up bright as day and I heard the crackle and whump of the big wand firing. The beam shot past off to our left and burned a twitching, shovel-wide scar in the wall, then steadied and swung toward us like a search light. I dove for the door with Lhan in my arms, and rolled into the burning hallway just as the beam swept over our heads, melting everything in its path.

Another tremor hit as we scrambled to our feet, and there was a huge crash back in the control room. It sounded like the ceiling had caved in. I nearly fell into the flames, but Lhan caught me and we went down on our knees in the center of the hallway, which was the only place that wasn't on fire. Everything else was going up like kindling—the walls, the ceiling, the dead guys that lay all around. The smoke was so low that if I stood up straight, my head was in it, and the fire was closing in on both side, tighter and tighter every second, cooking my naked skin like I was a piece of toast in a toaster. I was having a hard time breathing, and it wasn't just the smoke. My claustrophobia was kicking in big time.

Lhan took my hand. "Mistress, you must help me. I fear I cannot stand on my own."

I looked at him, bleeding and weak, and my panic started to fade. Maybe he meant it that way.

"You doing that on purpose?"

He raised an eyebrow. "Mistress?"

"Never mind. Let's go."

I pushed up and helped him to his feet. The floor was slanted under us. Shit was really not right with the temple.

Lhan pointed left. "The stairs were… this way, I believe."

The flames were too close on either side for us to go side by side, so I put Lhan behind me and told him to put his hands on my shoulders, and we went forward single file.

It was like walking through hell. The air was mostly smoke, and smelled like I was inhaling cancer with every breath. My tongue tasted like a burnt match.

"We're gonna die here, Lhan."

"If so, then I am well satisfied. The church has been dealt a killing blow, and I am with you."

I looked over my shoulder at him. Did that mean he'd changed his mind? Was he ready to let go of his bullshit at last? I was just about to ask when he pointed over my shoulder.

"There!"

I looked around. The stairs were just ahead to the left. Fine. Time for a heart to heart later if we got out alive. We hurried through the doorway and started down, then dropped to our hands and knees, hacking and coughing. The stairwell was completely filled with smoke, which was weirdly all rushing *down* the steps like upside-down rapids and howling like a hurricane.

"Gonna have to crawl down!"

"Yes! Crawl!"

We started down backwards, heads down, but halfway down there was another terrible crash and the stairwell crumped inward like a beer can crushed by a redneck. Lhan and I were slammed together and fell against the ruptured stairs, which continued to groan and twist.

"Okay, fuck this. Run!"

We bolted down like shit-scared schoolgirls and threw ourselves through the door at the bottom of the stairs into the hangar deck. It was just as bad in there. Everything was on fire, but that was only the beginning. There were bodies all around, and to the left of us, the ceiling had caved in, burying men and smashed fliers in burning rubble. Far to the right, there was a huge bulge in the metal floor, like some gigantic beam underneath was trying to poke up through, and all the vehicles around it had slid down the slope and smashed into each other.

Directly ahead of us the hangar doors were open, and that was where all the smoke from the stairs was going, funneling out like it was an exhaust fan. Lhan and I stumbled out of the flow and sucked in a few breaths of clean air as we tried to see past the tears in our burning eyes. There were a lot of priests running around, and more coming up the stairs from below every second, and they were all trying to get onto or into the few Jetson-mobiles that were still in one piece.

Some of 'em took off as we watched, the globe things on their undersides vibrating and glowing as they lifted off the ground, then turning toward the open doors.

I pointed. "We gotta get a hold of one of those things!"

But we weren't gonna get one without a fight. There were priests climbing onto every single one of 'em. In fact, most of 'em were so overloaded that they'd wobble up for a couple of seconds, then crash down again, with the priests punching and kicking and telling each other to get off.

I wanted one of the ski-doo ones that Ru-Sul had ridden. They looked the coolest and the fastest, and even better, you rode 'em like a Harley—even if you had to sit on a weird little priest-made booster seat to reach the handle-bars.

More clues to just how big the Seven were, I guessed. I just hoped I could make the damned thing go.

I looked at Lhan. He was still bleeding like a stuck pig, and looked pretty woozy, but his eyes were focused now.

"You ready?"

He pulled a crossbow off a dead paladin and cocked it. "As I can be, beloved."

"Okay." I pointed to the nearest ski-doo, which was struggling to get off the ground with twenty priests piled on top of it and more trying to climb on. "That one."

"As you say."

We took off at a dead run, and I knew we had it. They didn't see us coming. There was too much noise and movement and fire, and they were all way too focused on getting on and getting out, but before we got halfway there, the apocalypse happened. The big bulge in the floor off to the right went up like a volcano and blew the place to pieces.

Lhan and I were knocked fifteen feet to our left and missed getting fried to a crisp only because we landed on the far side of a broken vehicle and the fireball passed over us. Body parts and bits of hot shrapnel flew threw the air like confetti and pattered down all around us. I felt a burning in the small of my back and flailed around until a piece of burning metal fell off and clanked on the floor. My right ear was screaming like a steam whistle and I felt cooked all down my right side.

"Lhan, are you all right?"

For a second he looked up at me with absolutely no comprehension in his eyes and my heart flip-flopped. Had the blast knocked him stupid? Did he have a concussion? Was he brain dead? Then he frowned at me.

"Did you speak, Mistress?"

I breathed a sigh of relief. He was just deaf. That I could deal with. "I said, *are you all right*?"

"I—I… well, let us see."

He staggered up and looked down at himself. He was covered in cuts and scratches, and he had some massive bruises on his legs and arms, but nothing seemed broken. I was about the same. Good. It was time to get gone. Past time.

I looked toward the ski-doo. It had shifted ten yards to the left, but it was still floating, only with less priests on it now. The rest were all over the floor, mostly dead, but a few trying to crawl for the boat.

"Come on, Lhan. One more time."

It was hard to run straight. The deck was buckled, my bones hurt like I'd fallen off a cliff, and my inner ear was all fucked up. I felt like I was falling sideways with every step, but we made it at last, and I kicked up into the air, screaming like a banshee, and came down right in the middle of the boat. Of course I came down off balance and landed on my ass, but the swerving jolt as I hit sent half the priests slipping off to the floor.

I sat up, swinging around with my sword, and sent most of the rest after them, but then the guy at the controls kicked me on the teeth and I flopped back as he rose over me, shouting and stabbing with a sword.

A crossbow bolt thwacked into his chest, knocking him ass-first over the handlebars and sending three guys who had been riding the fender to the ground with him. That was it. Everybody was off.

I staggered up, holing my mouth, and looked back. Behind me, Lhan was fighting through the wounded, braining guys with his spent crossbow and hacking around with his sword and. I stepped to the edge, a little nervous the boat was gonna flip, and cleared his way with my sword, then hauled him up.

Another explosion thudded on the right, and people screamed somewhere in the smoke. I flinched, then then kicked back the priests who were trying to climb back on board and scrambled to the saddle with Lhan. "Here. Sit behind me."

I swung a leg over and instantly felt like that kid on the back of dad's Harley. It had looked weird when I'd seen the priests riding it, but it felt weirder, like *I* was the one that was out of scale. The booster seat at least allowed me to touch the handlebars, but it left my feet dangling, and I felt like I was riding a scoot with ape-hangers, which I'd never liked.

Also, I didn't know how to make it go. There was no clutch and no throttle I could see. In fact there didn't seem to be any controls of any kind. I couldn't have told you how to turn it on or shut it off. I kept feeling with my feet, hoping to find something I was supposed to push, but there was nothing, and shit was starting to blow up all around us.

"Goddamn it!"

I shook the handlebars in frustration and almost fell off as the boat-bike swerved around in mid-air. The handlebars! Duh! They were split, like the bars on those fancy exercise bikes where you pull with your hands the same time you're pedaling. I pushed forward on them. The bike jerked ahead and

Lhan almost fell off.

"Hold on, Lhan! I've got it!"

He gripped me around the waist and I leaned forward, pushing the right bar forward a bit more than the left to angle us toward the nearest hangar door. It was awkward as hell with the bars so high over my head, but I managed it, and we started to skim past the other vehicles.

Most of the priests who were trying to fly out were too deep in their own shit to notice us, but a few looked up and shouted. One raised a wand, but another blast ripped through the hangar and knocked everybody sideways—us included.

"The wall, Mistress! The wall!"

"Got it. Got it."

Actually I didn't, and I had to pull back hard on the bars to stop from slamming into the burning wall to the right of the door. The door itself was twisting and distorting like the mouth of somebody shouting in slow motion as the weight of the stories above started to crush it.

"Fuck!"

I reversed hard, then veered left and gunned it just as another explosion rocked the hangar. We shot out into the night sky with a fireball erupting behind us. All of Ormolu was laid out in orange and black below us, reflecting the fire that was eating the temple, and I could see crowds of people in the streets.

I looked back, terrified. "Is it falling? Is it falling?"

It wasn't, but we had another problem. Two other boat-bikes shot out of the fireball just as the hangar door crushed closed, and swooped toward us.

"I'm afraid we are pursued, Mistress."

CHAPTER FIFTY-TWO

DOG FIGHT!

I jammed the bars forward and the race was on. The other bikes were covered in priests, and slower than us, but that was changing fast. With every turn they made, more guys lost their grip and flew off, screaming, and they started to gain. Also, one of them had a wand, and started blasting at us.

It was then that I realized I didn't know how to go up or down. From my Ranger training I knew the basics of flying, but this was nothing like a plane. Pulling back didn't raise you up and pushing forward didn't lower you. What was it?

I leaned way forward to see if there was some other control hidden between the two bars, and all of a sudden we were plunging down like we were doing a bombing run. Lhan yelped in surprise and clung on as both of us lifted up off our seats. And as we did, we leveled off, and thumped down on the seat again, all wobbly and scared shitless, and about fifty feet below the other bikes.

Lhan clung to me, gasping. "That was... precipitous."

"Yeah. But why did it...?"

I looked at the bench under our makeshift saddle as I floored it again, and saw it was built like a wah-wah pedal. If I leaned far enough forward I'd press down the front of the bench and the nose would go down. If I leaned far enough back, I'd press the back down and the nose would go up, and the priests had built the bottom of the booster seat like a rocking chair so it would all still work. Talk about flying by the seat of your pants! Or no pants, in my case.

"Jae-En. They come."

A burst of wand fire carved a black line in the skin of the boat-bike, nearly cutting off one corner. The two fliers were angling down at us, and the guy riding bitch on the second one was firing over the driver's head.

I leaned forward hard and plunged straight for the ground, but this time I meant it. "Hang on, Lhan! We gotta ditch this thing, and fast."

I banked right around the burning temple, hugging the wall and trying to put it between us and that wand, but as we skimmed down the curve of the thing Lhan gripped my shoulder and pointed south.

"Jae-En! Look!"

I looked. Us and the priests weren't the only things in the sky that night. Off in the distance a bunch of airships were coming our way, and I thought I recognized Ku-Rho's warship, and Kai-La's repainted church ship among 'em.

I got a little thrill as I realized our friends were coming to rescue us, but a second later it turned to dread. Off to the east, more airships were rising into the sky from Ormolu's naval base.

"Holy shit! It's the whole fuckin' Oran navy!"

Lhan's fingers dug into my shoulder. "We must return to Kai-La. She has come for us and will die for it if we tarry."

I gritted my teeth and looked back. The boat-bikes were screaming down around the temple after us. They were zeroing in. "We gotta take these guys out first. That blue wand could bring down the whole fleet."

Lhan pulled his crossbow off his back and loaded it, then tried to twist in the saddle. "I will attempt a shot."

"Not yet, Lhan. We need the high ground. Lean back. Now!"

I pulled back hard on the handlebars and threw myself back. Lhan did the same, and we almost went off the back as the boat jerked up out of its power dive, then got thrown forward again as it jerked to a stop with a roar of reverse thrust. The stop was so fast it felt like we'd bounced off the ground and into a brick wall. The ski-doos had to veer left and right to avoid us, and one fishtailed right into the temple wall, smashing to pieces like a bike hitting a semi, and sending its riders flying as shattered cowling and smashed engine parts spun down toward the ground.

I angled after the other one, or tried to anyway. I felt like a kid trying to learn how to use a stick shift for the first time. I kept jerking forward, dropping, jerking forward, rising, stopping dead, swerving. It probably saved our lives. The guy on the back kept shooting at us, but I don't think even a targeting computer could have tracked us the way I was driving.

We couldn't keep playing dodgeball forever, though. We had to get going.

"Shoot 'im, Lhan! Shoot 'im!"

Lhan grunted. "Were you to hold steady for but a moment..."

"He'll kill us."

I swerved again and Lhan fell against me, banging my head with the stock of the crossbow.

"Ah, better. If I may lean on you?"

"Do it! Shoot!"

Lhan braced on my shoulders and fired over my head. There was a TWANG in my ear and the gunner on the last bike toppled off, a bolt sticking out of his back, and his wand falling with him.

"Yee-haw!"

The driver started taking evasive action, but I ignored him and floored it straight for Kai-La's fleet, screaming over the orange and black city like a hornet and keeping one eye on the Oran ships, which were all up in the air now, and slowly turning our way.

"Come on. Come on."

Pretty soon I could see people on the decks of Kai-La's ship, all standing at the rails and armed to the teeth, with more up in the rigging. Ku-Rho's ship was right beside Kai-La's.

"Hang on, Lhan. Almost there."

A sharp-tipped bolt like a fence post shot out from Ku-Rho's ship and nearly punched us out of the sky. I flinched aside and swerved all over the place in surprise. A bunch of crossbow bolts whizzed out after the flying stake, but all fell short.

"What the fuck? What are they doing?"

"They know us not."

I reined to a stop and stood up on the saddle, waving my arms. "Hey! It's Jane! And Lhan! It's us!"

There was a tense silence, and I was afraid they didn't believe me, or couldn't hear, but then I saw a little figure in red hop up on the rail of Kai-La's ship and put a megaphone to her mouth.

"Stand down, all! Stand down, Ku-Rho! These are friends. I'd recognize those tits anywhere. Come ahead, Mistress Jae-En!"

I breathed a sigh of relief and glided in easy, and saw Shal-Hau and Sei-Sien waiting for us at the rail in the middle of the crew. Well, Shal-Hau was waiting for us. Sei-Sien was staring past us at the burning tower with his face hanging out.

Shal-Hau spread his arms. "Welcome, pupil! Welcome, Mistress! I am overjoyed to see you alive. We thought the worst."

Lhan bowed, but was so wiped out he nearly fell off the bike. "Th-thank you, master. It is a joy to see you as well."

I bumped the rail beside them and reached out to hold steady. The crew stared at the boat-bike and edged back, but Burly whipped them into action.

"Don't stand there with yer gobs hangin' open. Bring our friends aboard. Can you not see they are hurt?"

The sailors were too weirded out to actually step out on the boat-bike, but they reached out to us and hauled us over the rail, then laid us down on the deck.

Shal-Hau stepped through them, and called for bandages so he could see to our wounds, but Sei-Sien kept staring out at the Temple of Ormolu, which was now bent at the top like a stubbed-out cigarette and still burning like a torch. Amazingly, it was also still shooting its stream of water up into the sky, but with the tip at an angle, it looked even more like a pissing dick.

Sei-Sien mumbled like a street crazy as he watched it burn. "They did it. 'Tis impossible, but they did it. The church is done."

I hadn't realized until then just how much I needed to stop moving, but as soon as I was on my back and Shal-Hau stuck a canteen in my hand, all I wanted to do was sleep. But not yet. I looked around for Kai-La, who was telling her crew to tie the boat-bike to the rail.

"You gotta get out of here, Kai-La. The navy—"

She smiled down at me. "Aye, we saw 'em. And we're away already. Not to worry. The she-skelsha can outrun anything in the sky, except maybe that little toy you brought with you."

She looked out at the temple, and the orange of the fire showed up the bones in her face. "I suppose that's your doing?"

"We didn't mean to set it on fire."

"A happy accident then."

Lhan lifted his head. "But the water has been freed. And not only here. All seven temples have given back what they stole."

Burly looked skeptical. "To the sky? It was the ground that needed it."

I was going to explain, but all of a sudden my head was drooping and I had to lay back again.

"Answered prayer," I mumbled. "Answered prayer."

Shal-Hau shook his head. "The poor thing is babbling. She must rest."

Kai-La gave me a sad smile, then waved to her crew. "Take them below and put them to bed, they're cluttering up my deck." She started back to the aft deck. "More sail, friends! Helmsman! Another point to the south!"

The last thing I saw as we were carried into the underdeck was the sailors scrambling up into the rigging and the sails on either side of the canopy creaking out to catch more wind.

CHAPTER FIFTY-THREE

RENEWED!

I woke up to trumpets blowing and for a second thought I was back in boot camp, with those asshole buglers blasting me out of my cot at oh-my-god thirty. Then I looked up at the curved wooden ceiling and remembered where I was. I groaned. It felt like my arms and legs had been tied in knots, then set in concrete. The real pain came when I moved, and every cut and scrape and burn I'd got from fighting naked for sixty or so floors started itching like I was covered in fire ants.

I looked over at Lhan and laughed. He looked like I felt, hissing and grimacing as he lifted his head at the horns.

"You find my pain amusing?"

"I'm just laughing to keep my mind off my own."

We were in Kai-La's cabin, set up on two little cots on the floor behind her dinner table. There was a lantern glowing on a hook above us, and the windows at the stern end of the cabin were dark. I was confused.

"Is it still night? Or is it night again?"

"I know not. I feel I have slept a full year."

The horns came again and we looked up.

"That is the call to battle."

"Ugh. I've always hated that tune."

We picked ourselves up and limped and groaned our way over to the window bench to push open the back windows. It wasn't night, just dark. The light was a weird grayish green, and as dim as a twenty-watt bulb, but it was still enough to see that the sky behind Kai-La's galleon was wall to wall airships. My heart sank. It looked like she hadn't outrun the Oran navy after all. They were right on our tail, less than two miles back.

I sighed. "Well, we won't be getting away from that."

"At least we will die knowing that our efforts have borne fruit after all."

I looked at him. "How do you mean?"

He pointed above the Oran ships. I looked up, then gaped. The sky was all clouds, heavy and gray and bulging down like the underside of a mattress with a fat guy sleeping on it.

"Holy shit. Did we do that?"

"I can think of no other explanation."

"Well, goddamn."

Kai-La's voice came from above, shouting orders, and I pushed to my feet. "Come on, we better go up and help."

Lhan nodded, but didn't get up. He just kept looking out the window.

"Mistress."

"Yeah?"

"Mistress, I would not fight again beside you before we have resolved what lies between us."

I sighed. "Lhan, I thought we went through this. I thought you were okay with what happened."

He turned away from the window, as grim as a hanging judge. "With your actions, I have no complaint. It is my behavior, from the moment of your return, with which I am not, as you say, 'okay.'"

I blinked as I worked that one through. "Huh? What are you saying?"

"I say that I have been a fool, and have made a fool's error. I have mistaken pride for honor, and it has divided me from she who I truly love."

I took a step toward him. "Lhan, don't—"

He held up a hand. "Let me finish, Mistress. Please."

I stopped and waited, though all I wanted to do was fold him up in my arms and squeeze him.

"In the tower, nay, in every place and every battle, you have shown me that honor has nothing to do with pride, but everything to do with defending the weak against the strong and protecting one's friends against one's enemies. I, by contrast, have named my vanities honor and demanded you give them the respect of law."

I shrugged, uncomfortable. "Forget it, Lhan. People stick to what they grow up with. You grew up in Ora, you're gonna have Oran values. You can't help it."

"Can I not?" He laughed. "Have I not flouted them in all else? Have I not spurned the path chosen for me by my father? Have I not slept on both sides of the bed? Am I not branded heretic? Have I not killed the priests and paladins of the Seven? Why then have I clung so fiercely to that particular part of Oran law which states that a dhan is sworn to defend his dhanshai's honor and protect her person against all dangers? Because I believed in it? I—"

He cut off in mid-flow, then frowned. "Well, in all fact, I do believe in it. That has not changed. What *has* changed, what *you* have changed in me, is that I now believe a dhanshai need not abandon her strength and valor in order to abide by her part of the sacred vow, or for her dhan to abide by his. Indeed, be their prowess equal, it should be right and proper that both defend and protect the other."

I stared at him. "Wait. So you believe we're equals now?"

Lhan laughed. "Equals? Hardly. You are so much my better in all the chivalric virtues that I would not allow myself to be mentioned in the same breath as—"

"Aw, can it, Lhan. Now you're just kissing my ass."

"I speak only truth, Mistress. You are stronger, braver, more noble—"

"Not to mention dumber, clumsier, uglier, and you can still kick my ass in a straight-up fight."

Lhan waved that away. "Do not make mock of yourself. You are a hero in every way that I am not—in the most important way. You do not permit your fears to turn you from doing what should be done."

I sat down next to him. "Lhan. I know you fucked up once. I know you let that boy be taken. But how many times have you made up for it?"

"Not enough."

"Okay, fine. Not enough. The point is, have you ever let fear stop you since?"

"I could not live were I to allow that again."

"Right. Exactly. You're handling it. You fucked up, and then you fixed it. You're never gonna do that again. I—" I stopped as a drawerful of Polaroids spilled across my brain. "I'm here because I can't handle my shit. I get mad and… and bad things happen. I go to jail. I kill some poor bastard. I… You know, I should be in the army right now. I should be off in Afghanistan being a *real* hero—I sure as hell trained hard enough to get there—but then I went and lost my temper and broke my CO's nose on my first week of deployment. Never saw action. Not once. Instead, I got sent home and dishonorably discharged, and ended up riding around on a Harley and gettin' into bar fights with other losers—all because I got no control. How fucking heroic is that? You tell me!"

He didn't get much of that last bit, so I put it another way. "Nobody's perfect, Lhan. *You* gotta fight your fears. *I* gotta fight my rage. And the thing is, when I'm with you, I can. I start to get my mad on and then I think, Lhan's gonna die if I go off like a rocket. I gotta keep it together." I shifted around and looked him in the eye. "Maybe that's the real secret of this Dhan and Dhanshai stuff. It's not just that we defend and protect each other, it's that we make each other stronger too."

Lhan held my gaze for a long moment, like he was thinking it all through, the suddenly he stood up from the window bench and bowed and crossed his wrists to me.

"Mistress Jae-En, I would pledge myself to you as a dhan of Ora should—heart, soul and arm. From this day forth, you will be my dhanshai and I will be your dhan. Your safety and well-being will be my only concern. Your love will be my only goal."

Just like the last time he'd done it, my first reaction was to laugh. My second was to say yes and pull him into my arms, but it needed more than that. I stood up too, then crossed my arms and bowed to him.

"And I would pledge myself to you as a woman of Earth—with my heart, soul and arm. From this day on, Lhan-Lar of Herva, you will be my dhan and I will be your dhanshai. Your safety and well-being will be my only concern. Your love will be my only goal."

Lhan looked a little shocked as I finished up, but then he smiled. "Ora may not find it proper or correct, but for you and I, it is as it should be. I accept your pledge."

"And I accept yours."

I spread my arms, but he stayed where he was. "May-may I have my balurrah back now?"

I laughed, then took it off my neck and held it out. "Come get it."

He reached for it, but I caught his hand instead and pulled him to me. We kissed. There was another horn blast above us, but neither of us looked up. It was a damn good kiss, and it was making up for a lot of lost time. It was also making me weak in the knees—and hot and slippery a little further up. Lhan seemed to be getting kinda excited too. We were still as naked as we had been when we'd escaped the temple, and I could feel him getting hard between us, and climbing up my leg.

I checked out the window. The Oran navy was about a mile away and closing fast. I looked into Lhan's eyes.

"If we're gonna die here, I wanna chance to make good on this vow of ours first. Whaddaya say?"

He tied his ballurah around his waist, smirking. "I say, I have never been propositioned with such poetry or romantic fervor. You take my breath away, beloved."

And then he pushed me back on the bench and buried his head between my thighs.

CHAPTER FIFTY-FOUR

TORRENT!

You know, I hope the Oran navy has binoculars, 'cause I really wanted the fuckers to see me leaning out that window ten minutes later, flipping 'em the bird as Lhan bent me over that bench and pounded the living hell out of me from behind. I wish they'd been close enough to hear me moaning and gasping. I wish they'd been close enough that I coulda told 'em I didn't care how many ships they had, or how many swords, or how many wands of blue fire, or that I was gonna die. None of that shit mattered, not one goddamn bit of it, because after being thrown around to Waar and Earth and back, and after all the fights and the fighting, I was with Lhan again, and this time it was right.

Five minutes after that, though, I completely forgot the Oran navy even existed. By then, Lhan was lying back on the bench and I was riding him like a pony on a merry-go-round, with molten honey bubbling and boiling inside me so strong I couldn't think thoughts or say words, just bounced harder and faster and harder and faster until, with Lhan bucking beneath me, I came like a steam hammer, jerking and grabbing the sill so I wouldn't fall out the window.

After a minute of just lying there, panting and half-out the window, I slumped down beside Lhan and we held and kissed each other and caught our breaths, sweat dripping off our bodies. But then I noticed it wasn't all sweat. Something was splashing on my face.

"Lhan, what are you—?" I opened my eyes, then squinted as wind and water blew through the open window. I stared, stunned.

"Lhan. Lhan, look!"

Lhan moaned and raised his head, still groggy. Then he stared too.

"Rain! Mistress, it worked. You've done it!"

And we weren't the only ones who noticed. A big cheer came from above us, and I could hear a lot of whooping and hollering.

"*We* did it, Lhan."

I gave him a kiss on the cheek, then pulled away from him and stood up, feeling better than I had since… since before the priests had sent me back to Earth.

"Come on, let's find some clothes and join the celebration. It'll be our last bash before we die."

***

But by the time we got up there, it was too wet for much of a celebration. The wind was picking up and the rain was blasting in under the canopy like a shower head, and the pirates were done whooping it up. Kai-La had half of 'em climbing up the shrouds to secure the sails, while the others were still at battle stations. Shal-Hau and Sei-Sien were huddled in the lee of the foredeck, staring out at the slashing rain. Sei still had the same look of dumb shock on his fine-boned face that he'd had when he'd been staring at the burning temple, but Shal-Hau beamed at us as we splashed out onto the deck.

"A miracle, friends! A miracle!"

I grinned. "Didn't we tell you? We freed the water!"

"Aye, but I did not believe it would bring the rain so quickly. You have saved all the farms in Ora."

Kai-La laughed and turned to us, water flying from her hair. "And us as well. Look!"

She pointed over the aft rail. Lhan and I looked, but there was nothing to see. In the few minutes it had taken us to pull on some clothes and make our way up to the deck, the rain had become a shimmering gray wall, so thick I couldn't see more than fifty feet out from the deck. The Oran navy had completely disappeared. Hell, it was hard to see the other ships in Kai-La's fleet, and they were right beside us. Even Ku-Rho's massive man-o-war was nothing but a smudgy ghost off to our left.

I shook my head, amazed. "Well, fuck me sideways. Visibility zero."

Kai-La clapped a hand on my shoulder. "You and your rain have saved our skins, lass. The navy will never find us in all this."

She turned to Burly, grinning through the rain. "Halan. Tell the signalers no horns. We wouldn't want the navy following our tune. Break out the flash lanterns, and give order to rise. We will take to the clouds!"

"Aye, Captain!" He turned to the crew, clapping his big hands and striding across the deck. "Haul out those lamps, lads and lasses. Lively now! And make ready to drop ballast!"

As the pirates hurried to follow Burly's orders behind us, Lhan and I stepped away from Shal-Hau and Sei-Sien and stood at the rail, letting the heavy rain wash over us. We stared out at the torrent for a long time, mesmerized, then Lhan looked down. I followed his gaze.

It was impossible to see the ground, just a gray vertigo of rain, dropping away from us, but I could imagine it—dry earth turning to mud, withered roots soaking up water, thirsty animals coming out of their holes and lapping at new puddles, farmers stepping out of their houses and staring up at the sky like we were staring down, little kids opening their mouths to catch the drops.

Lhan squeezed my hand. "You were right, beloved. One woman *can* change the world."

I squirmed, embarrassed, though I gotta admit I was pretty much saying the same thing to myself.

"I just hope it's changed for the better."

"Of course it is. How could it be otherwise?"

I got a sick feeling in my stomach, like he shouldn'ta said that, but then he wrapped his arms around my waist and kissed me full on, and my worries washed away. I kissed him back, folding him up in a big pink hug, and we just stood there, melting into each other, as the ship rose up into the clouds and the deck and the crew and the rigging disappeared one by one into a thick white nothing, until Lhan and I were the only things left in the world.

Acknowledgments

Thanks to my darling Lili for her patience and encouragement, to Howard, Sue, Grey, and Molly for early reads and showing me the way forward, to Ross for his understanding and insight, and to Bob for his perseverance and good cheer. Without all of you I'd still be rewriting the second act—again.

about the author

Nathan Long is a screen and prose writer, with two movies, one Saturday-morning adventure series, and a handful of live-action and animated TV episodes to his name, as well as ten fantasy novels and several award-winning short stories.

He hails from Pennsylvania, where he grew up, went to school, and played in various punk and rock-a-billy bands, before following his writing dreams to Hollywood—where he now plays in various punk and country bands—and writes novels full time.